DEFENSIVE ZONE

The Dartmouth Cobras

By
Bianca Sommerland

Edited by Rosie Moewe
Line Editor Lisa A. Hollett
Cover art by Reese Dante

Warning

This book contains material not suitable for readers under 18. In also contains scenes that some may find objectionable, including BDSM, ménage sex, bondage, anal sex, sex toys, double penetration, voyeurism, edge play, and deviant use of hockey equipment. Do not try this at home unless you have your very own pro-athlete. Author takes no responsibility for any damages resulting from attempting anything contained in this book.

Dedication

The game. 'nough said ;)

Acknowledgements

To Cherise Sinclair who made this a much stronger book. To the Toymaker and Eirocawakening for your beautiful Violet Wand scene—you have no idea how privileged I felt to be "there" with you for something so intimate. Your guidance and insight into the lifestyle was priceless. To Ebony Mckennie, Stacey Price, Genevieve Trahan, my precious beta readers. To Riane Holt for your support and guidance through the whole process. You tweaked the "Gossip Column" into something better than I could have managed on my own. To Rosie Moewe for your tireless work in the final hours, polishing words and lending a shoulder to lean on when I so desperately needed it.

Readers, your emails, comments, reviews, and investment in my characters make it all worth it.

And to my family who knows I'm crazy, but loves me anyway!

Chapter One

Celebrity Dish

by Hayley Turner

Silver Delgado has abandoned the spotlight—to run a hockey team?

I can't say I'm surprised. The child model and supporting actress for Take Me Home *started her career in Hollywood followed by rumors of sexy rendezvous with several players from her father's team, so it's obvious that she has a taste for stick welding hotties. The question is, why didn't her father, wealthy financer Anthony Delgado, delegate the team to his eldest daughter, Oriana? Rumors of her upcoming nuptials to the Dartmouth Cobras playmaker, Max "The Catalyst" Perron, say Oriana definitely knows how to handle a player, or three, quite well.*

Daddy dearest may regret his decision when Silver continues her shameless antics with the players who aren't "attached" to her sister . . . unless he's hoping she'll provide a little motivation. And who knows, if she gets bored, perhaps she can design a trendy line of heavy coats and boots!

Hollywood's loss is Nova Scotia's gain?

Silver Delgado crumpled the clip from the tabloid in her fist. A whitewash of cold ran over her flesh as she faced Daddy, but her smile never slipped. "Hayley is a jealous bitch—she thinks I fucked her husband."

"Watch your language, young lady." Her father's golden brown eyes narrowed as he leaned forward in his wheelchair. His red velvet smoking jacket, with its thick black silk collar, masked his frailty well, forcing her to focus on the austere expression which reduced her to the naughty little girl who had disappointed him yet again. "Did you?"

"Did I . . . ? *No!*" Her skin crawled as she pictured Mr. Turner, not ugly exactly, but definitely disgusting. He licked his lips so often whenever he talked to her it looked like he was drooling. "He hit on me a few times—my agent told Hayley that he was making me uncomfortable and she had to conduct any future interviews herself. Hayley refused to believe her husband would be that

1

'unprofessional.'"

"I see . . ." Shaking his head, her father rolled to the far end of his rooftop patio. He drew in a raspy breath and waved her over. Gazing out at the picturesque scenery, a clear view over the trees to Lake Banook, glowing under the early morning sun, he spoke quietly. "You earned this reputation, Silver. Whatever this woman has against you, everything in that article is the truth."

Everything? She bit back a grin. "So you want me to 'motivate' the players?"

He slapped his hand on the railing. "Don't be obtuse. I want *you* to behave professionally. This family doesn't need any more bad press."

"I know. But—"

"No buts. I hate asking this of you. If I had a son . . . if Antoine wasn't . . ." The lines in his face tightened. "You are all I have left. I need to know I can trust you to represent me, to prove that our family, that our *legacy*, is as strong as ever."

Chewing on her bottom lip, Silver rested her forearms on the railing and stared down at the manicured grounds below. "I'm not all you have, Daddy. Oriana—"

"Do not speak *her* name in my presence. What is it, Silver?" His trembling hand latched onto her arm. "Are you afraid of the responsibility? Please don't be. Think of it as playing a part. You're an actress, aren't you? Smile for the cameras, sign whatever my staff brings to you, and be pleasant with the investors. Learn enough about the game to carry on an intelligent conversation. It shouldn't be too difficult, even for you."

Yeah, thanks for all that trust, Daddy. "I'm sure I could do a decent job, but . . . Daddy, you can't be *that* mad at Oriana! She knows the game! She would be perfect for the job!"

"What did I say?" His face reddened and the stark blue veins at his temples throbbed. He slumped into his wheelchair and put his hand over his heart. "Do this for me and I will give you whatever you want. Do you like your condo? There's an extra room for an office so you can work from home whenever you want. My staff will accommodate you. If there's anything else you need, just tell me."

Silver blinked and shook her head. Her eyes teared up as she saw the strong man that had always intimidated her reduced to this. After seeing him in the hospital, inches away from death, all she wanted was to make sure he had time to heal. Did it really matter whether it was her or Oriana who took over the stupid team until then?

"Don't get upset, Daddy. I'll do it. Everything is perfect." She knelt by his side and held his hand to her cheek. "I'm just scared that I'll disappoint you. I don't know anything about hockey."

"Of course you don't, my precious little doll." He smiled and bent over to kiss her forehead. "But you can do this. Just be your beautiful self, keep your legs crossed, and everything will be fine."

Ouch. She bowed her head so Daddy wouldn't see her wince. "Okay."

"I like what you're wearing." He tipped her chin up and brushed his hand over her tight bun, his gaze raking over her grey and black pinstripe skirt suit. "If you dress like this every time you go out in public, people will forget your tawdry past and give you the respect a daughter of mine deserves. I suggest you burn the rest of your wardrobe. It killed me to see you strutting around in those trashy outfits. I was advised not to watch your movies. I hope you know you don't have to sell your body any more to make a living. You will receive a monthly allowance to cover all your expenses and more."

Damn it, I never 'sold my body'. Fine, some of the parts she'd taken hadn't required much of a wardrobe, but everyone in Hollywood had to start somewhere!

Not that Daddy would understand. So she simply nodded and smiled. "Of course."

Sitting back in his wheelchair, Daddy motioned for her to stand. "One last thing. I'm sure you've heard about the mess last season— last season being when the team was playing?"

She nodded. She wasn't completely brain-dead.

"Roy Kingsley was involved, but he is our biggest investor." Her father studied her face as though to make sure she understood what that meant. He continued at her nod. "If he approaches you, in any way, do your best to make him happy. And I don't mean by sleeping with him. But batting your eyelashes and being sweet may be enough to keep the dirty bastard from pulling his support of the team. Can you manage that?"

Flirt with the old guy, but don't fuck him. Yeah. I think I can manage. But hopefully she wouldn't have to deal with him at all. "I can do that."

"Lovely." His head jerked up as the patio door slid open. His jaw ticked. "*They* will have to go."

Silver looked up and inclined her head as Asher, her boyfriend, stepped out beside his boyfriend and tapped his watch.

"I'm very sorry to interrupt." Asher didn't look at her father. After Daddy's ranting about her "gay boyfriends" at the hospital, he knew better. "But we have to go."

"Not sorry enough not to." Daddy frowned at her. "If you don't go, I suppose there will be talk. Bring your sister the gift Anne bought her. We must keep up appearances. For now."

A quick nod and she scrambled to her feet. Anne, her father's— and now her—secretary, came out to roll him inside. For a split second, Silver was tempted to beg her father to come to Oriana's wedding. But after his last reaction to just hearing her name . . .

Yeah. Bad idea.

"You good?" Asher asked as soon as Daddy was out of hearing.

"I'm good." She moved away from him and stood by the tall, glass wall fountain in the center of the patio. It was new. Not something Daddy would have added on his own. She had a bad feeling Anne was making herself *very* comfortable here. "Let's go. I hate this place."

"Aww, doesn't it look the same as the fancy place you grew up in? What is it, new curtains? I'm sure it must be dreadful for you."

She should have kept her mouth shut. Asher had grown up poor. He'd gotten where he was today through hard work, his brains, and playing dirty. She respected him for that, but she wasn't stupid enough to think that he'd understand that her life hadn't been something to envy. As far as he was concerned, if you grew up with enough to eat every day, you had no right to complain.

And he was probably right.

"You're never late for anything, Asher." She gave him a sideways glance and smirked. "I wouldn't want to be responsible for ruining your *perfect* image."

"If I gave a shit about my image, I'd stay away from you." Asher grinned. "Come on. You've gotta get all prettied up. The sister of the bride should look her best, right?"

Pulling off the careless act was easy with Asher. She tossed her head and shrugged. "This is me. Would you expect any less?"

"Nope." Asher hooked his arm with hers and brushed his free hand over the front of his dark blue suit jacket. His crisp, light-toned cologne tickled her nose as he gazed longingly toward the entrance. "You know, it's too bad your father doesn't like me. He's got this Hugh Hefner thing going for him. I'd so drop you for him as a sugar daddy!"

"I *did* not just hear that!"

Asher smirked. "I've never done vintage."

"TMI, Asher." She tugged him inside, casting a pleading glance to Cedric who stood by the doorway, silent as a shadow. "Will you talk to him?"

"Why?" Cedric hunched his shoulders and followed a step behind as they made their way through the house. "He does who and what he wants. I'm just here to look pretty."

Uck, why do I bother? But at least Cedric's remark shut Asher up. He let her go and slung his arm over Cedric's shoulders. Thirty minutes later, Asher parked his town car in front of the condominium, then went inside with Cedric, straight into their room, and shut the door.

Silver paused in the hall by the door, wondering, like she always did when Cedric got like this, if she should have said something. What exactly, she didn't know. Cedric and her didn't talk much unless it was about legal stuff.

Asher can handle him. Go get ready.

Closing down and dealing with routine stuff, like getting all dolled up, cleared her head of all the drama with both her boyfriends and her father. Time to forget how sick Daddy was. And how miserable Cedric seemed sometimes. A mist of sweet perfume, a bit of powder on her face to illuminate her complexion, one would think she didn't have a care in the world.

The gilded vanity mirror before her reflected an utterly perfect face and body. Her bright green eyes were fake, but everything else was real, despite her agent's frequent hints about getting a boob job.

She turned from side to side. Yep, her pert breasts in the snug pink mesh tube top would get the guys drooling even though they weren't huge. She smoothed her hands over her loose hair and took a deep breath.

It's Oriana's day. All eyes should be on her.

Little wisps rose from her pale gold locks and she scowled. After spraying hair spray on a bristle brush, she brought it up and clenched her teeth when she noticed the brush shaking. She was shaking. She had to get a grip. A *lot* of the members of the BDSM club where her sister was getting married were players on the hockey team she now owned. If she was going to prance around in front of them looking like a whore, she better act comfortable with the image.

Not a whore. A sub. She snickered. As if any man could dominate her. She might pretend with Asher and Cedric, but that was just a game. A role she played when she was in the mood. Granted, she'd directed her sister to a Domme book when she'd had problems with her ex, but that was just because Paul seemed like the submissive type. Or a cheater, but she hadn't had the heart to tell her sister that. Men who didn't want sex either weren't interested in the woman they were with or they needed someone else to take charge. They could also be gay, but she knew enough gay men to rule Paul out. What she didn't get was how Paul had resisted Oriana. She had a natural beauty that might not make it on the runways, but made men think of more than fucking.

The brush clattered on her dresser top. She braced her hands on the ledge and bowed her head. Was she really going to get all worked up about this? Her sister was happy, and Silver was happy for her. Oriana needed the ring. And the collar.

Silver Delgado needed none of that. She was a self-made woman and she had two men who . . . cared about her. She was in control of her own life, and that was exactly how she wanted it.

Her pink silk clutch caught her eye. She opened it and took out a small vial, sealed with wax and full of white powder. Gritting her teeth, she shoved it back inside the purse and grabbed a lollipop from her stash. *I don't need that anymore.*

But she *did* need a drink. The cherry flavor felt cough-syrup thick on her tongue. She plucked it from her mouth and shouted.

"Cedric, bring me the rum!"

A couple of minutes later, Asher strode in and handed her the bottle. She smiled and fingered the buttons of his black silk blouse, hoping to distract him from a lecture. He had a thing about women drinking too much.

He took her purse and dumped the contents on the dresser. Picking up the vial, he gave her a sideways glance. "You're still hanging on to this? You know if you get hooked again, I'm not fronting the dough. It's a disgusting habit."

"I know that." She shoved her makeup and stuff back into her clutch without looking at him. "Don't worry. I just keep it around so I know it's there. If I don't, I start wondering where I can find more. It's complicated."

"Whatever. Are you ready?" He put his hands on his expensive black jean clad hips. "You look good."

"Thank you." She turned to the mirror and ran her hands over her thighs to make sure her pink booty shorts didn't ride up. Archer wasn't looking, but sometimes he did. He might be gay, but for some reason he was still interested in her. Which made him bi as far as most of his friends were concerned, but he joked that he wouldn't go *that* far. She was different. Not just another pussy.

She liked to think she was special. He loved Cedric. And just maybe loved her too.

"I've never played the Dom in front of anyone." Asher tucked his thumbs into his pockets and rocked on the heels of his shiny Italian loafers. "Anything I should know?"

As if I know? She slid open the top drawer of her dresser and grabbed the collar that went with her outfit. Pink and black studded leather. She held it out to him. "You do just fine showing the leather guys that you're the 'top.'"

"That's not the same and you know it."

All right, the dick chastity belt that Asher made Cedric wear to their meetings—which she couldn't attend—was a bit more than she wanted, but dominance was dominance, no? She just didn't want to seem available. She stuck the lollipop back in her mouth and wrinkled her nose. *Not to the "real" Doms.*

"Just pretend you own me. Okay?" She shoveled all her

belongings into her purse and sucked harder on the lollipop. "This is about Oriana."

"That's funny." Asher lifted her hair off her back and laid a soft kiss on her shoulder. "Because dressed like that, I'm thinking you'll get most of the attention. Which is exactly what you want."

"No it isn't! This is how subs dress!"

"For their *Master's* pleasure. So he can show off." Asher shook his head. "Why don't you wear that little red number you got from your shopping spree in Italy? It's quality and it's what I'd have you wear if you were really my sub. This outfit costs less than my socks."

"You're such a snob." She held her hair out of the way and let him put on her collar. "And I'm not your sub, so you don't get to tell me what to wear. That dress makes me look like a streetwalker."

"And this doesn't?"

"Fuck you!"

Asher laughed. "Not tonight, angel-face. I've already had my fill. Had to make sure Cedric was sated before I locked his cock." He chuckled at the face she made before leaving the room with a nonchalant, "You know I don't like sharing him."

Like you'd let me forget. Cedric wasn't even allowed to play with her much unless Asher was in the mood to watch him take her ass. Her thighs clenched as she recalled the last time. As usual, sex was good with either man, but . . . well, parts of her were neglected. Asher stimulated her clit to get her off, acting like it was a chore. Her "girly bits" did nothing for him. Of course, she had plenty of toys when she wanted to feel full in the most basic way, but it wasn't the same. For once it would be nice to have a man want her as a woman.

Which could happen tonight if that's what she *really* wanted. Asher wouldn't stop her from going home with another man, he wasn't possessive of *her*. The thing was . . . damn, finding a man at a BDSM club?

Taking a deep breath, she leaned closer to the mirror and tapped her bottom lip with a finger to make sure her lip stain was dry. Then she applied a generous coat of gloss and smacked her lips. *Perfect.*

She uncapped the rum and moved the lollipop to one side of her mouth so she could take a few good swigs from the bottle. Sweet fire burned through her, and she closed her eyes to absorb it. Once the sensation faded, she felt calm. In control.

Maybe, this time, she could be the one who did all the right things. She'd always been the troublemaker, the wild one, too irresponsible for anyone to ask for anything from. Maybe if she could prove she'd changed, Daddy wouldn't regret putting his faith in her. For once maybe *she* could be the good one.

You're going to a kinky club to watch your sister essentially marry two—three?—guys. And then there's your gay boyfriends. If you're going to be the good one, shouldn't you dump them and find a "normal" guy?

Well, Daddy didn't need to know what she did for fun. She took another swig from the bottle and winked at her reflection.

Never said I'd be that *good!*

* * * *

Leather, sex, and . . . carnations? Dean Richter rubbed his eyes with his thumb and forefinger, then undid the top button of his black dress shirt. Blades & Ice, the notorious hard-core BDSM club—*his* hard-core BDSM club—looked like it had been attacked by Martha-fucking-Stewart. White ribbons, flame colored bouquets, and a woven wood arch. Tim had opened the place at 5:00 a.m. so Max Perron, the groom, and, more importantly, the Dartmouth Cobra's best assist man, could set things up for his wedding. Max had been perfectly willing to rent a hall, but Tim had insisted the club was the perfect place for the ceremony.

Thanks, Tim. Dean leaned over the bar across from the insanity and glared at his half brother, who'd dragged the entire staff into decorating. *I'm going to make your wife twist your ball sack with rubber elastics, bro.*

A whimper drew his gaze to the doorway of a playroom just off the bar area.

Sloan Callahan, the Cobra's captain, forced Oriana Delgado, bride-to-be, to her knees. "You're spoiling the surprise. Max won't be happy."

"Please don't tell him."

"Give me one reason I shouldn't."

Oriana licker her bottom lip and her tone turned husky. "You're hurting me, Sloan."

Letting out a strangled laugh, Callahan released her. "Tease. We'll have our fun after the ceremony, not before."

"So we can't do *anything?*" Oriana undid the top button of Callahan's leathers. "At all?"

"Not unless you want to be upgraded from the flogger to the whip, love." Callahan smoothed his hand over Oriana's loose, shimmering bronze hair. "Dominik decided that was a fitting penalty."

"Oh no!" Oriana giggled and pulled the zipper down with her teeth. Her tongue darted out over the head of his cock. "To tell you the truth, I think he said that because he knows I'm ready."

Callahan's bare chest and stomach muscle tensed as he wound her hair around his fist. "Are you?"

Rather than answer, Oriana slicked Callahan's dick with her lips and tongue, taking him so deep Dean couldn't help but stare.

Damn. Out of Delgado's daughters, she's the last one I would have thought could . . . He tore his gaze from the pair and tapped the bar for another beer. No matter how often Oriana came to the club with her men, he still couldn't quite fit the image of the "sexually retarded" woman—as her ex-boyfriend and his ex-coach, Paul Stanton, had called her—and the beautifully submissive woman he'd come to know, in his head. Paul Stanton was the retard.

Then again, she wasn't submissive enough for his tastes. As long as she didn't break the club rules, it didn't really matter, but sometimes he found himself scratching his head when he saw what Dominik Mason, the Cobra's best blueliner and the man who'd collar her after Perron married her, put up with. Mason was a damn good Master—how could he let Perron and Callahan be so lax with discipline? The diminutive sub liked to top from the bottom, and even though she was usually reprimanded, Dean knew with Dominik alone she'd have been broken of the habit.

That's what you get for sharing a woman. He inclined his head to the scrawny bartender, who wore nothing but a leather cup and straps, and took his beer. Leaning one elbow on the bar, he surveyed the room with mounting disgust. The whole thing stank of a spoiled sub getting her own way. Only, Oriana *wasn't* spoiled and her Doms had tormented her excessively to get her to spill the details of her dream wedding. Which had been fun to watch. But the results had him on sugar overload.

"Bad time?" A young man in a stylish yet understated black suit—likely tailored to fit over those massive shoulders and long frame—took a seat across from him and gestured to the bartender for some of what Dean was having. His crew cut and the hard edge that stole some youth from his face gave him the appearance of a soldier on leave. A faint French accent and an easy smile lightened his stalk demeanor. "I have to admit, this isn't what I expected."

It took Dean less than a second to figure out who the man was. Landon Bower, the Cobra's new goaltender. Twenty-five and at the top of his game, Bower had been stuck on Montreal's farm team in Hamilton his whole career. The Cobras were desperate for a starting goaltender and Bower was everything they needed. Talented and kinky. The kink wasn't a requirement, but it made things easier. A good third of the team was in the lifestyle in one way or another. It wasn't exactly conventional for a team's general manager to seek out players with certain sexual . . . *leanings*, but it tightened the ranks, which was exactly what Dean wanted.

"This is not what my club usually looks like." Dean motioned toward the setup with his bottle. "Delgado's daughter is getting married to one of the players, and getting collared by another. My brother, your coach, thought it would be good for the team to do it here."

"And you don't agree?" Bower took his beer from the bartender and frowned when the man gave him a swift once-over. Straight then. He held the bartender's eye until the sub ducked his head and scuttled away. Then he swiveled in his chair to face Dean. "You have a problem with polyamory?"

"Not at all." Dean frowned. "You?"

"No. I've shared. I see the appeal." Bower paused and took a sip of his beer. "But I've never found a sub that would make the complications worth the headache. Takes a bit more work, in my opinion. One-on-one is hard enough."

"Very true." Dean tipped his beer bottle to clink it to Bower's. He liked the man already. "So you leave someone special in Gaspe or

Hamilton?"

"Would that be a problem?"

"Only if it distracts you from the game."

Bower grinned. "Nothing distracts me." He angled his bottle toward the club's packed entry. "Mon Dieu, I might find someone to help pass the time, though."

At the front desk, probably filling out the club's required waiver, a petite blond with an assto-die-for covered in snug pink booty shorts bent over.

Dean admired the view and thunked his fist on the bar. "Well now. Perhaps the night isn't a complete loss after all. I'll admit, Bower, this whole wedding things doesn't do it for me. But if it brings in some fresh meat like that—"

"I wouldn't want to alienate myself by competing with my GM for a woman." Bower cocked his head. "Not that either of us have a shot. Looks like she's taken."

Two slender men came up to fill in the forms beside the woman. The one in snug black jeans and a black silk shirt put a possessive hand on her waist, then laughed out loud and pushed her away. Then he moved in behind the man in leather chaps and a chastity belt, carrying a large white gift box topped with a huge white bow, and whispered something in his ear.

"Look a little closer, Bower." Dean's lips curved into a sardonic smile. "She's not taken. She's here with her gay friends. Probably a safety thing. Which makes her hot *and* smart."

Bower didn't say a word. Face impassive, he seemed to study the men like they were opponents in possession of the puck.

With her back still to them, the woman adjusted the collar of the apparent dominant's shirt and then rubbed her face against his arm like a kitten demanding attention. The dominant raked his fingers into her hair and pulled her in for a rough kiss.

"I'd say the dynamic of their relationship is a tad off-balance, but she's with them." Bower shrugged. "You've got unattached subs here, right?"

Dean kept his gaze locked on the woman and found he couldn't look away. His gaze trailed her as she made her way through the crowd filtering into the main room and settling on the long wooden benches that had temporarily replaced all the crosses and stocks and spanking benches. Something about her had every protective instinct within clawing past reason and demanding he see more. He considered himself an observant man. First impressions spoke volumes. Even from across the room, he could sense the connection between the men. The woman seemed like an afterthought, despite the passionate kiss.

You're reaching, Richter. Letting out a grunt, he nodded. "I've got plenty. I'll introduce you to a couple after the ceremony."

"I'm good with one," Bower said.

One brow arched, Dean regarded Bower, his tone dead serious. "You wanna make good with your GM? Do me a favor and take at least two off my hands. My most popular Dom and two of his trainees just took themselves off the market. There will be a number of needy subs, and I won't have them leaving here all depressed because they didn't get the coveted ring-collar-picket fence combo."

"Well since you put it that way." Bower grinned. "I suppose I can take one—or two—for the team."

"For the team." *Time to get down to business.* "I spoke to Noah—thank you for providing the reference, by the way. Your agent was smart to include a man I know personally on that very long list to vouch for you; it makes getting you settled in much easier. Anyway, he told me you're pretty good with electroplay. I've gone to few workshops, but I haven't gotten comfortable enough to start fooling around with the TENS or the wand. Think you could teach me?"

"Be glad to." Bower reached down, then lifted a metal case onto the bar. "I've got all the stuff for some demos, and I know a man who can supply you with more whenever you're ready."

"Perfect."

"Under one condition."

Dean's brow furrowed. "What?"

Bower took a deep breath. "Teach me how to use a whip. I . . . well fuck, I tried to convince myself I wasn't into giving pain. But I'm done pretending. I came out here because you guys offered the chance to accept who I am. I'm tired of playing with the light stuff."

"Electroplay isn't considered light."

"Yeah, well, I've always had a thing for the charge—I've been messing around with it since I was a kid. I learned a bit about the ropes and discipline, but I want more." Bower frowned at his bottle. "I want to be able to offer a sub whatever she needs. I've had a few who like playing hard and fast, and I hate sending them to someone else because I lack the skills. Sharing is one thing, but when you're doing it because you're not good enough—"

"I got it." Hell, why not? He liked training and this would work out well for them both. He'd learn a new skill, and he'd teach one of the most important men on his team not only how to wield a whip, but to accept the darker parts of himself. "Actually, unless I'm mistaken, the ceremony will end with one of my pupils using the whip on the new bride. Should be quite a show."

Bower's expression shifted, turning eager and almost feral. "I can't wait."

"You're gonna fit right in, Bower." Dean lifted his beer. "To the game, on and off the ice."

"To the game."

The faint music playing in the background changed. Romantic instrumentals to tell one and all things were about to get started.

And for the first time that day, Dean was looking forward to what lay ahead.

But as he made his way to the benches, the neglected sub in pink plagued his thoughts. Maybe he didn't understand her relationship with the men she'd come with. Maybe he was wasting his time.

Still, before the night was over, he'd meet her. Find out if he could give her what she needed.

Because the Dom in him knew, without a doubt, she wasn't getting it.

Yet.

Chapter Two

"**O**h my God, Oriana! You look amazing!" Silver burst into the small office turned changing room, the words leaving her mouth before she even saw her sister. Oriana had always been self-conscious about her appearance and had no sense of style, so Silver wasn't expecting much. Off the rack at best, hopefully formfitting?

She'd have something beautiful if she'd have let me help her.

Oriana hadn't wanted any help. She'd said Silver had enough to do with the move and the business. She'd insisted she and the men could handle it. As if men had any clue about wedding dresses!

They did a pretty damn good job setting up the club without your input. Fine, most of the people look like they're going to a kinky funeral . . . Almost everyone had either gone with black leather, suits, or outfits much like Cedric's. More than one sub, male and female, wore some kind of chastity belt and little else. She'd have stood out less if she'd stripped at the door. But the setup itself was pretty classy. *Some men have good taste. Look at Asher.*

Still, she would have liked to be involved. She'd hinted at Oriana needing a bridesmaid—all her sister's friends were in Montreal, and none had been able to take time off school to attend—but Oriana insisted she didn't need one. Fine, so Silver wouldn't "officially" have a place in the wedding, but she'd looked up some local caterers and florists anyway, emailing the information to Oriana just in case she needed them. She even gotten a bunch of wedding magazines and swung by Max's place to drop them off—with Dominik, after he told her Oriana was a little under the weather.

Oriana had called to thank her that evening. The phone call had been short and tense, but she'd pretended not to notice. Oriana was probably stressed because the press had latched onto the unconventional event, drawing the kind of attention her sister had always been uncomfortable with. Which she wouldn't want to talk to Silver about since she thrived on the spotlight.

Well, the press isn't here and Oriana deserves to be in the spotlight. Maybe she'll let me do her makeup . . . She fixed a cheerful smile on her lips and looked around. Oriana stood by the window, holding the thick black curtains together, head bowed. Then she squared her shoulders and turned.

The vision of her sister took her breath away.

In a long, white, one-shoulder gown, cut away to reveal the bottom halves of her breasts, Oriana looked like a bride more prepared for the wedding night than a walk down the aisle. A short zipper was the only thing holding the dress together, from the cutout to the point where the skirt was slit at one hip. Her natural olive-toned skin, which she'd inherited from their father, made her look exotic, like the woman in Silver's favorite painting, the *Gitana* by Fabien Perez, which one of her friends in LA bragged that she'd gotten from the artist himself. While some might envy Silver's fair, flawless complexion, she'd always longed for that honey-gold glow.

Her lips moved, but no sound came at first. Whoever thought Silver was the better-looking Delgado sister had never seen Oriana like this. She shook her head and whispered, "Wow."

"Thank you." Oriana gave her a tight smile and touched her partial updo, lightly fingering the wreath of baby's breath. "I take it you approve?"

"Oh, Oriana . . . " Silver held her hands out palms up as she approached her sister. "I always knew you'd make a beautiful bride. Max is a lucky man."

Oriana hesitated, then took her hands and squeezed. "What about Dominik? And Sloan?"

"Them too," Silver said, quickly. She didn't like Sloan, but now wasn't the time to let her personal bias show. And really, he'd chosen the better sister. "Is that what you've been so worried about? Did you think I'd judge you for being with the three of them?"

Shrugging, Oriana pulled away. "We were going to have a normal ceremony at first—for me and Max. Just so our father could . . . but he refused to come."

Silver bit her bottom lip. "Daddy's just old-fashioned. I tried to talk to him—"

"I *don't* need you talking to him for me." Oriana's eyes, only a shade lighter than their father's, turned hard and distant. "Stay out of it."

Silver swallowed and nodded. "All right." She fiddled with her clutch. "I was going to offer to do your makeup, but it's perfect."

"Yep." Oriana folded her arms over her chest. "I'm pretty much done here."

"That's . . . good. Do you want me to stay until things get started?"

"No. The ceremony will start in a couple of minutes." Letting out a sigh, Oriana moved toward the large desk and picked up her flowers. "Unless there was something you wanted to talk about? Have you settled in okay?"

"Yes." Silver moved away from the door and rested her hip on the edge of the desk. "Not that there was much setting up to do. The new condo Daddy bought was fully furnished. Once my stuff was shipped in from Hollywood, it felt just like home. I even managed to fix up the office in the forum. I haven't gotten a chance to go over all the paperwork, but with Anne's help it won't take me long to—"

"I'm sorry, I just realized I need a few moments alone." Oriana's clipped tone froze Silver's words like jagged lumps of ice in her throat. "If you could go take a seat with the rest of the guests?"

Silver blinked, nodded, and backed out of the room. Her shoulder hit the doorjamb and her lips formed another "I'm sorry," but Oriana had returned to the window.

Damn me and my big mouth.

She knew Oriana wasn't okay with her taking over ownership of the team for their father.

You just don't think.

Then again, that wouldn't surprise Oriana. Everyone knew Silver was spoiled and selfish. And she knew Oriana would forgive her, just like she always did. She stared at her sister's stiff back for a while, then retreated.

Making her way to the main room, Silver spotted Asher and Cedric seated near the end of the aisle. The Dartmouth Cobra players took up most of the front seats. By right, the sister of the bride should be up there.

But Oriana didn't need her family anymore. She had a new one. Loving and loyal. Exactly what she deserved.

So where do you fit in?

She didn't—not yet anyway. Reality hit her and she forced the tension from her body and leaned against Asher. Honestly, she shouldn't have expected everything to be all right with her sister—they'd hardly spoken since her return. Being like real sisters again would take some work.

Starting tonight, she would show Oriana she wanted that again. After all, she was the one who'd left, who'd decided she needed her freedom more than she needed anyone. She'd abandoned the sister who'd practically raised her, leaving her to deal with Daddy and all his issues alone.

But I'm back. And I'm not going anywhere.

* * * *

Dean rubbed his hands on his knees and sat up straight. Aside from the bride walking down the aisle in a dress that had several of the players adjusting themselves in their seats, the ceremony was as long and dull as he'd expected. It reminded him of an ex-girlfriend who'd been into soaps. She'd be sitting there, all teary-eyed, mumbling about how *finally* the current super-couple was getting their dream wedding. And he'd be forced to sit there, feigning interest while the priest went on and on for three episodes. Sappy personal vows would be exchanged, and the couple would rush out while the cast cheered and blew bubbles at them because rice was bad for the stupid birds.

Unless something interesting happened. Like the bride getting shot or someone in the crowd stood up and claimed to be having the groom's baby.

No such luck. Not that he wanted Oriana to get shot, but the minister . . .

Hell, is he reading the extended version?

The wedding ended. The collaring began. A bit more to the point, but Dominik seemed determined to cover everything. He included Max and Sloan in the ceremony, having Sloan cuff Oriana while Max braided her hair up and out of the way. She knelt and Dominik placed the collar around her throat. The small lock clicked and Dominik hung the key around his neck on a black ribbon.

"You belong to us, love," Sloan said, loud enough for everyone to hear. "Tonight you submit to our pleasure—whatever it may be. Do you give your consent?"

Oriana's cheeks glistened with tears as she tipped her head back. "Yes. But—"

Dominik frowned. "But?"

Well, this just got interesting. Dean leaned forward.

"I don't want to wait for your mark, Sloan." Oriana took a deep breath. "I want something tonight. Something that won't fade in a day or two."

"Are you sure?" Sloan laid his hands over her cheeks, using his thumb to wipe away her tears. "I'm happy to oblige, bunny, but I don't want you to regret it tomorrow when you're not all emotional. People could see it; it's still pretty warm out."

"I don't care—let them see." Oriana closed her eyes and touched her collar. "I need you to be part of this."

"I am." Sloan straightened. "And I will be. Dominik and Max will chain you for me, babe. Is that okay?"

Oriana shuddered. "That's perfect."

The foursome moved to a playroom, and the crowd followed as one without being invited. Dean stood in the doorway and glanced over at his brother as he and his wife approached.

"Was my wedding this long?"

Tim made a face. "Your divorce was longer. I think the four of them will make it work, don't you?"

Despite being bored out of his mind, Dean had to admit he could see the men really loved Oriana. And she loved them back without restraint. His wife had never been like that. She'd taken his ring and his collar, but she'd always held part of herself back. As soon as their daughter had grown up enough for her to gain some independence, his wife had decided she wanted the same. For years he'd told her to find her own interests, to be more than a stay-at-home mother—which she obviously hated being—and his sub. She'd insisted she had everything she wanted, then suddenly decided she wanted none of it. She walked out on him in search of a carefree life and ditched her daughter because, as she'd said, she'd never really wanted to be a mother. In front of their sixteen-year-old daughter.

Seeing the utterly crushed look on his daughter's face had hardened Dean's heart. He'd signed the divorce papers. But that hadn't been enough. His wife needed his money to have her fun. He'd resisted at first, but the long court battle had taken their toll on his daughter and he'd finally given in. Let the bitch have the money. His daughter needed to know someone still wanted *her*.

He'd been blind when it came to his wife, but he didn't think Oriana's men had that problem with her. She was as open and honest as they came.

"They'll work." Dean jabbed his thumbs into the pockets of his leathers and wrenched his thoughts away from the past. "Not what I'd want, but I've never met a woman like Oriana. It's hard to believe she's Delgado's kid."

"Can't argue that." Tim pressed a light kiss on his wife's brow. "But some of us are lucky and get the pick of the litter. My baby has a messed up family too, but she rose above it. You wouldn't want to know her siblings or her parents. But coming from them made her a strong woman you can't help but admire."

This was true. Tim didn't tell him much, but he'd done enough scenes with Tim's wife, enough aftercare before Tim took her away for the sexual stuff, to have learned a bit.

For the past two years, he'd kept scenes nice and impersonal. Platonic with Tim's wife, exploring a bit of pain, and purely sexual with the subs who came to the club not wanting a commitment. Maybe one day he'd meet a woman who would fit into his life in the way his wife never could, but he was perfectly happy without that now. He didn't need more.

Not yet.

Then again, he was open to the possibility. The woman in pink, for example. He hadn't seen her since he and Landon had watched her filling in the forms, but if she proved to be available as he thought she was . . .

Well, he might make an exception for her. He pictured her kneeling at his feet, naked, ready for more than just the vanilla with a bit of kink he'd settled for of late. A brief glimpse of what she had convinced him he had something to offer her. Even if only tonight.

* * * *

Silver swallowed convulsively, fighting not to jump every time Sloan's whip hit her sister's bare flesh. Her cheeks had heated slightly when Oriana had been stripped, and she hadn't wanted to look at first, but as each sharp *Crack!* got louder, she couldn't stop herself from staring at the long, red welts on her sister's back, butt, and thighs.

So far, so good. After all, Silver had been to plenty of BDSM and fetish clubs, she'd seen people whipped before. Of course, all the places she'd gone to had been more glamorous than Blades & Ice. The few men that had used a flogger or a paddle on her ass before fucking her knew better than to leave marks. She always had a list of limits a mile long when she played.

Looks like Oriana has a shorter list. A mocking voice said as she watched Sloan pause and kneel to kiss an unmarked spot on Oriana's hip. He stroked up her thigh and tipped his head back to say something only Oriana could hear.

Oriana nodded.

As Sloan straightened, a sick feeling of dread pooled in Silver's gut. She dug her nails into her palm and glanced over at Asher—who was kissing Cedric and completely oblivious to everyone else in the room. Other people were making out or . . . more. Apparently watching the scene had gotten a few people hot.

But these people didn't know Oriana. Oriana always put other's needs before her own. She would let Sloan push her further and further, never asking him to stop, if she thought it was what he wanted. And Sloan was just the type of asshole to take advantage of her passive nature.

Oriana's not stupid. Maybe this is what she wants.

Silver fumbled with her purse and took out a lollipop.

The whip snaked out over Sloan's head, came down in a black blur, and curled around Oriana's hip. Oriana gasped. A thin line of blood trickled.

Silver dropped the lollipop and rushed forward. "You son of a bitch!"

Sloan froze and stared at Silver. "What—"

Smack! Her palm went numb and she watched her handprint on his face darken to a bright red, shocked, but not satisfied. If only she was big enough, strong enough, to do some real damage. To make *him* bleed.

The crowd had gone silent. And not one member of the team Oriana cared about so much moved to help her. *Fucking cowards! Afraid to stand up to your captain?*

Well, she wasn't.

"Get away from her!" When Sloan didn't budge, Silver snatched the whip from his hand and threw it across the room. "She trusts you! How could you do that to her?"

His dark eyes narrowed. "Silver—"

"Don't 'Silver' me! You don't fucking scare me, Sloan." She poked him in the center of his bare chest. "The worst thing is, I was willing to give you the benefit of the doubt. But you're the same arrogant bastard you've always been. I think we both know exactly why you enjoy beating on women, don't we? Does Oriana know you're an impotent freak? Is that why she needs Max and Dominik?"

The area around the handprint on Sloan's face turned a darker shade of red. When he didn't say anything, she looked over at Max, who was standing in front of Oriana, speaking softly, and Dominik who was watching the crowd expectantly.

"Dominik, are you seriously going to put up with him treating her like this?"

The big black man ignored her.

Rage bubbled up inside and she moved to get his attention.

Suddenly, Sloan's hand shot out. He hooked a finger to her collar. "Who are you here with?"

"Excuse me?" She pried at his fingers in an effort to get free, but his hand seemed like one solid piece of iron. "Why does it matter?"

"Subs in this club don't disrespect Doms and get away with it." He jerked her collar. "Don't. Move."

All the blood left her face. She went still.

"Where's your Master?"

"He's there." She pointed at Asher, pleading with her eyes for him to come get her away from Sloan. *Fuck not being scared. This guy's crazy!*

Asher's eyes went big and round. He shook his head. "Look, man. We're not . . . I can't . . . Damn, she was just worried about her sister. Give her a break."

"Are you refusing to punish her?" Sloan threw his head back and laughed at Asher's nod. "Why am I not surprised? You treat BDSM like you do everything else, Silver? Like it's one big fucking game? Was coming here as a sub just your idea of playing dress up?"

"You better watch it Sloan," Silver said, doing her best to sound brave even though, for the first time in her life, she was the center of attention and really just wanted to disappear. Everyone was staring at her like *she'd* done something wrong. "I'm your boss."

"And I give a shit?" Sloan caught someone's eye, and Silver tried to twist around to see who. "You dealing with this or are we just kicking her out?"

"That's entirely up to her." The man's voice was deep, just gruff enough to be sexy, but it was the edge, the way he spoke as though obedience was a given, that made goose bumps rise all over her flesh. "I'll give you a choice, Silver. Sloan, you can let her go."

As soon as she was released, Silver shuffled away from Sloan, careful not to get too close to—*shitshitshit*—Dean Richter. Even over the phone, the man intimidated her, but it had been easy to come off as unimpressed without his sharp, hazel eyes locked on her, seeing everything she tried to hide.

"Are you listening to me?"

Silver evaded his steady gaze and tried to see around him. "Oriana?"

Dean glanced over his shoulder. "She's fine. Perron, Mason, would you please take Oriana to another room to come down?" He smiled. "It looks like she managed to stay in a good place."

Neither Max nor Dominik said anything, but moments later, a door at the other side of the room opened and closed.

Sloan stared in the direction of the door, then looked at Dean. "I'll leave this to you. I need to be there when Oriana's head clears."

"Go ahead," Dean said.

Once Sloan disappeared, Silver managed to hike her chin up and look Dean in the eye. "I want to go with them." Her pulse quickened. "Please. Just let me see if she's all right."

"So polite now." Dean circled her slowly, close enough that his leather pants brushed her thighs and his breath stirred her hair. "You're used to getting your own way, aren't you, Silver?"

As if that's a bad thing? "You said you were giving me a choice."

"I am." Dean stopped at her side. The fine lines on his cheeks smoothed away as his expression went blank. "Your choices are leave my club and don't ever come back, or accept whatever punishment I choose to give you."

"Punishment for what?"

"You're dating two lawyers and you don't know better than to sign something without reading it?" One brow arched, tone light, he seemed to be laughing at her.

A few people in the crowd did.

Deep, deep breaths and an eye roll kept the tears back. "I wasn't planning to do a scene tonight. I didn't think it was all that important."

"What you signed applies to every time you come here."

"Then I won't come back."

"Very well." He stepped aside. "You may leave."

For some reason, everything inside her rebelled against the very idea of walking out. And she couldn't quite figure out why.

Oriana. You're just worried about Oriana.

"I'm not going anywhere until I see my sister." She put her hands on her hips. "Things will be very unpleasant at work if you won't be reasonable."

"Don't threaten me, Silver."

"You should call me Miss Delgado."

Dean let out a gruff laugh. "I don't think so, pet. But while you're still here, I suggest you refer to me as either Master or Sir."

"Why should I?" She sniffed and gave him a swift, detached once-over. "Like Sloan said, I'm not a real sub."

"Aren't you?" He took a step forward and she took two quick steps back. He closed the distance between them and put his finger under her chin before she could move again. "Stop."

Her knees locked and she made a small sound in her throat as tiny fluttery things danced inside her belly at his command. She struggled against the clenching down low, but she couldn't stop herself from leaning, just slightly, toward him.

"There are things you could learn about yourself here, Silver. Things I and other Masters with experience could teach you. Have you ever been restrained?"

"Yes."

His eyes narrowed. "Respectfully, Silver."

She sighed. "Yes, Sir."

"Ropes or cuffs?"

"I hardly see why I would tell you—"

"You will tell me." His hand framed her jaw in a firm but not painful hold. "And you will *not* question me again."

Her mouth went dry. Her eyes wide. She was almost panting. "Cuffs. Handcuffs."

"What else have you done?"

Mind racing, she went over her considerable experience and tried to figure out a way to answer that wouldn't make her sound like a slut. His dark look didn't give her the impression she could make something up, so she went with vague. "Everything. I've tried a bit of everything."

"Everything?" His brow shot up. "How old are you?"

"Twenty-two."

People were laughing at her again. She wanted to scream, to throw something—but she had a feeling that would only get her in more trouble. Tears of frustration blinded her. One spilled down her cheek.

"Stay with me, pet. I'm the one you need to impress, not them." Dean used his thumb to wipe the tear away. "I've been in this lifestyle for about fifteen years, and *I* haven't done everything. You've barely had a taste."

"Fine." She wet her lips with her tongue. "But that doesn't mean I *want* to do more."

Dean let his hand fall to his side. "Then the choice is clear, isn't it?"

Yeah. Clear as fucking mud. Seriously, why even discuss all this with him? If she stayed, he would punish her. And it wouldn't be all fun and games. She could walk out with her pride barely bruised— impressing him didn't matter.

Shouldn't matter.

But it did.

"If I stay—"

"Silver," Asher called, warily eying Dean, who still hadn't moved. "Let's just get out of here. There are other clubs."

Several murmurs of accord came from the dwindling crowd. They were getting bored of her. No one wanted her here, and the entertainment value had passed.

"If you stay?" Dean prompted, as though he hadn't heard anything but her words. The flesh around his eyes crinkled slightly, and a dark strand escaped his neatly parted hair to rest on his forehead. The touch of grey over his ears gave him a distinguished look, but that unruly strand made him seem a little more approachable. And his tone wasn't mocking at all. Actually, it was warm, kinda nice.

Still, she shook her head. She couldn't finish that sentence.

He put his hands on her shoulders, and suddenly it seemed like they were the only two people in the room. Like his opinion *was* all that mattered. "Hear me now, Silver. I will be very disappointed if you take the easy way out. I think you're stronger than that. But I won't force you. You can go home with your boyfriends and have a pleasant evening."

She winced. Sure, going home with Asher and Cedric would be . . . pleasant. All she had to do was make sure they didn't forget she was there. Getting punished would be better.

She gulped as she resolved herself to her decision. *Maybe.*

"All right." She took a deep breath and rushed through the rest. "So long as it doesn't get too . . . personal." She forced a smile. "I'm not available."

"That remains to be seen," Dean muttered before he squared his shoulders and glanced over at Asher. "You may stay if you'd like. But I warn you, don't come here again playing the Dom if you won't follow through."

Asher nodded slowly. "Well, you see, things aren't really that way between Silver and me. If I decide to get involved in things with Cedric here, it will be different."

Wow. Thanks for completely abandoning me. Silver let out a strained, but light laugh. "Glad you made that clear, Asher."

"Silver—"

"You can go. I'll be fine."

Apparently, that was exactly what he'd wanted to hear. Because he left without looking back, Cedric following demurely on his heel. Which should have bothered her, but it didn't. Not at all. She didn't need anyone holding her hand.

"Give me your wrists." Dean slid his hands down her arms and forced her to focus on him as he undid a pair of cuffs from his belt. "I don't give safewords for punishments, but I won't push you any further than what you can take."

Oh, that's reassuring. She ground her teeth and let him secure the cuffs. "You sure asshole doesn't want to watch?"

"You will refer to him as Master Sloan in the club, pet. Preferably when he returns for his apology."

"Like hell, I will!"

"If you don't, your punishment will be even more severe." Dean's tone softened. "And you don't want that."

I really don't. But then she caught sight of the whip, laying like a dead black snake at the feet of the men in the front row, and her pride snapped back into place. Sloan, the fucktard, had used that whip hurt her sister. Dean couldn't beat an apology out of her no matter how hard he tried.

She folded her arms over her chest and sneered. "What will it be, ten lashes? Twenty? Bring it on. I'm not apologizing to that sorry excuse for a man."

"You're going to wish you didn't say that, pet." Dean sighed and took hold of her upper arm, towing her with him out to the main room. "Ten is a good number."

"I'm glad you agree."

He drew her in front of a large, throne-like chair and folded his arms over his chest. "Now strip."

"Strip?" She rubbed her arms and nodded. Fine, there was a crowd, but she had nothing to hide. All those women giggling and pointing could eat their fucking hearts out. She peeled off her top and shorts and faced Dean before letting out a flippant, "So what are you going to use?"

"My hand."

Aw, fuck.

* * * *

Dean struggled to keep his eyes on the mouthy little sub's face. Not that the pink number had left much to the imagination, but somehow she hid more in the swatch of cloth than most women could in a muumuu. Even naked, her posture and icy smile disguised the vulnerable woman he'd gotten a glimpse of earlier.

Why did the woman in pink have to be Silver Delgado? Why couldn't she have been someone a little easier to handle? Like . . . that Paris Hilton chick.

Not that high maintenance women ever appealed to him, but hell, maybe Silver wasn't what she pretended to be.

He pulled off his suit jacket and draped it over the high back of the large, oak throne. Then he pushed the padded, velvet arms out of the way. The piece was custom-made, used most often for spankings because it was damn comfortable, but the seat split down the middle to spread a bound subs' thighs wide for a good fucking. He glanced down at the seat and shook his head.

Not this time, Richter. She needs something else from you tonight.

Settling himself into the chair, Dean patted his thigh. "Come on, Silver. Let's get this over with."

She looked over her shoulder at the small gathering and inched closer. "Can't we do this somewhere a little more private?"

"No." He reached out and caught the short chain between her cuffs to pull her to him. "You had no problem disrespecting Master Sloan in front of an audience."

"He fucking deserved it."

Tired of arguing with her, he hooked an arm around her waist and dropped her over his left knee. As expected, she immediately kicked and tried to roll off his lap. So he pushed her knees down and held them in place with his right leg, all the while firmly gripping the nape of her neck to restrain her. "No. But *you* deserve this."

Without a breath of warning, he hauled back and laid a solid smack on her tight little ass. His hand was big enough to cover both cheeks, and a bright red mark blossomed over her pale flesh. She let out a screech which he cut off with two quick slaps.

"Damn you!" She bucked her hips and screamed when he responded with a resounding smack on her upper thigh. "You're hurting me!"

"That's the point, my dear." One more *crack!* and he decided to give her a little break. He petted her colorful bottom, speaking in a low, soothing tone. "There are rules here. You will learn to obey them."

"You think this will turn me into a good little sub?" She tossed her hair away from her face and glared at him. "Are you really that stupid, shithead?"

He had to clench his jaw to keep from laughing. *Shithead? I think you're ready for more.*

"You." *Smack!* "Will not." *Crack!* "Swear." *Slap!* "At me or any other member of this club."

"Fuck you!" She choked on a sob as his hand connected with the soft undercurve of her ass. "Stop! Stop!"

"One more if you promise to behave," he said.

"I promise!"

Finally. For a minute there, he'd wondered if she'd ever back down. He really didn't want to have to prolong her punishment, being that this was obviously the first time she'd ever been disciplined. Much as he enjoyed having her laid out, naked and available, she needed to know that accepting that she'd been in the wrong came with its own reward. He had a feeling a "good girl" would go a long way with her.

"Brace yourself, pet." He felt her tense up and waited. A bit of a headgame, but he couldn't help pushing her, just a little, to see how she'd react.

A few shaky inhales and she let her body go slack.

He gave her a solid *whack!* and set his hand on the small of her back as she absorbed the impact with a quiet dignity he admired. Gently stroking her tender bottom, he let his approval deepen his tone. "You did very well, Silver. I'm proud of you."

She went perfectly still. Abruptly her whole body stiffened up, and he had to tighten his grip to keep her from tossing herself to the floor. "As if I care? That's some ego you've got, Richter."

Well . . . he had to admit, that wasn't at all what he'd expected from her. He gave a curt nod and patted her butt. "In any case, your punishment is served. After you apologize to Sloan—"

Her laugh cut through his dwindling sympathy. "You've got to be kidding me. Did you miss the 'I'd rather take twenty lashes'?"

Stubborn didn't cover it. She had to be hurting! What was up with the continued defiance? "Silver—"

"Let me up," she hissed, squirming. "You got your kink on. I'm done."

"You're done when I say so."

"As if! You know, I could use you as a blueprint to build an idiot."

"Is that so?" He fisted his hand in her hair. "You've just earned yourself ten more. Sad thing is, I'd originally intended five because of your lack of experience."

"Oh yeah?" She wrenched her hair free and turned her head to curl her lips at him. "Well, experience this, asshole."

Bending down, she sank her teeth into his thigh.

The leather was thin enough for her to latch onto a nice chunk of skin. But the pain didn't reach the part of his mind that had locked on to the task at hand. He couldn't be angry at her, not when she was practically begging for more.

"Twenty it is."

* * * *

Landon took another sip of his beer and shook his head. Unlike most of the club's patrons, he didn't feel the need to get a front row seat for the woman's punishment, but still, he couldn't take his eyes off her. Despite her outrageous behavior, there was no denying she was submissive. Most women would have told Richter to take his club and shove it by now. Granted, she didn't have a safeword, but she didn't have to stay. No one would force her to go on with this, so somewhere, deep inside her, she wasn't ready for it to end.

But how long will she let this go on before she gives in?

He pushed away from the bar and moved closer to get a better look at her poor, abused bottom. Bruises had already formed, some purple around the edges, and Richter wasn't holding back. After another five he spoke softly to her, and some of the fight seemed to leave her as she hung her head and nodded.

The crowd had thinned. Whatever perverse pleasure they'd hoped to gain by watching Silver break had been denied. This could go on all night without her giving in completely. Most Doms would have shown her the door, figuring there was no way to get through that thick shell, but Richter was in another class and Landon had to give him props for not giving up on her.

I wouldn't either.

He finished his beer and sighed. Those kinds of thoughts would get him nowhere. He was positioned perfectly to see the effect the punishment had on Silver. The dim light caught the slick juices coating her thighs. Whether or not she was ready to admit it, Richter was getting to her. And he obviously thought she was worth the time and effort . . .

The play isn't over, Bower.

But with one last *Crack!*, the spanking was. He figured Richter would need a moment to bring her down from the twisted place between pain and pleasure, but circling around to where he could see clarity slash through the glaze of her eyes told him otherwise. He strode back to the bar and asked for a bottle of water. Then he asked a Domme by the bar where the sub blankets were.

Things were about to get nasty.

"I won't say it!"

Landon approached the throne, careful to avoid notice. Richter had Silver on her feet, his arm around her waist all that was keeping her at his side. Sloan Callahan had returned and was staring at her in a cold, detached way that seemed to steel her resolve.

"Pet, all this will be for nothing if you won't say you're sorry." Richter rubbed his forehead, as though trying to massage patience into his skull. "Whether you like it or not, Master Sloan is one of the men your sister has chosen. Your personal history with him is irrelevant. Can't you move beyond that? For her?"

Silver dropped to her knees with a hard thunk. She stared at the floor as she spoke. "I'm sorry if anything I did ruined tonight for Oriana."

Richter dropped his head back and muttered something to the ceiling before looking at Callahan. "Are you satisfied?"

"Yeah." Callahan shook his head. "I didn't come back for an apology anyway. Oriana asked me to tell Silver she was fine. And I needed to—damn it, Silver, I would never hurt her. I love your sister and—"

Head bowed, slender shoulders stiff, Silver muttered, "You *did* hurt her. And I'm sure you will again."

"I'm sorry you feel that way." Callahan scowled. "I've wasted more than enough time on this. She's your problem now, Richter. I'm going to take off and enjoy Max's honeymoon."

Every word out of Callahan's mouth seemed to have more impact that anything Richter had done. Landon saw the glisten of tears on her cheeks and had to fight the urge to go after Callahan. Not that the man was in the wrong, but damn it, she had her pride! What more did he want from her?

"Up we go, pet," Richter said.

Silver's eyes flashed as she shot to her feet. "Don't touch me!"

"It's over, sweetheart." Richter stroked her side, his jaw working when she jerked away from him and braced her hands on the throne. "Come sit with me for a bit. I know it was hard, but you did very well."

"I didn't have a choice, did I?"

"You didn't have to stay." Richter reached for her again, his hands hovering over her as she evaded him yet again. "You're a very strong woman, Silver. Come on, there's a good girl."

She let him touch her, let him pull her into his arms, surrendering for less than a heartbeat before she twisted away and lashed out. "No! I mean it, Dean! You've had your fun, now leave me alone!"

Her lunge forward came as a surprise, but Landon still caught her before she fell. Tucking her against his side, he wrapped the blanket around her shoulders and whispered, "Whoa there. Give yourself a second to get your bearings, *mignonne*. We get it. You're tough. That was still a rough scene, and your body needs some time to recover."

Richter's hard gaze locked with Landon's as Silver sobbed and pressed against him. He obviously didn't want to let her go, but the Dom in Richter understood he couldn't help her, not now when she still blamed him for whatever chaotic emotions tore through her.

Her bottom lip trembled. "I don't know you."

"Sure you do. You just signed off on a pretty decent contract for me to play for the Dartmouth Cobras as a starting goaltender." He drew her to a dark corner of the club, away from the lingering crowd, to a little nook behind a wood partition with a comfy sofa that offered some privacy. "Let's say I owe you."

"Sure." She sat up straight and eyed him as she took the uncapped bottle he offered. "But I don't get it. Are you a Dom?"

"Yes." He smoothed her sweat-slicked hair away from her face. "Why? Is that a bad thing?"

She frowned. "No. It's just . . . I was *bad.* Don't you guys look for the girls who want to lick your feet?"

"Right now—no offense—I'm not looking for submission from you." He grinned and leaned close as though they were sharing a secret. "Aftercare is part of my job. I've helped plenty of clueless husbands with it after a scene. He says or does the wrong thing and the wife is ready to walk out, but if I play with a woman, even if it's not sexual, I won't risk her dropping after and feeling bad about whatever happened."

"You had nothing to do with this . . . scene."

"Yes, but you plan to come back here, right?" He waited for her nod and pressed a soft kiss on her forehead. "Good. So do I. And I'd hate to think that what happened tonight scared you away."

"I don't scare that easy." She shifted, wincing as her hip pressed against his. But she relaxed against him, not resisting as he wrapped his arm around her shoulders. Such a tiny thing, quivering, smelling as sweet as the little flowers decorating the place, with the voice of an angel spitting venom. "So what is it? You figure if you're nice, I'll let you fuck me?"

Christ. Just holding her had him hard as fucking stone, but those words caused all the blood to retreat from his dick and rise up to pound in his skull. She really didn't see anyone wanting her for anything else, did she?

Much as he hated lying, he couldn't stop himself from reassuring her. It wasn't really a lie if it was partially true, right? "I try to do a good deed a day. Would it hurt your feelings if I tell you I have no intention of sleeping with you?"

Her muscles hardened under his arm. Then went slack. She laid her head on his shoulder and let out a heavy sigh before taking a sip of water. "Oddly enough, no. It's not insulting. You really do this with women you don't have sex with?"

"Yes." He pressed his eyes shut and rested his cheek on her soft, tussled hair. "You ever snuggled with a straight man that didn't want to fuck you?"

"Honestly? No." She snuggled a little closer. "So you're saying you don't want to fuck me?"

This time he could answer with the truth. "I don't want to fuck you."

"Good." And with that she let herself go. "That's a nice change."

Those words wouldn't have left her mouth if she wasn't feeling so raw, so exposed, but he'd take it. He made sure she drank the full bottle and held her arms when she tried to stand. Her legs shook and she let out a weary laugh.

"It still hurts."

"It will—for a while." He licked his bottom lip and forced an easy smile. "The question is, what do you want now? Should I call you a cab?"

"You probably should. But . . ."

"But?"

She kept herself pressed against his side, thankfully nowhere near the stiff erection that saluted her between his thighs. Her focus was on Richter, at the bar tipping back a shot. His eyes hadn't left them once. The man hadn't liked Landon taking over aftercare, but, as a Dom should, he put the sub's needs before his own.

"As a . . . friend—not that I should be telling you this at all—"

"Tell me." He watched Richter stand and approach the bartender before heading to a small corridor that led to the private rooms upstairs. The ones he'd been told right away were for Richter alone. "That way I'll know I haven't lost my touch."

"I don't want it to be over. Not now." She burrowed her face under his arm. "Not like this."

"You want him."

Lie to me, babe. I don't usually allow it, but I will now.

But he'd gained her confidence, so she replied with complete honesty as she stood. "I do. And I take what I want."

"As you should. They say life is short." He kept his eyes on her. Legs steady. Fully aware of her surroundings. She knew what she was doing. "Go for it."

"I think I will." She spared him a carefree smile. "Thank you for this. I was feeling . . . a little weak. You made the ground solid again. I don't have the words to say it better."

"You've said it just fine, pet." He wanted to use a more personal endearment, but he had a feeling she needed nothing more. From him anyway. "I'm glad I could help."

"You did." Her brow furrowed as she looked around. "Damn, where's my purse? I want to leave you my number. I don't usually, but I want to hang out some time. For coffee or something."

"You left your purse with your clothes." He pretended not to notice her blush. She'd forgotten that she was wearing nothing but a blanket. "Tell me your number. I won't forget."

She told him, then laughed. "This is stupid. After the way I acted, he'll tell me where to go."

"I doubt that." *I wouldn't.* "You'll never know if you don't put yourself out there."

"True." She squared her shoulders. "Maybe if I show him how good I can be—"

"Be you." Landon pushed his own feelings aside and gave her the best advice he could, all the while wishing he was in Richter's place. "He won't say no."

"I hope you're right."

"I am."

"Okay." She took a step, then paused. "See you . . . soon?"

"Of course." He forced a smile. "I'll give you a shout tomorrow."

"That would be great. I need a friend here."

He watched her slide up the shadowy stairwell and nodded to himself. *You've got one, sweetheart.*

Chapter Three

By the time Silver reached the top step, her nerves had taken a hike. She combed her fingers through her hair, fluffed it, and took a deep breath. A butt clench brought back the sharp pain from the spanking and the mess of emotions that had come with it. Rage, mortification, disgust—mostly in herself. For a split second, her mind had gone to a place where she actually wanted Dean to punish her, where she felt like she deserved it.

They do say crack kills brain cells. She smirked, rubbing the tiny vial in her purse through the fabric, and tightened her grip on the pale blue fleece blanket Landon had wrapped around her. Really, it was no wonder that she'd gotten all confused down there—Dean was a hunky piece of manflesh. She liked it rough sometimes, and he could definitely scratch that particular itch.

Before she could change her mind and consider just how rough things might get, she lifted her fist and rapped softly on the door.

"One minute!" Dean called.

A *bang!* followed by cursing, made her wince. *Okay, maybe this wasn't such a good idea.*

The door flew open just as she was about to retreat. "Wh— Silver?"

His gaze swept over her and instinct took charge. She stepped forward and let the blanket fall.

He shook his head. "Silver—"

"I've taken all the humiliation I can stand for one night, Dean." She flattened her hands on his chest, fingering the buttons of his shirt and keeping her eyes downcast because she knew he'd like that. "Don't make me beg."

Letting out a skin-tingling chuckle, he wrapped his hands around her waist and pulled her against him. "As if you would."

"If that's what I have to do for you to take me . . ."

"Take you . . ." He ran his thumbs over the soft curve of her stomach, and sparks with wings skittered around within. Her muscles jumped and he tilted his head slightly, studying her. "Are you sure?

The spanking shook you pretty bad. You wouldn't even let me—"

She put a finger over his lips. "I'm still pissed at you about that. Don't remind me. All you need to know is I know exactly what I'm doing."

"Do you?" He drew her away from the door and swung it closed. Then he pressed his eyes shut and gave his head a little shake. "Damn woman, I hope that's true, because I'm in no condition to be the sane one here."

A throaty laugh escaped her. She rose up on her tiptoes and spoke with her lips close to his. "Are you drunk?"

"Not quite." His eyelids lowered and his lips curled. The hint of alcohol on his breath made her mouth water. He flicked his tongue over her bottom lip. "But I've had enough to accept your offer, even though I should make you get dressed and send you home in a cab." His hot breath caressed her lips. "Even though we'll both regret this tomorrow."

We will, won't we? Doubt crawled into her mind, but she squashed it like a gnat. She smiled, her mouth just over his. "I wouldn't want you thinking I took advantage of you. Call a cab if you want."

"Not likely." With that, he claimed her mouth with a fierce kiss that promised all she'd come for. She moaned as his teeth tugged at her bottom lip. He clenched his fists in her hair, and his tongue delved deep into her mouth, thrusting, possessing, driving her mad as the rest of her body screamed for the same attention.

Together they stumbled into his living room. He helped her remove his shirt without breaking his assault on her mouth and then fell onto the sofa. She undid his pants, pulled out his dick, and explored the hot, thick length with her hands while he dug his fingers into her shoulders and practically dragged her into his lap.

"You've had me fucking bursting at the seams since the moment you walked into my club—before I even knew who you were, I wanted you." He let his head fall back and groaned as she fisted her hand around his cock and rubbed the head against her wet folds. "And when you took everything I could give—"

"Not everything." She slid to her knees and flicked her tongue over the tip of him, tasting her own musky arousal mixed with his salty pre-cum. "Not yet."

In one smooth, practiced motion, she had his full length in her mouth, hitting the back of her throat as she bobbed her head. His pulse pounded against her tongue and she swallowed, sucking harder and harder until he grunted and jerked her to her feet.

"Enough. I want more than your mouth." He belied the comment by taking her mouth, stealing her breath and her strength with a kiss that slammed the door on her illusions of being in control. "I have condoms in my wallet."

She shook her head and looked around. Her purse was on the floor by the blanket. She fetched it and dug inside for her stash. "I come prepared."

His expression darkened, but he held still as she covered him. He didn't speak until she climbed onto him and moved to take him inside her. "Stop."

Eyes wide, she stared at him. "What?"

He grabbed her wrists and roughly drew them behind her back. Holding them with one hand, he patted her thigh with the other. "Open."

A shudder passed through her as she tested his grip. He might as well have shackled her. Part of her rebelled, wanting to take charge, but lust spilled over and she surrendered to it, willing to let him lead the way if it would end with her being filled up and satisfied.

She spread her thighs as far apart as she could and whimpered as he angled her back. He slipped a finger between her folds and drew it over her clit.

"Look at that pretty pussy." He opened her with his finger and thumb. "You're so wet, sweetheart." He slowly pushed one finger inside her. "Hot and tight. I think you've been needing this for a while, pet."

She gasped and threw her head back as she thrust her hips forward. "Yes!"

"How long has it been since you had a nice, hard dick in your cunt, Silver?"

"Too long! Please!"

"Soon." He lowered his head and caught a nipple with his teeth. Exquisite pain speared straight down, and she let out a desperate, keening sound. He teased the tip of her nipple with his tongue, then glanced up at her. "Sensitive nipples. Do you think your men will notice if I leave them nice and red?"

"No." Her eyes teared up and she swallowed. The last few times Asher had fucked her ass, he'd left her shirt and bra on. Her breasts didn't interest him. "Dean . . . I don't want to talk about them."

"Poor baby." He shook his head and lapped a circle around her other nipple. "Forget them." His finger pushed in deep and he curved it forward, holding her still as she squirmed. "Right now, you're all mine. And I happen to love your breasts."

She panted as he sucked her breast into his mouth. *Fuck!*

Too much. With just his finger in her cunt and his lips on her breast, he made her feel more than she could ever recall feeling. She bucked and quivered as he fucked her languorously with that one finger, licking and nibbling at first one breast, then the other, until the nerves in both burst into flames. Her core clenched around his finger, and she tumbled into a fast, hard orgasm. The pleasure blanked her mind and she collapsed onto him, hardly even noticing that he'd released her hands as she clung to him.

"I'm not done with you." He pressed her head against his chest. "But I think you need a minute."

She squeezed her eyes shut and shook her head. "No. More. Please."

"No more?" He laughed when she sat up straight. "I'm teasing, pet. Clasp your hands behind your neck. I need to be inside you."

Shifting to give him easier access, she twined her fingers under her hair, not caring anymore that he'd taken over. The way he took away her choices, they way he forced her to slow down, made her *feel* more of what he was doing to her. She'd never been so aware of her body. So aware of the man she was with. His hand on the small of her back, his other around his dick, made her throb with anticipation. He helped her rise up just enough to slip himself into her entrance. Then he grasped her hips and yanked her down hard.

"Oh!" She dropped her head onto his shoulder, shaking as her body adjusted to him. A little too long, a little . . . too . . . thick. He stretched her more than any man she'd ever been with. "Wait. Wait."

"Yes. I can tell." He let out a gruff sound and held her tight. "Jesus, Silver, hold long *has* it been? You should have told me." He put his hand under her chin and kissed her. "Why? Why would you do this to yourself?"

No, no, no! She gulped against the tightening in her throat. He couldn't do this. Not now. He was a means to an end. That was it. Her relationship with Asher and Cedric was none of his fucking business.

A little honesty would get him moving. "You're a lot . . . bigger than I'm used to. But you've got me so wet, I think I can—"

"You can." He glided his lips down her throat, then laid gentle kisses over each of her breasts. "I would grab your ass and make you take me deeper, but that would hurt. And I don't want to hurt you anymore. I just want to feel you around me."

Her hips rose. She lowered slowly. And sucked in air as his dick forced all the delicate tissues within to expand. "You aren't hurting me You're driving me insane. I want you fuck me hard on the floor. I want to be under you—"

"That's not happening tonight, love" He stroked her bottom, pressing lightly with his fingertips until she moaned at the sweet bite of pain. "If you're under me, all the pressure will be on the bruises. If you weren't so tight, I'd try it, but together, it's too much. Lift up a bit. Take me, baby."

She lifted up and braced herself. "Don't hold back."

"I won't."

He fucked up into her, harder, faster, his fingers digging into her flesh as he made her meet every violent thrust. All the while she kept her hands locked behind her neck, never questioning his control. Only once she reached the edge of another climax did he slow, easing her back just enough that the denial became torture. He lifted her a bit higher and teased her sporadically clenching entrance with the head of his cock, penetrating her over and over until she gasped a wordless plea.

"Ask me, Silver." He stroked in a bit deeper, then resumed his shallow thrusts. "Ask if you may come."

Her lips parted and her tongue stumbled on the words. "Let me. Please let me."

"Say 'Please let me come, Sir'."

Everything inside her tightened and she screamed. "Let me

come, Sir!"

"With pleasure." He slammed into her and held her down, rocking his hips, drawing her orgasm out until the ecstasy gained a sharpness that bordered on pain. His dick throbbed and she cried as the pulsing within yanked her up to the peak yet again. He reached between them and roughly manipulated her clit. "Give me another one, baby. Just one more. Give it to me now!"

Tears spilled down her cheeks as she came violently, the glorious agony ripping through her so abruptly that she collapsed onto him and made a sound that scored her throat. Every tiny movement within made her wince. She brought her hands down and pressed her clenched fists to his chest.

"Don't. Move." She rubbed her wet cheeks against his shoulder and tried to remember how to breathe. "I'm begging you. Sir. Master. Whatever. Please don't move."

"Shh." He stroked her hair and her back, whispering. "I won't move until you're ready."

"Thank you." She closed her eyes and let herself go slack as exhaustion took over. "Oh, thank you."

* * * *

Dean tucked Silver into his bed and eyed the bottle of whiskey on his nightstand. He wanted to blame the alcohol for what he'd let happen, but that was a cop-out. Granted, his inhibitions had taken a beating, but even stone cold fucking sober, he doubted he would have turned her down. Sainthood had never been on his to-do list. Then again, fucking his boss's daughter hadn't been on there either. He considered himself an intelligent businessman, and being with Silver Delgado was a bad idea on so many levels.

Not that he could find it in himself to care.

You're a fucking hypocrite, Richter. He thought back on telling Mason off for getting involved with Oriana months earlier and sighed. At least Mason had been serious about the girl. Things between him and Silver had gone way too fast.

What am I going to do with you, little one?

He stretched out at her side and brought a strand of pale gold hair to his lips. She looked damn good in his bed, her lips swollen and red from his kisses, long black lashes resting lightly on her flushed cheeks giving her an almost innocent allure.

A snort escaped him. Silver was anything but innocent. Her inexperience in the lifestyle didn't change the fact that she'd been around the block a time or two. She took what she wanted, and for some reason, she'd wanted him.

But he wanted more. The things he would do to her, if given a chance—his dick hardened at the thought of having her wrapped up in his ropes, completely helpless, her responsive body available to him, her mind shut down, nothing in her head except for what he'd make her feel.

For what seemed like hours, he lay there, determined to let her rest. But as he drifted off to sleep, she shifted and his hand glided down from her hip to the hot, moist slit between her thighs. He had to force himself to roll away from her long enough to find a condom, but as soon as he was covered, he gently drew one of her legs over his hip and slid into her.

"Mmm, Dean." She wiggled and turned her head, her eyes still closed as she sought his lips. "I like you inside me."

He kissed her and twined their hands together, drawing them up between her breasts as he held her tight. His lips skimmed over hers as he whispered, "I enjoy being inside you. I debated leaving you alone for the rest of the night, but you tempt me without any effort at all."

She giggled and slipped her lips down to his throat. "It's a natural talent. My photographer told me I have a fuck-me face."

Dean decided if he ever met this photographer, he would make him eat his fucking camera. "A fuck-me face. Hmm. What about the men who want more than a quick fuck, Silver? Surely you've had a few?"

"Yes." She nipped his neck. "But I tend to avoid them. The drama isn't worth it. You're not one of those sappy, we-had-sex-and-I-want-to-keep-you types, are you?"

"Who me?" He let out a dry laugh. "I don't go for the drama either. I'm usually careful about choosing subs from the club to play with—some get attached after you make them come. I take it you're not that kind of girl."

"Nope." She moaned as he fully sheathed himself in her hot, wet cunt. "Should I put that on my club résumé?"

"We will not discuss your finding another Dom now." He thrust in, letting his pelvis hit her abused butt hard enough to remind her of the bruises he'd left. "You've already taken on more than you can handle, pet. I'm not usually this nice."

"*Nice?*"

"Nice. I'd love to see how far I can push you, but I'm feeling generous. Just enjoy it."

"That sounds lovely." She ground her hips down and took him deeper. "I've imagined so many different positions with you, Dean. This wasn't one of them, but I like it."

He worked himself in and out of her at a lax pace, wondering what those positions were, and when she'd imagined them. Someday soon, he'd make her tell him. For the moment, it was enough that she'd lowered her guard enough to say what she had. "Good. Because I plan to take my time with you. I will know your body better than you do."

Her pussy squeezed him, but it wasn't quite erotic. She was trying to pull away from him, not physically, but emotionally.

And just like that, her guard was back up.

"Let's keep this about sex."

"Why?" He smoothed his hands up her sides and over her breasts, molding them and brushing her nipples lightly with his fingertips. Gentle pleasure to soothe her. "What are you afraid of, Silver?"

She went utterly still, then gyrated her hips in a way that told him they were done talking. "Fuck me, Dean. Fuck me hard and fast and make me come. That's all that matters."

He couldn't fuck her the way she wanted him to without hurting her, and something told him that wasn't what she really needed. So he pulled her flush against his body and kept a steady rhythm, ignoring her efforts to make him go faster.

"I want you, just like this." He chuckled and kissed her throat when she groaned. "Keep fighting me and I won't let you come at all. I'm close. I can be a bastard and just take what I want without giving you anything."

"I don't doubt that."

"Enough. You're in my bed, in my arms. I'm deep inside you, and I can feel how much you're enjoying this. Don't force me to pull out and find my cuffs."

She squeezed him tight. "Handcuffs?"

"No. Something that will hold you without damaging you."

"Handcuffs never hurt me much."

"Because they were just a prop." He drove in and stayed there, gripping tight to her waist so she couldn't move away. "When you wear my restraints, you'll know the difference. I would love nothing more than to have you spread-eagled on my bed, completely open to me."

"You're really into the dominant thing, aren't you?" She closed her eyes and rested her head back in the crook between his shoulder and his neck. "You don't have sex without being in control."

"No. I don't." He took her wrists, pinned one under his body, and held the other between her thighs. "And you don't really enjoy sex unless the man takes control."

"That's not true."

"It is. I know you don't want to talk about them, but I think you should. Does Asher play the Dom with you? Does he hold you down and takes your ass despite your protests? I can imagine you getting off on that. Then you don't have to think about how he's using you."

"No, it's not like that!"

"Yes, it is." He released her hand and slipped his between her butt cheeks. "Play with yourself, Silver. I'm going to finger your ass."

"Don't!" She clenched as he worked his fingers between her butt cheeks, using her own juices as lube as he forced his fingers into the tight hole. "My pussy is all yours. But please, please don't do that."

"I won't fuck your ass. Not tonight." He pushed his thick fingers into her and moved them in time with the thrusting of his dick. "But I will take all of you. You enjoy this. You're a little ass slut, aren't you? That's why you thought your gay men could satisfy you."

"Oh! Oh!" She bucked and cried out. Her asshole clamped around his fingers. "I didn't know!"

"Didn't know this was all they would give you?" He slipped his dick out of her cunt and continued fucking her with just his fingers in her asshole. He was tempted to put his cock in there, but she'd been used that way too often to truly enjoy it now. "I'm bigger than they are; I could take you there and make you feel like an anal virgin." He thrust into her pussy until his dick filled her completely. "But, if given a choice, I prefer a nice, wet cunt."

"Don't stop!" She panted. "I like that. I like you taking it all."

He frowned as he drove his fingers and his dick in harder. "You're with two men. Don't they ever—"

"Never. I've asked, but Cedric can't really get off with a woman . . ." She hissed a curse. "Why are you doing this? I don't want to talk! I want here and now!"

"I won't always give you want you want." He pounded in, feeling her pussy grasping at him as she came. "But like I said, tonight I'm feeling generous."

He hugged her to him as he found his release, cursing himself as she sobbed and curled into a little ball before he'd even drawn out. He'd given her pleasure, but, at the same time, he'd made her acknowledge things she wasn't ready to face.

Sometime during the night, she shifted in sleep and snuggled up to him, a shuddery breath escaping her as she burrowed her face between his neck and his shoulder. He rested his cheek against the top of her head, sharing her pillow, amazed at how good it felt just to hold her. He couldn't remember the last time he'd looked forward to seeing a woman in the morning light.

His lips twitched into a smile as he inhaled the honeydew scent of her hair. *When's the last time a man served you breakfast in bed, sweetheart?*

Chapter Four

Silver fingered the lapel of her light grey suit jacket and flipped through the pages of the tome she'd been reading for—she glanced at the clock over the door in Daddy's office and groaned—just an hour? Incredible. How in the world was she supposed to learn anything about the game if all the stupid facts bored her to tears? She'd gotten here early, *despite* her crazy night, all motivated to take on the role as the new owner, but no matter how hard she tried, she just didn't get it. It was a game. Big strong men got suited up in bulky equipment and bashed each other around while trying to get the puck in the net. Sometimes the guy standing there stopped it. Sometimes he didn't.

And she was paying millions for these guys to mess around on the ice? Seriously?

She sipped at her coffee and made a face at the cold mouthful. Pressing a button on her phone, she waited for Anne to answer, tapping her fingers on the desk at the silence. *Hell, am I paying anyone to actually work around here?*

Pushing away from the desk, she stood and strode to the door. Throwing it open, she shouted. "Anne!"

"Yes, Miss Delgado?" Anne scurried out of the bathroom across from the reception area, still doing up her skirt. "I'm sorry. I can't seem to go for more than five minutes without having to pee . . . oh . . . you didn't need to know that."

Well, don't I feel like a bitch? Silver plastered a smile on her lips and held her hand up. "It's okay. Being pregnant must suck. I just wanted a fresh coffee."

"I'll get it now," Anne said.

Silver shook her head. "No. Take it easy. Just tell me where to go—"

The elevator dinged and Silver smiled as Asher stepped out with two coffees in hand and a small paper bag. His expression told her he planned to do some sucking up.

Perfect.

"Never mind!" She held the door to Daddy's—no, *her*—office and then joined Asher inside. "This is a nice surprise."

"Silver . . ." Asher placed the tray on the desk, his blue eyes wide as he turned to her. "I'm sorry. I was an asshole last night. You didn't give me a chance to apologize when you came home to get ready for work—I couldn't leave things weird between us. I never should have left you at the club."

The club. She closed her eyes and saw it all. The spanking, escaping from Dean in a haze and sitting with Landon, who'd taken care of her when she was ready to fall apart. Then leaving him for some hot sex—some *really* hot sex—with the man that had beaten her ass. What the hell had she been thinking? Dean Richter, of all people? A fucking Dom! She'd almost lost herself to him . . . almost, but not quite. Her brain had made an appearance before dawn. She'd left him a nice note to wake up to.

Yeah, I'm sure he loved that.

Too bad. She seemed to recall telling him she wasn't into guys that wanted to "keep her." And he'd said he understood.

Making her way around her desk, she let out a shallow laugh. The rich aroma of coffee had her feeling very forgiving. "I made it clear I wanted to stay, Asher."

"So you're not mad?"

The coffee burned her bottom lip so she pressed her finger to it. Sitting reminded her of worse pain and she frowned, leaning forward to take some pressure off her butt. "I didn't say that."

"Damn. How bad did he hurt you?" Asher came to her side, took her coffee, and set it aside before pulling her to her feet. "Let me see."

"Here? You've got to be kidding!" She brushed his hands away and straightened her wide-legged grey trousers. "I'm fine. My butt's just colorful. No big deal."

Asher cocked his head. "You've got the professional thing going for you. But I've got to ask." He grinned as he opened the front of her jacket. "What happened to your shirt?"

Well, fuck. Silver had hoped no one would notice. The jacket buttoned up high enough to completely cover her bra. Her face heated up. "You starched it. I tried it on, but it felt weird and I don't have any other shirts that go with this suit."

"You're so cute." He did up the buttons, then cupped her cheek in his hand. "So, how's your first day so far?"

"Horrible." She plunked into her chair and clenched her jaw when her butt throbbed in protest. "I'm going to go crazy if I don't do something. I know I need to learn more about the game, but there's got to be more to this job than signing checks."

"Depends." Asher picked up one of the magazines she'd left on the corner of the desk. "*Cosmo?*"

"For my free time."

"They have a hockey feature." He flipped through the pages and whistles. "There's a sniper from Florida who made the sexiest bachelors top twenty. He looks familiar . . ."

A sniper . . . Daddy had left a message on her phone last night, and among a lot of incoherent grumbling, had mentioned the team needed a sniper. Googling the word told her a bit—basically it was a "great goal scorer." All right, Daddy hadn't specifically said he wanted *her* to get the "sniper," but why else would he have called?

Your job is to run the team while he can't. So do it!

Silver sighed and took in the full page image of the heartthrob as Asher held out the magazine. Oh, yeah, she'd buy season tickets to watch him play. Too bad the Cobras didn't have more men like that. Fine, they had Max, but he was taken. Dominik was a little too intimidating for her tastes, and Sloan . . . well, he was just an asshole. A few guys on the roster were worth a second look, but this guy . . .

"That's it!" Asher smacked the sports rag from the pile onto the desk in front of her. "He's a free agent. And he's made waves making it clear that he's looking for the best offer. You've got space on your cap for him and another high-profile player."

She bit her bottom lip. He'd lost her. "My cap?"

"There's a limit on how much you can spend on players. From what I know about hockey, a sniper is always a good investment." Asher ran his finger down the center of the picture, pausing over the soaked white boxer concealed crotch of the man in question. "Want me to make the call?"

"I don't even know how this works." She wrinkled her nose at the big dusty book that hadn't helped her at all. Where was the book that would tell her whether the hot guy was any good? "Shouldn't we look at his stats first?"

"Sure." Asher flipped open the sports magazine and pointed at a long list of names and numbers. "Pretty impressive if you ask me."

"You're a lawyer; what do you know about player stats?"

Asher rolled his eyes. "It's not complicated."

Right. It might as well have been Chinese. But she'd asked Asher to come work with her because she trusted his advice. Mostly. He'd never screwed her over when she was signing his paycheck anyway. "Do we just make an offer?"

"Sure." Taking out his phone, Asher glanced at her as he dialed. "I'll find out who his agent is. If this is what you want . . ."

The whole paying insane amounts for players had escaped her, but suddenly it kinda made sense. It was just like casting parts for a movie. Big names brought extra exposure. And this man was obviously a big name.

"Go for it." She squared her shoulders and took another gulp of coffee. Daddy had chosen her to take over for a reason. Maybe this was it. Much as she loved Oriana, she couldn't very well make unbiased decision with three of her men on the roster.

And *Sloan* was one of those three men. The only reason she'd woken before dawn was because she'd dreamed of him using the whip on her sister. But in the dream it was much worse than at Oriana's wedding. So much blood—Sloan asking if Oriana wanted more. And through lips bitten clean through, Oriana had whispered *"Yes."*

Oriana's not stupid. She won't let Sloan go that far.

Did it need to go *that* far? Dominik and Max obviously wouldn't stop him.

But maybe I can.

Speaking of which . . . "When you're done with that, find Sloan Callahan's contract. I want to know how long we're stuck with him."

"Got it."

While Asher made himself familiar with all her daddy's files, Silver leaned back in her chair and finished her coffee. *Maybe this won't be so hard after all. People want entertainment. Hot guys who can score. I can give them that. And this is a family business. For once, it's me looking out for them.*

Fifteen minutes later, a contract was drawn up and placed before her for her signature.

She signed on the bottom line with flourish, enjoying the feeling of power.

Damn, I love my job.

* * * *

"Sir?"

Dean glanced over at Guy Bolleau, the assistant general manager, and shook his head. "I've asked you not to call me that, Bolleau."

"Sorry, Mr. Richter." Bolleau quickly stepped aside to let Dean pass. The approaching season left Dean with little time for pencil pushing, so the ever practical man had temporarily taken over Dean's office.

He was probably the only person Dean would let infringe on his territory. Even after spending the whole morning hard at work, Bolleau managed to keep the place looking undisturbed. The man was like a very efficient ghost, invisible except for how smoothly he kept things running.

After shedding his suit jacket and hanging it in the small closet beside his desk, Dean settled into his large, leather chair and gestured for Bolleau to take the seat across from him. "What is it, Bolleau?"

Bolleau approached the chair, fiddling with the pen in his breast pocket as he eyed the papers on the desk. "I'm not quite sure how to tell you—"

"Spit it out, man!" Dean pressed his lips together and immediately regretted snapping at the man. Bolleau didn't do nervous. Whatever he had to say must be bad. "I apologize. Training camp has revealed several . . . weaknesses in the team I had not foreseen. Including my brother's tendency to coddle rookies—which we have in excess. I may have to replace him if he doesn't smarten up."

"I see." Bolleau sat and fidgeted with his tie. "Well, I'm afraid the coaching staff is the least of our problems. The Dartmouth

Cobras made an . . . inadvisable acquisition this morning."

Leaning back, ankle on his thigh, Dean folded his hands over his raised knee. "Excuse me?"

"Scott Demyan." Bolleau held his hand out toward the papers on the desk. "His contract was faxed earlier this morning. He should arrive sometime tomorrow."

Icy calm flowed through Dean as he picked up the contract and looked it over. A cursory glance at the signature gave him the sensation of chewing tinfoil. He took his time going over the small print. All in order. Already approved by the commissioner.

The bastard was likely on the green somewhere, laughing his ass off at the joke the Cobras had become. If the contract had been obscene, he would have been forced to refuse it, but a one-year deal at 2.5 million for a player of Demyan's caliber didn't warrant his concern. That an ignorant, twenty-two year old girl had signed the contract made no difference. She had the legal right to sign anything she wanted.

Revenge? He tapped his fingers on the contract and discarded the idea. Silver had snuck out early, leaving a short note assuring him she'd "had fun," promising the return of his shirt as soon as she had it dry-cleaned. Impersonal and straightforward. What had passed between them was nothing but a one-night stand.

Not his first, but . . . *damn.* No woman had ever made him feel so thoroughly used.

Mentally putting the thought on ice, Dean focused on the problem at hand. Anthony Delgado had meddled in team affairs more than most owners, but even he rarely went against his advisors. Emotion-based decisions could usually be put off until he was in the right mind to see reason.

Why the hell had Dean thought Silver would be as easy to handle? He should have anticipated her unpredictable, self-indulgent attitude. Had he really been stupid enough to believe she'd demurely sit in her father's office and wait for Dean to make decisions for her?

Actually, he'd expected to have to hunt her down and coax her into accepting the barest minimum of her responsibilities. She didn't really care about the team. For years she'd been oblivious to it.

Anthony had thrust his Judas child into the deep end to fend for herself. She couldn't be more unprepared for the task at hand. But she hadn't run away—from her father anyway. Not that it mattered. He had to concentrate on her motives.

She's doing this for "Daddy." She wants to prove herself.

Too fucking bad. He refused to let her run *his* team into the ground with idiotic moves like this.

He lifted the contract and handed it to Bolleau, needing it out of his sight. "File this. And contact Demyan's agent. I expect him at training camp by Wednesday morning. Fax him the schedule."

"Yes, Mr. Richter." Relief smoothed the deepest wrinkles from Bolleau's face. "I will be in my office if you need me."

"That's fine." Dean's jaw ticked and he clenched his fist to maintain his controlled demeanor. For just a few moments longer. "You may go."

As soon as Bolleau closed the door behind him, Dean shot to his feet and swept all the contents off his desk, barely stifling a roar between his teeth. His muscles jumped under his flesh and his pulse beat at his skull. He pressed his hands to his desk and hauled air into his burning lungs.

Get a grip, Richter. He nodded as though the words had been spoken out loud by another—perhaps his mother who'd had the makings of a Domme, who'd run her polyamorous household the way a general would run an army barrack. Even her "alpha" lovers had bowed to her efficient rule of the household. When she'd said "Come here," the children marched into her presence.

Assured of his control, he left his office and headed to Delgado's. He threw the door open without knocking and glanced dismissively at Asher, Silver's lover and apparent co-conspirator. "Get out."

"Hey, you." Silver took one look at his face and frowned. "All right, is this how it's gonna be? Fine. But just so you know, Asher is the president, so he outranks you. And this is *my* office."

"The president? I assume you didn't know I already hold that position along with that of the general manager of this team?" Dean arched a brow at her confused expression and shook his head. "You really need to hide behind him?"

"Hide?" She let out a sharp laugh. "From who? You? Do you

think I'm afraid of you?"

You should be. He almost voiced the words but decided against it. This was business. "We're not at the club, Silver. I was hoping we could be professional about this."

"But . . . after last night." A flush spread over her cheeks. "So you won't touch me?"

"No. I won't touch you." His nostrils flared. Egotistical little bitch. Did she seriously believe he'd come here as a jilted lover? "*Last night* is irrelevant."

She blinked and gave her head a tiny shake. "Irrelevant? Then why are you—"

"I'm going to get us some lunch, Silver." Asher patted her shoulder and moved away from the desk. "Good luck."

Silver glared at Asher's back as he walked out, then jumped when Dean slammed his hands on her desk.

"Please explain something, because I'd really like to understand." He watched her lips move soundlessly, continuing when she nodded. "What possessed you to make a 2.5 million dollar deal without consulting me? When we spoke on the phone months ago, you admitted that you knew *nothing* about hockey. Have you suddenly become an expert?"

"Scott is a good player." She sat back in her chair and folded her arms over her chest. "He'll be an asset to the team."

"According to whom? Do you have any clue what the team needs? Are you aware of the fact that we just brought up three rookies that can play his position?" He groaned at her blank stare. "Do you even know what position he plays?"

She jutted her chin up. "He's a sniper."

Dean snorted. "And what does that mean?"

"He can get the puck in the net." Her fingers dug into her arms. "You don't have to be a genius to know that's a good thing."

"Maybe not, but we have half a dozen players who can do that as well, if not better, than he can. We are in desperate need of defensemen." He stepped back and lowered wearily into the seat in front of the desk. "You've screwed up the available cap, Silver. I've spent months reviewing prospects, and now I'll have to trash all my plans and start over."

"If it's just about the money, I have an easy solution." She leaned forward and flipped open a file on her desk. "Sloan Callahan is making five million a year. Get rid of him."

Dean's eyes narrowed. "Get rid of him? Are you serious?"

"Why not?" She slid the folder toward him. "Think about it. Me and Asher went over his stats. He's still worth something, but he's not half as good as he used to be."

"He's recovering from an injury. He hasn't been back long enough to know whether his performance will improve."

"So what?"

Deep, deep breaths. The image of hauling her over the desk and baring her ass for another good spanking flashed behind his closed lids, but he'd asked for professional. As ill-suited for the job as the girl was, she was still the owner. "So he's an asset to the team. I'd considered trading him when it seemed like his ego was causing a rift between the coach and the players, but the fact is he's a good leader. And an asset to the team."

"But there are other 'good leaders.'" Her forehead creased as she bent over the desk, running her finger down a long sheet that contained the team's stats. "Dominik Mason had almost as many goals as he did last season. And he's a defenseman. Why not just make him captain?"

"Have you checked his penalty minutes? He's got a temper and makes a damn fine enforcer, but unless we want the whole team to turn into a bunch of thugs, a leadership role is out of the question." Dean rolled his shoulders and gave her a tight smile. "Admit it. You want to get rid of Callahan because you don't like him."

"Why should I? He's an asshole." Her bottom lip stuck out. "Shouldn't I like my players?"

"You should want your players to win and leave your personal opinion of them aside." He rolled his eyes. "And what you just said sounds pretty silly considering you've contracted Scott Demyan."

"What's wrong with Scott?"

It irked him that she used his name so casually, but he pressed on. "Demyan recently claimed the spot of the most hated player in the league. He's a PR nightmare. His exploits constantly make headlines. He's been charged for solicitation five times since he went pro."

"And?"

"And he won't fit with the team. Everyone on our roster wants to prove themselves. To live up to fan expectations." Tension settled in the center of his brow at her stubborn look, and he did his best to rub it away. "This team is floundering. It took years to convince the league we could support a franchise in the Maritimes. If we don't get attendance up, the team will be shipped to somewhere like Vegas. This wasn't a good investment for your father, but he believed in it enough to put his entire capital on the line. He trusted me to make something of this team. Can you trust me to do the same?"

Her expression softened and her eyes lit up. "Oh, Dean. I'm not questioning you. I just want to do everything I can to live out Daddy's dreams. You understand that, right?"

Now they were getting somewhere. He could work with this. Granted, she'd messed up, but she'd been dumped into a role she wasn't equipped for. "I understand."

"Good." She grinned. "So, where are we sending Sloan?"

The question caught him off guard. Hadn't she heard a word he'd said? He placed his hands over hers and met her steady gaze without blinking. "We're not sending him anywhere."

"Yes, we are." She jerked her hands free. "Make it happen, Dean, or I will replace you."

His brows shot up. "Will you?"

"Yes, I will." She fiddled with her papers, all business once again. She put on a good act anyway, but he noted the tremor in her hands. "I'm not a puppet. Get used to it. I will have a say in how this team is run. My father chose me for a reason. You don't have to like it, but you will do things my way."

Holding back his laugh took every ounce of control in his being, but he managed. As he stood, he straightened his tie and gave her a curt nod. "Thank you for making that clear."

"You're welcome." Her nose wrinkled. "About last night . . ."

His went still. "What about it?"

"I hope you know it was just a one-time thing." She frowned at her desk, as though it had denied her the right words. "I'm not usually like that . . . but as you pointed out, I've never seriously gotten into 'the lifestyle.'"

"That was pretty obvious to everyone in attendance," he said. "Have you heard from your sister?"

"Of course I haven't heard from her. She's still on her honeymoon . . ." Silver chewed on her bottom lip. "I'm sure we'll talk when she gets back. I'm a little surprised she didn't call me after what happened though . . ."

"Why do you think that is?"

"I don't know."

"Bullshit." Dean smiled. He'd already taken off the kid gloves. Silver didn't need them. "Oriana is a submissive through and through. You made a spectacle of yourself. She may wonder if you wanted the attention."

"I didn't!" Her defensive posture had his protective instincts sitting up, but her next words shoveled them under disgust. "I exposed Sloan for the sick freak he is. She's just not ready to face it."

"Sick freak? Sloan gave your sister *exactly* what she needed."

"Says you."

"Yes, says me." His lips curled away from his teeth. "I proved last night how capable I am at reading a submissive's needs."

"You're so fucking full of yourself. You had a hard dick. That's *all* I needed."

"Apparently that's all you *ever* need."

Silver sucked her teeth and nodded. "Yeah, well, how about we just forget it ever happened."

"I plan to."

"Good!" She stood and pointed at the door, shaking so hard her teeth chattered as she spoke. "Now get out of my fucking office!"

"Gladly." He stormed out and slammed the door behind him. The echoing *bang!* reverberated in his bones as he strode toward the elevator. Silver's sob slammed into his gut.

She's feeling sorry for herself. Don't worry about it.

He knew it was true, but still, something inside urged him to go back and comfort her. He'd been cruel.

His legs locked as the elevator chimed. He reminded himself of the folder on her desk. One of his men needed him to stop her from messing up his career and his life on a whim. She neither wanted, nor needed his help.

Asher stepped off the elevator with his arms full of take-out bags and drinks. Dean forced himself to step inside.

She's got everything she wants. Men. Money. He cracked his neck and glared at the doors as they slid shut. *She's not getting my team.*

＊ ＊ ＊ ＊

Landon wiped the sweat from his face with a towel, holding his cell phone to his ear with his slippery palm. Training had his pulse thumping, but it seemed to pound a little harder as the phone rang. Silver probably wouldn't answer. Who knew how many guys she gave her number out to? And she'd disappeared with Richter—

"Hello?"

"Hey!" He glared at a man who'd rolled up a towel, looking ready to whip it at him. The man held up his hands and shuffled away to torment the younger rookies. "It's Landon—the guy who brought you the blanket?"

"I remember." Her tone sounded tight. She was probably busy and wondering why he was wasting her time. "What's up?"

Moving away from where most of the team huddled around the refreshment table, making all kinds of noise about how *this* was the year they'd claim the Cup, he did his best to keep his tone casual. "Not much. Just wanted to see how you were doing."

"Oh." The line went quiet. "That was nice of you."

Yep, that's me. All kinds of nice. She probably thought he was a loser. But . . . hell, he really needed to know that she was okay. And if she needed a friend as much as she'd let off last night. *Seriously? You're good with the friend label?*

Took him less than a second to answer himself. Absolutely.

"Listen. I've got an hour to chill before getting back on the ice. I was wondering . . ." He hated how unsure he sounded. He could maintain complete control between the pipes, in a scene, in every other aspect of his life. But this was something new. He'd never been friends with a girl. "Do you want to have lunch? Or maybe we can have drinks later?"

She let out a curt laugh. "If you want to fuck me, Landon, you don't need to try so hard. I'm easy. Ask anyone."

He almost dropped the phone. "What?"

"Where and when?"

Is she serious? He could honestly say he'd never been less aroused in his life. "Look. I don't know if I gave you the wrong impression—"

"Are you gay?"

Holy shit! Really? "This was a mistake. I'm sorry I called."

His finger was on the "end" button when she spoke. "Wait! Please, please don't hang up!"

He put the phone to his ear, waiting.

"Are you still there?" Her tone sounded small, desperate. "Landon?"

"I'm here."

"I'm sorry. You must think I'm a real bitch." Her exhale came loud and staticky through the phone. "I'd love to have lunch. Can you come pick me up?"

"I don't know if that's a good idea." He pressed his eyes shut, ignoring the shouts from the players speculating about "The Honeymoon." Maybe he'd been wrong about the girl. He was new here. There was a lot he didn't know. "I don't say shit I don't mean. You said you needed a friend. If you don't—"

"I do!" Her voice hitched. "More now than ever. If you meant it—"

"I meant it."

She sighed. "Good. Then please, come get me. Without a friend, right now, I might lose my mind."

"Where are you?" His pulse quickened. Something in her words made him nervous. She'd done her best to pass them off as light, but she meant them. Something had happened. The girl was going to snap. He dressed in street clothes and kept talking. "I don't get how people think you're easy if you make it this hard on your friends to ask you to hang out."

"I don't . . ." She swallowed audibly. "I don't have any friends."

"Then what does that make me?" *Keep talking, sweetie.* He elbowed past the crowd blocking the door and ignored the reporters. *I'm on my way.* "Do you not want friends?"

She laughed. "Are you for real? Who doesn't want friends?"

"Hold that thought, buddy." He grinned and fished his keys from his jean pocket. "You might want to rethink that after we hang out a few times. I like playing darts and I'm a sore loser. We'll get along better if you're not any good."

"I've never played darts."

"Well, I'll teach you." He slid into the front seat of his rented Jeep and started it up. "But you've got to promise me one thing."

Giggling, which made him feel much better, she asked, "What's that?"

"If you get better than me, you'll still let me win. I wasn't kidding when I said I was a sore loser."

"You've got it!" She laughed. "But you explain it to my victims when I shoot wide."

"Hey." He hooked his cell up to his Bluetooth and maneuvered out of the parking lot. "What are friends for? I'll distract them while you slip out."

"Sounds good." She paused. "Shit, I never told you where to pick me up!"

"Then tell me!"

"I'm at the forum." Poor girl sounded so lost. "And I'm in way over my head."

"I got that." He tightened his grip on the steering wheel. "Get out of there. Meet me outside."

Chapter Five

Silver almost felt guilty about leaving Asher after he'd gone out and gotten all her favorite foods, but the guilt couldn't stand up to her anger. She drained half a flask of rum, stuffed it in her purse, and fished out a cherry Tootsie Pop as the elevator descended. Sugar, caffeine, and liquor mixed together made her jittery, yet kinda mellow, almost the perfect balance. There were other things that could give her a better fix, but she wasn't going there ever again.

As she made her way across the main floor, her resolve weakened. The cold dismissal from Dean had hit her hard. Not that she'd *ever* consider fooling around with him now that she'd gotten him out of her system—*Have you? Really?*— but damn it, she hadn't expected him to react the way he had. The team mattered more to him than she did.

Get over it. It's not like you've never felt this way before. She realized she'd worked her hand into her purse to cup the tiny vial in her palm like a cherished memento. Jerking her hand out, she clipped the purse shut. *You don't need his approval. Or anything else from him. You just need him to accept that you're in charge.*

Still, that weak, needy part of her she usually ignored refused to shut up. Not because of Dean—*forget him!*—but because of Asher. More and more often he showed, in little ways, that she wasn't all that important to him. He loved Cedric, and she wanted to believe he loved her too, but . . . hell, she might as well admit it. He didn't. So where did that leave her?

Alone. Her sister hadn't answered the one concerned call she'd made. Her father wouldn't want to hear about her "drama."

Her simple, five inch heels clipped briskly on the marble tiles. The points found a wide gap and she stumbled. Dropping to one knee, she glanced around to see if anyone had witnessed her humiliation. The security guard pointedly focused on his newspaper. Not one person passing even paused.

I might as well be invisible.

A few years ago, she would have screamed to get someone's attention. Would have bitched about the tiles and demanded they be fixed *immediately*. People would have scurried around, ready to cater to her every whim . . .

But she didn't make a sound. She stood and straightened her pants, wincing at the dull throb in her knee. Limping, she made her way to the door, her vision warped by tears. The cool outside air smacked her face as she pushed it open.

A big hand smacked the door over her head. A wall of muscle in a snug grey T-shirt and faded jeans blocked her path. Before she could react, Landon spoke, his deep, gruff voice softened around the edges by his accent. "Hey. You all right?"

Doing her best to stand up straight, she nodded. "I just tripped. My pride hurts worse than anything else."

He curved his hand under her elbow and guided her past the doors, helping her lean against the wall before crouching down. "I'm not surprised, but I'd like to take a look anyway." His light grey eyes met hers as he curved his fingers under one pant leg. "Do you mind?"

"No. Go ahead." She pressed her eyes shut as he gently rolled her pant leg over her knee and sucked in a breath as the material peeled away from broken flesh. His freshly-showered scent hit her like a gust of wind rising from a summer rain. His calloused fingers brushing alongside the wound distracted her from the pain. Distracted her a little *too* much. She smirked, sure it was intentional. "Like what you see?"

"Not at all. Torn flesh and blood just isn't my thing. I'm a breast man, myself." He straightened and grinned at her. His grin turned to a frown when she evaded his gaze. "Did I say something wrong?"

She sniffled, hating that she couldn't pull it together. *A breast man? Just great.* All she seemed to hear lately was that no one wanted her. "I have tiny boobs."

"I would argue that, considering I've seen them." Landon winked and she couldn't help but let out a watery giggle. "But right now all I'm thinking about is patching you up. You won't take offense if I tell you the only thing I want to put on you is a Band-Aid, will you? I've got some good lines to practice on you after if you want."

"Really?" She allowed him wrap to his arm around her shoulders, encasing her securely against his solid body. Such a big, hot—*very hot*—man. She peeked up at his face. His smile was playful, without a hint of lust. She wasn't sure whether she should be disappointed or not. He did want to practice lines on her after all. "I'm pretty sure I've heard them all."

"Damn." He led her to a Jeep and held the door open as she climbed in. "So is 'Any more than a mouthful' lame? Could you help me come up with new material?"

"Why would you bother asking? I—" She cut herself off. *He almost hung up on you about twenty minutes ago for suggesting he wanted to fuck you. Don't go there.* He'd been insulted. He was the only person being nice to her. Time to attempt her first normal conversation with a man she wasn't related to. "Yeah. It is kinda lame. You want some friendly advice? Don't comment on breasts when you're with a woman with small ones. Not until you've got her naked. At that point, worshiping them works."

"So if she's got massive hooters I should remark on them at once?"

"Only if you wanna get slapped."

His deep laugh sent a warm rush straight through her. "Maybe I'm kinky that way."

You sure he doesn't want to fuck you?

How could she be? She didn't think it was possible, but Landon made her forget her suspicions as he quickly cleaned her wound and gently covered it with a large Band-Aid. He kissed the top of her knee in a way that seemed so automatic she didn't even try to read anything into it—though her skin tingled where his lips had pressed long after he rolled her pant leg down.

Damn, it felt . . . nice. Not sexual. Nothing sexual had ever been so tender.

I really hope he doesn't want to fuck me.

Music started up the second he turned the key. Before long, the upbeat dance tune had her swaying and singing along, tapping her lollipop hand on her knee in time to the beat. They drove for a bit without a word, both enjoying the music. At a stoplight, Landon looked at her with an unreadable smile on his lips.

"So," he spoke loud over the music. "I hear you're an actress? Is singing part of the job description?"

She winced. Asher told her all the time that she couldn't carry a note. "Depends. If I started younger, maybe, but most of my parts didn't involve much more than a willingness to show a bit of skin."

His brow shot up. "You're not a porn star, are you?" He held up a hand before she could come up with a biting response. "Don't take it the wrong way, but I have an unhealthy addiction to pornos, and I would remember you."

Heat spread over her cheeks. "Are you serious?"

He snorted. "No. Do I look like some kind of perv?"

At that point, she really couldn't say one way or another. But if he was a perv, he was a cut above the rest. He'd passed the fifteen minute mark without leering and groping. Which earned him some serious brownie points.

She stuck her lollipop in her mouth and sucked hard. Then shifted it to one side of her mouth. "Why the question then?" She crunched on what was left of the candy and dropped the stick in the empty ashtray. "Not that I'm all that surprised, but why even mention porn star?"

"You brought up showing skin." He shrugged. "You've got a nice voice. I think you sold yourself short."

Oh, he's so full of shit! She shook her head and smiled. "I do not. But you're sweet to say so."

"I get the impression that you don't believe me." He eased the Jeep into a space on a grungy, low-end shopping district street and shifted into park. "Me and you are gonna do karaoke one day. Maybe you'll believe the drunken, cheering crowd."

Her eyes went wide. "Not now? I'm not up to—"

"I think I mentioned darts." He got out and went around the car to open her door. "Maybe we can hit a karaoke club this weekend."

"Maybe . . ." Singing in public wasn't high on her to-do list. She really, really hated being laughed at. "But I thought we were going out for lunch."

He glanced over at the bar he'd parked in front of. "This place serves food. I hope you weren't expecting anythin' fancy?"

He brought me out for greasy bar food? She wrinkled her nose. This had to be the oddest date she'd ever been on.

It's not a date.

Right. Still, if she ate here, she'd be obliged to sign up for a local gym. Her Dartmouth "owner" career had gotten off to a rocky start. And Daddy would take the reins back any day now. If she wanted to maintain her independence, she might want to start looking for work soon. And her body was the only thing she had that was worth anything.

"Do you think they serve salads?"

"Oh, no. You're not allowed to do that. We're hanging out as friends." Landon folded his arms over his broad chest. "Save the 'I'll just have a salad' for the men you're trying to impress. With me, you're gonna eat normal. You're not allergic to French fries, are you?"

"No, but—"

"Do you like them?"

Well . . . To be honest, once in a while she did enjoy scarfing down all kinds of naughty, fattening foods. French fries became a comfort food when she quit sniffing. But after gaining three pounds in a week, she'd gotten back on her no carbs diet.

"I like them . . ." She drew her shoulders back. "But I have to be careful. You must get that? You know about keeping in shape."

His expression turned serious. "Very true. So how about after we stuff our faces, we walk to the forum? That should burn all those nasty calories."

"You'll be late getting back to training."

"I like living on the edge." He held the bar door open for her. "I just got here. I don't want the coaching staff to think I'm predictable."

She arched a brow as she paused by his side. "How much am I paying you again?"

"Way too much." He chuckled and gave her a little shove. "But I won't let you down so long as you don't expose my strategy. I plan to be an old-style goalie. A little weird. You good with that?"

With his kind of weird? Oh, hell yeah! She had no clue what would happen on the ice, but right here, right now, he was everything she needed and more. He didn't take anything seriously! And he made her feel like it was okay for her to do the same.

"I reserve judgment." She gave him a sideways smile. "I should be honest. I'm a sore loser too. I will so pull the 'a gentleman would let me win' card."

"Will you?"

"Yes I will."

He hugged her against his side and whispered in her ear. "Then I suggest you find yourself a gentleman. Because otherwise I will kick your ass without thinking twice."

＊ ＊ ＊ ＊

Landon put the dart in Silver's hand and pointed at the board. She seemed to have forgotten everything he'd taught her after hitting the wall a few times. "It's really not that hard. Aim for the center. If you hit anywhere on the board, you'll get points."

Silver swayed into him, her three beers already testing her endurance. "Show off. You bought me that last beer because I got close."

"Shh!" He steadied her with a hand under her elbow. "Don't share my nefarious secrets! I just bought that guy in the corner a pitcher. I plan to go all dart shark on him."

"Dart shark?" She took a firm hold on his shirt and pressed her eyes shut. "Are you for real?"

"Are you okay?" He hadn't taken Silver for a light drinker, and after a good meal, he'd thought a few beers would be okay. But she was acting like she'd had more. "I like winning and all, but I've got some standards. If you can't see the bull's eye, you win by default."

"Yay!" She folded into him and tipped almost off her heels. "Then I win!"

"You win." His teasing took a hike and his protective nature rose to the forefront. "But I demand a rematch after you sleep this off."

"Sleep this off?" Her brow wrinkled. "Do you think I'm drunk? Seriously? A bit of rum and beer ain't enough to make me tipsy. I'm not a cheap date."

"Damn." *Rum? When had she had rum?* He led her to their table and leaned her against the table as he grabbed her suit jacket. That she was prancing around in a bra and dress pants should have given him a clue, but some of the waitresses were wearing just as little and he didn't take Silver as the shy type. After she'd shed the jacket, she'd relaxed. It had taken him a little longer to unwind—how the hell could he *not* be aware of all that creamy, exposed flesh? But this was how she was used to people seeing her. He refused to judge. He'd just wanted her to be comfortable.

But maybe he *should* have said something.

"Damn?" She glared at him—well, more like glared at his shoulder, but apparently she wasn't seeing straight. "Are you surprised that I'm not a cheap date?"

Cheap dates don't start drinking before lunch. He considered saying as much, but decided against it. He knew players who drank before games because they couldn't take the pressure. Could be a problem—especially if it got to the point that they couldn't deal with getting up in the morning without a drink in their hand.

Was Silver like that? A lot of people might see her charmed life as nothing to get stressed about, but after seeing her with her boyfriends, and after hearing a bit about her dad . . .

"I don't think you're a cheap date. But I feel like an ass for not asking what had you ready to fall apart when I called." He did up her jacket buttons. "You want to talk about it?"

She shook her head, then made a choked sound. "I fucked up. I wanted to prove I could handle the job, but the more I think about it—Dean was right. I never shoulda hired that guy."

"Hired?" He frowned. "Did you hire a new president?"

"Oh, well that too." She swallowed and teetered a little. "Do you think that'll be an issue? I didn't know Dean already had the position! He's the general manager! And I figured Asher would make a good president. He can read contracts. I'm too stupid."

"You know, I really hate people insulting my friends, so . . ." He tipped her chin up with a finger and looked into her over bright emerald green eyes. *Contacts.* Nothing about the woman was what it appeared to be. Including her confidence. "Don't call yourself stupid."

"Okay." Resting her head against his chest, she spoke so quietly he had to bend down to hear her. "Do you know Scott Demyan?"

Oh no. "Not personally, but I've heard of him. Why?"

"I got him for the team."

All righty then. He could see how Dean would have been pissed. No way would he approve of that showboating, chirping, antagonizer on the roster. They had *at least* one rookie who fit the bill already. Not that it mattered now. "Why did you do it?"

"Seemed like a good idea at the time." Her brow furrowed as she sniffed into his shirt. "You smell nice."

"Okay, now I know you're wasted."

"Am not."

"Are too." Redirecting her to the door, he did his best to hide her wavering walk so the bar patrons wouldn't stare. Her legs gave out when they hit the sidewalk, and he carried her to his Jeep. "Would it be too forward of me to ask you for a favor?"

"Nope." She laughed. "I've been waiting for it."

Every muscle in his body tensed, but he refused to let her drunken rambling get to him. "Good. So no more rum for breakfast?"

"Huh?"

"You heard me."

She sighed and slumped into her seat. "Fine. But only if you tell me something."

"Ask away." He did up her seat belt and swiped away a tear that had spilled down her cheek. "I'm an open book."

"Why do you care? You're hot. You could get a girl with fewer issues." She pursed her lips. "And what's with the 'friends' thing?"

"Maybe I've got issues too. And maybe I need a friend." Flattening his hands by her shoulders, he leaned in close. "You're a lot less messed up than some people I've known. I've made my share of mistakes, and they had way more impact than anything you've done."

Her hand found his and she blinked as though trying to see him better. "Tell me about it."

"I will." After patting her cheek, he stepped back and closed the door. He didn't speak again until he'd pulled into the midday traffic.

"If you promise to let me get you home and fix you up a pot of coffee before I leave, I promise to go into overshare mode the next time we go out. Deal?"

"Deal. But . . ." Her head in her hands, she whispered, "You've got to give me something. Why did you sound so worried on the phone?"

A lump the size of a boulder lodged in his throat. "Because the last time a woman called me to tell me she was about to lose her mind, I laughed it off and said I didn't want to hear it. And I've been paying for it ever since."

Chapter Six

The heart monitor at Delgado's bedside beeped a steady rhythm. Dean's presence hadn't caused him any stress so far. Hopefully he could keep it that way. At least the man was well enough for home care.

"So, how is my baby girl doing so far?" Delgado pushed himself up on his stiff gold silk covered pillows and smiled at Dean. "I trust you're leading her in the right direction and not letting those fags speak for her."

Dean kept his eyes on the rise and fall of the red line on the monitor, choking down the urge to remark on the man's bigotry. "I do believe Silver is quite capable of making decisions on her own."

"I'm not sure if you're implying that this is a good thing."

Might as well get straight to the point. "It's not. She made an acquisition without consulting me. And she is determined to make a trade that I object to."

Delgado dropped his head onto his pillows. "Is she?"

"She is."

"She can't . . ." Delgado pressed his eyes shut and the bleeping sped up. "I want my lawyers. Get me my lawyers, Richter. I want a clause in there than prevents her from running the team on her silly little girlish whims. And get her here too." He groaned and pressed his hand over his heart. "I should have seen this coming. She's just like her mother."

Dean took a deep breath. He knew enough of their family history to object to Silver being compared to her mother no matter what she'd done. "Surely not like her mother, sir. I can't believe—"

"Believe it. Both women were coddled and spoiled all their lives." Delgado took a shallow breath, and the monitor let off an ear piercing sound which made Dean frown. The stupid thing must be hypersensitive. His father's heart rate had become much more erratic before the alarm went off. And he hadn't been able to speak as Delgado still was. "Silver is the spitting image of her mother. I hate that she got her license. Do everything in your power to keep her from driving anywhere. You never know—"

"You must be clear with me, Mr. Delgado." Dean held his hand up to the nurse that rushed into the room. "What exactly is it you are asking me to do?"

"Keep my daughter alive, Richter." Delgado's eyes rolled back into his head, and the nurse quickly injected something into his IV. "I can't lose her. Not again."

The nurse shooed him out and Dean took a seat on the bench that had been set up in the hall outside Delgado's bedroom, jaw clenched so hard his muscles ached. He should feel some sort of pity for the man, but it was difficult after seeing his father go through the same thing just a few years back. Both men had been given the same advice to improve their quality of life. Regular exercise, a special rehabilitation program, a healthy diet—Delgado refused to do any of it. Dean's father had lasted two years, two wonderful years, before his heart gave out for the last time. The way Delgado was going, he wouldn't last another month. But he lashed out at anyone who suggested he fight to live. He'd fired two nurses and replaced the consulting doctor when they tried to reason with him.

"I'll finally be with my wife. And . . . my son," he'd said.

With no thought to the children he'd leave behind.

Dean had to call the lawyers, no doubt about it. But part of him hurt for Silver. She probably thought what she was doing would give her father time to get better. But her father didn't see her as his daughter. He saw her as the woman he'd lost. A mere reflection of the woman he hoped to join in death very soon.

And where did that leave Oriana? If anyone should be running the team in her father's place, it should be her. But the man didn't see it. He behaved as though he'd only ever had two children. And the favorite was dead.

Any mention of Oriana was forbidden by the doctor as well as a long list of "stressors," which left Dean with no way to improve the situation. All he could do was stop it from getting any worse.

Silver's temporarily replacing her mother, and the team is temporarily replacing his son. Someone has to be thinking long term, Richter.

Heaving out a heavy sigh, Dean took out his phone and called Delgado's lawyers. After a short, cordial chat, he hung up and prepared for an unpleasant conversation that couldn't be put off any longer.

No answer. When the voice mail came on, he kept his tone crisp and professional. "Silver, when you get this message, come to your father's house. He'd like to speak to you."

Ending the call, he shoved his phone in his pocket and let out a sound of disgust that startled the butler, causing the man to appear a bit less like one of the many antiques stationed around the house. The butler's grayish skin dropped a shade as he stared at Delgado's door like his employer would come out any moment and tear into him for breathing too loud. This whole ordeal stank of the kind of drama he'd closed himself off from after his wife left him. Of course, he still had to deal with a certain amount from his teenage daughter, but . . .

Silver isn't that much older than Jami. The thought made him groan and he massaged his temples as a dull ache settled between them. He should have considered that before sleeping with the woman, but something about her seemed worldly beyond her years. It was hard to believe Silver was in the same generation as his defiant, yet still so innocent, daughter.

Laughing dryly, he considered another *big* difference between the two. There was no guarantee Jami would respond to a request from her father to see her.

He didn't doubt for a second that Silver would be here within the hour.

* * * *

A mallet swung rhythmically inside Silver's head, each strike pacing her pulse. She squinted at the digital clock on the night table by her bed—the red blur strengthened the blows against her skull. Looked like four something. The scent of coffee beckoned and she stumbled to the kitchen, blindly pouring herself a cup and hissing when some spilled on her hand.

Shit! She brought her hand to her mouth and laved away the burn with her tongue. *Landon must have left hours ago! Why is this so hot?*

Quick sips of coffee and some stretching got her feeling more bruised than beaten. As she splashed some cold water from the kitchen sink on her face, the coffee machine caught the corner of her eye. The time had been fixed and the brew was set on automatic. Apparently for two hours after she'd crashed.

I so owe Landon a great big hug! She smiled and polished off her coffee, her spirits rising as she thought back on their lunch together. Maybe this being friends thing was a good idea after all. The men she fucked were never this considerate!

Two vitamins and some orange juice had her feeling steady enough to hop into the shower. Almost back to normal after she dressed and fixed her hair, she decided to brave her phone. The first message was from Landon.

She didn't bother listening to the rest before calling him back. She got his voice mail.

"Hey, you!" She fiddled with her hair and tried to find the right words to express her gratitude. "Damn, I don't know what to say—and if you knew me better, you'd know that's rare. Thank you. For everything. I'm feeling a lot better and I'm looking forward to hanging out again—I'm mean—well, when you're not busy. Okay, I should erase this message. I sound pathetic, don't I?" She giggled and rolled her eyes. "Yeah, yeah, I know. Don't insult your friend."

She listened to the silence, wishing she could hear Landon's voice. She wanted that feeling again—the one that she'd had the entire time she was with him. Was this what it was like to have a friend? A real one?

"Okay, before I get all sappy, I'm gonna hang up. But . . . well, give me a call."

Jerking the phone away from her mouth before she could say anything else, she eyed the phone. If she pressed two, the message would be erased. But she held her breath and pressed one.

"If he doesn't think I'm a freak after lunch, this won't faze him." She gave a firm nod and played the rest of her messages. One from Dean—her throat tightened. Daddy wanted to see her.

The next message made her skin crawl.

"My name is Charles Lee. I represent Roy Kingsley, one of the team's investors." The man said smoothly. "I would like to meet you at your convenience to discuss the coming season. It would be in your best interest to schedule an appointment within the next few days."

Sure, I'm right on that. She pressed "end" and stuffed her phone in her purse. Then took it back out. She could ignore that last call—*let Dean deal with the creepy investors*—but she wouldn't ignore Daddy.

Her hand slipped over her little vial, found a tiny pack of licorice, and fisted around it. *I disappointed him once by taking off. I won't do it again.*

Half an hour later, she strode up to Daddy's front door, straightened the skirt to her new suit, and pressed her finger on the doorbell.

The butler, whose name she'd never gotten because Daddy didn't approve of chatting with the staff, let her in with a courteous, "Your father is expecting you, Miss Silver."

"Thank you." She inclined her head, then clipped across the grand room and hurried up the stairs. She ignored Dean, who was waiting in the hall, and burst into Daddy's room. "Daddy, you're looking so much better!"

His cold look stopped her in her tracks. "What have you done?"

"Oh, don't worry about that now." She slapped a bright smile on her lips. "How soon will you be strong enough to get out of that bed?"

"Maybe never." He sat up and slammed his fist into the rumpled blankets. "I trusted you! How dare you take it on yourself to make decisions for the team without consulting the advisors I provided for you! What were you thinking?"

"But you said we needed a sniper . . ." A blank look. Didn't he remember leaving the message? She barreled on, willing to take the heat for following his directions to avoid agitating him more than necessary. "We have to entertain the fans, Daddy." She sat on the edge of the bed and took his hand. "I know how to do that. I thought that's why you chose me?"

"No. I chose you because there was no one else."

"But—"

"Shut up!" The veins in his neck swelled and his face reddened. Her hand hovered over her throat as she prepared for him to collapse, but his face shifted into a chilling calm. "I have made

Richter your partner. Because of your stupidity, I was left with no choice but to give him proxy control of fifty percent of the team. Fortunately, the doctor found me fit to make the decision. Otherwise, you'd still have the power to destroy everything I've built!"

Destroy it? Her eyes teared up. "Daddy—"

"I said 'shut up.'" His monitors made a frightening sound as he dropped back onto the bed, quivering with rage. "You do nothing unless Richter approves it. Do you understand?"

"Yes, Daddy." Tears spilled down her cheeks, and she hastened to wipe them away. "I'm sorry."

His shaky smile took her off guard. "I know you are. You're a good girl. I will forget everything you've done in the past if you can do this."

"I can." She clenched her fists at her sides. "I will."

"All right." He settled into the bed and the monitors stopped making that awful noise. She noticed the nurse hovering but kept her focus on her father as he spoke. "Why don't you get some renovations done in the boxes? Maybe hire a new PR agent. I've asked Richter to let you handle those kinds of things. Much as I hate it, you do have some experience with the media. Make them happy."

She rubbed her wet nose and nodded. "I can do that."

"I know you can." He patted her hand as his eyes drifted shut. "Make me proud."

Whatever it takes. She vowed as the nurse waved her away.

Dean met her at the door. "Silver—"

"Unless it's about business, you have nothing to say that I want to hear." The soreness in her throat burst into sharp little shards of anger. So much for an amicable working relationship. She wouldn't give him his own way, so he'd found a way around her. "I never took you for a tattle tale, *Richter.*"

His shoulders squared as he looked down on her. "This isn't high school, Silver. You wouldn't listen to me. I knew you'd listen to him."

"With him in that condition? Of course I'll listen to him. This upsets him so much . . ." She crossed her arms over her chest, hating that with him this close, she was tempted to move in for the hug he looked tempted to give her. "Just stay out of my business, all right? Like Daddy said, I'm in control of renovations. And more importantly, PR. I wonder how long you can hang onto Sloan after it gets out that he can't play for shit anymore."

"I believe you are in for an unpleasant surprise if that's what you think."

"We'll see." She gave him a sweet smile. "And as for Scott, I hope you can handle him. He's the kind of man fans want."

"As if you know what the fans want." His lips curled into a sneer. "Learn the game. Then we'll talk."

You want to hit below the belt, Mister? Hell, his ratting her out cut deep enough to scar, but as long as the marks weren't physical, she could ignore them. They ranked as high on her scale of importance as her lingering attraction to him. Or her insane longing for his respect. Their verbal battles worked on so many levels. They kept him at arm's length where he belonged. *And I've got a few low blows of my own.*

"I don't have to know the game to understand men." She thrummed her fingers on his chest. "Men idolize those who can get any woman they want. Scott can do that."

"Can he?" Dean leaned forward and spoke low. "Will you be on his list of conquests?"

"May-be." She smirked and shrugged. "He'd be a step up from the last guy I fucked."

She felt his eyes on her back as she spun on her heels and made her way down the stairs. Confident as he was, she sensed that she'd taken this round. If he wanted to keep up with her, he better up his game.

Chapter Seven

The kid circled sideways and waved his stick in Landon's face, his latest, lame-assed attempt to distract Landon a bit more effective than his previous efforts, but no less annoying. Landon shoved Carter aside and skidded across the blue ice to make an easy pad save.

Carter whooped and patted Landon's helmet with a gloved hand. "Not too bad, Bower."

"Yeah, thanks." *You pain-in-the-ass.* "You're not too bad yourself." *You're lucky you're on my team, or I'd make you swallow your teeth so you look like a pro.* He watched the younger man take his position for the puck drop and decided to take his revenge. "So how long before they send you back to the farm team?"

Carter didn't look at him, but the distraction kept him away from the net long enough for Landon to get a clear view of the puck. He snatched the snap shot out of the air a second before Coach blew the whistle.

"Slick." Carter shot him a gun-shaped glove salute before skating away.

Slick. Right. Landon nodded at the guys who skated by to give him halfhearted props. Aside from Carter, the team was still a bit stiff with him, but he didn't blame them. Goalies held the fort. The last one had thrown games for profit. They trusted the backup goalie, but he just couldn't cut it as a starter. Which meant they had to put their faith in Landon.

He hadn't earned it yet. But he would.

After lingering on the ice long enough to make sure the locker room would be mostly empty by the time he went in, Landon lumbered down the hall, stopping short at the sight of shapely, tanned legs gripped around the waist of the big defenseman, Dominik Mason.

"What did you say to me, bunny?" Mason wrapped his hands under the woman's knees, hefting her up a little higher. "Sure sounded like 'mentally challenged.' What do you think, Perron?"

"I think we should give the lady a chance to explain herself." Perron grinned around the mouthpiece he was chewing on. "So what do you say, sugar? Did we hear wrong?"

"Yes!" Oriana squirmed. "I was talking about someone else!"

"Were you?" Mason's tone dropped, taking on a hard edge. "First of all, I do not tolerate lying. Second, your response was to my question of 'who are you waiting out here for, dressed like that?'"

Perron shook his head. "You've gotten yourself in a heap of trouble, Oriana. Might as well come clean."

Oriana let out a squeak, then a moan. "Please, Master. Don't do that here."

"Then be honest with me," Mason said, nuzzling her neck.

"Fine." She sighed as he set her on her feet. "I insulted you. I lied. I'm a very bad girl." She bit her bottom lip. "I beg you to take me home to punish me."

Mason rubbed his chin. "Well . . ."

"No." Perron held a finger up and frowned when Oriana sputtered a protest. "You've been mouthier than usual lately. I think a few nights pleasuring yourself while we watch should get the point across. Then, to make sure you don't forget, perhaps a public scene at the club?"

"I wasn't *that* bad!"

"Really?"

Oriana shuffled her feet, head down, the perfect depiction of a contrite little sub. "I'm sorry."

Landon couldn't hold back a smile. Such natural submission was a beautiful thing.

"You're lucky Landon is too much of a gentleman to embarrass you by making his presence known, bunny." Mason lightly cuffed her chin, then gave Landon an offhand salute. "Would you like her to apologize to you for this willful display, Master Landon? On your knees, pet."

Brow furrowed, Landon quickly shook his head before Oriana could kneel in front of him. "That won't be necessary. I won't—"

"The offer was for a simple apology, Landon." Mason's jaw hardened. "Do you honestly think we'd pass her off to someone else as a punishment?"

Landon's eyes narrowed. "If you have any experience in the lifestyle, you know it happens."

"If?" Mason laughed. "You're awfully young to claim much experience, Bower."

"You're awfully narrow-minded for a man in the middle of a ménage."

"Is that so——?"

"Actually, most would consider it a polyamorous relationship." Perron arched a brow at Mason and pulled Oriana to his side. "So, you've both proved you've got long shlongs. Can we bring our baby home so we can watch her play with the new toys I got her?"

Heat spilled over Landon's cheeks. Pretty ridiculous, getting into a pissing contest with his teammate. Granted, people in the lifestyle commenting on his youth often got his guard up, but that was no excuse. "Excuse me. I meant no disrespect."

"Don't bother." Perron smacked his shoulder. "Dominik is in thug mode. You'll be grateful for it on the ice, but it's a pain in the ass because he gets stuck in the role for hours after a game."

Oriana giggled. "Which is why you got me the kinky ref outfit."

Mason rolled his eyes. "I think Bower's heard enough. Say goodnight to the nice man, pet. We will finish this in private."

Breathe quickening, Oriana moved closer to Mason and mumbled, "Goodnight, Sir."

Landon watched the trio walk away, shook his head, and went into the locker room. The captain, Callahan, was sitting on the bench in front of Landon's stall.

"You did really good out there." Callahan stood and moved aside to give Landon space to get changed. "But you were late coming back from lunch. Paul told me you had an impeccable attendance record for training with your last team. Something going on I should know about?"

"Not at all." Landon peeled off his sweat-dampened practice jersey and tossed it onto the pile in the corner. "Just lost track of time."

"I see." Callahan sighed. "Fuck, man, you've got a shitload of pressure on you, and it sucks, but this team is recovering from a serious blow. To top it off, I just found out Scott Demyan was added to the roster. We've got a spoiled little diva running the show and—"

"I consider Silver a friend, Callahan, and I'd appreciate it if you don't talk about her like that." Landon grinned at Callahan's stunned look. "I get that it was a bad trade, but so what? One man doesn't make us less of a team." He shrugged. "And who knows, he may surprise us and make her look like a genius."

"I doubt that."

"Hey, don't give up on the guy before he even gets here. He agreed to play for the team. That's got to mean something."

"Yeah, it means no one else wanted him." Callahan massaged his eyes with his fingertips. "Look, he's my problem. I'll figure it out. My main concern is making sure you're comfortable with the men in front of you. You let me know if there's any way I can make this easier for you."

"Will do."

Callahan nodded and headed for the door. Halfway there, he paused. "And Bower?"

Landon looked up from where he was undoing his pads. "Yeah?"

"Don't be late again."

Chuckling, Landon shed the rest of his equipment and then made his way out to the empty player's lounge. He liked the captain, even though he seemed like a bit of a tight ass. Perron seemed pretty cool—though he couldn't fathom a honeymoon that lasted less than twenty-four hours being shared . . . And then there was Mason. He couldn't read the man. His reputation at the club was sterling, but he was a different animal on the ice. He'd reserve judgment.

After changing into street clothes, he pulled out his phone and checked his messages. One from Silver and one from his sister.

He called Silver first.

"Hello?" A man, probably Asher, answered in a brisk tone.

"Hey, is Silver there?"

"Who's asking?"

"Landon." Landon waited for Asher to call Silver, but was met with silence. "She called me."

"She's not accepting calls right now. But I'll give her a message if you'd like."

"No, that's all right." Landon shoved his feet into his shoes. "Thank you."

Hanging up, Landon headed straight out, one destination in mind. He didn't need the pompous asshole giving Silver a message for him. He was perfectly capable of delivering it himself.

* * * *

Silver hugged her knees to her chest, rocking back and forth, oblivious to the shards of glass littering the floor. Alcohol created puddles on the kitchen tiles where she'd missed the sink and the scent beckoned.

"I don't have time for this, Silver." Asher's soles crunched in the glass as he paced in front of her. "You knew I had plans with Cedric."

Her bottom lip quivered. "Then go! I wouldn't want to be an inconvenience!"

"Don't be like that." Asher threw his arms in the air. "This isn't fair! I do my best to split myself evenly between you two, but you're an attention whore! The world doesn't stop turning because you want it to! The rest of us have the right to keep living!"

Cold spilled over her flesh and she turned her tear-burned eyes up to him. "Is that what you think of me?"

"I've always known who you are." Crouching in front of her, Asher held out his hands, palms up. "And I accept you. I'm just not crazy about all the drama."

All the drama? She shook her head. Their whole relationship had been all carefree and fun, going to parties and schmoozing with the rich and famous. The lifestyle Asher liked, but couldn't get on his own. Until her father had his heart attack, she'd never asked Asher to deal with any family drama . . .

He dealt with you coked out of your head. And your diva tantrums. Maybe this is just too much.

True. She sighed and pressed her forehead to her knees. Her throat ached from screaming. Her chest felt hollow and sore. And for what? Getting Asher's attention didn't make her any more important to him. It just proved him right. "It's okay, Asher. Really.

You and Cedric go out." Her voice hitched. "Tell him I'm sorry. I didn't mean to freak out like that."

"I'll tell him." Asher ruffled her hair, and then the sound his heels grinding glass drifted away. The door opened and Asher spoke with uncharacteristic hostility. "Can I help you?"

"Where's Silver?"

Landon? Silver's eyes went wide, and she dragged herself up the counter to see down the hall. Little sparks danced inside her belly as she caught sight of him, towering over Asher.

"There you are!" Landon elbowed past Asher and came toward her with a strained smile planted on his lips. "You called?"

"I did." She raked her teeth over her bottom lip, looking around at the mess she'd made. "But that was before—"

"Before you decided you needed to tidy up a bit?" Landon grabbed the broom leaning against the wall in the hall and crunched through the glass until he was standing right in front of her. "No problem. I'm not much of a neat freak."

His words made her smile, but still, she shook her head. "Landon—"

"I told you she wasn't taking calls," Asher said.

Landon nodded. "Yes, but I'm not on the phone, am I? If she wants me to leave, she can ask me herself." He swept some glass away from her socked feet and arched a brow at her. "So what do you say?"

Her chaotic brain calmed at his level tone. She had no right to ask Asher to put up with her like this. She had even less right to ask Landon. But the word came despite her reasoning.

"Stay."

"All right. Up with you." He picked her up and sat her on the counter. Then he glanced back at Asher. "Don't let us keep you. There's a man waiting for you in the hall. Hot date?"

"None of your business." Asher went to the coat rack by the door and grabbed his coat. "Listen, you. If you hurt her—"

"You'll sue me?" Landon laughed and the sound was ragged, like a knife hacking at wood. He gave Asher a look like the other man was shit he'd found stuck to his shoe. "Sorry, pal, but the whole building heard exactly how you feel about this situation. Not like

Silver doesn't know exactly what most people see when they look at her, but you needed to make your point loud and clear."

Asher snorted. "Whatever, man. Honestly, I hope she tears your heart out and eats it raw. You're stupid enough to deserve it."

Landon ran his tongue over his teeth and nodded slowly. "Got it. Anything else?"

"Don't be here when I get back," Asher said before striding out and slamming the door behind him.

"We'll see." Landon swept up the rest of the mess without looking at her. "Now that he's gone, you want to tell me what happened?"

"Anne, the secretary, told Oriana she overheard that I had plans to trade Sloan. Oriana called me and . . ." Tears spilled over and her throat locked. She struggled to get out the rest. "She asked what else I planned to take away from her. I tried to explain that I didn't want any of this, but she hung up on me. She hates me."

"I doubt that." Lips in a thin line, Landon stared at the colorful pile of glass of the floor. "So, after she hung up, you threw a few bottles?"

"Not exactly." Silver brought her fingers to her mouth and nibbled off the opal colored polish. This was it. This was the moment when Landon would decide he didn't want to hang around her anymore. "When I tried to talk to Asher, he closed his bedroom door in my face."

"Some boyfriend."

"No, it's not like that. You don't get it. I can be very . . ." She dropped her gaze to her toes. "Demanding."

"So let me get this straight," Landon said. "You got the door slammed in your face, so you just came in here and started breaking things."

"No. I knocked."

"What did he say when he answered."

"He didn't."

"Ah." After patting her jean-clad knee, Landon resumed cleaning up the glass. Then, without a word, he turned and headed for the door.

Don't go. She pressed her hand to her throat and whispered the words.

Landon stopped. "I'm sorry, what did you say?"

"I said—" Her voice sounded weak. Pathetic. She swallowed twice to get it back to normal. "Please. Don't leave yet."

"Why not?" He returned to the kitchen and rested his hip against the counter. When she didn't answer, he tapped his fingers on the countertop. One dark brow arched, he waited a little longer before calmly saying, "This is called an adult conversation, Silver. It goes both ways."

Condescending bastard. Her spine went stiff and she scowled at him. "Forget it."

"No. I won't forget it. You could have hurt yourself here because Asher didn't have the decency to answer you. Not that I'm saying the way you reacted wasn't a little over the top, but you don't need a daily reminder that you don't matter to him." He pressed his fingers to her lips before she could object, bending down a bit to her eye level. "How about next time, you call me. If I don't answer, leave a nice long message—get it all off your chest. I will *always* call you back as soon as I can."

"You really mean that, don't you?" She cocked her head, studying his face for any hint of a catch. "So what now?"

"Now, how about you go put on something comfy and we settle in for a movie marathon." He strolled into her living room like he owned the place and found her DVD collection. His brow shot up. "Are these Asher's?"

She hopped off the counter and went to check. "No, those are mine."

"You like old Westerns?"

"Yeah. So?"

He grinned. "So we have a lot in common. Rock, paper, scissors for who gets to pick first."

Ridiculous, but she went along with it, lost, and settled into the sofa while he set up *The Good, The Bad, and The Ugly* in the DVD player.

Then he handed her the remote. "Just give me a sec. I'm going to raid your kitchen for snacks."

"Landon—"

"One word about your figure and *I'm* going to spank you."

Ten minutes later, he plopped down on the couch, setting down a bowl of popcorn and two bags of chips on the cushion between them.

"If it's not too late, maybe we can watch *Butch Cassidy and the Sundance Kid* next?" She popped a piece of popcorn in her mouth and glanced over at him. "It's one of my favorites."

"Sure. Then *Tombstone?*"

"All right . . ." She chewed slowly, leaning forward, her mouth watering as he ripped open a chip bag and then slipped an all-dressed chip between his lips. Spices sprinkled over his bottom lip and chin. She had to tear her eyes away from the tasty sight. "How long you planning to stay?"

"Not sure." He winked. "But I fully intend to be here when Asher gets back."

Chapter Eight

Loud moans woke Silver moments before her alarm went off. She glared at her clock, missing the days when 6:00 a.m. was bedtime. Not that she really *had* to get up now. Owning the team meant setting her own schedule but showing up late would only prove that she wasn't taking her job seriously.

Which means Dean wins. So not happening.

Pushing up from the bed, she gave a cat-like stretch, rolling her eyes as the moans grew even louder. Asher and Cedric were obviously having fun. And probably wanted her to join them. Arousal sped up her pulse and she nibbled at her bottom lip. Some makeup sex would be a good way to start the day. She hated fighting with Asher, and he hadn't been too happy to find her asleep on the sofa with her head on Landon's lap.

Maybe he's jealous. The thought made her smile; he wouldn't be jealous if he didn't care. She'd never wanted him to be all possessive, but things had changed. They'd either drift further apart, or they'd take their relationship to the next level. The idea scared her a little, and yet . . . she didn't want to lose him. Most of the last eight months were a blur, but that first moment when she *really* noticed him would stick with her forever.

Laughter all around her as she explained to the judge she thought the no parking only applied during the winter like some signs back home. This lawyer at her side, paid on a promise of a retainer once her agent finalized her latest gig. Hot guy in a light grey Armani suit. He'd put a comforting hand on her shoulder and rose, clearing his throat.

Armed with a photo of the faded sign, Asher had approached the judge and pointed to the illegible words. "Seasonal parking is one possibility. Or maybe no parking during earthquakes? Hurricanes? Signage shouldn't be a guessing game, Your Honor."

Once the case was dropped, Asher had brought her back to his place, and they spent the night having hot sex. Cedric showed up that morning after a business trip, and Asher had introduced him as his boyfriend. Slightly awkward, but Cedric hadn't seemed to mind. Two weeks later they were both living with her.

We had something. We just need to find it again.

After shedding the pink plaid pajama pants and white tank top she'd slept in, she made her way to Asher's room. A grunt made her pause. She held her breath and stepped into the open doorway.

Asher's tanned flesh glistened with sweat as he grasped Cedric's hips and slowly eased his dick between Cedric's quivering ass cheeks. He thrust in to the hilt and pressed his chest to Cedric's back, kissing the nape of his neck and panting as he drew out.

"I love your ass. You're still so fucking tight." He rocked forward and raked his fingers into Cedric's messy brown hair. "I could spend the day inside you, just feeling you clenching around me."

Cedric pressed his forehead to the mattress and jutted his ass up, spreading his thighs to take Asher deeper. "More. Give me more."

Silver swallowed as Asher rose, gliding out, then slamming back in. They really were beautiful together, slender bodies, pale gold sunlight accenting their faded tans. Cedric had a softness to him, sweet passion in contrast to Asher's animal lust. And that lust seemed so harsh at times, devoid of love, but for Asher to let himself go like that with anyone was something special. He used to let go with her . . . but not anymore.

Give him a reason to! Put yourself out there!

She whispered his name, just loud enough to be heard over Cedric's pants. "Asher?"

Asher turned his head without slowing, looking right at her as he spoke. "It's all yours, love. Take it. Tell me how much you want me."

"I want you!" Cedric gasped as Asher pounded into him. "Pleasepleaseplease!"

Licking her lips, Silver stepped forward. "I—"

Asher smoothed his hands down Cedric's sides and went still. "You what? If you couldn't tell, we're in the middle of something."

"I know, I just—"

"Just what?"

"Do you want me to . . ." Suddenly, she felt ridiculous. They obviously didn't need her. Seeing her, standing there naked, had no effect on Asher. And Cedric didn't seem to notice her at all. *What a stupid idea.* She took a step back and shook her head. "Never mind."

Digging his fingers into Cedric's hips, Asher narrowed his eyes at her. "What is it, Silver? You're feeling needy? Maybe you should have had your 'friend' take care of that last night."

He is jealous. Hope sputtered to life and she dropped her hands to her sides. "It's not like that with him, Asher. I'm sorry if you—"

"Damn it, why not?" Asher gently eased out of Cedric's ass and stood. "I've never stopped you from doing whatever you wanted with other guys!"

"I know that." She frowned, confused. "But you know it doesn't mean anything. I love you!"

"Silver, I'm gay."

"And? That's never mattered before!"

"And how long did you think we could go on like this? *Seriously?*" He sighed and raked his hair away from his face. "Look, we've had fun, but I'm done. You need things I can't give you. I'd hoped you'd find someone before—"

"Before what?" She ground her teeth and looked from Asher to Cedric, who'd covered himself with the bed sheet. "Are you breaking up with me?"

Cedric hunched his shoulders and muttered, "We're getting married."

The weight of his words hit her gut like a cement block. "You're what?"

"I proposed last night. Cedric said yes." Asher's tone was steady, almost defiant, as though he expected an argument.

Closing her eyes, Silver leaned against the doorframe and did her best to fill her lungs with air. *I put myself out there for this? For a "we don't want you anymore"?* "This doesn't make any sense. The way you acted last night . . . I thought . . ."

Asher sighed. "Silver, I still care about you. I don't like that guy. He's pushy and arrogant, and if it gets out that you're fooling around with the players after what happened with Oriana—"

"Fooling around with the players?" She let out a bitter laugh and locked down on her emotions. They were fucking useless anyway. Her tone became a cold, mocking thing oozing between her lips.

"Because I'm hanging around with one guy?"

"People will talk."

"Let them. I really don't give a fuck." Her lips curled. "Think of the publicity. It'll be good for the team."

That's right. The team is all that matters. It's all Daddy's ever turned to you for. And he wanted you to get rid of Asher and Cedric anyway.

"It wasn't when Oriana did it." Asher took a step toward her, brow furrowed, eyes strained. "Don't do anything stupid, Silver. I know you're pissed, but with your reputation—"

"My reputation." Giving him a curt nod, she swiveled on her heels, tossing words over her shoulder like she didn't have a care in the world. "About time I lived up to it, don't you think?"

* * * *

Silver considered going straight to the locker room when she got to the forum. The images of stripping right in front of all those big men, still soaked with sweat from practice, had her pulse racing. The elevator doors closed twice before she forced herself inside and jammed her finger on the button for the fourth floor. In her office she paced back and forth, back and forth, willing herself to feel nothing, but all the while feeling too much. Erotic images filled her mind—Asher with Cedric, which hurt because they were moving on without her. Then she recalled her night with Dean . . .

No! Not Dean. Don't think about him. If he knew . . .

Groaning, she left her office and went to the bathroom. She wet her hands with cold water and smoothed them over her throat, ignoring the droplets that scattered over her hot pink silk shirt. Hands braced on the edge of the sink, she tried to bring order to the chaos in her mind. Why did this bother her so much? Fine, she felt a little used, but in all honesty, she'd used them too. For almost a year she'd called them her boyfriends, enjoying both the stability and the freedom of having them in her life. Asher understood that when she had a bad day, some rough sex would make it all better. Better sex than drugs, right?

But she should have known, should have suspected, that one day their carefree little arrangement would end. Leaving her alone.

Stop it. She scowled at herself in the mirror. *You don't want a relationship anyway. You want a good fuck.*

Yes. A good fuck and everything would make sense again.

So where to? A snarky voice in her head demanded. *The locker room or the closest bar?*

"Uck. When did you get so desperate?" She turned her back on her reflection and fished in her purse for ... *there,* gummy bears. A mouthful got her thinking clearly again. She really wasn't up to throwing herself at another man. Not after Asher rejecting her. Not after what had happened with Dean.

Why the hell couldn't she get him out of her head? She had the strangest urge to see him. And it wouldn't go away. Back in her office, she buried herself in her work. But then considered going to ask him about the budget for the renovations.

The numbers are right there. Figure it out.

But she couldn't focus. Every time she blinked, she pictured him, holding her down, telling her he could give her what she needed. Taking control and overriding all her objections. The images made her just as wet as his actions had. She wanted him again, no matter how often she tried to tell herself otherwise.

Did you forget him ratting you out to Daddy?

No. She hadn't forgotten. But they needed to be able to work together. And to tell the truth, she'd forced his hand.

You're just looking for excuses to see him.

Maybe she was—she stood and undid the first few buttons of her shirt. Not that any excuse would matter. One look at her and he'd know exactly why she was there.

You might want a legitimate one, just in case. That way you won't be completely humiliated when he rejects you too.

* * * *

Dean trudged into his office and threw his suit jacket over his desk chair. Usually he hung around during training camp to see how the men were doing, but he just couldn't focus today. All he kept hearing, over and over, was his daughter saying "I hate you."

Why? Because her mother had called, making her monthly effort to show interest in her only child, and he hadn't found out until *after* he lectured Jami about staying up all hours drinking with her friends. Hell, he hoped she was just drinking. The way she'd blown up at him, screaming for him to "leave her the fuck alone," made him wonder. After she'd broken down and told him her mother was pregnant ... damn it, the right words just wouldn't come. She refused to let him hug her or tell her it didn't matter. She blamed him for everything, told him he was a control freak and that's why her mother had left them.

And maybe she was right. Macy had been interested in being a submissive when they first got together, but her interest waned— having a Dom in real life didn't live up to what she'd read in romance novels. He'd loved her so much he'd done his best to fit into the vanilla lifestyle she seemed to want, but it wasn't enough.

Thank God that's over. At the very least he didn't have to pretend anymore. Dominance wasn't a game for him, wasn't something he could switch on and off at will. Nor would he. Even now, just thinking about taking one of the many willing subs at the club eased some of the tension from his body. A shallow relief, because none of them belonged to him, but there were benefits to that as well. He didn't have the time for a 24/7 style relationship, what with a team to run and a daughter to raise.

And yet ... he shook his head and let out a gruff laugh. Ever since he'd seen that woman in pink—even after learning that woman was Silver—the idea of taking on a sub of his own had taken root and wouldn't be shaken. Not just any sub either.

You can't have Silver. She doesn't want this.

His office door creaked open and he looked up.

Silver stared at him, lips parted, eyes wide. "Dean?"

He smiled and rested one hand on his desk. "Can I help you?"

"No." She licked her bottom lip, one hand on the doorknob, knuckles white. "I don't know."

Like hell, she doesn't want this. The woman he saw before him wasn't the one who'd fucked with his team, who'd cursed him out, who'd left his bed in the middle of the night. She was the vulnerable woman who'd attracted him at the club. The one who needed what he had to offer. He straightened and held out his hand. "Come here."

She took three steps before losing her nerve, but he met her halfway and circled her waist with his arms, backing her into the door to close it as he claimed her lips. She moaned in his mouth as he explored her with his tongue, and the sound tore a growl from his throat. Her small body trembled and pressed against his, begging without words. He ground himself into her soft belly, letting her feel the effect she had on him.

Then he slid his lips along her jaw and whispered in her ear, "Tell me what you want."

"Fuck me." She curved her neck against his mouth and raked her fingers into his hair. "Just fuck me."

His eyes narrowed, but he kept his lips on her throat so she wouldn't catch his response to her crude demand. His tone was gruff when he spoke. "And what do you need?"

"Need?" She whimpered as he bit into the flesh above her collar. "What do you mean?"

He brought his hand up to frame her jaw and forced her to look at him. "You came to me, pet. There are other men, but you came to me. I won't make this easy on you."

"I don't care." She met his steady gaze for an instant, then her wet lashes fluttered shut. "Tell me what to do. I don't want to have to think about it."

He hated that word. *Want.* But what she wanted and what she needed were one and the same at the moment, so he let it go. Bracing her with one hand under her elbow, he stepped back.

"Strip."

"Here?" She watched him lock the door, and her throat worked as she swallowed. "But . . . I'm wearing a skirt."

Dean folded his arms over his chest. "I won't repeat myself, pet."

"Pet." She shook her head even as she brought her fingers to the buttons on her blouse. "Will it always be like *this* with you?"

"Yes." His lips curved slightly. "But that isn't a problem, is it?"

"Not now it isn't." She removed her shirt, then her skirt, hesitating when he arched a brow. "Everything?"

"Everything." He reached out and touched her cheek with his

fingertips. "You're not ashamed of your body. Why deny me?"

She closed her eyes, removed her bra and panties, gasping in air as though the question had stolen it from her. "I feel more naked with you."

"Good." He latched onto her wrist and drew her to his desk, sweeping papers aside before lifting her up and sitting her on the edge. "I want you naked. Physically. Mentally." He curved his hand around her throat with just enough pressure to open her eyes and quicken her pulse. "Don't try to hide from me, Silver. I won't allow it."

Shaking her head, she grabbed his collar and leaned forward. "You don't get it. I need to be fucked hard. That's it."

"That's not all you need." He grabbed her hands and tugged, laying her out on the desk. "Listen to me, pet. We will *not* fuck." Admitting it out loud made his dick throb painfully, but he continued without pause. "I will take my time and enjoy each and every inch of you. And when I'm done, you'll thank me."

Her hands fisted and she tried to sit up. "Like hell, I will!"

He chuckled and smoothed a hand over her quivering belly, lowering his head to lick one very hard little nipple. "Or maybe you'll thank me before I'm done. After I make you come once, twice—it doesn't matter. You'll say the words. Or scream them."

A gasp escaped her as he thrust his fingers into her hot, wet pussy. When she wiggled her hips, he sucked her nipple into his mouth and bit just hard enough to warn her to stop moving.

She took the hint and went perfectly still.

"What do you say, Silver?"

"Yes." Her body bowed as he drove his fingers in deep. "Yes, Sir!"

You're mine, sweetheart. He used his thumb to stimulate her clit and rose up to kiss her swollen lips. *You just don't know it yet.*

* * * *

The desk warmed under Silver's body, and her sweat slicked the glossed wood surface. Dean's fingers inside her, his lips on her breast, his hand holding hers high over her head—all kept her from moving much. But her heart fought to beat free of her ribcage and she squirmed restlessly as he teased her to the brink, slowing before she could throw herself over the edge. This wasn't at all what she'd planned, and yet, it felt too good to let protests leave the wide O of her lips. Dean was right. Somewhere, deep within, she'd known what he would demand from her. He'd told her once that dominance was part of the package—not in so many words, but she couldn't act like she didn't know what he was about. Maybe it would be an issue if things went long-term—*which they won't, so don't even go there*—but right now surrendering meant not thinking. And she didn't want to think. She needed to feel.

He slapped her pussy and she cried out as painful pleasure ripped through her. "You're leaving me, little one. You will be with me completely, or I will take you off my desk and see you to the door."

No! I can't leave! She twisted her trapped wrists and tossed her head. "I'm sorry. I'm here. I was just thinking—"

"Don't." His thumb pressed hard on her clit, and her hips jerked as the sensation electrified her. He lowered his lips to her belly and found a spot that had her twitching and gasping uncontrollably. "You will have to think about this later. For now, all you need to know is you are mine. And, lucky for you, I'm in the mood to play."

"Good!" Air caught in her throat as his fingers curved and found just the right spot to turn her brain to mush. Clinging to resistance didn't make sense any more. "After. After I don't know . . ."

"But I do. You intrigue me, Silver." He bent down and laved her lips with his tongue, thrusting in deep while he looked into her eyes. "Do you want to know why?"

She shook her head as her vision blurred and her body took over. "Why?"

"Because you're not as detached as you pretend to be." He smiled down at her. "I am surprised that you didn't have more success as an actress, though. I've never met a sub so difficult to read."

"I'm not a sub. And maybe that's a problem, but . . ." How she managed the words, she couldn't say, but they came out, putting up a safe wall between her and Dean. "I just need you to get me off."

"You need more." He closed his lips over one nipple, sucked hard, then moved to the other and stretched it with his teeth. When a strangled scream left her, he released her and chuckled. "But hold back all you want. I'm up for the challenge."

"Stop. Talking." She thrust her hips up and took his finger deep inside her. Pride sneered at her and she spoke just to appease it. "You're boring me."

"Am I?" He released her hands and gave her a hard look when she moved to bring them down. "Latch your fingers to the edge of the desk."

"Why——?"

A hard *smack!* on the side of her breast made her buck and cling to the edge of the desk. Heat and pain flared downward, spilling moisture which he spread with his fingers before dipping them into her. He fucked her hard and fast with two fingers, then three. The violent, erotic sensation dragged her up, up—then he stopped.

"Look at you." The edges of his lips quirked as he fisted his hand in her hair and made her face him. His thrusting resumed, slow and shallow, engaging the tight ring of muscles at her entrance. "One minute you hate me, the next you're laid out on my desk like a fuckable buffet. I know why I want you, but why do you want me?"

Her ass lifted rhythmically off the desk and her nails scraped the edge of the desk. "Because you can give it to me rough. I do hate you, but you're good, okay? Satisfied?"

"Not quite." He pressed his lips together, released her hair, and gave first one nipple, then the other, a brutal twist. "But you're right about one thing. I can give it to you rough."

He drove his three fingers deep, his knuckles slamming into her as he pistoned in and out. She let out a silent scream as she came, and he slapped her breasts while rubbing his wet fingers over her clit. Her insides rippled, sore, yet already craving more. Pleasure slashed through her and erupted over and over. A third climax latched on before the intensity of the first two had dwindled.

"Oh, fuck. Dean, please . . ."

"Thank me for making you come, Silver." He kissed the edge of her lips, then whispered in her ear. "Thank me, and I'll let you come one more time."

She shook her head as tears rolled down the sides of her face. "I'll thank you if you fuck me."

"I won't fuck you." He rubbed her pussy with his palm, torturing her with just enough pressure to keep her on the precipice, but not enough to let her take that last dive into ecstasy. "But I'll finish this if you say the words."

Damn you! She clenched her thighs around his wrist and gasped out. "Thank you for making me come, you son of a bitch."

"Bad girl." He slapped her aching nipple and clucked his tongue. "Say 'Thank you, Sir.'"

Defiance caved under desperation. She pressed her eyes shut. "Thank you, Sir. Thankyouthankyouthankyou!"

"Much better." He bit one nipple, pinched the other, and shoved his fingers inside her.

The orgasm fractured everything within into a million white-hot shards. She bit her tongue until she tasted blood to keep from howling out her satisfaction. The aftershocks carried on long after Dean pulled her into his arms, holding her close as he rocked back and forth on his chair, murmuring meaningless words like "beautiful" and "precious."

She somehow managed to speak after what seemed like forever. "I should go."

"Not just yet, sweetheart." He kissed her cheek and whispered, "Stay with me for a bit."

Cradled there, with her cheek cushioned on hard muscle covered in surprisingly soft white cotton, she couldn't imagine anywhere else she'd rather be.

Until reality hit her like a steel bat cracking the back of her skull. Stay with him? No. She couldn't. The control she'd given up to him already was a big huge sign that she better not go there.

I came to get fucked. Not for . . . this.

Whatever *this* was.

She pushed away from him and quickly gathered her clothes, dressing without looking at him. Confidence never failed her when she was naked, but it did now. It wouldn't take much for him to change her mind.

He doesn't want Silver Delgado, Über Diva Bitch Extraordinaire. About time she made an appearance, don't you think?

"That was . . . interesting." She gave him a cold smile. "But stupid. You got nothing. And I'm not the type to care about returning the favor."

"I wouldn't say I 'got nothing.'" Dean leaned back in his chair and folded his arms behind his head. "And I'd never expect you to return the favor. You'll do so when you're ready."

You're in for an unpleasant surprise. She smirked. "If you say so. I just hope you can be discreet?"

"Of course." He stood and picked up a folder from his desk. "I took the liberty of listing all the reputable PR agents in the area. Let me know if you need any help choosing one."

She snatched the folder and jutted out her chin. "I can manage."

"I'm sure you can." He sat on the edge of his desk and hooked his thumbs to his belt. "I'll be at the club on Saturday, if you're interested."

"Oh, I might swing by." The conversation felt stilted, weird after what they'd done, but his nonchalance made her want to take one last jab. "But I won't be there for you."

"Really?" Folding his arms over his chest, he looked her over and shook his head. "So who *will* you be there for?"

Shrugging, she turned away and opened the door. "Oh, I don't know. So many men to choose from . . . and I want to get to know the team better. There are twenty-three guys to go through, Dean. I really can't say."

"I see," he said, his tone telling her nothing. "Well, good luck."

In the hall with the closed door against her back, she ground her teeth and cursed at the ache in her chest. Why the hell did it bother her that he didn't seem to care?

He will. She squared her shoulders and strode to her office, slamming the door behind her. *And really, does it matter?*

It did. But it wouldn't, not for long. Even if she had to fuck the whole team, she'd prove to him, to herself, that she didn't need him.

I am Silver Delgado. She took a deep breath and dropped into Daddy's chair. *And he has no idea what I'm capable of.*

Chapter Nine

Four pans spit and sizzled and smoked on the stove. Landon sighed as he dumped another burnt pancake in the trash and cleared his throat into the phone tucked against his shoulder. "Becky? You were saying?"

"What are you doing?"

"Making breakfast. I figured I should use some of the food my sweet sister stocked my fridge with." He poked the bacon with a fork, then frowned at it. Damn stuff cooked too slow. "I'm tired of eating out, and I miss the breakfasts you used to make me."

"Yeah, you were spoiled." Becky laughed. "But don't you have a girlfriend to do that for you? We both know you can't cook."

"No, you just wouldn't let me. I think I can manage."

"And the girlfriend?"

"I don't have a girlfriend." The dryer in the closet down the hall beeped. Landon spooned some batter onto the hot frying pan, then checked the hash browns in the oven with the bacon fork. His knuckles grazed the red hot element. "Fu—fudge!"

"What happened?"

"It's hot!" He chuckled as she muttered under her breath, clenched and unclenched his throbbing fist, and headed to the washer-and-dryer nook to retrieve his laundry. "I know you and Mom think I need a woman to take care of me, but I've been managing just fine on my own."

"Landon, it's been two years—"

"We're not discussing this." He dumped his clothes into a laundry basket and straightened to shake out his dress shirt before it wrinkled. "Hey, guess what?"

Becky was silent for a few minutes, breathing the way she did when she was counting to ten in her head. Finally, she replied, "what?"

"I did my own wash—separated the colors from the whites and everything." He smirked at her long-suffering sigh. "Aren't you proud of me?"

"You are such a pain in the ass. Fine, you don't need a girlfriend." She said it like she didn't really believe it, but she probably wanted to move on to nagging about something else. "There is more to life than hockey though. Please tell me you do more than work out and practice."

"I do more than work out and practice."

"Like what?"

He thought of his trip to Blades & Ice and grinned. "You really want to know?"

"Oh. That." She sighed. "Well, at least you have a hobby."

A hobby? He snorted. *I guess you could call it that.* "So what about you? Dickhead start paying child support yet?"

Her sharp exhale sounded loud in the phone. "We are so *not* discussing *that*."

"Fair enough." After bringing his clothes to his room, he laid a fresh suit out on his rumpled bed. "So how's Mom? Her and Dad back from their—what is it, third honeymoon?"

"Not yet. They . . ." She paused, then groaned. "What are you doing now?"

"About to get changed." He looked down at his faded jeans, with the left knee ripped and the right almost worn through. His outfit for his early morning jog. Not something he could wear to his first preseason game. Or any games. Richter had included a pretty strict dress code in his contract. "I want to head to the forum early to meet the new goalie coach, so I can't—"

"You're cooking, Landon. You should stay in the kitchen."

"Yeah, yeah." He rolled his eyes and started down the hall. His eyes widened as he caught sight of the flames rising from the frying pan. "Shit!"

"What—?"

Tossing the phone onto the table in the hall, he darted into the kitchen, rushed to the sink, and filled a coffee mug with water. The damn bacon was crispy now—he tossed the water and threw himself back as a huge fireball flared up.

"Holy fuck!"

The smoke detector screamed and black smoke filled the room in waves. Scrambling down the hall, he grabbed the phone.

"Landon!"

"I'll call you back." Without waiting for an answer, he hung up and dialed 911 as he abandoned his apartment to the fire.

* * * *

Sitting on the sidewalk, Landon turned his phone in his hand and stifled a cough with his sleeve. A medic approached him, but he waved her off. He didn't need to go to the hospital—unless it was to have his head examined. How the hell could he have been so stupid?

The entire building had been evacuated as a precaution, but thankfully the fire had been contained to his apartment. Still, it made him sick to see the mother with her baby pacing outside in her pj's, trying to soothe the infant as the firemen rushed in and out of the building and the sirens wailed. Again his actions could have cost someone their life.

His phone vibrated in his hand. He checked the number, then brought it shakily to his ear, his voice raspy as he spoke. "Good morning, Silver. How you doing, beautiful?"

"Fine, I just—" She cut herself off. "Are you okay?"

"Just had a little mishap."

"What kind of mishap?" She didn't wait a breath before snapping. "You told me to call you if something was up. You said we were friends. Doesn't that go both ways?"

"Yes, but—"

"Uck! Men are such hypocrites!" She let out an angry cat growl. "You better start talking, mister."

He clenched his jaw to keep from smiling. *Damn, I'd love to see that girl all riled up.* "You're right. I would have been pretty pissed if your house caught fire and you didn't call me. Can I make it up to you by letting you buy me breakfast?"

"Your—you—What?" This time she hissed, "Where. Are. You?"

He gave her directions, remained silent as she cursed at him, then hung up after promising not to go anywhere. Only after staring at the phone for about ten minutes did it occur to him that he never let *anyone* speak to him like she had. And she was a sub to boot.

Not your sub.

He stuffed his phone in his pocket and scowled at the thick hose snaking across the lawn and into the apartment.

Right. Mustn't forget that.

＊　＊　＊　＊

"Why are you just sitting there? Why aren't you with the medic?" Silver glared at Landon and slapped his chest as he stood. "Do you have any idea what smoke inhalation can do to you?"

He caught her wrists and smiled down at her. Soot and stubble darkened his cheeks, stealing some of his disarming charm. "I'm fine."

Her body shook with fear and rage. Damn it, she could have lost him. They were just getting to know each other and it could have been over. Her vision blurred and she sucked in a deep breath as a hand settled on her shoulder. The way Dean steadied her reaffirmed her decision to call him on the way here. Most times she wanted to scream and throw things at him, and after yesterday she should know better than to let him get close, but at the moment, she welcomed his strength.

"She's right, Landon." Dean moved to her side and gave Landon one of those don't-bother-arguing looks. "And with what she's invested in you, I suggest you do as she says."

Landon's jaw hardened. He straightened and opened his mouth.

"Don't." Silver pressed her fingers over his lips. Men and their stupid pride. "Please, just do this for me. I let you take care of me. If the medic says you're fine, I'll drop it. But I need to know for sure."

His eyes softened and he leaned down until his forehead touched hers. "Fine. But after that, we're going to have breakfast."

She laughed. "Yes, I remember. And I'm buying." Glancing over at the apartment, she swallowed. The big brick structure looked untouched except for a single, broken window. Lingering smoke formed a paste on her tongue and a coal-like lump in her throat. "I guess you lost everything . . ."

The moisture in her eyes helped clear away the scratchy sensation, but she knew she was way too close to getting silly emotional. Landon was okay. That was all that mattered.

"Hey." Landon took her hand and squeezed. He smiled when she looked up at him. "It's just stuff. Most of my valuables are in storage at my parents' place. I didn't lose anything that can't be replaced."

"But—" Silver cut herself off as an elderly couple ambled by. She tightened her grip on Landon's hand as he watched them pass, guilt casting shadows over his face.

"How did the fire start?" Dean's tone had a sharp edge. He avoided her glare and focused on Landon. "If you don't mind my asking?"

Landon's brow furrowed. He stared at his grey sneakers. "Grease fire. And my own stupidity. I tried to put it out with water."

"Jesus." Dean shook his head. "You're lucky. Are you sure you didn't get burned?"

"Wait? What's wrong with putting a fire out with water?" Silver bit her lip when Dean muttered under his breath and massaged his temples with his fingers. "*What?*"

"Remind me to keep you both out of my kitchen." Dean laughed, groaned, and fiddled with his tie. "I've got to get back—the new guy should be joining the team today, and I want to see what I'm dealing with. Can you stay with him?"

Wow. Silver nodded, speechless. He actually trusted her to take care of their most valuable player? Would wonders never—

"I won't keep her long," Landon said. "She's got stuff to do—"

"Yes. And I believe her priorities are well in hand."

"I don't need a babysitter."

"That remains to be—"

Silver threw her arms up in the air, then grabbed both men's hands to pull them away from where the firemen were dragging the hose out of the apartment. "Stop it. Both of you. Dean, you've got my number. I'll check in later." She turned to Landon and put her hands on her hips. "We are friends. Do we have to go over how things work both ways?"

Lips twitching like he wanted to laugh, Landon shook his head and hooked his thumbs to his pockets. "*Non, mignonne.* I've got it."

"Good." She gave Dean a distracted nod when he said goodbye, her gaze locked on the angry red blotch covering the knuckles of

Landon's right hand. "You liar!"

Landon blinked and frowned. "Excuse me?"

"I will not!" She shackled her hand around his wrist and stomped her foot. "You . . . you . . . Arg! I thought you said you didn't get burnt!"

"Ah . . ." His tongue traced his bottom lip. He gave her a disarming smile, and she wanted to strangle him. "That."

"Yes. That." She dragged him toward the ambulance. "We are getting this looked at right now. And if you argue with me, I'll . . ." She scowled at his chuckle. "I'll have Dean bench you for a month."

That sobered him. For a split second. Then he grinned. "Bench or scratch?"

"Both!" She backhanded his hard chest when he laughed. "Oh, I am so going to learn that stupid game so I can punish you when you don't behave."

He cocked his head as they stood by the back of the ambulance and reached out to tuck a strand of hair behind her ear. "I can teach you."

Her cheeks warmed and she checked to make sure the fire was really out. Besides some thinning smoke, it seemed to be. She wrinkled her nose. "I'd like that."

A medic approached, her professional mask slipping as she looked from Silver to Landon. "Have you changed your mind, Mr. Bower?"

"Yes, he has." Silver tugged his arm and pushed him to sit on the bumper of the ambulance. "Sit."

He made a funny expression, as though a great big conflict was going on in his head. Suddenly calm spread over his features and he nodded. And sat.

Chapter Ten

The warm, buttery croissant left little flakes all over Silver's white suit jacket, but she hardly noticed as she sat flush against Landon's side, rubbing his arm to warm his goose-bumped flesh. The cold from the ocean washed over them, but he seemed too entranced with the view to notice.

"I don't think I'll ever get used to this. It's beautiful. Peaceful." He smiled and reached over, wiping away some foam from her latte off her upper lip with his thumb. "Did you miss it when you went to Hollywood?"

"Not really. I never spent much time enjoying the view." She rested her head on his shoulder and, for the first time, really took in the beauty laid out before her. The boats swaying lazily on the tide, the sun caressing the water in a gentle glow. Thin clouds gave the sky a grayish cast, but it only added to the early morning serenity, making everything seem quiet and still. The color reminded her of Landon's eyes when he looked at her in a way that made her feel calm. Just being here with him slowed the rush of life, and the restlessness that always wound around her was gone. She found herself inhaling deep and absorbing everything, holding it in because this couldn't last.

"Why?"

"Why?" She blinked and tipped her head up to find him watching her, his head tilted slightly, as though his entire focus was on her. "Well, I was too busy. My mother got me in dancing lessons when I was very young, then singing. I was a model when I was a kid—it's in my portfolio. She did everything to make sure I'd succeed. I won a few competitions because of her. If you ask Oriana, she'd probably tell you all our mother cared about was socializing and shopping, but she did all that for me. She tried to get Oriana into it, but Oriana wasn't interested. She was a tomboy and loved sports, and our mother didn't know what to do with her . . ."

Her chest tightened. She never talked to anyone about her childhood—well, besides her agent and that was just background stuff. Going over it all, she realized Oriana had always been a daddy's girl—but Daddy only saw his son.

Landon slid his arm around her shoulders. "How old were you when your mother died?"

"Seven." She thought back and . . . the details were fuzzy. Her mother had cried all day, finishing off two bottles of wine while staring at the second place ribbon Silver had won, muttering that a tap dancing routine would have gotten them first place.

"Three girls sang 'Tomorrow!' Three!" Her mother had moaned and rocked back and forth while researching something on her laptop. "Next time, you'll dance. I think there's another competition next week. If it's not too late to sign up . . ."

"I'm sorry, Mommy." Silver had hovered by her mother's side, wishing she could say something to make her feel better, wishing she hadn't failed her. Her insides hurt and her stomach felt full of curdled milk. Bouncy curls weighed heavy on her shoulders and mascara streaks made her face sticky and dirty. She wanted to rub her eyes, but making them all red would make mother mad. "I'll practice every day, I promise."

"Yes, you will." Her mother had slammed the laptop shut and lurched forward, scaring Silver. The laptop crashed to the floor and Antoine came running.

"Mom? Are you okay?"

"I'm fine."

"You should go lie down."

"I said I'm fine! Watch your sisters. I'm going out."

"No. You're not. Let me call Dad."

Silver jumped as Landon's grip tightened on her shoulder, dragging her back to the present. "Hey, where'd you go?"

"Sorry." She shook her head hard to clear the haze of memories. "I was just thinking about my mother. The day she and my brother died . . . well, I messed up. Daddy had my brother, who was always coming home with medals and trophies. And she had me. She wanted me to be the best and I wasn't. I just wish . . ."

"Don't do that. I'm sure she would be proud of who you've become."

"Who I've become? Most of my acting gigs were cheesy B movies, flashing my tits and reading corny dialogue. I kept up with the dancing and the singing, but I never used either." Inhaling deep, drinking in the fresh ocean air, she shook her head. "But it doesn't matter. She's gone and Daddy needs me. This team can make it, right? Maybe this will be the year we win that cup."

"Maybe." Landon trailed his fingers through her hair. "But what do *you* want? You can't live for your parents. Don't you have any dreams of your own?"

Did she?

Uck, the talking about serious stuff was not her thing. Dean had forced her to do that. She didn't want it from Landon too. "Okay. Moving on. I called Dean and we agreed. You're taking a few days off."

Landon groaned. "Why'd you go and do that?"

"Because I could." She smirked and stuffed a piece of croissant in his open mouth to keep him quiet. "The doctor said you were fine, but as a precaution, you should rest for a few days. And that's exactly what you're going to do."

He gave her hair a little tug. "All this power is getting to your head."

"It is not."

"Well, how about, to make things fair, you have to do what *I* say now."

Her breath hitched and her heart beat into overdrive. She took a big gulp of cold latte. Swallowed. Stared at him. "Umm . . ."

Power sparked in his heavy-lidded eyes as he leaned close. "What's wrong?"

"Nothing." Her gaze slipped to his full, soft lips. Then snapped back up. "I just forgot."

He chuckled. "Forgot what exactly?"

"That you're a Dom."

"Really?" He cocked his head to one side. "Is that a problem for you?"

Maybe. She finished off her latte and went perfectly still as he framed her jaw with his hand. "I don't know."

"If I gave you an order, would you obey?"

Yes! God yes! She pressed her eyes shut and dug her nails into her palms. A boat horn sounded and she started, speaking in a rush. "Please tell me you're teasing me."

"I'm teasing you." He patted her cheek and let his hand fall to his lap. "Actually, I was going to *ask* you to come to the forum with me tonight to watch the game."

The request completely deflated her, and her pulse slowed to a discordant thud. Some part of her wished he'd, well, been serious. Which was crazy. She had more than enough dealing with one Dom in her life. A Dom she *could* resist.

Sometimes.

Snap out of it, Silver. Landon is your friend. Pursing her lips and jutting her chin out, she slapped his arm. "You scared me, you jerk. Yes, I'll come watch the game with you. You promised to teach me more about it anyway."

"Yeah, about that . . ." He scratched his scruffy chin, his expression abruptly shifting to the playful one she'd gotten used to. "I need to pick up another suit. My sister helped me stock my wardrobe—I'm a fashion dud. Do you think you can spare some time to go shopping with me?"

"Are you kidding? I'm a fashion queen! I know just the spot, and I know just the style and color to complement your body and your eyes and—" Smacking her hand over her mouth, she blushed. "That came out wrong."

"Damn, and you had me thinking that I'm not butt ugly." He sighed and stood, taking both their cups to the trash by the bench. "Guess all the simpering fans are only after my money."

"Oh, shut up." Rising gracefully, she lightly brushed the croissant crumbs from her jacket and straightened her skirt. "You know very well that you're a stud."

They made their way along the pier arm in arm, Landon seeming to chew on her words as he admired the view once again. They'd reached Silver's car before Landon stopped and turned to face her.

"So you think I'm a stud?" His brow creased slightly and he held up his hand. "Wait. Don't answer that. I don't want to know."

"Then you shouldn't have asked." She shoved him toward the passenger side, then climbed in behind the wheel. All settled in, she gave him a sideways once over. "I'd do you."

Landon groaned, covered his eyes with his hand, and muttered, "Brat."

"Yes, Sir."

The lighthearted remark stole all the fun from their banter. For the first time, Landon couldn't seem to find a joking retort. And Silver couldn't get past how easily the formal address left her lips.

* * * *

Hours later, Silver left Landon in the player's lounge to take a nap and headed up to her office to see if she had any real work to do. Anne stood and intercepted her with an armful of files and a few messages.

"Mr. Richter would like to speak with you when you have a moment." Anne shuffled back to her desk and added distractedly, "Oh, and there's a man waiting for you in your office. He called several times while you were gone—he said your cell phone was turned off?"

Silver's heels scraped the tiles as she swiveled toward Anne's desk. "What? No, it wasn't! I had it on in case Dean called!"

Anne shrugged. "Well, he mentioned asking for an appointment. He's an investor, you know. You really shouldn't ignore him."

An investor? She recalled the message left on her cell days ago and shuddered. "You sure he doesn't want to talk to Dean?"

"He asked for you."

Uck, I really don't like you. Anne had always seemed so pleasant, answering her phone calls sweetly before transferring her to Daddy. But after she'd gone and told Oriana that Silver was looking into trading Sloan . . . yeah, the woman was a bitch. And probably a gold digger too. She'd spent an awful lot of time at Daddy's bedside over the summer.

"You know, Anne." She put a tight smile on her lips and approached the desk. "My ex-boyfriend is a lawyer, and he's been going over the contracts of the employees here. I'm no expert, but I do know what a non-disclosure agreement is. You've already breeched that, so I would suggest you be very careful from now on. I'd hate to fire you, what with a new baby on the way and all, but if you don't show me some respect, that is *exactly* what I'm going to do."

Anne paled and nodded. "Yes, Miss Delgado."

"From now on, you do not let people into my office without clearing it with me first. Understand?"

"Yes, ma'am."

"There's something sexy about a woman who knows how to take charge." Dean's deep voice and hot breath had all the hairs on the nape of her neck standing on end. His tone dropped to a whisper. "If you weren't so sweetly submissive, I'd peg you for a Domme."

It took every ounce of strength she had not to melt back into his arms. She sucked air through her teeth and glanced over her shoulder. "You wanted to see me?"

"Yes. But it can wait until after we see to your uninvited guest." He pressed lightly on the small of her back to get her moving toward her office. Stopping at the door, he held her shoulders and turned her to face him. His lips curved slightly as he flicked a flake of croissant from her jacket. "May I make one request before we go in?"

A request? Be still my heart! She wrinkled her nose and stared at his gold hockey stick tie clip. "Sure. What?"

He tapped her nose and chuckled when she skidded out of reach. "Stop looking so terrified. I have no intention of molesting you."

She let out a sigh of relief. "Oh, well, that's good."

"Tonight."

"Ugh." *Infuriating man!* Arms folded over her chest, she glared up at him. "I hate you."

"Again?" He slid his hand around her throat and drew her close for a light kiss. His brow arched when she rose up for more. "And now?"

The minty taste of his mouth lingered, leaving a hot and cold sensation on her lips. She glared at him as she reached out to open the door. "I want to kill you and bury you in an unmarked grave."

"Liar." He pushed the door open and his entire bearing changed so abruptly she shivered. This side of him, pure raw power unleashed, scared her. More than a little. "Can we help you?"

The short, pudgy man shot out of her chair and quickly moved away from the desk. "Ah . . . I'm sorry. I expected to speak with Miss Delgado alone. You are . . . ?"

"Dean Richter. The general manager of the Dartmouth Cobras." Dean thrust his hand out. "I understand you are one of the team's investors?"

"Charles Lee." He handed Dean a card. "And I am simply a representative of Kingsley Enterprises." His gaze flicked from Silver to Dean, and he winced as he shook Dean's hand. "My client is naturally concerned with the changes in management and asked for some assurances—"

"Naturally." Dean gave the man a cold smile and put his hand on Silver's shoulder. "Miss Delgado is young, but the league would not allow her to take on the responsibility if she did not have advisors to back her. Aside from that, her father has given me a share in the team to run by proxy, which means very little will change."

Mr. Lee's lip curled slightly. "Really? So am I to understand you approved the team's acquisition of Scott Demyan? I find that hard to believe."

"And why is that?" Dean asked.

"To be frank, the man doesn't fit with the team's image. That aside, Miss Delgado signed the contract, not you." Mr. Lee smirked and continued. "Obviously, as the owner, she has more say than you do. My clients need to know the team is stable."

"You may assure them it is." Dean stepped away from Silver and loomed over the man in a way that made Silver wonder if she should grab him before things got violent. His fist clenched at his sides . . . and stayed there. "And you may also inform them I am well aware of Kingsley Enterprises' part in the *situation* with Coach Stanton last season. No charges have been filed—yet. They would do well to avoid bringing any further attention to themselves. They will profit from the success of the team. Nothing else."

"I'm sure I don't know what you mean." Mr. Lee paled and glanced toward the door. "But I will convey your message. If you'll excuse me?"

Dean gestured dismissively toward the door. Mr. Lee scurried out.

Then Dean turned to Silver and she gasped. The rage in his eyes tempted her to follow the potato in a suit out the door.

"Don't ever meet with that man alone—or with anyone associated with him." He grasped her wrists, making her drop all her folders, and pulled her toward him, trapping her wide eyes with his hard gaze. "Promise me."

"I promise." She trembled and tugged at her wrists. "But you have to tell me what's going on. What did he really want?"

"I don't know." Dean relaxed his grip and stroked his thumbs over her inner wrists. "I'm sorry. Did I hurt you?"

"No." She nibbled on her bottom lip. "But you're kinda freaking me out. You must have some idea of why he came if you're this upset."

Dean crossed his arms over his chest and turned, moving away from her to take a seat in front of her desk. He pressed his eyes shut and inhaled roughly. "You must have heard that Oriana's ex—Paul—was involved in a scandal."

"I might have heard something." She frowned and went to perch on the edge of the desk in front of him. "Oriana didn't tell me much, but people are talking."

"People?"

"Anne. She's a gossip."

"Ah." His shook his head. "Investors paid him to rig games so they could bet on them. He involved the goalie I traded and the defenseman whose contract I bought out so he could retire. Paul disappeared—it seems like he got roughed up by his 'partners' in the hospital. He tried to blame Max Perron, your new brother-in-law, for the injuries but then screwed himself over by asking another doctor to clear him to coach an important game. The police looked into it and found discrepancies in his initial exam and his condition hours later. The charges against Perron didn't stick."

"That's good." She smiled and pictured Max with Oriana. They were sweet together and she liked Max. "He makes my sister happy."

"So does Dominik. And Sloan." His brow arched when she mumbled her grudging accord under her breath. "I'm not surprised that you don't like Sloan, but what's your problem with Dominik?"

Well, that's easy. "He's an über Dom."

"An über Dom?" Dean laughed. "Don't you read all those kinky romance books? Aren't über Doms exactly what women like you want?"

Kinky romance books? She shook her head and giggled. "Seriously? I'm so not the romance type. I've read some nonfiction BDSM. Mostly because I had a part I was trying out for... there's this movie coming out based on some popular BDSM book, and I wanted to get an idea of what the appeal was. My agent asked me not to read the book—she wanted me to have my own take on the character from the script. I started going to kinky clubs when I was nineteen, so I thought I knew everything. Those books proved me wrong."

His brow creased slightly. "Have you ever been with an 'über Dom'?"

Her thoughts slipped to the one time she'd almost fallen into that trap. The man had been hot, powerful, intimidating. She found herself wanting to obey his every command, and that had her saying her safeword before he even snapped her cuffs together. The things she might have let him do to her—she shuddered.

"Once... almost. But I'm not a real sub. I like playing around sometimes, but it's never real. He almost made it real."

Dean rose from the chair and approached her slowly, as though she was a skittish little kitten. "Before he made you feel that way, were you attracted to him?"

"He was attractive, but..." Damn, how to explain? To Dean of all people? "I would have fucked him, just normal-like, but when I fool around with the kinky stuff, it's with guys I know I can control. I totally top from the bottom. I know all the definitions, and that's why I know I'm not a sub."

"You keep saying that." He cupped her cheek. "Stand up."

She stood and gaped at him as he curved his hand around her throat.

"Let's test your theory, shall we?" His lips quirked at her frown. "What? Afraid that you're wrong?"

"I'm not wrong. I'll admit I never saw Oriana as a sub, but she shows all the signs of being one and it makes her happy. Which is awesome." She hooked a finger into the buttons of Dean's shirt.

"But I'm not like that. I've never been sexually repressed, so if the whole being tied down and spanked thing really got me off, I'd know."

"You were wet after I spanked you." Dean crowded her against the desk and put a bit more pressure on her throat. Her insides liquefied. "I slapped your breasts and pussy, and you responded in a beautifully submissive way. I believe you've focused too much on what a 'real' submissive is, concentrated on all the ways you didn't fit, because you don't know what would happen if you truly surrendered to a dominant man. Any more than you know what would happen if you got into a serious relationship."

"I was in a serious relationship with Asher and Cedric."

"As in you no longer are?" His steady gaze held sympathy. "I'm sorry Silver. I didn't know it was over. I had the impression that you had an open relationship—and despite the fact that I didn't feel that you were right together, I knew they meant something to you. When did this happen?"

"Yesterday—or . . . well, this morning I guess." She shrugged as her throat grew tight. Then frowned at his shiny black shoes. "It doesn't matter. I should have seen it coming."

"Perhaps." His shoes moved closer, and his hand came into her line of sight. His fingers brushed up her jaw and into her hair. He kissed her cheek, then her nose, then her lips. "But you still have the right to be upset about it."

She groaned and latched onto the back of his neck before he could back away. For good measure, she hooked her ankles behind his knees. "I'm not upset—about that anyway. I am annoyed at you though."

His eyes crinkled. "May I ask why?"

"You know why." She reached into his jacket and grabbed his belt. "You make me forget that I don't like you when you get me thinking about letting you fuck me."

He pushed her hands down and shook his head. "I'm not going to fuck you."

"Arg!" Slapping her hands on the desk, she released him and scowled. "You keep saying that! Why the hell not?"

"This isn't the place for this discussion, Silver." He went over to the files she'd dropped and quickly put them in some semblance of order before bringing them to her desk. "Which is actually why I wanted to speak to you. We really should keep things professional at work. I don't want whatever is going on between us to distract you."

Sliding off the desk, she straightened her jacket with an agitated yank. "There's nothing going on between us. Not even sex because you keep turning me down. But thank you for reminding me what a condescending asshole you are. Makes things much easier."

His jaw ticked and he shot her a cool look. "Don't be childish. I'd like to establish an amicable working relationship. We got off to a rough start, but I think we both want what's best for the team."

"Yes, we do." Her whole body shook as though she'd just taken an espresso shot. The dampness between her thighs pissed her off. She really, really wanted to throw something at Dean for making her feel this way again, but she wouldn't be "childish." She just had to remind herself that there were other dicks around to be had. And worse came to worst, she had an arsenal of toys at home. "Is that all?"

He shook his head, started for the door, then paused. "I meant to tell you . . . the way you handled Landon—I was impressed. People say that you're selfish. But they're wrong."

The door shut behind him. She couldn't move. All the air in the room had rushed out with him, but the temperature had gone up. She pressed her hands to her hot cheeks and bit back a smile.

Impressing him never occurred to her. Never.

But she had, and damn if it didn't feel good.

Chapter Eleven

Dean crossed the hall with long strides, his rubber soles creating a brisk tattoo on the tiles, remnant of his brief military stint. He put his thoughts in order with regimental efficiency, stacking wayward emotions in the back of his mind where they belonged. The game tonight had to take priority. He had a mission and . . .

He shook his head and quietly laughed at himself. *It's a preseason game, Richter. Not combat.*

Regret speared his chest and his cadence faltered. He'd enlisted in his late teens to attend university fully funded in return for forty-eight months of service. What had started out as a way to receive the education he couldn't have afforded otherwise became a way to get the structure he craved. Unfortunately, his pastime of playing street hockey ended his career. An awkward fall tore the ligaments in his right knee and reconstructive surgery, while essentially successful, wasn't enough for him to pass the medicals. After his discharge, he'd turned his focus to the game he'd loved as a boy. He couldn't coach, but he'd been successful as a scout and had worked his way up to assistant general manager of the Washington Capitals.

When Delgado offered him the position of general manager, he'd jumped on the opportunity. As much as he'd loved his team in the States, his ambitions had him packing his wife and daughter and moving back to his birth country. While his marriage fell apart, he took comfort in the fact that twenty-three men relied on him to see to their futures. It was almost like being an officer again—only without the prestige and honor of fighting for a cause. Or such a *big* cause. They still fought for something, in a way.

Maybe his love for the game made it seemed grander than it was, but it satisfied him. He pushed his men hard. Granted, they weren't putting their lives on the line for their country, but there was some national pride involved. Canada lived and breathed hockey, and he would see his team flourish and become one of the legendary franchises.

So long as *he* didn't let anything distract him.

Pausing in front of the elevator, he pressed the down button and groaned. Reaffirming his goals didn't help. His dick strained against the steel-toothed cage of his zipper, and his flesh recalled Silver's soft skin, her brief submission . . . and, worst of all, her strength. She cared for Landon, and the fear of losing him had almost paralyzed her, but she'd set that aside to see to his needs. How could he not respect that?

You told her you didn't want to distract her, the cold, logical voice within said. *Be honest. You're afraid she'll distract you.*

No. Nothing could distract him. But that didn't mean he couldn't enjoy her away from here, at the club where he was in complete control, where nothing unexpected could be thrown at him that he couldn't handle . . .

Speaking of which, it was time for him to meet their new player.

The elevator doors opened. He stepped forward. A woman with a CBC press badge pinned to her chest stepped out, forcing him back.

"Are you Dean Richter?"

"Yes." He glanced at her badge and ground his teeth. "Rebecca Bower. Are you here to see your brother?"

"No." The petite woman looked him over and pursed her lips. "I'd like to speak to you first."

"Of course." He held out his hand toward the elevator. "I am heading down to the rink to meet our new acquisition. You may join me—if you keep this off the record."

"Sure." She backed into the elevator and fiddled with the amethyst pin on her lapel. She seemed nervous, but she pounced when the doors closed. "You have a game tonight. I need to know there's no chance of my brother playing."

Dean inclined his head and smiled. "You do know he's been cleared?"

"I really don't give a shit. I may have agreed to off the record, but if my brother is put on the ice, I'll dig in deep and find a way to expose your team for putting your players at risk." Rebecca pulled her cell phone out of her serviceable black purse. "The fire made the headlines. I've been fending off calls offering sympathy for my brother's demise all day. He left a message while I was on my way here, saying he was fine, but that's not good enough. I've already spoken to the doctor he saw at the hospital. He was advised to take a few days off to make sure there weren't any lingering symptoms from smoke inhalation."

"Ma'am, I make a point of being informed of my players' medical conditions. I apologize if you've made this trip for nothing, but Landon is being well cared for."

"My trip wasn't for nothing." Her cheeks reddened slightly. "My editor approved it hoping I'd get a story. I refuse to make one out of my brother being an idiot. But an exclusive with Scott Demyan will satisfy him."

Dean nodded. "I can arrange that. The team will hold a press conference about the acquisition tomorrow, but I see no harm in you providing a preliminary report. Last I heard, your brother is resting in the player's lounge. He's a dedicated player and sticks to his routine. I'd prefer not to disturb him if you will accept my assurance that he's well."

"Thank you, Sir." She ducked her head, and his inner Dom instantly acknowledged her tone and submissive behavior. For some reason, this seemed natural for her. And accepted. He refused to guess on her involvement in the lifestyle, but she was clearly comfortable with it. Unlike Silver— Rebecca cleared her throat to regain his attention. "May I ask you a question? Still off the record?"

"You may."

"Are *all* your men Doms? I only ask because I need to know Landon will fit in here."

"Why wouldn't he?" His eyes narrowed when she looked away. "Answer me."

Her breath hitched. "He was eighteen when one of his professors introduced him to the lifestyle. The man was hard-core, a leatherman, but even after he learned that Landon was straight and dominant . . . well, he didn't care. He taught Landon everything he knows. They became close friends, and the only thing Landon cared about as much as hockey was becoming the 'perfect Dom.'" She scowled at her patent leather pumps. "His girlfriend at the time pretended to be submissive to keep her hooks in him. He felt guilty for not being able to give her the time she needed because of his dedication to the game, so he gave into her every demand when he wasn't on the road. Things ended . . . tragically." She paused and made a face, as though suddenly realizing she'd said too much. "If he wants you to know more, he'll tell you, but I just wanted you to know . . ."

"I understand." Dean wanted to push her for more, and with how vulnerable she was after nearly losing her brother, she'd likely tell him anything he wanted to know, but he wouldn't take advantage of her. "And I'll keep an eye on him."

"Good." Her nostrils flared with a sharp inhale. "Because there are rumors spreading about him and Silver Delgado and I don't want her to—"

He straightened and put his hand on her arm as the elevator stopped and the doors slid open. "Landon is a big boy, Rebecca. I will do my best to make sure he doesn't get into a bad situation, but you'll have to trust him to make his own decisions. And Silver won't hurt him."

She glared at him and yanked her arm free. "So you say."

"Silver is the reason he's not playing tonight."

"Oh."

"Yes. 'Oh.'" He smirked. "You really don't need to protect your brother from her. From what I've seen, she considers him a friend."

Rebecca followed him to the training room, muttering softly, "The friend status with that woman is a good thing."

Dean sighed and pushed the door open. He expected to see Demyan on one of the bikes, warming up for the game. Instead the man was face down on a table, groaning as one of their only female trainers massaged him.

"Right there—oh, yeah." Demyan shifted and cast the petite Asian woman a hooded look. "You've got magic fingers, babe. I can breathe all right now. You wanna see what else I can do?"

Before the trainer could answer, Dean spoke up. "I would. Perhaps you can join your teammates and get dressed for the game?"

"Coach didn't tell you?" Demyan let out a fairly convincing hacking cough. "I'm not in the lineup tonight. I'm sick."

Like hell you are. Dean studied the man, ignoring his cynical thoughts. His skin did seem a little flushed, and he was breathing hard—accusing him of faking would start their working relationship off on a bad foot, so Dean let his suspicions slide and waved the trainer away.

"I'm sorry to hear that. Have you seen the team doctor?"

"Naw, he's busy with some kid—Tyler Vanek?" Demyan rolled over and stretched. "I'll be fine for the last preseason game; I just need to rest up a bit."

Vanek? Dean shook his head. The boy wouldn't be fit to play until midseason, if that. His head injury was so severe the doctor had told Dean, quite frankly, that his career might be over. The fact that he was young and in good shape leaned in his favor, but it was too soon to do more than pray for a good outcome. *After* he'd had time to heal.

Dean would have to speak to him.

"You have to pass the medical evaluation before you can play, but if you rest up tonight, I think you should be fine for Friday's game." Dean reached out and patted the wiry man on the shoulder. He wasn't even warm. "We'll be holding a press conference tomorrow to show you off to the fans." He glanced over at the pile of clothes by the table and pressed his lips together. Ragged jeans and a white wife-beater. Real classy. "I expect you to be wearing a suit."

Demyan chuckled. "A suit? Yeah, I don't do suits."

"You do now." Dean did his best to keep his tone neutral. He already didn't like the guy. "I suggest you go over your contract with your agent. All players must dress appropriately for team functions. This includes all games and press conferences. Not exceptions."

"Really? We'll see about that." Demyan sat up and wrapped the white towel draped over his groin around his hips. He looked ready to make a smart-assed remark, but then noticed Rebecca, standing a few feet behind Dean. "Hey there, cutie. Sorry the GM is being rude—he should have made introductions before he started nagging." He held a hand out. "I'm Scott Demyan."

"Rebecca Bower." Rebecca strode forward and grabbed Demyan's hand, shaking it hard before blurting out. "I would like to ask you a few questions, if you don't mind."

Raking his gaze over her professional attire like he was stripping each piece off with his eyes, Demyan nodded slowly. "Let me take you out to dinner, and I'll tell you anything you want to know, babe."

"I won't be here that long." Rebecca gave him a sweet smile and pulled her wallet out of her purse. "I left my daughter with my parents, but I promised to be back in time to tuck her in. My flight leaves in an hour. I miss her so much. Isn't she adorable?"

The way Demyan stared at the picture of the sweet little girl with curly pigtails proved that Rebecca had chosen the right escape route. Men like him didn't fool around with women who had "baggage."

Demyan cocked his head to one side. "Can't your husband tuck her in?"

Rebecca held out her left hand, wiggling her fingers with an amused expression on her face. "I'm divorced."

"Get your parents to do it then. I swear, it'll be worth it."

That did it. Dean didn't want this scumbag on his team. Unfortunately, he was stuck with him.

"A fifteen minute interview shouldn't make your *condition* any worse." Dean slapped Demyan's shoulder hard enough that both he and Rebecca winced. "This will show the fans how *dedicated* you are."

Demyan grumbled something under his breath and squared his shoulders. "Fine. What do you want to know?"

Rebecca dropped her purse on the table after taking out a notepad. She glanced at it, then shot off her first question. "You've been involved in several scandals, including one that involved two prostitutes. Should the Dartmouth Cobras expect the same behavior here, or have you changed your ways?"

Gut check! Dean grinned. Not only had Rebecca turned the slick asshole down quite effectively, but she'd gone right for the jugular to begin her interview. He'd heard good things about the Bower family, and he already liked Landon. Perhaps he should send Rebecca off with tickets for the first at home game so he could meet them all.

Shoving himself off the table, Demyan scowled at his clothes. "Mind if I get dressed before the interrogation?"

"Not at all," Rebecca said. "I'll wait for you in the hall."

Dean followed her to the door, then glanced over his shoulder at Demyan. "My assistant will be present for the interview, since we're presently between PR agents and we don't want you to say anything that would damage your—or the team's—reputation."

"Wouldn't want that." Demyan pulled on his jeans, looked up, and let out a weak cough. "After that I'm heading home. I'll swing by around noon for the press thing."

"It's scheduled for 10:00 a.m."

"10:00 a.m. it is then." Demyan rolled his eyes. "Anything else, Richter?"

"No, that will be all." Dean smiled. "Ms. Bower will meet with you in the player's lounge. I think she can handle things from there."

And sometime between now and then, I'll have to speak to Silver. He closed the door behind him and hesitated beside it. *She screwed up. She needs to know the press will rub it in.*

For some reason "I told you so" didn't even register. All Dean could see was the coming media circus. All he could think of was ways to protect her from it.

Even though she'd brought this on herself.

* * * *

Landon uncapped a bottle of beer and passed it to Silver. They'd sat silently in the owner's box through most of the first period while she remained fixed on the play as though he might give her a pop quiz when it was over. He relaxed into the cushy leather sofa and fought the urge to play with her hair as she leaned forward and held her breath.

Down on the ice, several players brought up from their farm team jostled for the puck. Callahan and Perron rested on the bench, red-faced and exhilarated, even with their limited play time. Preseason was a time to get the team ready for the real games and to test the rookies to see who was ready to take their place on the team. The best players took the ice for a couple of games and the results meant nothing. Still, he would have liked to have been down there with his new team. It didn't matter that the stats didn't count. He was itching to prove himself.

Silver tugged his sleeve and let out a tiny growl as Luke Carter, a rookie power forward, took a nasty hit into the boards. "That can't be legal! We have to go down there and—"

"It was a late hit." Landon's lips quirked. So she *had* been paying attention. "But if the refs don't see it, it doesn't count."

Minutes later, the ref blew the whistle.

"Bullshit!" Silver stood and approached the glass, pointing like she was condemning the ref to the farthest reaches of hell. Adorable in all her indignant fury. "You said offside was when the player crossed the blue line before the puck! He didn't!"

"The left winger did."

"He did not! I was watching!" She put her hands on her hips. "I don't like these refs. Let's get new ones."

Inwardly, Landon roared with laughter. Outwardly he managed a straight face. "We don't get to choose the refs, *mignonne*. And besides, that was the linesman."

"Oh . . . can we fire them?"

"No. The officials don't work for the team; they work for the league." He patted the seat beside him and draped his arm over her shoulder when she sat. His mouth watered as he caught her scent. The woman always smelled like flowers and candy. "If you're getting this worked up now, imagine what you'll be like during the regular season. This is nothing."

"I'm going to need a prescription for Prozac." She shot off the sofa as though a spring had propelled her. "That hit was bad. You said hitting the numbers—oh no! What if he's out for the season? He looks like he's hurt!"

Landon stood and moved to her side. Carter again. Not surprising, the kid had been chirping the entire game. But he got to his feet without any help and made it to the bench. "He's fine. And look, Pledich is headed for the box."

"He should be thrown out!" She glanced over her shoulder as the assistant general manager snorted. "What's so funny?"

"Nothing, ma'am." The man pushed his glasses up with his thumb and went back to his paperwork, muttering, "Women don't get it."

"*You,* I can fire." Silver bared her teeth and jerked on the hem of her white suit jacket. She turned to Landon. "I don't get it. I'm the owner, but I have no say over what goes on down there?"

Damn, can I take the Fifth? "That's not *entirely* true."

"Then how can I make this team better? It doesn't take a genius to know they're not doing good. Five goals in ten shots. Is that normal?"

Okay, maybe it would be better if she hadn't been paying attention. His answer wouldn't satisfy her, and her passion was driving him to distraction. "*Non, mon chou*, but we're playing a goalie from the minors against one of the best lineups in the league. We'd be doing better if I was out there—"

"You said these games don't count."

"They don't."

"And we need you playing your best during *real* games."

"True."

"Then sit down and shut up!" She faced the glass and threw her hands in the air. "What's wrong with him? We don't need a penalty now!"

Dominik Mason headed to the box after an interference hit on Pledich. The crowd roared and stomped their feet.

"Idiots!" Silver spat like an angry little cat. "Why are they cheering?"

"It's very hard to explain anything while you're fuming over every call, Silver." Landon hooked his fingers into the pockets of her slacks and pulled her back to the sofa. Beside him, only after he thought better of placing her on his lap. "Take a seat. Breathe. And listen."

Silver's whole body trembled with agitation, but as she turned and lifted her gaze to his, something inside her seemed to latch onto his calm. She settled down beside him and folded her hands on her lap.

"Okay. I'm listening."

Landon smiled and tapped her nose. "There's a good girl. Now, one thing you have to understand about hockey, even if you can't fully grasp anything else, is that it's not just about scoring, or even winning. Of course, that's important too, but pride and respect stay with you even if you're with a team that can't contend for the Cup—"

"But—"

"Don't interrupt." His eyes narrowed slightly at her huff. It took everything he had not to latch on to her token submission. But he barreled on. "When you're out there on the ice, you've got to be able to trust that the other men have your back. For passes, or, if you're a goalie, to keep your line of sight clear. Works better if you're all gelling. That also means if someone takes a cheap shot, you're going to want to make them pay. Having every guy on the team going for revenge would be a mess, but that's kinda Dominik's job. I think he'd do it anyway, but at least the other teams know they won't get away with targeting our players." He shook his head and watched Carter skate by the opposition's bench, getting just close enough while he chirped to tempt them to make a grab for him. *Punk!* "Whether they deserve it or not."

"So this is what you consider a good penalty?" Silver held her tongue between her teeth and tilted her head slightly. "Like when that defense guy got a tripping penalty?"

She's catching on. He nodded. "Yes, exactly. You've got to know the rules. And you've got to know when to break them."

The door to the owner's box opened, and Landon glanced over distractedly to see who'd come in. His eyes widened as he watched his sister stride toward him, her eyes spitting fire.

"*Tu es stupide! Tu mériterais une claque en pleine face!*"

Silver scrambled to her feet when it looked like Becky might slap him like she'd threatened to in French. "Excuse me, who are you?"

"Miss Delgado, I appreciate you forcing my brother to stay off the ice, but this is between me and him." Becky gnashed her teeth together in the way she did whenever she got really mad. The sound made the hairs on the back of his neck stand on end. He stood before she could shove Silver aside, and she latched onto the collar of his shirt. "*Suis-moi.*"

"*Non. Calme toi un petit peu.*" He pried her fingers loose and held a finger up to Silver as he drew his sister to the back of the room, speaking low in their birth language. "What are you doing here? Where's Casey?"

"Staying with Mom and Dad. And by the way, you're lucky I didn't tell Mom why I came down or she would be here beating you upside the head for being such a moron!" Her voice rose and she ignored his efforts to quiet her. At least no one could understand what she was saying. She cracked him upside the head and kept ranting. "Who leaves the kitchen while they're cooking? You could have died! I can't lose you!"

Landon pulled her into his arms and let her stifle a sob against his chest. "I'm okay. And I'm sorry I scared you. I swear I'll be more careful from now on."

She sniffed and shook her head. "It only takes once. Just once. You don't always get lucky."

A massive fist took hold of his heart and squeezed. It wasn't surprising that Becky was this upset. She was the most levelheaded person he knew, but something like this would trigger all too recent memories. She'd almost lost her daughter because her now ex had left their toddler alone in the bath "to play" while he entertained his new girlfriend.

Patrick had called her from the hospital and Becky had called Landon on the way there, almost falling apart as she asked him to join her because she wanted him to take her husband out like the trash he was. Landon had no problem with that. Yes, accidents happened, but that wasn't the first time he'd neglected his daughter for a piece of ass.

"Becky, look at me." He dried her tears from her face with his palms and kissed her cheeks. "Would it make you feel better to slap me a few times?"

Becky let out a watery laugh. "Yes, but I won't." She stood back and looked him over. "Are you sure you're all right? No burns?"

"Well?" Landon lifted his bandaged hand. "Just a little one, but that happened before the fire."

"Ugh." She gently took his hand in hers and shook her head. "Swear to me you'll never try to cook again. Either order out or find someone to do it for you." Her nose wrinkled as she glanced over at Silver who was pretending not to watch them. "Just not her."

"Hey, for all you know, she's a great cook!"

"Really? Well, then, how about I bring Mom and Dad and Casey down for your first home game. She can cook us supper and convince me that she won't kill you." Becky reached into her purse and brought out some tickets. "That would make me feel much better."

"But we're not—"

"Make your big sister happy and don't argue." She elbowed past him and approached Silver, switching fluidly to English. "Sorry about that. I was on the phone when the fire started, and I had a mini panic attack." Her hand jutted out and Landon winced as her nails dug into the back of Silver's hand. "We haven't been properly introduced. I'm Rebecca Bower."

"Silver Delgado." To Silver's credit, she didn't even wince. A pleasant mask slipped over her features, and she arched a brow at Landon as he joined them. "I freaked a little when Landon told me he burned down his apartment, so I can only imagine how you felt."

"Yes, well, thank you for taking care of him."

"He's a good investment."

"I'm glad you think so." Becky finally released Silver's hand and gave her a tight smile. "I hope you don't mind, but the family will be coming down in a few weeks to watch Landon play, and he said you can cook, so we'll be swinging by for an early dinner before the game."

"I never—" Landon snapped his lips together at Silver's glare, then tried again. "Becky—"

"That would be wonderful." Silver eyed the rink and cleared her throat. "I look forward to meeting your parents."

"Good." With a curt nod, Becky turned away from Silver and reached out to give Landon a stiff hug. "I have to catch my flight. I feel much better knowing you're okay and in good hands. See you in October."

"You want me to drive you to the airport?" Landon followed his sister to the door and held it open for her. "I'm not really busy."

"I'll be fine. And I have a feeling she needs you here." Becky's lips quirked as Silver made an aggravated sound at another "bad call". "She's really clueless, isn't she?"

"She's learning."

"I thought you had better taste."

"Did you?" He stared at her until she looked away. She knew better than to assume that after his last relationship. "Really?"

"Okay, okay, you're right. But . . . Silver Delgado? Seriously?"

She flattened her hand on his chest. "What the hell are you going to do with a girl like that?"

Her presumptions irked him, because no matter what she thought, he and Silver were just friends. But even worse, she didn't think Silver was worthy of him.

He bent down and whispered, "I hated Patrick, but I never judged you for being with him. He was a mistake, but he was your choice. I get that you're gun-shy, but you don't even know her and you're not being fair."

Becky nodded slowly. "So you're saying she's not a mistake?"

A mistake? No. The only mistake is not making her mine. "I've known her less than a week, but I can tell you, right now, any man would be lucky to have her."

"Okay. I'll take your word for it." Becky sighed and patted his chest. "Just don't be as stupid about her as you were about cooking bacon."

"I won't." *Liar!* He clenched his fist against the door. "Have a safe trip home."

After his sister left, he returned to Silver's side, his palms itching to touch her even though he knew he shouldn't. Silver solved that problem by slipping her hand into his.

"Dominik did it again." She smiled up at him. "And this time, I got it."

I knew you would. He pulled her back against his chest and wrapped his arms around her, resting his chin lightly on the top of her head as they observed the rest of the play in silence. *I just wish that I got you.*

Chapter Twelve

After the game, Silver strolled down the short hall away from the concession stands and groaned as Landon broke off a piece of his huge pretzel and held it to her mouth. The man couldn't seem to stop feeding her! Every time they hung out, her strict, self-imposed diet took a nosedive out the closest window. But the approving smile he gave her was worth every pound she'd have to burn.

Stepping lightly, she pictured the game in her head and chewed fast. "You know, even though we lost, I think we played pretty good. I mean those two last-minute goals were . . ."

"Sweet." Landon fiddled with his tie and undid the top button of his off-white shirt. "If they hadn't disallowed the last one, we would have tied it up. I think we've got a strong season ahead of us."

"With you in net?" Silver tugged him past the elevator, toward the stairs. "We would have buried them! And we're going to bury all the other teams!"

"You haven't seen me play yet, *mignonne*." He held the door open for her and followed her down the first flight. "For all you know, I'm horrible."

"I doubt that." Reaching the door to the main floor, she stopped and turned to fix his new grey tie. His fans would be out there. He had to look perfect. Her lips twitched up as she ran her gaze over his barely-there brown hair and his charming smile surrounded by a scruffy shadow. *He always looks perfect.* She gulped as his gaze turned knowing and her pulse quickened. "That word, *'mignonne'*, what does it mean?"

He tucked a strand of hair behind her ear. "Cutie."

"Ah." *Open door. Keep moving.* She backed up and this time held the door open for him. "And *'chou'*?"

"Cabbage," he said, hooking his arm through hers to lead her through the parting crowds.

Digging in her heels, she jerked him to a stop. "Cabbage?"

"Yes. It's a common French endearment."

"Yeah, well, could you use something else?" Her nose wrinkled as she tried to imagine how "cabbage" could be considered an endearment. "I hate cabbage."

"How about, *mon lapine*?"

"Which means . . . ?"

"My rabbit."

She punched him lightly in the gut. "No freakin' way. I'm your boss, not your puck bunny."

His teeth flashed in a broad grin. "Touché. Shall we go with *mon chaton*?"

Her brows shot up expectantly.

He leaned in close and whispered in her ear. "Kitten."

Little tremors ran over her flesh, causing all the tiny hairs to rise. Heat flooded her cheeks and she forced her eyes not to drift shut as she shook her head. "You shouldn't call me things like that, Landon. We're friends. Just friends."

"I know."

"You don't want more, do you?"

The skin around his eyes creased as he brought her hand to his lips. "I want us to have this, Silver. I love hanging out and talking. I love you calling me on my shit. More would change everything."

"You're right." *But, but*—A little voice in her head whimpered as she slammed a mental door in its face. He was right. And things were complicated enough with Dean. "So, about dinner with your parents . . ."

Landon groaned and released her hand to run his own over his hair. "I'm sorry about that. When Becky gets something in her head—"

"That's not what I'm worried about." She bit her tongue, then laughed. "I'm no better at cooking than you are! What are we going to feed them?"

He chuckled. "I'm sure we'll think of something."

"Maybe we can get Dean to play chef." Where the hell had that come from? Arms folded over her chest, she watched the crowd thin and quickly changed the subject. "Umm . . . where are you staying tonight?"

Before Landon could answer, a voice called out from the other side of the room. "Bower! I was looking for you."

"Hey, Perron." Landon shook hands with the man. "What's up?"

Max glanced over at Silver. "Hey, sis." He continued before she could stutter out a coherent word. "We all heard about the fire. I'm sorry you're laid up, but glad to hear you made it out okay. Where are you aiming to crash?"

"There must be a good motel around here?" Landon apparently didn't notice her trying to get his attention with her wave and throat clearing, because he just kept talking. "I was about to ask Silver, but she probably doesn't know anywhere cheap." He gave her a one-armed hug. "No offense, I wouldn't want you staying at a place like that anyway. Your dad probably had you all set up when you moved back, right, *ma chérie?*"

Uck, I need a translator for this guy. What's he calling me now? The French words sounded familiar. *Pricey?* She elbowed him in the side. "I'm paying you enough for you to stay somewhere nice. And besides, I was going to say—"

"I have to replace *everything,* Silver. I'm not wasting money on a hotel."

"Then—"

"Why don't you stay at my place?" Max put his hand on her shoulder and squeezed. "A man has his pride, darlin'. And I've got plenty of space, Bower. I reckon Sloan and Dominik won't mind having you around."

Landon nodded slowly. "What about your wife?"

Max snorted. "She'd take Sloan's whip to me if I didn't make the offer. Seriously, man, we're a team. We look out for each other."

"Thank you. It shouldn't be for more than a week," Landon said.

Silver ground her teeth. "Are you sure you have enough rooms?"

"Vanek moved in with Carter, so we're got a spare." Max seemed to be trying very hard not to laugh. "If you're concerned, you can swing by and check it out."

Damn it, Landon can stay with me! She wanted to kick Max. He obviously thought she would rather take his word that Landon would be fine than face Sloan and Oriana. Her family. More people who couldn't stand her.

But he obviously didn't know her very well.

She smiled sweetly. "I'd love to."

Eyes wide, Max looked at Landon as though expecting him to object.

Landon smiled and took her hand. "I was hoping you'd say that. We can swing by your place and pick up a few movies. We've got a few Clint Eastwoods to go through to finish our marathon."

"Oh yeah! I fell asleep during *Unforgiven*—I really wanted to see that one!" She batted her eyelashes at Max. "You don't mind, do you, *bro*?"

* * * *

Silver flicked her French manicured nails, one at a time, against her thumb as she gazed up at the blocky, modern two-story house from the driver's seat of her car. A light breeze came through her open window, and the cold bit through her thin, sporty fall jacket. She'd changed at her place while Landon picked out the movie, going for a casual look in jeans and a plain white cotton T-shirt, but now she wished she'd stuck with her regular, high fashion wardrobe. Louis Vuitton didn't leave her feeling vulnerable and young. Heels gave her stature.

Sneakers made her small and insignificant.

Landon patted her knee. "Open the door, *chérie*. You'll see; it won't be that bad."

Right. I'm sure they've got the welcome mat laid out. She shook her head and sighed. "You don't get it. Oriana isn't speaking to me. This is her house and—"

"She's your sister." Landon frowned at her shrug and got out of the car. He came around to her side and opened her door. "Come on. You'll feel better after you two hash this out."

She sincerely doubted it, but she took his hand and joined him on the sidewalk before slamming her door with resounding finality. Landon was wrong, this wouldn't make anything better, but at least she could say she'd tried.

His solid grip on her hand gave her strength as they approached the house, but as they started up the stairs and the door opened, she jerked her hand free. Holding on to him would make her look even more pathetic.

Landon paused and looked back from a step ahead.

"You okay?" He mouthed.

Giving him a curt nod, she forced herself onto the porch and smiled at her sister who held the door open for them. "Hey."

"Hey." Oriana pressed her lips together, then turned to Landon with a brilliant smile. "I'm so happy you took Max up on his offer. Come in. I'll show you to your room."

"Thanks." Landon reached back and put his hand on the small of Silver's back, propelling her forward with him. "I really appreciate this, but . . . well, maybe Max can show me the room while you two talk?"

"That's a mighty fine idea." Max came to Oriana's side and whispered something to her before gesturing to Landon. "It's not the biggest room in the house, but I think you'll be comfortable."

The men disappeared behind a door just off the large living room. Silver nibbled at her bottom lip and tried to ignore the fact that Oriana was glaring at her. "Look, I know you're upset, but—"

Her phone buzzed in her purse.

"You should get that." Oriana turned away and said lightly, "Would you like something to drink? I have wine—not the stuff you're used to, but it's pretty good."

Silver swallowed. "No, that's okay."

At another buzz she reached in her purse and checked her phone. Dean's number flashed on the screen.

"Diet Coke? Beer?" Oriana called from the kitchen.

"Diet Coke, please." Silver glanced over to where Sloan watched her from the sofa and decided to take Dean's call. She held the phone up to her ear and tried to keep her voice level. "Hello?"

After a brief pause, Dean spoke, his tone gruff. "What's wrong?"

"Umm . . . ." She peered up at Dominik as he sauntered down the stairs halfway across the hall. "I'm going to take this outside, if you don't mind?"

"Go ahead."

Outside, she took a deep breath and let out a light laugh. "Why would you think something's wrong?"

"Silver, don't play games with me. You sound tense and so far you've failed to make one smart-assed remark."

"Ah." She giggled and wrapped her ponytail around her hand as she gazed up at the pinprick star laden sky. "Sorry. How's this—miss me already?"

"Of course. Why wouldn't I miss your sass?" He chuckled, but for some reason she didn't think he was joking. "I know I told you I wanted to be professional at work, but neither of us is at work now. I'd appreciate some honesty."

"Honesty? Well, I'll give you one thing. You have excellent timing."

"How so?"

"I'm at Max's place and . . . things are a little awkward." *To put it lightly.* She made a face. "Oriana isn't happy I'm here."

"I see." Dean paused, then sighed. "Why are you?"

Resting her hip on the railing, she tried to put her thoughts into some semblance of order. "Landon thought it would be a good idea for us to talk—but that was after I'd already agreed to come hang out. Max invited him to stay and . . . I guess told me I could come along expecting me to say no."

"So naturally you didn't." Dean snorted. "I would have liked to have been there to see his reaction."

Silver let out a sharp laugh. "I would have taken a picture if I could have. But now—I mean, it seemed like a good idea at the time . . ."

"What is the problem exactly? If you don't mind me asking?"

"Oriana found out I'd considered trading Sloan."

"So what?"

So what? Her brow furrowed. This from the man who'd almost blown a gasket when she'd brought it up? "You're kidding, right?"

"Silver, you know how I feel about the matter. Still, Oriana knows enough about the game to know these things happen. If we decided trading Sloan would benefit the team, he would be traded." Dean waited, as if to gauge her response, then groaned when she didn't say a word. "You both have to understand something, and I will tell her myself if you don't. This can't be personal. If I can analyze my own brother's performance before deciding whether or not he's suitable as a coach, she'll have to accept that I will do the same for the players, whether or not they're in a relationship with the owner's daughter—or sister." He amended. "Do you understand?"

"Yes, but . . ." Silver held the phone with her shoulder and braced her hands to the railing. "She hates me for even thinking about it."

"That's her problem, not yours." He spoke softly, soothing her with his deep timbre. "I would assure her that you won't make the decision based on your own opinion of Sloan as a person, but you cannot promise that he won't be traded just because he is, in essence, your brother-in-law."

"Legally, he isn't."

"Don't be petty, dear, that won't help your case." He cleared his throat. "Now, I called because I sent you a text about the press conference tomorrow, but I wasn't sure if you'd seen it."

She vaguely recalled the text. Hadn't she replied? "I got it and I'll be there. You don't need to worry, I'm good with the media."

"Yes, but this isn't Hollywood. The press will come down on you hard for signing Demyan." He exhaled sharply into the phone. "I thought you should be warned that he'll likely prove that you made a mistake."

Uck, not this again! "Dean, I know you don't like him, but give the guy a chance. You haven't even seen him play yet!"

"No, but I should have today. He decided he was too sick."

"Oh . . . well, people do get sick."

"He was faking, Silver. He felt well enough to hit on a trainer and Bower's sister."

Silver winced. She didn't know the trainer, but she'd noticed the press badge on Rebecca's jacket. The guy was either cocky, or stupid, or both. "How do we deal with this?"

"Let me deal with it. I just wanted you prepared. Most of the league knows you made this trade without me."

"So I'll look stupid."

"Not at all. I've made it clear I support the trade."

Blinking fast, Silver straightened and shook her head. "Why would you do that? You didn't support it!"

"And?"

"And why should you look bad because of my decision?"

"Don't worry, I'll survive." He chuckled again and goose bumps rose on her flesh. "We've got a good team. This is nothing. At worst, we make him a healthy scratch for most of the season. That should get him in line."

Not that she had any clue what a healthy scratch was, but his support had her ready to go along with anything. "Good. I can agree to that. But . . . I'm sorry if I made things harder for you."

"Just promise not to do it again."

I can't do it again. Daddy made sure of that. But he wasn't rubbing it in, so she quickly agreed. And looked inside to see Landon in the living room speaking with her sister and the other guys. "I promise. But I should go in now. See you tomorrow?"

"About that . . ." Dean inhaled roughly. "I think we should meet before the press conference and make sure we're on the same page. I know a place that serves crepes if you'd be okay with a breakfast meeting."

She bit back a smile. "I'd like that. But I've got to say, I'm surprised you'd go out for breakfast since you seem to be such a good cook."

"What gave you that idea?"

"You said you wouldn't let me and Landon in your kitchen. Must mean you think you can do better than we can."

"That's not hard. Apparently neither of you can cook without hurting yourselves."

"I still can't picture you cooking."

"Really? Maybe you should come to my place in the morning."

"Sure. What time?"

"It will have to be early. Can you make it to my place by six?"

Movie marathon and breakfast at 6:00 a.m.? It was already after ten. Still, she didn't want to cut her night with Landon short or miss seeing Dean bent over a hot stove. Her mouth watered as she imagined him in some low riding pajama pants—or boxers. Unlikely, but . . . *hell, sleep's overrated.*

"I'll be there. Can you text me your address?"

"Will do," he said. "And Silver?"

"Yes?"

"Chin up. I wouldn't rub it in, but keep in mind, you sign these guys' checks."

After a quick goodnight, she smiled at the phone and stuck it in her purse. Dean made her feel . . . worthy. Of the team and more. She reentered the house with her shoulders back and her head held high.

"—I know you aren't cleared for practice, Landon." Sloan was saying. "But I try to get the guys to hit the sack before midnight. You should get used to it."

"I've got some pretty good routines set up, Captain." Landon grinned at Silver and held out a Diet Coke. "But today's been a trying day. Max invited Silver, so I hope you don't mind if she hangs out with me in my room for a bit." He winked at her. "We'll be careful not to disturb anyone."

Silver took a sip and choked a little at the implication in his words. His teasing didn't usually bother her, but did he have to make it sound like they'd be . . .

Sloan muttered under his breath, "Why am I not surprised?"

Landon patted her back and arched a brow at Sloan. "What can I say? Silver cracks me up with her impersonations."

I do? Once, during a Clint Eastwood movie, she'd repeated a line. Okay, maybe more than once. But she'd tried to be quiet. Had he really "cracked up" because of her?

Dominik laughed, put his arm around Oriana's shoulders, and inclined his head to Silver. "Apparently it runs in the family."

Oriana pursed her lips. "Well, I don't know about the rest of you, but I'm going to bed. Landon, do you need anything? You're about the same size as Max—maybe he can lend you some pajama pants?"

"Naw, I'm good," Landon said. "Thank you."

Before Oriana could leave, Silver stepped forward and blurted out, "Can we talk?"

"Go ahead," Oriana said, tersely.

"Alone?"

Her sister folded her arms over her chest. "No. I know what this is about, and I'd rather not talk about Sloan behind his back. If you have something to say, have the guts to say it to his face."

"Fine." Silver ran her tongue over her teeth and recalled Dean's words. *Chin up.* Landon's presence steadied her resolve as she faced Oriana. "I'm sorry you heard about the trade I considered from Anne, but I won't apologize for considering it. And I can't promise that I won't consider it in the future. But if the general manager and I decide selling his contract would benefit the team, I will let you know before you hear it from anyone else."

Sloan grunted and held up his beer in a sarcastic "cheers". "That's good to know."

"I'm sorry, Mr. Callahan, were you expecting special treatment because you hooked up with a family member?" She watched Dominik and Max through the corner of her eye and relaxed when she saw at least they got it. "The Dartmouth Cobras are just like any other club, and I think you have enough experience to know what that means. You'll be a free agent at the end of this year. There will be a lot of discussion over whether or not to re-sign you. It's nothing personal."

Lips drawn in a tight line, eyes narrowed, Sloan nodded.

Oriana slid her hand down Dominik's arm to lace her fingers with his, then reached out to put her free hand on Sloan's shoulder. "So you won't go after him just because you don't like him?"

"No."

"Okay." Oriana closed her eyes and inhaled. "Okay. I can accept that." Her eyes met Silver's, still slightly guarded, but not resentful. "Do you want me to show you how to set up the DVD player? Or get you some snacks?"

A peace offering? Despite how easily Oriana had forgiven her before, this time she'd wondered if she'd gone too far. But Dean's advice had saved her. She wasn't hungry, but she could hear Landon's stomach growling. The corners of her mouth lifted. "This man eats for twenty. I'll come help you get the snacks. I'm sure he can figure out how to set things up."

All the men seemed to let out a sigh of relief as one. In the kitchen, Oriana pointed out the cupboards with the snack foods while she put together a plate full of sandwiches. After a long span of silence, Oriana came to her side and nudged her with an elbow.

"So, what happened with the lawyers?"

Silver put some freshly popped popcorn in a bowl and shrugged. "It didn't work out."

"Oh." Oriana frowned and set the plate on a large silver tray. "And you and Landon . . . ?"

"Are just friends." Suddenly she wanted to tell her sister everything, but she had no idea where to start. She'd never had any trouble giving her sister all the gritty details, and yet, well, there weren't any. Her nose wrinkled. "It's . . . different, but good. And neither of us wants to ruin what we have by . . . you know."

Oriana blinked. "What? You've *got* to give me something. I'm usually begging you to stop sharing and—"

"There's nothing, sis. Landon wants to stay friends. So do I. It's pretty simple."

"Is it?"

Nope. Silver shrugged again, picked up the tray, and headed to Landon's room, trying not to think about how good it felt just to be near him, about how hard it was to ignore the way her body reacted to his touch. She never answered her sister, but as Landon sat up from the bed and took the tray from her, she answered herself.

It's not simple at all.

Chapter Thirteen

*B*zzz:
    Dean shook his head as he rubbed his hair with a towel and glanced at the clock. 5:30 a.m., now *that* surprised him. He took Silver for the type of girl who'd show up late just to make an entrance. Not to mention the time it took her to get all primped. Two hours was standard for most of the women he dated. She probably hadn't gotten much sleep, if any.

This isn't a date, Richter.

He acknowledged the unwelcome thought with a nod and made his way to the door, hesitating for a moment to consider his unbuttoned white shirt. Whatever people said about Silver, one thing was certain—she took her job seriously. If she considered this a business meeting, shouldn't he keep up appearances?

*B*zzzzzz!

Impatient little thing. He sighed, unlocked, then opened the door. "You're early."

"Oh." She tongued her bottom lip and stared at his bare chest. "I'm sorry. I lost track of time, and I didn't want to be late." She shifted the black suit bag slung over her shoulder and ducked her head. Her hair, usually perfectly styled, bobbed in a hastily done ponytail. "I was hoping I could get ready here—if you don't mind . . . ?"

"Not at all." He let her in and smothered a grin as he looked her over. T-shirt and jeans, both so rumpled he was willing to bet she'd slept in them. *Probably not in her own bed.* His withheld grin vanished. "I just took a shower, so you might want to wait a bit for the water to heat up."

A blush spread over her cheeks. "You'll let me take a shower?"

"Why wouldn't I?"

"I don't know—I just—well, you don't want to—" She swallowed. "Uck, I'm going to shut up now."

Apparently the Delgado princess wasn't the woman who'd come to his door. She'd show up if Silver got too nervous, but he'd keep her at bay as long as he could.

Shaking his head, he traced her bottom lip with an index finger. "I do want to, Silver."

She hissed in air and her tongue touched his fingertip. "Then . . ."

"You will give yourself to me at the club, pet. Not before."

"Says who?" She looked away and crossed her arms over her breasts. "Even if I go back, why the hell would I hook up with you? Been there, done that. We're both here now. It's convenient."

"I wouldn't say that."

With perfect timing as always, his daughter slunk out of her room, her blanket creased face pale and a little grey. "Coffee, Dad?"

"Try some orange juice first, sweetie." Dean moved away from Silver and grabbed his daughter's arms as she teetered in the general direction of the kitchen. "Vodka?"

"Tequila." Jami groaned as he helped her to the table. "Never drinking it again."

If only . . . He went to the fridge and took out the orange juice. At the counter, he poured his daughter a tall glass and glared out the window while he regained his composure. It was just a phase, not a reflection of his parenting. Still, as much as he tried to convince himself this was true, part of him knew it didn't matter. He was failing his daughter. And he had no idea what to do about it.

Asking Silver to come here had been a mistake.

"Try this." Silver took the seat at his daughter's side and handed her a banana from the fruit bowl on the table. "If you're not still feeling pukey, it should help."

Jami twisted her lips and laughed. "Who the fuck are you? One of his 'pets'? He doesn't usually bring them home."

The muscles in Silver's jaw tensed, but her expression didn't change. "I'm your daddy's boss."

"So he's *not* fucking you?"

"Jami!" Dean stepped up between the women and shook his head. Damn it, he'd raised her better than this! "Apologize this instant!"

"No." Silver held up her hand and leaned close to Jami. "You really want to know, or are you just hung over and pissed off? I'm guessing you're at least eighteen because otherwise Daddy wouldn't let you go out and get plastered, would he? You've got all the freedom you want, and you know what? That's fine. But if you fuck up, that's your problem, not his. Be a big girl and own it, Jami."

"Who the hell do you think you are?" Jami pushed away from the table and almost tripped over her chair. "You don't know me! You don't know what my life is like! How dare you judge me!"

"I'm not judging you." Silver shrugged and peeled the banana. She took a big bite, chewed, swallowed, and smiled. "But I don't see Dean raising a stupid kid. You'll get it eventually."

"Whatever." Jami grabbed her orange juice and headed back to her room. "Give me five minutes and I'll be out of here. Hopefully you two can restrain yourselves that long."

Dean ground his teeth and pressed his eyes shut as her door slammed. Neither he nor Silver moved until Jami returned, moments later, and stormed out of the house.

His apology froze on his lips as Silver's chair scraped across the tiles, and she went to toss the banana peel in the trash. She licked her fingertips, her tone light as she fetched her things. Almost completely detached, except she was shaking like she'd had too much coffee. "Sorry about that. I should have kept my mouth shut. You should go after her. I'll—"

"Silver, sit." When she immediately sat, he let himself breathe. "*I'm* sorry. She's been relatively pleasant over the last few days. I wasn't expecting this. You did absolutely nothing wrong."

"I'm four years older than her—she'd resent her dad's girlfriend lecturing no matter what, but—"

"'Her dad's girlfriend?'" He braced one hand on the table beside her and wrapped her ponytail around the other. With a light tug, he forced her head back. "Is that what you are, Silver?"

"That's not what I meant."

"Are you sure?" Bending down, he kissed the edge of her lips, chuckling when she tried to turn her head for more. "Be still. I'm still waiting for an answer."

She latched onto his shirt with both hands and strained against his grip on her hair. "If you don't kiss me, I'm going to hurt you."

"So demanding." He chuckled again, gliding his lips to her ear, letting her feel the scruff on his jaw lightly scrape her soft cheek. "You know that's not how it works with me."

"Dean . . ." Her pulse quickened under his tongue as he sucked on the delicate flesh of her throat. "Please."

"Much better." He caged her chin in his hand. "Open."

As her lips parted, he gently pulled on her bottom lip with his teeth, increasing the pressure a little more as she gasped, rewarding her with a shallow thrust of his tongue as she trembled with the effort to hold still. Her tongue flicked out to meet his and he pulled away.

Rather than object, she let out a little sigh and let her eyes drift shut.

"Have I told you lately how beautifully—" he traced her top lip with his thumb. "—submissive—" he pushed his thumb into her mouth, tempting her to suck on it by pressing down on her tongue "—you are?" Her lips and tongue remained passive to his invasion, but her breaths sped up to a pant as he whispered to her. "I won't fuck you. But I will kiss you since you asked so nicely."

* * * *

Sweet and hot and all that Silver wanted. Somehow, with just a bit of pressure under her jaw, Dean brought her to her feet and had her body flush against his in a firm, one-armed embrace. As he stole all the strength from her body with one long kiss, she reached up to find something to hold on to, hesitating before clasping her hands around the back of his neck.

"Go ahead." He slid one hand around her waist and under her shirt, pressing against the small of her back to support her. "Hold on tight."

No man had ever said that to her unless he was about to give her a rough ride, but what Dean did with just his lips and tongue on her mouth fired up every nerve ending, until she melted, evaporated, would have floated away if she hadn't anchored herself to him. His tongue caressed hers, guiding it in a slow, deep kiss, his fist in her hair pulling just a little whenever she tried to take over or speed up. Each inhale heated up as their ragged breaths mingled between them.

And at the very moment when she couldn't take any more, his lips left hers and returned to her throat.

Desperate little whimpers escaped her. Her nipples tightened and jabbed into his unyielding chest. He bit her hard and the sharp pain folded her knees and almost completely undid her. If he didn't take her now, she would go completely insane.

"Silver, you will focus on breathing and my words." He lowered her to a chair and pressed a finger to her lips before she could scream or beg. "Breathing first."

Breathing? I'll give you fucking breathing! She breathed through her nose hard and fast. Which made her sound like an angry bull. She made herself stop.

"Much better." His eyes creased and he gently stroked her swollen lips with his fingers. "I need you to know I want you, pet, so much that it's painful, but we will wait until tomorrow night. It will be worth it. Can you trust me?"

Her lips curled bitterly as his fingers left them. "Trust you? You just got me all worked up for nothing! I'm tired of you playing with me!"

"I'm not playing with you." His jaw ticked as he shoved away from her. "I suppose I should apologize again. The kiss was a mistake."

A mistake? She frowned. *Mind-blowing. Frustrating, maybe. But not a mistake.* She bit her lip as he moved across the kitchen, taking out a frying pan and several mixing bowls. She expected him to slam them, but besides some rigidity in the set of his shoulders, he seemed utterly calm.

"Are you allergic to strawberries? Nuts?" He leaned into the fridge, speaking without looking at her.

"No. I don't think I have any allergies." She stood and approached him cautiously. "Umm . . . can I help?"

"Do you know how to beat eggs?" He held out a carton.

She snorted and took it. "Of course I do. How many do you need?"

"Two."

At the counter, Silver palmed two eggs and spoke lightly as she looked around for something to break them with. "Ah, where are your knives?"

"Just use the edge of the bowl."

The cook that had worked for Daddy when she was a little girl always used a blunt knife. But people on TV used Dean's method, so it shouldn't be too hard. She hit the egg on the edge of the bowl and groaned as half the egg and shell ended up in the bowl, and the other half on the counter.

She glanced over her shoulder to where Dean was slicing apples at the table. "Can I have a spoon?"

"A spoon?" He set down the knife and stood. "What—"

"I've got it!" She hunched over the mess and shifted from side to side as he tried to see around her. "Just pass me a spoon." Her elbow slipped in some egg slime. "Eww. And a towel."

He folded his arms over his chest and gave her "The Look". "*Silver.*"

She shivered, but the grossness dripping down her arm stole some of the effect he had on her. She mimicked his tone. "*Dean.*"

Shaking his head, he put his hands on her shoulders and turned her to face him. His eyes took in the yolk on her shirt and her hands. His lips quirked. "Have you ever cooked anything before?"

Damn it, you had to ask. Her brow creased as she stared at her feet. *He's going to think I'm a spoiled little princess.*

Most people did, not that she cared, but it was different with Dean.

"Don't make me repeat myself, Silver."

She stomped her foot and glared at him. "No, all right? I've never cooked for myself. I don't know how to clean or wash clothes or do anything."

"Now, I know that's not true." His head titled slightly. "I figured you weren't the domestic type, but you don't do any of your own cleaning?"

"I'm not a slob or anything—I just, well, I pay someone to tidy up my condo twice a week."

"And what do you eat?"

Shrugging, she brought her fingers to her mouth and chewed on the flesh along her thumbnail. "Cedric cooks sometimes."

"Really?" He shook his head and pushed her hand down.

"You're a horrible liar, little one. I think all that acting for the camera makes your face even easier to read. Must make sure every nuance is picked up."

Just to prove him wrong, she shifted her expression into one of pure bliss. "Honestly, Cedric is a wonderful cook. Why, just last week he made a stew and I completely forgot about my diet and stuffed my face until I was ready to burst!"

Dean's brow furrowed and his lips drew into a thin line as he studied her face. "I stand corrected."

She smirked and gave him a mock bow. "Thank you."

"But I still know you're lying."

"Yeah, right." Letting out an aggravated huff, she went to the sink and snatched the rag hanging over the faucet to clean up the egg. "You're guessing."

"True. I am making an educated guess on what I know." He came up behind her and slid his hands into the back pockets of her jeans. "You never had dinner with Asher and Cedric at home. Maybe Cedric cooked for Asher, but never for you."

Her spine stiffened. How did he know?

"Not that it matters." He kissed the nape of her neck. "I'd be happy to cook for you."

"I want to learn to do it for myself." She tilted her head to one side as he nibbled up the length of her throat. "But you did promise me breakfast."

"That I did." His warm breath sent tingles over her moist flesh. "Go take your shower. I'll finish up here."

Shower. Yes, a nice long cold—throbbing between her thighs cut her off—*no hot shower. And a few minutes to take care of . . .* Her breath hitched as she pictured him joining her. Oh yeah, with that image in her head, it shouldn't take long. "Okay. You finish and I'll—"

"There's something I need to do first." He moved his hands, flattening one on her stomach while the other covered her aching breasts. He deftly undid her jeans and slid his fingers into her panties. "I thought so."

Oh, God! His fingertips slipped over her clit, and a shock of pleasure had her writhing against him.

"This should tide you over until tomorrow night." He bit her and thrust deep inside her, curving his fingers until he found the trigger to set her off. Holding her tight as she bucked and cried out, he withdrew his fingers almost completely, speaking over her moaning protests. "Much too easy. Give me another, pet. I want to hear you scream."

She almost screamed right then. Her clit pulsed and swelled and wet heat flooded his palm. He worked three fingers into the tight confines of her jeans, prodding gently at first, slicking them up, then pushing until she opened for him. He pinched her nipple through her shirt and drove his fingers in as far as they would go, then strained as her body resisted.

"Still so tight. Relax, I want to see how much you can take."

All of it! She wanted to take all of it! His fingers were thick and skilled, but she remembered how it felt to have his dick pounding into her and she wanted that now. Her insides convulsed around his fingers, and she twisted as he teased her opening with all four.

"Brace your hands on the counter."

Her hands slapped the counter and she almost fell forward as he released her. Her thighs quivered as he jerked her jeans down and removed them. Finally. Finally he would fuck her.

"Look at that beautiful ass." She heard him kneel behind her and tensed up as he sank his teeth into one butt cheek.

What was he—

Her nails scratched the counter as he cupped her pussy. "Spread your thighs as wide as you can."

Lost in the moment, she obeyed. Whimpered as he filled her with all his fingers. And bowed her spine as he slapped her thigh.

"You're not ready for fisting, but with some work . . ." He grunted as he pressed his knuckles against her pussy. "Jesus, you're so hot and wet. I want to taste you."

He thrust one last time, hard enough that she screamed as the climax ripped through her. He lifted her up so her thighs balanced on his shoulders. Her arms shuddered under the strain as his tongue speared her. Fiery spikes shot deep inside, over and over with each thrust of his tongue. His fingers dug into the back of her thighs, and vibrations brought the erotic sensations to a fierce boiling ecstasy as he groaned into her pussy.

Her palms slipped on the counter, and she was sure she'd crack her head and knock herself out. But he caught her just in time and cradled her in his arms.

"There we go. Shh." He kissed her forehead and rocked her as she buried her face into his chest. "You ruined my plans for this morning, sweetheart, but I just can't seem to keep my hands off you."

"I don't want you to." She flicked her tongue out to taste the beads of sweat glistening on his steel-wrought pecs. Sweet mother, the man was hot. In more ways than one. She let her hand drift down to his crotch and squeezed his very erect cock. "But I still don't understand—"

"You want more?" He sounded so surprised, she wanted to say yes. But she was too sore.

"I will, just give me a bit." She wiggled off his lap and winced when her butt hit the tiles. "Ouch! How hard did you bite me?"

He grinned as he stood and held out his hand. "Hard enough to leave a mark. Does that bother you?"

Surprisingly, it didn't. She wouldn't be doing nude shots anytime soon and, as her body adjusted to the lightly throbbing bruise, she found she kind of liked it.

Weird.

"What was that look?"

No way. Do not tell him. "What look?"

"Like you're savoring something." He covered her ass cheek with a hand and squeezed. "This, perhaps?"

She yelped. Then bit back a groan as the throbbing intensified. "No. I was thinking about that shower."

"I'm sure." He sighed. "We'll work on this truth thing. I would punish you for lying now, but I'm pleased with you."

"Why?"

"Because you took what I gave you and didn't ask me to fuck you once."

Holding her tongue between her teeth, she picked up her jeans and moved to put them on. "What's the point? You already told me you wouldn't."

He put his hand on her wrist before she could pull her jeans on.

"Strip here, Silver. I want to see you. I think I've earned the pleasure."

Dropping her jeans, she straightened and gave him a sly smile. "I think you're right."

Her hips swayed to a sultry song in her head as she peeled off her T-shirt and tossed it aside. Unclasping her bra, she turned away from him, backing up until her butt rubbed against his erection. She let her bra fall and arched to look up at him, molding her breasts with her hands as he stared.

"Don't you wish you didn't have to wait?" She smirked and sauntered away from him.

He yanked her back by the wrist and bent her over the table.

Whack!

"You cockmunching son of a bitch!" She howled as he smacked her again. "Stop! Ow!"

"Behave, Silver." Another hard slap struck her inner thigh when she tried to kick him. "I would have stopped at one for the sass, but I do not tolerate insults."

"You better get used to it, limp-dick!"

"Limp-dick?" He laughed and ground himself hard against her already sore ass. "Sweetheart, I am never 'limp' around you."

Oh oh oh! Sore as she was, her insides clenched at the idea of having him inside her again. Maybe another verbal shove would do the trick. "Well, you're a fucking asshole anyway."

He sighed. "I think you enjoy being spanked too much for it to be a very effective punishment. Don't move."

For a few seconds, she stayed in that position, face down on his table, staring at the bowl of sliced apples which for some reason hadn't turned brown. Just as he returned, she realized she'd done what he'd told her to and tried to fix that by skirting away.

Something hit her, hard, and her breath caught in her throat. That wasn't his hand.

He laid the flogger on the table. "Don't make me use it again, pet."

Something wet squirted between her ass cheeks. Her eyes went wide. "No. Oh, hell no!"

"Brace yourself."

Cold. Hard. Big. Pressing against her asshole. "I said no!"

Dean's big hand massaged the sorest spot on her butt. "Have you forgotten your safeword, pet?"

"No, I haven't fucking forgotten."

The flogger disappeared. *Crack!* She grunted through her teeth as her body absorbed the sting.

"Manners," Dean said.

"I haven't fucking forgotten, Sir!" *Really? Then say it!*

So twisted, but she really didn't want to. Her eyes teared up as the big thing—probably a butt plug—was forced into her. Burning, burning, then a plop as it was seated snugly.

"There we go." He pulled her to her feet. "Take your shower and leave it in. I may take it out before you sit down to eat if you tell me how sorry you are."

"I'm not sorry."

He frowned as though frustrated with her response. "You know what? I believe you. I may have been very wrong about you. Do whatever you want."

Fine, I will. Not like it mattered what he thought. She laughed in his face and scampered to the bathroom before he could use the flogger again. The plug was just big enough for discomfort, but nothing she couldn't handle. He should have gone for a bigger size if he really wanted to punish her.

Size didn't matter much as the heavy plug weighed on the snug ring of muscles. Irritating, but worse, a constant reminder of how things had shifted from their talking and then their lusty play. Under the hot spray she felt her defiance wash away. Part of her wanted to push him, to test him, but . . .

But what?

The way he'd looked at her, that disappointment, which only darkened after she'd laughed, ruined everything. Maybe she'd pushed him too far. She didn't want him to stop caring.

Why? He's not your Master. You don't want a Master.

Well, playing with one once in awhile might be interesting.

Find another one. Shouldn't be that hard.

But, she didn't want another one.

She wanted Dean.

Which scared the hell out of her. Dean was too intense. Too . . . real. Who knew how far she'd go with him at the club if she went there and let him dominate her. What if he proved that she was submissive? What then?

Her fingers, slick with some fresh spring-scented soap, found the tiny bumps on her ass where he'd bitten her.

What if I just get off on the pain?

Only one way to find out. For now, she could submit to him— another hour wouldn't kill her. Then tomorrow she would test her pain theory. With someone a little less . . .

Über Dom! She giggled and finished washing. After drying off, she cracked the door open and called out, "Sir?"

Dean came to the door and arched a brow at her.

"I'm really, truly sorry. Calling you names was immature and rude. I mean, you invited me for breakfast and gave me a fucking amazing orgasm and—"

"All right, that's enough, pet." He shook his head and backed her into the bathroom. "Apology accepted. Grovelling doesn't suit you."

"Then—"

"Hands on the bathtub."

She put her hands on the bathtub and braced for him to take the plug out. He pressed on it and her body shuddered.

"It will take some work to wear you out, won't it, baby?" Stroking her spine, he curved his fingers into her while keeping pressure on the plug with his palm. "You'll come again when I take this out."

"No, no, no! Ah!" The orgasm slammed into her as he gently eased the butt plug out. She sobbed at the empty, empty feeling but his fingers saved her, giving her something to clench down on. The last wave drained her and she dropped to her knees, not moving as he found a cloth and cleaned her, though whispers of humiliation escaped her. "Don't, oh don't."

"It's all right, sweetie. We're done." He pressed her head against his thigh and petted her hair. "I put your suit on my bed. Get changed in my room and join me for breakfast. Things will be all back to normal."

He was right. Shortly after, dressed and primped, with her damp hair in a nice, neat bun, she was able to sit at the table across from him without one thought of all she'd let him do. Or all she wanted to let him do. She could almost pretend this was actually a normal breakfast with a coworker. Except for when Dean fed her the first, delicious mouthful, which reminded her of decadent apple pie without the thick, flaky crust. Or when she watched Dean lick a bit of apple filling from his bottom lip. Or when she wished he would kiss her again.

"What would you think of cooking lessons?"

Almost certain they'd been discussing the press conference—or had that been before she'd distractedly mentioned her ideas for renovating the VIP boxes—she washed down a mouthful with a sip of milk and tried to get her thoughts back on track.

"Cooking lessons?"

"You said you wanted to learn." He set his fork on his empty plate and leaned back. "I'd be happy to teach you."

She tore her gaze away from his chest and filled her mouth again so she wouldn't recall how good he tasted. "You don't have enough to do with teaching me about the team?"

"The offer's on the table." Dean stood and cleared the table. "Let me know what you decide."

"I'd love it; I just don't—" She cut herself off. He obviously couldn't hear her over the water blasting into the kitchen sink. So she answered herself. *Maybe he wants to spend time with me.*

The concept of a man wanting to spend time with her to do something other than fuck was still a little strange, but Landon had already shown her how pleasant it could be. Could she have something like that with Dean? Did she want to?

Spotting a cloth hanging from the stove, she went to fetch it and approached the dish rack. "Is it okay to use this to dry the dishes?"

"I can do it."

"But I want to." She picked up a fork when he nodded and chewed her bottom lip as she rubbed it with the cloth until it shone. "Thanks for breakfast. I really enjoyed it."

"You're very welcome." He glanced over at her as he washed the frying pan. "So, you were saying the colors in the VIP boxes are too drab?"

She nodded. "I'm thinking something a bit more modern. I've called in a designer and a contractor. I know they're already all sold for the season, but there's space for two more if we cut down on seats—I mean, with all the empties we've always got near the back—"

He smiled, shut off the water, and rested his hip on the counter. "You've done your homework."

"Well, what do you think I do in the office all day?"

"I wasn't sure, but I'd like to know what else you've come up with."

Warmth filled her as she looked into his eyes and saw he really, truly meant it. "How much time do we have? This could take a while."

He checked his watch. "We have an hour."

"That's not enough." She quickly finished putting away the dishes and waved him over to the table. "But I guess I can tell you about the magazine."

"The magazine." He blinked and sat across from her. "I'm not sure—"

"Please hear me out. I think this will be great for the team, and they need all the publicity they can get, just . . ." Inhaling deep, she watched his face to make sure she hadn't lost his interest already. She hadn't. "Promise not to laugh."

Reaching across the table, he held his hand out, palm up. When she gave him her hand, he squeezed it. "I will never laugh at you. I may not always agree, but I will always take you seriously." He released her hand at her nod and straightened. "Now, tell me about the magazine."

She told him about it. And about the charity events, speaking in a rush, sure he'd eventually get bored.

But an hour and a half later, *she* was the one who noticed the time. And he made *her* promise they could discuss her plans further after the press conference. They made it there just in time, and she was sure she'd have to powder her face for the cameras because she must be glowing, she felt that good.

Unfortunately, her only appearance in front of the cameras was to tell the media the press conference was cancelled.

Scott hadn't bothered to show up.

Chapter Fourteen

The swarm of reporters slowly thinned until only a couple from the gossip columns remained. Dean watched them with his arms folded over his chest as they hovered near Silver, practically frothing at the mouth, waiting for her to say something they could use. These kinds of leeches didn't usually come to press conferences, but it wasn't too hard to figure out what had drawn them. Two celebrities, the first Silver herself, the second the infamous Scott Demyan.

Moments ago, Silver had begged for a break to get a glass of water. He'd tried to intercede and tell the vermin it was time to leave, but she'd caught his eye and mouthed, "Let me deal with it." So he stood back and watched, feeling useless for the first time in his career. Much as he publicly supported Silver, nothing he could say or do would make this acquisition okay. And as much as he wanted to protect her from the aftermath, she seemed determined to handle it on her own.

His chest tightened as he watched her turn away from the reporters, blinking fast and swallowing hard. He took a step forward.

She spun around and smiled at the young man in the cheap twill jacket and the middle-aged woman who looked like she moonlighted as a hooker. "All right, now that the rest of them are gone, I do have a little tidbit to give you, but you *have* to promise not to share it with your editors until this afternoon."

Close enough to listen, but not close enough to intrude, Dean's eyes widened as she laid out the "real" reason why Scott hadn't shown up. Both reporters scribbled notes and nodded vigorously as Silver admonished them once again not to tell *anyone*.

Once they were gone, Dean strode up to her side and pulled up a chair, forcing her to sit when he noticed her trembling. "Do you need anything? More water?"

"Just hand me my purse, please." She thanked him when he did and felt around inside it. Her hand came out with a licorice stick. Chewing thoughtfully, she glanced toward the door to the conference room, then leaned forward. "You were right. This is *nothing* like Hollywood. They were asking me about things I know nothing about. I felt so stupid. One guy laughed at me when I said the minor goalie we used was really good and we might keep him. I don't know what was so funny. If he wasn't good, we wouldn't play him right? I know he didn't do well last night, but he'll get better?"

"He will get better, but he's only eighteen and he'll need to play a few years in the farm team before he's ready to play for us in the regular season. But don't worry about that. You did great."

"I didn't say anything I shouldn't have?"

"No, but we're going to be hard-pressed to get everything set up." He checked his watch. "I'll have to make a few calls, but there's something we need to handle first."

Her lips curved in a slow smile. "'We'? So you're coming with me to give Scott the good news?"

You're a vicious little thing, aren't you? He held out his arm and felt his own lips curl up as she hooked her arm to his. "I wouldn't miss this for the Cup." He laughed and shook his head. "Okay, that's not true, but you know what I mean."

"All hail Lord Stanley." She bit her bottom lip and shot him a questioning glance as though making sure she'd gotten it right. At his nod, she grinned. "Shall we?"

"After you, Miss Delgado."

* * * *

Silver couldn't keep her eyes off Dean as they drove to Scott's apartment. The plan had been so last-minute, so crazy, that she would have bet he'd tell her off for being impulsive and not clearing it with him. But, so far, aside from when she'd contracted Scott and considered trading Sloan, he'd . . . respected her input on everything. She couldn't help but wonder when he would brush her off or treat her like a silly girl who had no business sticking her nose in a man's game.

He's not Daddy.

The disloyal thought lodged a lump in her throat. Yes, Daddy was old-fashioned, but that didn't make him a bad person. He'd trusted her enough to give her his most prized possession.

But why not Oriana?

There was no easy answer. But she couldn't think about that now. Every time she considered how unfair it was that Oriana had been overlooked, she felt guilty, and that made it harder to do what needed to be done. Like today. This plan *so* wasn't Oriana's style.

Of course, Oriana *never* would have signed someone like Scott.

"We're here," Dean said, pulling over to the curb.

Action.

She giggled and shook her head when Dean frowned at her. He wouldn't get how she turned doing things like this into a movie she had a lead role in. Most people probably wouldn't. It just came so automatically, most times she didn't have to think about it. Only this time, she knew there would be no second take. If she didn't put Scott in his place, he'd ruin her reputation.

The cool sea breeze lapped her gently as a sun-soaked wave as she clipped up the cobbled steps and pressed the buzzer for the concierge. A stooped old man opened the door and Pine Sol clashed with the salty air.

"Can I help you?"

"I'm sorry to disturb you, but we work with Mr. Demyan and we're very concerned." She curved her hand around her throat and blinked fast. "You see, he's been so sick that he can't even play and he isn't answering our calls. I tried buzzing him, but he isn't answering. I need to know that he's okay."

"After last night, I'd say he's fine. I got three calls about music and women screaming, but he ignored me when I knocked on his door." The old man grunted and unhooked a nest of keys from his belt. "I didn't want to bother the cops with nonsense. But if you're worried about him, go for it. And tell him the landlord is considering throwing him out."

"I will." Silver held the bundle of keys by the one the concierge showed her and put her hand on his shoulder. "And if the landlord needs to throw him out, tell him or her not to worry. He has friends he can stay with. We'd hate for him to bother your other tenants."

"I say, are you Silver Delgado?" The man squinted at her. "You are! He's no good for the team, talk to Mr. Richter, he's a smart guy.

He'll set you straight."

Dean moved up behind her and put a hand on her shoulder. "Miss Delgado and I are working together to make sure the team meets fan expectations. This includes Mr. Demyan. I think you'll be surprised at how dedicated he really is."

"I hope you're right, sir." The old man straightened as much as he could and looked from her to Dean in a way that made her wonder if Dean's *support* wasn't a bad idea. "She's a young thing and I know the damage a pretty miss can do. I've got two lookers of my own. Heaven help the men they reeled in."

Door five. Silver didn't wait to see how Dean would reply. Seriously, if any woman could be accused of messing with a man's head, it would be her. That aside, she was perfectly willing to mess with Scott's head. He didn't deserve her pity.

She unlocked the door and wrinkled her nose at the stench of rotten food and sex. Mere steps away from the door lay Scott, limbs tangled with two women and mismatched, stained sheets. Silver crept by them and paused by the tiny kitchenette to put her finger to her lips as Dean stomped in. He scowled, then nodded.

Scott hadn't been here long, but he'd managed to make the entire apartment into a place she'd be ashamed to invite guests. Much as she wanted to embarrass him, she couldn't bring the press in here and pull off the misunderstood philanthropist act. Which meant she had to get him out of bed and dressed. Fast. And the sleazy chicks would have to go.

None of his dishes were clean, but she found a bucket under the sink that hadn't been used. She filled it with cold water in the bathtub and carted it out to the living room. With one last glance at Dean's open-mouthed stare, she tossed the cold water onto the sleeping trio.

The women screamed. Scott woke with a start and reached under his pillow. Her bucket landed with a *clunk!* as he pulled out a gun. "Come get me, you fuckers!"

Silver froze. Her blood turned to ice. The last time a man had pulled a gun on her she'd been with Asher. A client he'd failed wanted revenge, and she'd been caught in the crossfire. The gun went off and she couldn't hear in one ear for a month. But that hadn't affected her as much as the flesh wound which had left a small, hidden scar a few inches above her ear. So easy to hide, but a constant reminder that if the man had wanted to kill her, she'd be dead. Asher talked him down after, but that nervous twitch on the trigger could have ended her life. Her fingers found the smooth spot covered by hair. Her eyes locked on the black barrel aimed at her head.

"Are you fucking insane?" Dean pulled her behind him and picked up a crowbar. Why the hell was there a crowbar by the door? "Put it away!"

The gun shook and again that man was screaming at her. Screaming at Asher.

"No, no, no!" Her mind went blank. She went deaf again and the sound blasted in her skull. "Please! I didn't know! I don't know! I won't say anything!"

The sound came over and over, ripping through her. She crouched down and suddenly she was floating, leaving the place where the sharp stench of gunpowder took over and left her helpless. Maybe she was already dead. She hung around bad people. All the drugs and the deals would catch up with her. Asher lied. He couldn't protect her!

"Silver!" Dean's voice came through the fog and she latched onto it. "Please talk to me. I don't know if this is a movie you starred it that hit you bad or from real life. Talk to me!"

"Real. Too real!" She shook her head but the buzzing from the past remained. And the doctor, telling her the bullet didn't do any real damage. "But my ears hurt. I can't breathe!"

"I got you, baby."

Something was closing around her, trapping her. She lashed out, freed herself, and lunged for the door.

This time she was fast enough to get away.

* * * *

Dean moved to follow Silver. Scott grabbed his arm—ducking just in time to avoid getting a fist in the face. Red flashed in Dean's vision, and he forced himself to drop the crowbar before he was tempted to use it.

"Get out of my way," Dean said.

Scott stashed the gun back under his pillow, then held his hands up. "I'm trying to help, man. I didn't mean to freak her out like that, but she's having a panic attack and you grabbing her will only make it worse. Get her to walk around the block or something."

Giving Scott a curt nod, Dean headed out the door. He called back over his shoulder. "You better be dressed when I come back."

Outside, Dean had to run to catch up with Silver. She stopped when she noticed him, and he watched her slip a calm mask over her face. A good act, but neither her breathing, nor her pulse had slowed. The way her gaze darted sideways told him she still wanted to run.

"Hey . . ." Her tongue traced her upper lip as she gave him a little smile. "Sorry for acting like a spaz. I have this thing about guns."

Clearly. He had so many questions he wanted to ask her, but now wasn't the time for an interrogation. He knew more than a little about panic attacks from the club and his stint in the military—forcing someone to talk while they were having one could make things worse.

"You need to do something for me, sweetie." His jaw ticked as she rubbed her arms. He wished he could hold her, but after what had happened last time—Demyan was right. He settled on taking her hand while paying close attention to her pale face to see how she'd react. So far so good. He gently stroked her knuckles and focused on keeping his tone neutral. "You're breathing fast. Too fast. Slow it down a little."

"Yes. Yes I should." She shook her head quickly and resumed walking. Her grip on his hand tightened. "Can't seem to manage it though."

"You can. All you have to do is listen to me and do exactly what I say."

She laughed and a bit of color returned to her cheeks. "Or you'll tie me up and spank me?"

He smirked. "After this morning, I think I'll use spanking as a reward."

Rolling her eyes, she sighed. "You're too much. So what do you command, oh great and mighty one?"

"Breathe and count with me. And let me know when you're ready to head back."

"Back . . ." She groaned. "Damn it! I have to get Scott ready! The press will—"

"Inhale. Now exhale: five, four, three—you're not counting."

"That's not the way I learned to do it." Staring at her feet, she mumbled under her breath. "I like 'I'm safe.'"

Already her breathing had calmed somewhat, but her admission made him want to keep it going a little longer to make sure she stayed level. He brought his hand up, very, very slowly, so not to startle her, and cupped her cheek in his palm.

"Do you feel safe?"

Her eyes drifted shut. Her lashes rested on her cheeks. And she smiled. "Yes, I feel safe. That never would have happened with you. You're smart. And careful."

What wouldn't have happened? He swallowed against the question he couldn't voice and simply nodded. "Let's try it your way then. Inhale. Now exhale. I'm safe."

They continued this way for a few blocks, whispering those two words, walking at the same pace, breathing as one. As they headed back toward Demyan's apartment, Dean realized he didn't want to kill the man anymore. He would find out why the hell he slept with a damn gun, but even that didn't seem that important right now. All that mattered was Silver wasn't faking anymore. She really was fine.

"I suppose I owe you an explanation," she said, glancing toward the news van that had pulled up across the street. "But we don't have much time, so maybe after . . ."

"Whenever you're ready." He took one last deep inhale. "I don't imagine you want to go back in there. Care to stall the press while I fetch our newest altruist?"

"That would be great." She tugged on his hand before he could walk away. "Thank you."

Rising up on her tiptoes, she gave him a quick kiss on the lips, then blushed and hurried across the street to meet the reporters.

Dean shook his head as he entered the building and made his

way up to Demyan's floor. With all they'd done—never mind their one-night stand, but just this morning—why in the world would she be all shy about kissing him? Was she afraid the press might catch her? No, more likely she wasn't sure if she could instigate a kiss since he was a Dom. Did she think she needed permission?

He snorted at the thought. As much as he believed Silver was submissive, she wasn't *that* submissive. She had no problem trying to instigate sex.

One hand on the doorknob, he brought the other up to rest his fist against his lips. Suddenly he knew why this kiss had been different.

This kiss had nothing to do with sex.

A faint clicking behind the door drew his attention. He knocked.

"Come in," Demyan called.

Dean stepped into the apartment. The women were gone. The lights were off. And Demyan was sitting in the dark, hunched over on his sofa, wearing a rumpled suit, opening and closing the gun's chamber.

He didn't look up as he spoke. "Is she okay?"

"She's fine. But we need to talk."

"So talk."

"Why don't you put away the gun?"

Demyan laughed. "I probably should. Hell, after that, I should probably get rid of it. Guess it doesn't matter that the thing isn't loaded."

It didn't, but Dean shrugged. "I'm slightly less tempted to beat you to a bloody pulp for pointing it at her." He took a seat as Demyan stuffed the gun between the sofa cushions. "Now, since we came in uninvited, you were technically within your rights to defend yourself and your property. And so long as you've got a licence for it, I've got no say in you possessing it. But you can't bring it on road trips, and I would really appreciate you telling me why the hell you need to sleep with a gun."

"I probably don't. Not anymore." Demyan stood and approached the window. He winced as he peered through a slit in the curtains. "So you decided to bring the press here?"

"Yes. And Silver made excuses for you not showing up for the initial press conference." Dean stood and brushed some crumbs off his pants. "I expect you to go along with them."

"Sure."

"And the gun?"

"After, man." Demyan smirked as he straightened his tie and sauntered past Dean. "I don't owe you an explanation. But I do owe her one. I don't mind if you sit in on it."

For a split second, he'd almost felt sorry for the man. Thought maybe he'd misjudged him. He was still pretty young, and who knew what kind of trouble he'd gotten himself into? Maybe he needed help.

But that temporary inclination was gone. There was no misjudgement. Scott Demyan was an asshole.

And Dean and Silver had to somehow convince the media he was a bleeding-heart superstar.

"Silver, love." Dean muttered to the empty room. "I hope the man can act."

Chapter Fifteen

Hours after the press conference, Silver sat with her sister on the floor in Max's living room, watching Scott on the big screen while she nibbled on a slice of pizza. Behind her, Landon played with her hair while he chatted with Max about how Scott might actually be a decent guy.

Silver leaned over and whispered to her sister, "That man deserves an Oscar for that performance."

Oriana winked at her and rose up on her knees to lay her head on Dominik's lap. "You and Sloan are being awfully quiet. Aren't you excited that you get to play tomorrow? For such a good cause?"

"I'm looking forward to it, pet." Dominik smiled down at Oriana, the gold in his eyes glowing in the light from the TV. "But I think the wrong person got credit for the idea."

"What?" Landon tugged Silver's hair and frowned when she glanced up at him. "You didn't seriously put this together to make him look good?"

Her teeth dented her bottom lip as she eyed her sister. She hadn't gotten a chance to talk to Landon since last night, what with her and Dean rushing to organize everything. Actually, she was supposed to be having supper with Dean, but his daughter had called and he'd reluctantly asked for a rain check. Not that she'd minded too much. She knew he'd want to talk about the gun thing.

Which she wasn't ready to discuss. Avoiding unpleasantness with her sister was easy, she'd been doing it for years. But Dean wouldn't let her and Landon . . . Landon made her want to tell him everything.

Thankfully, with the other men around, she could avoid getting into anything serious. A little tricky without blatantly lying, but Scott's next words on screen gave her an out.

"I'm so grateful to be part of a team that gives me the opportunity to do some good."

Sliding into a position that almost mirrored Oriana's, she grinned at Landon and pretended not to notice his frown. "We gave him the opportunity to change his image. I mentioned the Leukemia

Foundation event this weekend and asked Dean if it was too late to put a game together between the Cobras and their farm team. He said it was cutting it close, but he thought we could pull it off. Scott jumped on the idea." *Stretching the truth isn't actually lying.* "There was no time to prep him for the interview, so all those words are his own."

Scott came out with another gem at exactly the right moment. "My niece was diagnosed with leukemia when she was five years old. She . . . she didn't make it, but funds like this have made a lot of progress in treatments since she passed away. Hopefully the money we raise will result in more children beating this. I plan to contribute whenever possible. This is just the first step."

She had to believe this part of his interview was real. And what he'd told her and Dean after convinced her it was. He carried a gun because his brother was a heavy gambler, and when his brother failed to pay his debts, the thugs he dealt with went after Scott. His brother was too proud to ask for his help, even when the medical bills threatened to put his family out on the street. Scott had handled his brother's debts, but that hadn't been enough, because his brother wouldn't stop borrowing to feed his addiction. Losing his daughter, then his wife only made it worse. So Scott had continued to pay until one day he'd had enough. He ignored the phone calls and met "the collector" at the door with a gun of his own. The guy hadn't expected it, so he backed down, but that only bought Scott a bit of time.

He still expected the goons to come after him.

What if they do?

"Silver." Landon snapped his fingers in front of her face. "What are you thinking about? You just went white."

"The pizza." She leapt to her feet and rushed to the bathroom. And bent over the toilet as her excuse became the truth. Someone crouched behind her and gathered her hair away from her face.

She prayed it was Oriana.

"You will tell me what's got you so upset," Landon said. When she sat up, he wet a facecloth in the sink and knelt to dab her lips. "Once you're feeling better. Do you think you can stand?"

She nodded and made it to her feet before the floor tilted like it was trying to pitch her off. But Landon caught her and the world steadied as she settled into his arms and laid her head on his shoulder.

"*Ma pauvre petit*, you've had a rough day, haven't you?"

"Uh uh. Just tired." She pressed her eyes shut and sniffed his throat. "Mmm, I like your cologne."

"I'm not wearing any."

"Oh." She huffed out a breath and sighed as he lowered her somewhere soft. "I think I need to sleep."

"I agree." Landon's fingers delved into her hair, plucking out all the bobby pins she'd used to secure her bun. "I'll crash on the sofa. You can stay here."

Landon's bed. She was in Landon's bed and she really shouldn't be. "Give me a few minutes and I'll get up and go home."

"In a few minutes, you'll be fast asleep."

Probably. She burrowed her head into the pillow. The darkness behind her closed lids swept her away. And narrowed until she was staring into a circular hole. *Bang!* She jumped and her eyes shot open. "What was that?"

"What?" Landon strode across the room and took her hands, rubbing them as though they were cold. "You fell asleep, Silver."

"No, I wasn't sleeping." Shaking her head, she looked past him. The other men and Oriana were speaking softly in the living room. The TV had been turned down low. "I heard something loud, like a door slamming or—" She tried to sit up, but he pushed her back down. "You didn't hear it?"

"No. Oriana came in awhile ago to check on you. After I told her you were sleeping, she went out and everything has been really quiet since." He fingered the collar of her shirt. "You were probably uncomfortable in all this. Why don't I get your sister to bring you something comfortable to sleep in?"

She started nodding, but when he stood, acidic fear spilled up from her gut. Her nails dug into flesh, but she didn't feel pain. She looked down and let go when she saw the bloody half moons on the back of Landon's hand.

"I'm sorry, I didn't mean to—"

"Don't worry about it." He pinched the flesh between his eyes and shook his head. "I hate feeling useless, *mignonne*. Tell me what you need."

"I need—" *Just say it!* She scooted over and stared at the empty space on the bed. "Could you stay with me?"

He nodded, then went to the small pile of clothes on the dresser. He returned with a T-shirt and some boxers. "Get comfortable. I'll be right outside—"

"No!" *Pathetic! You're so pathetic!* Damn it, she didn't care. "I promise, I'll tell you everything tomorrow. Just don't leave me."

His lips pressed together, he studied her for a moment. Opened his mouth a few times. Then spun around and spoke with his back to her. "How's this?"

"Perfect." Changing quickly, she left her clothes on the floor and slipped under the blankets. "It's safe now."

"Do you want the light on or off?"

What am I? Two? Some cruel voice inside seemed to be laughing, but Landon wasn't. She considered for a moment and realized, with him beside her, the darkness wasn't all that scary.

"Off."

The lights went out. The mattress creaked as Landon climbed into the bed. For a while, the only sound was his steady breaths, rhythmic and comforting. As her eyes adjusted to the darkness, she saw he was lying on his side, stiff as a board, watching her.

"You don't look comfy." She inched closer to the wall. "There's plenty of space."

"I'm not sure . . ." He groaned. "Look, I don't want things to get awkward between us."

"Oh." She really wasn't being fair. This was his bed and they'd both agreed to stay friends. And friends didn't share beds. "This was a bad idea. You've got to get up early for the game tomorrow, and I should go—hey! What are you doing?"

Yanking at the blankets, Landon nudged her aside and spread them over both their bodies. Stretched out on his back, he curved his arm under her shoulder and dragged her toward him until her head rested on his chest. She wiggled a little, bending her knee over his thighs, deciding that he made a very good body pillow.

He took her hand and held it over his heart. "Much better."

As the heat from his body and his steady pulse and his presence lulled her to sleep, she smiled.

Yes. Much.

Chapter Sixteen

L andon's head weighed on his pillow, still heavy from a slumber he was reluctant to shake. He groaned and scrubbed his hands over his face. The scent of some kind of pastry beckoned, along with the sweetness of Silver's laughter. Cuddling up with him last night seemed to have done her some good.

Hell, he couldn't remember the last time *he'd* slept so well. His body had tried to make an issue of it at first, but his conscience won out in the end. Knowing Silver trusted him enough to fall asleep in his arms without even a question of him wanting more—that was enough.

That would have to be enough.

Friends, Bower. Maybe you should have it tattooed on your ass so you'll see it when you pull your head out.

He grunted and pushed off the bed, swinging his legs over the side to stand. No one should be expected to think straight in the morning until they'd had at least two cups of coffee. He padded into the hall in the long black shorts he'd picked up the day before for lazing around the house—modesty and all since it wasn't his place—and straightened his tank top to cover the bulge of his semi.

"I still can't believe you made these from scratch! Mmm!"

The sound of pleasure Silver made tightened his balls. And when he stepped into the kitchen, he knew he was a goner.

Loose bedroom hair caught the sunrays from the kitchen window and cascaded the glow in a wave down her back as she bent over the ironing board, chewing on the strawberry turnover her sister had fed her. His large white T-shirt hid her curves, but when the light hit her just the right way, the shadow of her body revealed everything. Then her legs—fuck! How had he missed them last night? Or when he'd held her at the club, completely naked. Was it those evil red shoes she was wearing that made him wonder . . .

Moving up behind her, his fingers twitched as he fought to keep them out of her hair, fought to keep his hands off her body and his dick from pressing against her ass. His every inhale was a struggle.

He exhaled fast and hard, right by her ear.

She went perfectly still.

"Silver." His lips brushed that soft, soft flesh and he wrestled with the urge to taste it. "Please go get dressed."

After carefully placing the iron in the holder at the end of the board, she turned and looked up at him with wide eyes. "I was just getting your shirt ready for you. You only have two and they're both wrinkled."

"She did a really good job too." Oriana slinked over, her own nightclothes covered as usual with a large robe. She held out the plate of turnovers and waited for him to take one before she continued. "She doesn't know how to work a washing machine, but she can take the creases out of anything. I can't even get a collar that perfect."

"That looks great, thank you, Silver." He tried to catch her eye so she would do as he'd asked. He didn't want to say anything that might embarrass her in front of her sister.

Silver sidled away from him and unplugged the iron. "I find things look fresher when you iron them before putting them on. I do it every morning." She glanced over at Oriana. "Thanks for helping me with the washing machine. I couldn't have worn the same clothes again. I know you think I'm a snob—"

"I do not."

"You do too! You said it every day when we were kids!"

My cue to leave. "Excuse me, ladies. I'm going to go hop in the shower—"

"Max is using the one downstairs and Dominik is upstairs." Oriana nodded toward his untouched turnover. "You'll have just enough time to eat and get dressed. Sloan said he wanted to get to the rink by ten since the game's at twelve."

"You don't smell bad." Silver picked up the shirt and stepped up to him. "If that helps."

Helps? Hell no, it doesn't help. His heart raced like he'd just run up a flight of stairs in his goalie gear as she held out the shirt for him and her breasts brushed his arm. "Why are you wearing shoes?"

"The floor's cold. I didn't have socks."

Oriana had gone back to the stove. He took the opportunity to pull Silver close and spoke in a firm tone. "I would appreciate it if you'd go get dressed."

"I don't see what the big deal is."

"Silver—"

"You're wearing less than I am."

"Silver—"

This time a snarl cut him off. Well put together in a charcoal suit, black silk shirt, and tie, Callahan stood in the doorway, scowling at him. Then at Silver. "Can we save the foreplay and fuck-me-shoes until *after* breakfast?"

Silver's eyes narrowed. "Why? Are they giving you ideas?"

"It's too early for this shit." Callahan strode up to the table and grabbed the newspaper. "Be nice if you had enough respect for your sister not to strut around like that."

Bright red blotches spread over Silver's cheeks. "Fuck you, Sloan."

"For the—what is it, tenth time?" Callahan smirked. "The answer is no."

Landon smoothed his hand down Silver's side, trying to calm her even though he wanted to lay his fucking captain out for being such an asshole. He let Silver nudge him into a seat and grinned when she swiped the turnover plate out from under Callahan's hand and offered it to him.

"Stop it you two." Oriana frowned at Callahan when he opened his mouth. "Why don't you go in the living room? I'll bring your breakfast in a minute."

"I don't need you serving me," Callahan said.

Oriana poked him in the chest. "You serve me supper every night."

"I serve supper at the kitchen table. That's hardly the same."

"Ugh! You're impossible in the morning!"

While the couple bickered, Silver began creeping toward the door. Landon hated Callahan embarrassing her, but at least she'd come back covered up and his sanity would be saved. He took another turnover.

And dropped it when Silver screamed.

Landon shot to his feet. Perron burst out of the bathroom in nothing but a towel. Mason thundered down the stairs in a pair of boxers.

Callahan burst out laughing. "A spider, Silver? You're incredible."

Eyes flashing with rage, Silver pried off one of her shoes and threw it at Callahan. The other was slapped down on the spider and quickly followed the first. "I hate you!"

"I'm heartbroken, really," Callahan said dryly.

Without another word, Silver stomped down the hall into Landon's room and slammed the door.

No one moved. Landon looked to Oriana, expecting her to go comfort her sister, but she was too busy glaring at Sloan. He turned away from them all, his teeth clenched so hard his jaw hurt. Focusing on the dull ache kept him from cursing them out.

"Leave her for a bit," Oriana said, her tone dangerously low. Then she continued, sounding so fucking pissed he turned again to make sure she wasn't talking to him. "I can't believe you just did that."

Callahan's eyes widened. "Me? You're joking, right?"

"I know you two don't like each other, but you *laughed* at her! That was . . ." She shook her head and hugged herself. "That was unbelievably cruel. Even for you."

"Oriana." Mason stepped forward and slid his hands under her elbows, easing her arms apart. "It might have been cruel if he knew how she'd react. Or why it would bother her so much. But he doesn't."

Perron came up behind her and wrapped his arms around her waist. "Talk to us, darlin'."

She opened her mouth, hesitating as she finally noticed Landon, standing there. The way she looked him over made him feel like an ant under a magnifying glass that a child might study or fry. "This is personal."

Leaving them alone to discuss this would be the decent thing to do. But Oriana had these three men and Silver had . . . just him. He gave Oriana a tight half-smile. "Not to be crude, but I really don't give a shit if it's 'personal.' Silver's hurting and I'm her friend."

Callahan snorted.

The muscles in Landon's forearms twitched. "Captain, I'm real close to making sure you're listed with an upper body injury. Due to a broken nose."

His captain's eyes darkened. "Do I need to remind you you're a guest here?"

"So is Silver."

"All right! Enough!" Oriana dropped her head back and leaned on Mason. "Our father used to laugh at her. She'd do something girly, like scream at a spider or cry over a broken nail, and he'd laugh. If his business partners were around, he'd call her his silly little doll. And they'd laugh with him because she'd—she'd scream and ask him if he loved her at all and if he did why didn't he help her? I know it probably sounds stupid, but it got worse as she got older. Every time she came to him with a problem, he'd make her tell him in front of other men, and then he'd make a joke out of it. I asked him once why he did it . . . she was eleven and she'd just gotten her period. I never talked to her about it because . . ." She made a face and focused on her slippers. "I started mine after her. I never even thought about it. Anyway, he told me she needed to toughen up. What I didn't get is why she still went to him, even after he humiliated her . . ."

"She wanted the man to act like a daddy," Perron said softly. "She still does."

Landon's stomach twisted into a knot as tight as the fist pressed to his sides. He pictured Silver, that beautiful woman, as a little girl, tiny, fragile. And alone.

"I'm going to see if she's okay." He sucked his teeth when Callahan stepped in front of him. "Try and stop me."

"That's not what I'm doing." Callahan closed his eyes and sighed. "Just tell her . . . tell her I'm sorry. I'd tell her myself, but I don't think she wants to see me right now."

"I'll tell her."

When he stopped by the door, he realized his hands were still fisted and forced them open. Unclenched his jaw. Relaxed his features so she wouldn't take one look at him and see the rage boiling within. The extreme reaction wouldn't make sense to most people, but all he kept thinking of was his dad, hugging Becky and treating her like she was special. Hell, he'd done the same for Landon. Granted, he'd gotten the men don't cry lecture, but as a little boy his tears had been kissed away as his father gently reminded him he wasn't a man yet.

Why couldn't someone have done that for Silver?

As composed as possible, Landon opened the door, prepared to do all the hugging and kissing needed to make things right. But the woman who faced him wasn't his sweet, vulnerable Silver. She was the closed-off, untouchable Silver Delgado.

"Oh! I'm glad you came. I really didn't want to go back in there and deal with the drama to say goodbye." She wrinkled her nose in a way that seemed scripted and fake. "One thing I miss about Hollywood. It kept me too busy to come down for all the family mess. Maybe, if I don't cut it as the owner, I can go back."

"*Mignonne.*" He reached out for her, but she skirted away and burrowed in her purse for a lollipop. His sleepy cock woke a little at her provocative sucking, but his concern kept his blood pumping in his heart and his head where it belonged. "Don't slip into some role and pretend it's all right. It's not all right."

"What's not all right?" Holding the lollipop in one hand, she licked her lips and gave him a slow once-over. "Landon, you're a sweetheart, but you worry too much. My family's not like yours, but that's okay. And really, it could be worse. Look at me. I'm fine."

He looked at her. Perfect hair. Perfect makeup. Her clothes were all fresh, and if she had a flaw, he couldn't find it. The shiny shield she never held up to him was firmly in place. "Don't do this."

"This? Landon, think about it. You held me while I fell apart last night and I appreciate that, but I'm not as damaged as you think. We'll talk more later, but now . . ." She checked her phone. "Uck, I have to hurry. See you at the game?"

No use in pushing any more. She wasn't ready to let him in. He nodded. "Sure. We can hang out in the bleachers."

She let out a light laugh that reverberated up his spine like a knife scratching porcelain. "Sloan didn't tell you? You've been cleared to play! I get to watch you between the pipes!"

"That's great." A shallow buzz of excitement rushed through him, diluted by the fact that holding him at arm's length wasn't enough. She was pushing him further and further away. "Maybe after we can—"

"You're going to the club tonight, right?"

"Yes."

"Well, I guess I'll see you there." Her mask slipped and she groaned. "My shoes—could you get them for me?"

He nodded and left the room, walked stiffly to the kitchen, and returned without a word to anyone. Not that anyone had tried to speak to him. He had a feeling they all knew who waited for him in that room.

After slipping into her shoes, Silver gave him a quick peck on the cheek. When their eyes met, she tripped away from him. "I—I really appreciate everything."

Another vague nod. He had no idea what to say. This was goodbye.

But as he watched her from the front door, getting into her car and waving gaily at the shoddily hidden camera crew, something inside him snapped into place.

Not goodbye. Not for long. They were friends and that wasn't going to change.

This woman might be Silver Delgado. The actress. The infamous playgirl.

But she hadn't met Landon Bower. The man who played to win.

It was about time she did.

Chapter Seventeen

The arena wasn't fancy; it didn't even have press boxes and only had a quarter of the seats the Delgado Forum held, but in twenty-four hours, they'd filled it. Every man, woman, and child stood as the local Canadian Idol finalist sang the anthem. Silver trembled with anticipation as she watched Landon take his place between those red metal bars. Sloan met his younger counterpart at center ice. The puck dropped. And all those big, strong bodies collided.

Silver leaned forward, restraining herself from pressing her face against the glass as the farm team—The Queen's Vipers—took control and plowed the net. A firm arm around her shoulders held her together as she cringed. Landon sprawled under a pile of bodies and lay on top of the puck for three long seconds. The ref blew the whistle.

"This wasn't a mistake, was it?" She tipped her head up to see Dean whose focus seemed to be on keeping her warm instead of on the ice where it belonged. "He's ready?"

"He's ready." Dean hugged her tight, then leaned down to whisper in her ear. "That isn't your baby out there. He's your friend and a full-grown man who's dedicated his life to standing between those pipes. I understand your concern, but you need to know I wouldn't risk an asset to our team, or a man's career, to put on a show. The doctor checked him out. He's in good shape."

My friend. Do not forget. Must not forget. If she showed too much concern, people might wonder. "Looks like a lot of money to me, Dean. Maybe I'm not that good at numbers, and I'm woman enough to admit it. But I'll take your word for it."

Seconds later, she almost retracted her words. Carter, their cocky young forward, iced the puck. He won the face-off, but almost put the puck in his own net. The Viper's sharpshooter caught the rebound. Dominik knocked Landon over trying to cover the right side of the net.

Landon rose and gave him a hard shove. He gestured to the blue ice with his stick and waved his blocker in front of his face, shouting something she couldn't quite make out. Dominik shook his head and moved to skate away. Landon grabbed his arm.

"Shit." Silver pressed her hand to her throat and glanced over at the bench. The coach, Dean's brother Tim, called to the men, but Dominik and Landon ignored him. *Someone* had to do something. She turned to Dean. "Can't you—"

"Not my job, sweetheart." He nodded toward the rink. "But it's being taken care of."

Her lips curled as she watched Sloan get between the men. Both Landon and Dominik looked ready to start swinging and she secretly hoped they would, now that Sloan might catch a stray punch or two. But Dominik backed off after just a few words from Sloan, and the game resumed without any further issues.

It took a while, but eventually Silver found herself completely engaged in the game, no longer flinching when Landon fell, or smiling in satisfaction when Sloan's body was crushed against the boards. She whispered questions to Dean less and less frequently as the pieces of the game formed a complete picture in her mind. The intensity of each play sent her heart to pounding as though she was the one out there, flying across the ice as Scott did so effortlessly. Or Max who passed the puck with foresight and precision, resulting in rapid-fire shots on net, and finally, the first goal.

The steady din from the bleachers erupted. Silver covered her ears and laughed as Dean grinned down at her. His eyes were wide and bright, and the pure joy made him look younger somehow. He truly loved this game, and for the first time, she could see why. It was starting to grow on her too.

"So, we've got some good prospects out there? That kid who almost scored—"

Dean's brows shot up. "Kid? If you're talking about Hart, he's three years older than you are."

"I thought the guys on the farm team were younger than the guys on the team."

"No, that's the juniors. There are thirty-year-olds on the farm team. Some men spend their entire careers there. Hart's not ready for the NHL, but he's decent if we ever need to bring someone up."

Dean pointed to another young man who managed to steal the puck from Dominik and dart between Carter and Max. "Collin Gail. He's eighteen, and he's got some growing to do, but I think he'll be our top scorer in a year or two."

"A year or two." Silver wrinkled her nose. "What good does that do us now?"

Before Dean could answer, she gasped and bunched her hand in his shirt. Collin feinted to the left, waited until Landon came out to meet him, and skidded to the right. Blasted a shot at the open net—

Landon dived and her mouth dropped open as he snatched the black blur out of thin air.

A gruff laugh at her side brought her head up as the crowd lost their freakin' minds. Dean was shaking his head. "Landon just robbed him. That was one hell of a save."

She smiled so wide her cheeks hurt as she rested her forehead against the glass and watched Landon stand. He looked right back at her as his defensemen hit his pads with their sticks, congratulating him. Even with the distance between them, she could make out his face, all shiny with sweat. And his beautiful grey eyes.

He winked.

Her heart sputtered and she forced herself to back away from the glass.

Friends. Just friends.

She hadn't acted like much of a friend this morning. It was just . . . uck, she couldn't say for sure, except over the past week it had gotten easier and easier to let her guard down with Landon. Which had been nice at first, but she finally saw how weak it made her. She was losing control of her emotions and almost falling apart in front of Sloan, of all people, told her enough was enough.

Not that she wanted to stop being friends with Landon. Only cool it down a bit before it turned into something more than either of them could handle. She liked Landon too much to let him get involved with a girl like her.

Dean touched her arm and bent down to be heard over the ruckus surrounding them in the in-between period rush for refreshments. "Would you like a coffee?"

She shrugged. "How about a beer?"

He frowned and shook his head. "Coke?"

Frowning back, she jerked her chin up. "Why can't I have a beer?"

"You think it would be good for the press to see you drinking on the job, at a charity event?"

Gah, why does he have to be right all the time? "Diet Coke, please."

His lips tilted up as he nodded, and she blinked against the image of what those lips had done to her body. Might do again tonight if she let him. Which she really, really wanted to—after she figured a few things out about herself.

He must have read something in her expression because he leaned over, his body language seeming carefully controlled, but his words anything but. "You have no idea what I want to do to you when you look at me like that."

Her breath hitched and she stared after him as he made his way through the throng and out of sight. The way he did that, switching from business partner, to Dom mode, to seducer, and back made her head spin. If she let herself think about it, she might even admit— admit what? There was nothing to admit.

Still, she had fifteen minutes to kill.

The crowd had thinned in the stands, but they flooded the small concession area and stood in long lines outside the bathroom. Their urgency was contagious. None of them wanted to miss the puck dropping for second period, and she found her own pace quickening to match those of the people around her. So many bodies in such a small space—the stadium was a third of the size of the Delgado Forum—made it stuffy and she felt a little claustrophobic. She joined the crowd trickling out to the parking lot.

The sun blinded her as she stepped past the heavy metal doors. She fetched her sunglasses from her purse and slipped them on. A thin cloud of smoke hovered over the small group of smokers, and she held her breath before she was tempted to take a whiff. Smoking was the only bad habit she'd managed to ditch before it did any serious damage, but sometimes she still got cravings. And stifling the urge to smoke brought on worse urges.

She'd almost reached the corner of the building, past the stands set up for donations and the area where children were getting their faces painted and taking pictures with the teams' mascots, when she spotted a familiar face. Dean's daughter, Jami, snuggled up on a bench at the edge of a line of evergreens with a man big enough to be a member of one of the teams. Silver was pretty sure he wasn't a Cobra. They passed a cigarette—no, a *joint*—back and forth between them, and Jami giggled as the man cupped his hand around his mouth and blew smoke into her face.

None of your business, Silver. She's an adult.

Which was true. But she was also doing drugs way too close to where kids could see her and Silver was responsible for the event. Maybe if she put it the right way . . .

Squaring her shoulders, she approached the pair. "Hey, Jami! I'm glad to see you here. It's really nice of you to show support for your father. But if you're going to get high, you need to do it somewhere else."

Jami giggled again. "Why? We're fine here, thank you very much."

"There are *families* here."

"Yeah, way over there." Jami pointed toward the front of the building. "We're not bothering anyone."

So much for being nice. "You're bothering me. Either put it out or leave."

The man took the joint from Jami and notched it on the edge of the bench before she could protest. He smirked at Silver. "Better?"

"Yes. Thank you." Something about the way the man looked at her made her nervous. It was like he had a secret he was just dying to share with her. And it wasn't anything good. She formed her lips into a neutral smile and stuck her hand out. "We haven't met. I'm Silver Delgado. Are you on one of the teams?"

He let out a dry laugh as he shook her hand. "No. I'm a bartender. The name's Ford."

"A pleasure." She tried to sound sincere, but he laughed again in a way that made it obvious she hadn't succeeded. "So, are you and Jami—"

"He's my boyfriend, so hands off." Jami draped herself over Ford and glared at Silver. "I've heard about you. Apparently you went through the whole team before you left for Hollywood. And now that you're back, you're starting over at the top. Does my dad know what a slut you are?"

Aww, how sweet. Stoned out of your freakin' mind and still looking out for daddy. Silver shrugged. "It's not exactly a secret. You want to know what happened the night we met?"

"Eww!" Jami hid her face in her boyfriend's leather jacket. "Seriously, just go away."

"Glad to," Silver said. She slid her sunglasses down a bit and kept her eyes on Jami until the girl sighed and lifted her head. "But just a friendly piece of advice before I go. You fucking reek. You might want to make yourself scarce before your father gets wind of you."

"Ha-ha." Jami flipped her the bird, then stood and dragged Ford to his feet. "Come on. I don't want to deal with my dad's fuck friend anymore."

Ford tucked Jami against his side and nodded to Silver. "Until next time."

Silver watched them walk away and rubbed her arms as a chill crawled over her flesh like a thousand icy little worms. Apparently, Jami was going through one of those phases, and since she'd gone through a few herself, she refused to judge. But that guy was bad fucking news.

Tell her father. Let him deal with it.

Yeah, not likely. She hadn't stooped to the level of rat just yet. But Jami's words reminded her that Landon probably wasn't the only one she should cool it with. Dean really *didn't* know much about her. He knew her as a businesswoman and as a sub. And she wasn't really either of those.

Was she?

Spinning around, she decided she'd had enough "fresh" air and headed back to the stadium. A horde of toddlers surrounded her and she froze, scared to step on one of them. An older kid, maybe seven or eight, stared at her with something like hero worship. She stared back and stuttered when he held out a Dartmouth Cobra cap.

"Luke Carter," the little boy said.

Someone behind her chuckled. "I think that's for me, hot stuff."

She sidestepped and watched the young forward who she

remembered from the preseason game, and the club, who everyone called Carter, crouch down to sign the boy's hat.

"You play?" Carter asked after putting the cap on the boy's head. The boy nodded vigorously but didn't speak. "Oh yeah? What position?"

The boy squeaked. "Left wing. Just like you."

"Good man." Carter cuffed the boy's chin and straightened. "Where are your parents? You want to take a picture or something?"

Eyes wide, the boy glanced over his shoulder and shouted, "Mom! Mom, it's Luke Carter! Luke Carter!"

A woman with a baby carrier and a stroller rushed over, patting her tiny infant's head as it wailed. In the stroller, a little girl with sweet tiny pigtails echoed the baby's cries. "Peter, I told you to stay with me!"

"Luke Carter!" The boy pointed at Carter and rolled his eyes at his mother who'd managed to stop the baby's hollering with a pacifier. "I couldn't stay with you while you drooled over Sloan Callahan! Carter is my favorite player!"

The woman blushed and glanced over at Silver. "I wasn't, I just—" Her eyes widened. "Oh! Aren't you Silver Delgado? I loved your last movie!"

Heat spilled over Silver's cheeks. Not many people recognized her from her movies. Most were low-budget and cheesy. The last had been all right, a comedy romance with a star people actually knew, but she'd played the slutty best friend and it wasn't anything to brag about. "Thanks. It was pretty good."

"Pretty good? Oh my God, I know you were playing a minor role, but I really felt for you. Sex was the only way you knew how to connect with men, and I could tell you were so afraid to get involved and get hurt. I was hoping they'd make a sequel so we could find out what happened to you."

Something about the woman's assessment made her very uncomfortable. The part had been pretty easy to play, but she hadn't gone for all the depth the woman apparently saw. She'd just followed the script. "I'm so happy to hear you enjoyed it, but unfortunately, the movie wasn't popular enough for them to consider a sequel."

"Oh . . ." The woman rolled the stroller back and forth, tensing as the little girl let out a piercing scream. "You'll do other movies though, right?"

Silver shrugged and eyed the stroller-bound toddler. Opening her purse, she peeked inside and took out a lollipop, careful not to let the girl see it. She glanced at the mother. "Is it okay . . . ?"

"Go ahead." Rocking on her heels and murmuring to the baby, the woman came to Silver's side and watched her offer the little girl a bright pink lollipop. "Go ahead, Sandra."

A little hand plucked the lollipop from Silver. Big brown eyes met hers. And Sandra's adorable face broke into a heart-melting smile. "Thank you."

"You're welcome." Silver smiled back, then straightened. "We should go in before you're late, Carter."

Carter looked at his watch. "Ah sh—shoot. Yeah. But I promised the kid a picture."

The mother quickly took out her phone and snapped a few pictures with Carter and the boy. Then she snapped one of Silver. "I hope you don't mind. My friends will never believe I met you in person without evidence!"

"That's fine." Pictures she could handle. They'd once been part of her daily routine. "It was very nice to meet you."

After saying goodbye, she and Carter hurried into the stadium. There were few people hanging around, which meant the game was about to start.

Carter stopped her with a hand on her shoulder before she could return to the bleachers. "You were great out there."

"So were you." She took a moment to really see him, this young man who was about her age, who drove the other players, and the ladies, nuts. Decent looking, with short blond hair and nice blue eyes, but it was the edge of laughter, the ne'er-do-well appeal, that set him apart. He was the perfect kind of guy to have a bit of fun with. "Are you going to the club tonight?"

"Yeah." His lashes lowered into a hooded gaze and he leaned forward. "I'm learning a few new tricks. Why? Are you?"

"Yes." She fingered his collar and licked her bottom lip. "See you there?"

"I'll find you." His hand lifted, and when she didn't object, he trailed his finger down her throat. "Maybe I can give you a taste of what I've learned."

"I'd like that." She checked to make sure no one was watching and then got up on her tiptoes to whisper in his ear. "Just promise me one thing."

"What?"

"You'll give me everything I ask for."

"Baby, that *won't* be a problem." He nuzzled his face into her hair. "Just don't expect breakfast in the mornin', okay? I'm not that kinda guy."

"Good." She stepped back and patted his cheek. "Because I'm not that kinda girl."

* * * *

Landon slammed his blocker into his sports bag, on top of the rest of his equipment. Sweaty, half-naked male bodies moved around the tight confines of the locker room, stinking it up since most of the men didn't want to use the showers. The floor was covered in a puddle that smelled like sewage.

Winning had put most of the men in a good mood, with a few notable exceptions. Callahan avoided everyone as he changed and stormed out with a don't-fuck-with-me look on his face. Mason followed shortly after, relatively quiet, though he paused to tell their youngest players they'd done well.

Perron sat on a table in the corner of the locker room, speaking softly. "She looks fine, sugar. Yes, Dean was with her. No, she hasn't spoken to him yet—I wouldn't worry . . . okay, so why don't you call her?"

He was probably talking to Oriana. About Silver. And Landon was pretty sure his name had been mentioned.

Before coming in here to get changed, he'd tried to find Silver, but she was already gone. Leaving Richter to deal with wrapping up the event. Richter looked distracted, which troubled Landon. He'd already decided Richter was the best man for her, and he wouldn't come between them, but all that was based on the fact that Richter could take care of her. Which he couldn't do if he wasn't with her.

Chill, Bower. Richter's got this. Stick with the program.

The program being showing Silver she needed him. Because she did.

She needs you or you need her?

A bit of both. But so what? They had fun together, and he liked knowing she could come to him with anything that bothered her. Which he wasn't so sure of anymore. Not because of anything he'd done—not that he was aware of anyway. He hadn't pressured her in any way, hadn't done the one thing he knew would scare her off . . .

Or maybe he had. It wouldn't take much. The wrong look. A touch. If she thought he wanted more than friendship she'd—she'd put up a wall between them.

He pressed his eyes shut. Damn it, he *had* fucked up. Those little moments that came so naturally added up to all he'd tried to avoid. He should have tried harder. He'd done exactly what he'd promised he wouldn't. There was no doubt about it. All that he'd tried to hide came out in actions rather than words.

And she knew.

Maybe he could fix that by showing her the other side of him. If she saw him at the club, as a Dom, one who hadn't laid claim on her—maybe then she'd relax. He made a face at the thought of taking another woman when all he wanted was—

Get a fucking grip!

Right. He wouldn't go there. What he wanted didn't matter. She could find a man to fuck anywhere. And hopefully, if Richter was half the man Landon thought he was, she would get much more.

So where did he fit in?

We're friends. Nothing will change that. The word had turned into a goddamned mantra. Without them, he might have put up a fight. Done everything in his power to get Silver to see him and all he could offer. But it was too late. His sister called him stubborn. Whatever. He'd set his course and he wouldn't waver from it. Silver desperately needed a friend, and he would give her one.

"So, Carter. I saw you out there with Silver." Demyan's voice cut over the lingering chatter from the other men. "Looked like you two were getting pretty close. You next in line?"

Carter cocked his head. "You hit a dry spell, man? Need to hear about my sex life to get off?"

"Ah, I was right. You are going to fuck her." Demyan folded his arms over his bare chest and propped himself against the lockers. "She's not picky, is she? Can't wait to show her what a real man feels like."

"Oh yeah?" Carter stood. "Well, think what you want, but I'd make other plans if I were you. The girl's got standards and you are so below."

Demyan laughed. "You think so? Kid, let's clear something up. She didn't bring me here because she thought I'd be good for the team. She took one look at me and creamed her panties. Makes me feel a little cheap, but I'm sure being balls-deep in that hot cunt will help me get over it."

Landon didn't recall standing. Or moving. The next thing that reached him was the crunch of bone under his fist. A spray of blood. And the feral satisfaction of feeling a fist hit his jaw before Demyan's body dented the locker behind him.

"You broke my nose, you fucker!" Demyan threw all his weight into his forward lunge. "I'm going to put you in rehab."

A blocked punch. A swift elbow to the ribs. Hands tugging at him. Blood blurring his vision.

"Talk about her like that again and I'll fucking bury you." Landon struggled against the arm locked around his throat. "You're dirt! You're fucking scum! If you ever touch her—"

"I'll touch her all right!" Demyan spat on the floor and twisted to free himself from Carter and the backup goalie, Ingerslov. "I'll fuck the bitch so good she'll scream my name whenever she lets you fuck her. You're pathetic. Crushing on that little whore."

"Let me go!" Landon thrashed, stopping himself inches from driving his elbow into Perron's gut. He didn't want to hurt Perron. The man was decent. But when he got his hands on Demyan—"He's dead! He's fucking dead!"

"Get him out of here!" Perron grunted as Landon slammed him into the lockers. "Now!"

It took Perron and two other men to restrain Landon as Carter and Ingerslov dragged Demyan out. Landon growled and wrenched away from them for a split second before Perron punched him in the face.

Black and red spotted Landon's vision as he slumped onto the bench. His head rang.

Silver. Keep Demyan away from Silver. He lurched to his feet.

Perron shoved him back down. "Get a grip!"

"That bastard doesn't get to talk about her like that!" Landon panted, his lungs searing worse than they had during the game. "He doesn't get to touch her!"

"Listen to me." Perron crouched in front of him. "I'll talk to Oriana. Tell her what Scott said. I get it; he's an asshole and she doesn't need him messing with her. But this won't help anything."

Landon groaned and hung his head. Jesus fucking Christ, what the hell was wrong with him? Perron was right. This wouldn't change anything. But neither would getting Oriana involved. "Silver won't listen."

"Then she's going to get hurt." Perron slapped his shoulder and shook his head. "It sucks, I know, but all you can do is be there for her. Oriana said you two are just friends. Is that true?"

"Yeah." Landon stared at his bloody fist and nodded. "Just friends."

Just fucking friends.

Chapter Eighteen

"**N**o, don't come pick me up. I'll see you there." Silver carefully applied another coat of lip stain. No chance of smearing it when she started doing naughty things. "Speaking of which, there's something I should tell you."

"Yes?" Dean sounded much, much too calm over the phone. Kinda made her nervous. "What is it?"

"Tonight I'm . . ." *Find the right words. Damn, there are no right words!* "I'm not going as your sub. I can't—not yet. We've had fun, but if I'm going to explore my . . . submissive side, if I even have one, I have to do it my way."

"I see." He went silence for exactly five seconds. "Which means what? Just so we're clear."

She bit her lip. Stupid. Now she'd have to put on another coat. "Which means if I get involved in a scene, you don't interfere. That's how it works at your club, right?"

"In other words, this . . . *scene* won't be with me."

Well, at least I don't have to spell it out. "No. It won't be. And I know you won't like it—"

"Why should I care?"

Ouch! She frowned at her reflection. "I'm not saying you should. I just wanted to be up-front with you. This whole lifestyle may work for me. I doubt it, but hey, you gave me a good time. Maybe someone else can. Someone who won't ask me to kneel and lick their feet."

"When have I *ever* asked you to do that?"

"You're too intense, all right! I want the dummy 101 version, not the advanced."

"Well, I'm sure that won't be too hard to find." He let out a harsh laugh. "It is my club, so if you change your mind, I'll be around."

"Sure, but . . ." She had to speak fast. She had a feeling he was going to hang up on her. "This changes nothing at work, okay? We'll still be cool?"

"Of course."

Dial tone. Wonderful. Her excitement about the night dimmed like a half dead light bulb. Her body was still raring to go, but her head was doing that "what if?" thing. Stupid brain. This didn't need to be all complicated. She owed Dean *nothing*. Absolutely nothing.

So why did it feel like she was planning to cheat on him?

Single lady? Got it? Get it? Good!

Dean didn't own her. No one owned her.

Wandering around her apartment, she froze beside the empty room and closed her eyes. Asher and Cedric had moved out. No big fuss, they'd just packed their things while she was gone and left a note. Or, well, Asher left a note. Cedric wouldn't. Over the last year, she'd imagined a connection, but it was gone like thin smoke in the wind. As make-believe as their entire relationship.

Asher wanted to keep in touch, but the bastard probably just wanted his job back. Dean could handle the position of GM and president as he had for years, but the team still needed a lawyer.

Tonight, none of that mattered. This wasn't about work; this was about getting off. Something she could probably do alone with one of many toys, but last weekend, and all her time with Dean, haunted her. Maybe she had some freaky needs. Some she'd never considered. Except once. But back then, she'd panicked. Tonight she wouldn't because Carter wasn't . . . *über*. He was just a man who got kink. Like she got kink. Who could give her kink.

Sounded good anyway.

She checked herself out one last time in the hall mirror. Strappy black fuck-me-shoes—*eat your heart out, Sloan; chew real good*—and a pink checkered dress with the sides cut out that fit like a glove. She was a cover model for Wet-Dreams-R-Us, and a man would have to be dead to resist her.

Carter wouldn't be able to. But she couldn't keep his face fixed in her head as she pictured a man stripping her of her expensive dress, pulling down her thong, bending her over . . .

Dean's face came first. Then Landon's.

Too much. Her brain needed to go on vacation. Time to let her libido take charge. For tonight, she was a wet pussy in high heels.

And nothing else.

Less than fifteen minutes later, she parked in front of the club, then sauntered out, all smiles for the invisible cameras. The bouncer recognized her and let her in without a second glance. She'd seen him flirting with the men behind the red-roped barrier, so she didn't take offense. *He* didn't need to notice her.

A strangled scream stopped her in her tracks.

Fuck. I hope Oriana's not here!

She surveyed the crowded room and found the screamer. Not her sister. Just a woman riding a contraption with a dildo sticking out of it while a man yanked on a chain attached to her nipples and a woman pressed a vibrating rod against her clit.

Silver's thighs clenched and her nipples twinged. She concentrated on the music, wild wailing guitars and a heart pumping drumbeat, and wandered deeper into the main room. The sounds around her became part of the music. She kept her gaze locked on the bar, avoided looking left or right, pretending this was just another bar and nothing scary was happening in the shadows.

"I've got a spot ready for us." A hot breath stirred her hair, and she jumped as though the air contained an electric charge. Carter chuckled. "Need a minute?"

She tilted her head back and smiled at him. "Not at all. Do you?"

"No." He took her hand and led her to an empty station at the back of the room. Nothing special, just an ottoman with chains. Occupied by two women and another man.

"Chicklet, I can't." The other man, who looked like a cherub with his golden curls, someone she thought she recognized but wasn't sure, knelt and pressed his forehead against a very tall woman's thighs. "I'm sorry; it's just too weird."

"It's okay, Tyler. But Laura needs a top. Can you handle her for tonight?" The big woman, Chicklet, petted the head of the cherub and drew the other woman to her feet. "She deserves a reward."

Tyler gazed up at Chicklet with nothing short of worship. "She'd rather get it from you. And so would I."

Laura's lips parted. Then snapped shut. She glanced over at Silver and her cheeks reddened.

"Eyes down, Laura." Chicklet smiled when the petite woman dropped her gaze to her bare toes, then brought her attention back to the young man on his knees. "I know you both enjoy spending time with me, but you need some bonding time, and I promised I'd help Carter out. I'm one of the few experienced Dommes, and the boss man has decided I know enough to train him."

"Tell Callahan to do it."

"Callahan is busy. And I always work with Carter. You know that."

"Yes, but with *her*?"

Chicklet frowned. "You're pushing it. I don't have to explain myself to you. You wanted to step it up. Have you changed your mind?"

"No!" Tyler shook his head and bowed down low, kissing his mistress's booted feet. "I'm sorry. I need . . . I don't know. But I haven't changed my mind."

"Then go." Chicklet pursed her lips as he shot to his feet and ambled away with Laura a step behind. Then she ran her hands over her leather-clad hips and faced Silver. "Sorry about that. I'm Chicklet. But you should call me Ma'am. Dean is big on protocol."

"Got it." Silver moved to shake the woman's hand but thought better of it and let her arms hang at her sides. "So what do I do?"

"You've asked Carter to top you, so I suggest you kneel and wait for him to take over." Chicklet arched a brow at Carter. "Any time now."

Carter ducked his head and grabbed some ropes from beside the ottoman. "Yeah. I figured we'd start with that corseted thing you taught me, but we haven't had a chance to negotiate."

"Then maybe you should." Chicklet stared Silver down until she recalled the *suggestion* and dropped to her knees. "Forget I'm here. Do you know the club safeword?"

"Red." Silver looked from Chicklet to Carter. This was so wrong. Not at all what she'd expected, but . . . maybe it would get better once they "negotiated". "I guess I need to tell you what I want?"

"Tell me what you need," Carter said, looking to Chicklet for approval.

Chicklet groaned. "This is starting off well."

Silver ignored her. "I . . . I don't understand how I reacted to being spanked. It hurt, but . . . I liked it. I want you to . . ."

"She wants you to hurt her." Chicklet smirked. "You're pretty good with a flogger. Wrap her up and have some fun."

"Fun?" Carter grinned as he unwound the rope. "Not a problem. But I need something first, pet."

Silver wanted to laugh. The whole scene seemed like one ridiculous parody. Like something she might do in one of her worst films. "What?"

Carter's expression changed. His eyes narrowed as he loomed over her. "Strip."

"Already?" She snapped her lips shut at his frown and rolled her eyes. Pushing him was no fun. Not that pushing Dean was *fun*, but something about him made her want to test her limits. With Carter, she felt like either she had to play along or they'd get nowhere. She stood gracefully and shed her clothes, much the same way she would before a photo shoot or a scene in a movie. It was part of the job. Might as well get it over with.

As he circled her, she did her best to stand up straight and hold in a weary sigh. They had a few gawkers, two naked men wearing harnesses and two Dommes standing behind them, leashes in hand.

From behind her, Carter moved close enough for the crease in his dress pants to brush her calves. He whispered, "What are your limits?"

"No blood. No sharp things. No anal." She blushed at the last. Why the hell had she said that? Anal wasn't a hard limit. And had she just given him permission to fuck her?

Why not? He's hot.

"You're fucking gorgeous, you know that?" He gently wound her hair around his hand and pulled her head back so he could kiss her. A nice, deep, kiss. Decent. Really. "I can't wait to see you in my ropes. Move exactly as I say and don't speak unless you're uncomfortable. Understand?"

She nodded and followed his instruction as the soft ropes slid across her body, white and bright blue, above her bare breasts, over her shoulders like bra straps, then around and around her waist with a complicated pattern over her ribs and all the way down to her stomach. Snug, but not in a bad way. His practiced movements, his soft touch, and the caress of the rope stirred her blood as the first hint of arousal heated her core. He pulled her arms behind her and bound her wrists in the trailing rope.

"That's lovely, Carter." Chicklet stared at her as though entranced by the rope work. "Better than what I showed you. Where'd you learn that?"

Carter pressed his lips to Silver's shoulder, then stepped in front of her to admire his work. "Callahan gave me some pointers."

Bile rose in Silver's throat. For fuck's sakes, was that man everywhere?

He's not ruining this.

"What should I do now?" She groaned at the snap in her words.

He doesn't need to. You're managing just fine.

"Kneel up in front of the ottoman." Carter helped her lower to her knees, then eased her face down onto the cool leather surface. "I'll start slow, warm up your flesh at bit before we start anything heavy. If it gets to be too much, just tell me. Yellow means slow down, but you might forget if you're into it."

Yeah, yeah. Can we get started? She pressed her forehead into the leather and muttered, "Yes. I understand."

The first pass of the flogger tickled. The next tickled more. She shut her eyes and tried to imagine reaching that space she'd reached with Dean. A place where her brain wasn't working so hard to convince her body to enjoy itself. But Dean never gave her a chance to think about much. His intensity swept her away with a glance.

Warming her up seemed to take forever. Finally she sat up and shook her head. "This isn't working. I'm not—I can't—"

"Shh . . . it's all right. I didn't want to move too fast, but we can try something else if you want?" Carter crouched down at her side and brushed her hair away from her eyes. "What would you like me to do?"

Fuck, hit me like you mean it! She studied his face. He would do anything she wanted. All she had to do was ask. "Can we try something?"

"Absolutely."

Speaking low enough so Chicklet wouldn't overhear, she told him. His eyes widened. He started to look at Chicklet, as though to asked permission. But then his jaw firmed and he nodded.

She rose up on her knees and braced herself.

* * * *

Dean did one last round of the club and returned to the far end of the bar, where he could observe Silver without her seeing him. The moment she arrived and let Carter lead her away, he'd wanted to grab her and throw her over his shoulder, make it clear to one and all she was *his*. But she'd made it clear she didn't want to be his. So all he could do was stand by and watch to make sure she didn't get hurt.

Carter was gentle, attentive, and way too young and inexperienced to put someone like Silver in the right headspace to enjoy what he was doing to her. They both went into the scene as though it was something any two people could just do, but the whole thing was painfully awkward. Silver rolled her eyes and sighed and Carter didn't react. The ropes seemed to help a little, but Carter might as well have been working with a volunteer from the crowd at a workshop.

"You going to stop them or should I?" His brother, Tim, freakishly observant as always, took a seat by his side and stole his beer. "She's already topping from the bottom. Carter is going to let her talk him into something stupid."

"I doubt that." Dean tried to laugh like it didn't matter, only, it did. Silver was going to ruin this for herself. "She's going to get bored, and he's going to give up. Chicklet looks like she's falling asleep."

But Chicklet woke with a start at the loud *Smack!*

The room passed him in a blur as he cut across the distance between him and Silver. He already felt Carter's throat under his hands, as it would be in seconds when he got to him.

Chicklet blocked him. Tim grabbed him from behind.

Silver noticed none of them. She blinked as the huge handprint on her cheek turned a bright red. And whispered, "Again."

"I can't." Carter tripped backward. "Fuck. Red. Fucking red. This isn't—I can't—"

"Why not?" Silver's eyes spit fire as she stood. "You asked me what I wanted and I told you! I guess it's wrong, right? Too fucked up for you?"

"Enough!" Dean shook with rage, but not at Carter. The poor, stupid kid was in way over his head. He focused on Silver. "He said red. That means it's over. Find someone else to play with."

Silver laughed. "Like you?"

His nostrils flared. "At the moment, I wouldn't touch you if you begged me. That kind of manipulation makes me sick. I suggest you get dressed and go home."

* * * *

Silver hung her head as Carter fumbled with his knots, his icy fingers making her shiver. The ropes didn't loosen, instead seemed to tighten, putting more pressure on her lungs, so much that she couldn't breathe. Only it wasn't the ropes constricting her airway. It was something else that weighed heavy on her chest.

Guilt? Her nostrils flared. No way. She hadn't done anything to feel guilty about. Negotiations between her and Carter had gone well; he'd just freaked out after his hand hit her cheek. The shock on his face told her he'd gone past his own limits without realizing it. She gave him a sidelong look. Brow furrowed, he concentrated on the tangled mess he'd made of the ropes around her wrists. He seemed all right. Except for his shaky hands. And the twitch at the right edge of his mouth.

"Carter, let me take care of her." Chicklet put her hand on Carter's shoulder. "Go for a walk."

"I'm fine," Carter said.

Chicklet's fingers dug into his shoulder. "No. You're not. Go. Walk. We'll talk when you come back."

Carter walked. Leaving Silver alone with Chicklet.

Meeting the Domme's steady gaze, Silver shrank a little. Tied up, exposed and shamed by the club owner, now at the mercy of Carter's mentor. Might be a good time for *her* to safeword out.

"Stop looking so scared. I'm not going to hurt you." Chicklet took a knee behind her and sighed. "Wow. You really fucked with that kid's head. These knots were perfect. I don't know what he did, but I'm not going to be able to untie this." She fetched a small black bag from the side of the ottoman and took out a pair of clippers. "Hold still; I'll have you out of that in a minute."

As the pieces of the rope fell away, a strange sensation came over her, like being on a roller coaster without restraints. Her pulse beat too fast. Air came in short little bursts, metal and leather, dark and thick and sweet.

Chicklet snapped her fingers in front of Silver's face. "Stay with me. I'm almost done."

Done. Then Silver would be free to leave. And she had to leave. She didn't belong here; they'd all made that perfectly clear.

After helping her to her feet, Chicklet shoved her dress at her. Grinning, she pointed toward the small hall to the bathrooms across the room. "Get dressed, then go splash some water on your face. This is going to take some grovelling, little girl."

Me? Grovel? Like hell! Silver pulled on her dress and panties, then tossed her hair to give it some life. "What are you talking about?"

"Carter had no business topping you, and you had no business asking him to. I shouldn't have let it go as on as long as it did, but I figured one of you would smarten up before it went too far." Chicklet shrugged. "My bad."

"Why shouldn't he have topped me?"

"Because you have a top already, and it wasn't fair to use Carter to hide from him. You're lucky Dean didn't get to him. If that kid had gotten hurt, I'd have dragged you into the alley and shown you what a rabid bitch I can be." Smiling pleasantly, Chicklet lowered herself to one of the leather chairs and rested one ankle on her knee. "Hopefully that won't ever be necessary. I like your sister, and you must be all right if Dean likes you. Not convinced, but you'll work on that, right?"

"I still don't get it. Why is what I asked for so wrong?" Lips pursed, she searched the room. At the spanking throne, she saw what she was looking for. A man grabbed his lover's jaw, said something to her, then hauled back and slapped her at least twice as hard as Carter had hit Silver. "Why is it okay for them?"

Chicklet snorted. "They've been married for ten years."

"So you can't have fun here unless you're married?"

"No, but face slapping is a bit extreme for a first scene with someone. There was no telling how either of you would react, but you're good at using your looks to get your own way. Which of course reflected badly on Carter, not you." Chicklet sucked her teeth. "But whatever. It happened. And hit a trigger for *him*. And you didn't care enough to notice. To make it worse, you asked for more. Hope it was worth it."

Silver winced. Okay, put that way, maybe it hadn't been her finest moment. Some could even call it selfish. Reckless.

Heartless.

"Should I go talk to Carter? Apologize?"

"No. You're either going to make things right with Dean, or you're going to call yourself a cab and go home." Chicklet pulled something out of the small pocket on her vest. Her namesake. She popped a piece of gum in her mouth and chewed hard. "If Carter sees you with Dean, he'll get it. He won't feel like a failure. I'll find him an experienced sub to play with, and things will be peachy keen."

Lovely. Silver sought Dean out in the crowded bar. There, showing a young woman how to hold a whip. He moved on to scrutinize a—Silver almost bit through her tongue—wax play scene. The colorful spill over the woman's breasts, the lick of fire on the wick, held so close, hardened her own nipples as though they shared the sensation. And enjoyed it.

Dean bent down, whispering something to the woman that made her smile.

Silver's eyes slitted. She put her hands on her hips and spun around to face Chicklet. "Dean told me to leave."

"No." Chicklet smirked over the fist where she'd propped her chin. "He suggested it. You choosing now to be obedient, missy?"

"Maybe . . ."

"Coward."

"Fuck you."

Chicklet arched a brow. "I could flog you for that. And I promise you wouldn't enjoy it. Might want to run along before I decide *I* would."

Yikes! Silver didn't even try to fake not being afraid of the woman. Her attitude wasn't holding up, and she couldn't very well charm the woman into liking her, not after the whole thing with Carter. A punishment from her would be straight-up, no-nonsense, without anything sexual to dampen the pain.

At least moving fast kept her from seeing any more scenes. She knew Landon was here, and if she saw him now, she'd forget about putting space between them and walk straight into his arms. He would get what she'd been trying to do. He'd warn her to be careful, but then he'd hold her and make everything better. She wouldn't feel stupid, or alone, or . . .

So why are you even considering going to Dean? Chicklet was right! You'll have to kneel and beg his forgiveness. But with Landon—she cut off that thought. One slip with Landon and they wouldn't be friends anymore. They'd be lovers. Then they'd be nothing.

In the bathroom, she splashed water on her face, not worried about ruining her makeup since everything was waterproof. Two women chatted in the stalls, nothing but white noise at first. Until she heard one mention Landon's name.

"He's new, and oh my God!" The woman sounded like Minnie Mouse on crack. "My husband arranged to do a scene with him!"

"I saw him, you lucky bitch." The second woman squealed. "Do you mind if I watch?"

"Not at all. He says he doesn't do 'penetration' when he's doing scenes with couples, but my husband will make him a deal. He might be old, but he gets me *everything* I want. And that stud is mine!"

"I'm so jealous!"

"Don't be. Maybe I can slip you in somehow."

"You are a true friend!"

Both women laughed. The doors unlocked.

Silver slipped out before they spotted her. In the hall, she gouged her palms with her nails and counted down to calm her breathing. She hated the idea of those women using Landon like a piece of meat, like their own personal toy. But what could she do? It was none of her business who he fucked.

Which didn't mean she couldn't look out for him. She slipped into the main room and circled toward the bar, keeping her eye out for Landon. Unable to find him, she watched the hall, and when two women emerged, nonchalantly followed them to a roped-off area in the darkest part of the club, some distance away from the dance floor. All it contained was long, red padded table with restrains hanging from the top and bottom.

There he was, speaking to an older man as he opened a metal box. As the women, both naked, approached, he straightened. They dropped to their knees before him within the rope barrier. Landon's expression darkened, and one of the women scrambled to her feet and ducked under the rope.

That *look*. Silver swallowed and hugged herself. Oh yeah, he was definitely a Dom. Even concealed behind the curious onlookers gathering on this side of the ropes, she could feel his . . . presence. The only thing that she could compare it to was when she'd gone camping with her parents and her siblings—she couldn't have been more than six—and Daddy had spotted a wolf close to their tent. Her brother and Oriana went out to get a better look, but Silver had stayed in the tent, simply peeking out, afraid to get too close, but needing to see it. She knew she was safe; the wolf paused for a second before disappearing into the woods, but she'd been aware of it on a primal level.

As Silver watched, the woman laid herself out on the table and let her husband and Landon strap her down. Landon petted her bare stomach, whispering as he held up something with a thick black handle and a thin glass tube. He manipulated the handle and the tube glowed with an iridescent purple light. Then he traced a circle over the area where his hand had passed.

In a trance, Silver inched closer until she could see the tiny white sparks hitting the woman's flesh and hear the faint crackling of electricity. The woman made sharp little cries as Landon drew the tip of the glass up to her breasts, lifting it a little above one nipple so the tiny white bolts snapped at it. He continued to tease her with the thin tube, paused, then went to his box for a large glass orb. The people around her *ohhed* and *ahhed* over the beautiful blue color of this one.

All Silver saw was the glistening between the woman's thighs as she jutted her hips up and grunted. Landon was using the orb along the woman's inner thighs, and she moved like she was getting fucked.

"Oh, please! Please!" The woman slammed her head on the table. "I want you!"

"Hush. Don't fight it." Landon held the orb over her cunt. "You're close. Come for me. I want to see you lose control."

The woman looked like she might, but instead her eyes opened wide and she glared at her husband. "Earl!"

The old man pulled out his wallet. "How much will it cost? It shouldn't take you more than two minutes. Like you said, she's close."

"We discussed this earlier. I don't charge, and I don't fuck those I demonstrate for."

Around her, the crowd began mumbling. She wasn't sure what they were saying. She was waiting for the man to back down. Or for Landon to stop.

But his focus was on that cunt. Who was completely ignoring him.

A light throb began in the base of Silver's skull, gaining strength and wrapping around her throat until she couldn't breathe.

Let Landon handle it.

"You told your husband you needed this. He doesn't know how to give it to you, but I can teach him." Landon waved the old man closer. "See the way her muscles clench. If you trigger the right pressure points, you force her to open and close in a way that simulates sex. It's even more intense with the TENS."

"Earl!"

The old man shook his head and shoved a handful of money at Landon. "Take it!"

"Oh!" The woman opened her mouth wide and screamed. "Oh, fuck me! Fuck me!"

"He said no!"

Silver didn't know how she'd gotten past the ropes, or why her hand was wrapped around Landon's wrist. All she knew was when she looked up, she really wished she'd stayed put.

Landon switched off the wand. "Kneel."

She dropped to her knees before her mind could respond. Head bowed, she listened to Landon as he put his tools away.

As he spoke to the couple. "I'm sorry the scene was interrupted, but I was about to end it anyway. My terms are not negotiable. You should find what you're looking for elsewhere."

The woman cried and the old man grumbled, but they both got out of there pretty fast. Now Silver could hear the muttering from the crowd. They didn't like how Landon had been disrespected either. Several soft voices seemed to commend her interference, but harsher, stronger ones spoke over them. According to them, she'd had no right to get involved.

Not that she didn't know that already.

"Stand up."

At Landon's command, she scrambled awkwardly to her feet, teetering on her heels. He would scold her, that was for sure. But she didn't expect what came next.

"You never interrupt a scene in this club. Never." He curved his hand under her chin, and her eyes went wide at what she saw there. This wasn't her sweet friend Landon. His stare was unforgiving and cold. "I don't appreciate you forcing me to punish you. But I will."

Punish me? No! Not you! Her eyes teared and she shook her head. "Landon, please. Let someone else do it!"

"You interrupted *my* scene. You apparently didn't think I could manage it on my own." He pressed his eyes shut and shook his head. "I think I've earned your respect."

"You have!" *Fuckfuckfuck.* How had she made such a mess of *everything* tonight? "But—if you—we can't—"

"Punishment doesn't equal sex, pet." Landon's eyes opened, stormy and distant. "I won't fuck you."

Her legs almost folded as he repeated Dean's words. And that *endearment.* She didn't—she'd *never*—wanted Landon to fuck her. She wanted to keep what they'd had. It was precious and this would ruin it.

"You can't stay here if you won't accept your punishment." Landon stepped back, leaving her to hold herself up. "Decide now."

Can't stay and what else? Would they ever get back to that place, where they could talk and laugh and just hang out, if she refused? This was part of him. A part she had to accept. And the punishment couldn't possibly be as bad as the sheer disappointment in his eyes.

"I'll take it." She held her breath, but he didn't say anything, simply stood there, looking down at her, making her feel so small and helpless. Her words came out in a rush. "Do it. Do it before Dean finds out."

Are you fucking brain-dead? She wanted to take it back, but it was too late.

Landon reared up to his full height and laughed. "Why? Do you think he could punish you worse than I will?" His hands snaked out and he latched onto a handful of her hair, dragging her against him as his lips curved into a vicious smile. "When I'm done, you're going to wish it was him dealing with you. Bend over and hold on to your ankles. Ten is standard."

When he released her, she bent automatically into the position he demanded. Humiliating, but a spanking and it would be over. Later they could talk, after he held her, all wrapped up in a blanket, and became her friend again.

He must have sensed something, in her posture, or in her shallow submission, because he growled. "And I won't be using my hand."

Her legs quivered as he folded the bottom of her dress up over her ass. He didn't touch her G-string. From behind the shield of her hair, she watched his boots move away. Return. Part to shoulder width.

"Count."

At the first slice, she almost choked on her tongue. Fire cut a straight line across her upper thighs. Long and thin, whatever he'd used rested against her. Disappeared.

Trembling, she whispered, "One."

Snap! Snap!

Raw, searing pain. Her lips parted. The words lodged in her throat.

Snap!

"Two, three, and four. Say it, pet."

"Please, please—" Hot tears spilled down her cheeks. "I can't—it hurts!"

"Say it."

"Twothreefour!"

Snap!

Agony ignited and all the lashes seemed to come together and split open. She sobbed and dropped to her knees. "Landon—"

"Take a minute to compose yourself." Landon came around to stand in front of her. "Then you may lean on the table to make it easier."

Begging, crying, none of it reached him, so she just sat there until the burning eased into a dull throb. His gaze didn't shift from her face as she swiped away her tears and dragged herself up on the table. Part of her wanted to scream at him, to tell him it wasn't fair—and yet another part steeled within, determined to show him she could do this.

To show him she could take whatever he dished out.

Come on, buddy. Show me what you've got.

Her nails scratched grooves into the table padding. She threw her head back and inhaled deeply.

"Five. Which means there's five left." She smirked when his stony expression faltered. "What are you waiting for, *Sir?*"

His lips drew into a thin line. "Careful, Silver."

"Ah, yes. Manners." She rolled her eyes. "Pretty please, *Sir.* Get it over with."

He shook his head. "This means nothing to you, does it? You have no idea why what you did was wrong, and you couldn't care less."

"That's not true. I know I pissed you off."

"Pissed me off? No. What you did was dangerous. Yes, I'm disappointed that you disrespected me, but your utter disregard for the rules is so much worse." He laid a long, thin black cane with a silver handle on the table in front of her. "The pain you're in is *nothing* compared to what could have happened to that woman if I'd made the wrong move when you barged in. She could be in the hospital with serious burns and I could be in jail, facing charges. But all you can think about is that I might be mad at you."

Selfish. You're spoiled and selfish. Not spoken out loud, but she imagined him saying it, like everyone else did. And that hurt much worse than her abused ass.

"Maybe you're right." He turned away from her. "Maybe

someone else should do this."

She grabbed his wrist, then released it. Doing that *again* wouldn't help matters. Her wet lashes clung together as she blinked.

He waited, silently, for her to speak.

At a loss, she picked up the cane and held it out to him. "I'm sorry. Don't give up on me. Please?"

"I should add another five for the attitude."

For some reason, she got the impression he wanted this over with as much, if not more than she did. Not that it showed. He was a Dom and she deserved to be punished.

And she finally agreed.

Fuck, doing the right thing is going to hurt.

"Another five, Sir. Please. Should I start at one?"

"Yes."

Snap!

This time, she absorbed the pain and let it blank out everything else. At least she could do this with some dignity. "One."

After three more, dignity took a hike.

* * * *

Dean's nostrils flared as he escorted the couple out of his bar. His fists clenched and unclenched as her pitiful screams rose above the music and the equally loud cries of ecstasy coming from every other station.

Chicklet patted his shoulder and tugged him toward the bar. "I think you need a drink."

He shook his head but didn't resist. "I don't need a drink. I need to know what the fuck happened."

"I've already told you. And so has everyone else."

A wretched sob almost undid him. He groaned and slumped onto a stool. "She shouldn't be here."

"No, she shouldn't be here alone. Not when she already has a Dom willing to teach her." Chicklet smacked the bar to get the bartender's attention. "You are willing to teach her, aren't you?"

"Of course I am. But she didn't want me to."

"Ah, I see. So most subs get what they need, but Miss Silver

Delgado gets what she wants. Got it."

"What if I'm wrong?" He didn't want a beer, but he accepted the one the bartender brought just to have something to do with his hands. "What if she's not a sub?"

Chicklet shrugged and jerked her chin toward the back of the room. "She handed him the cane. You tell me."

His eyes widened and he spun around on his stool. Even from here, he could see the bright red welts on Silver's delicate flesh. His first instinct was to cross the room and beat the shit out of Bower for hurting her, even though he had every right to. He rose and let his Dom side take over as he approached them, keeping in mind what Chicklet had said. He observed her stance, the way she cringed every time the cane came down, but never shifted or tried to escape it.

Bower could have restrained her for the punishment, but he'd left her to accept it or not on her own.

And she was accepting it.

After the last strike, Silver bowed over the table and sobbed. Bower lifted a hand over her, almost touching her . . .

Then stepped back. His head snapped up and he looked right at Dean.

Shit. No goddamn warning, the man just expected him to take over. As if Silver was Dean's sub. Dean's responsibility.

No fucking problem. I've got her.

Long strides brought him to Silver's side. He scooped her into his arms seconds before her legs gave out. Glaring at Bower, he covered Silver's ear with one hand and spoke low. "If you weren't willing to finish this, you shouldn't have touched her."

"It wouldn't have been necessary if you hadn't let her wander around on her own." Bower hefted a large bag on the table and began packing his equipment. "You might want to invest in a collar and leash."

If Dean's arms hadn't been full with Silver's trembling body, he would have crushed the younger man's face in with his fist. "I read you wrong, boy. I thought you were her friend."

Bower went still. "If I wasn't her friend, I'd have her bent over the table with my dick in her cunt. She wouldn't fight me now, would she?"

No. Right now, Silver wouldn't fight anyone. The pain had gone beyond what her body could easily process. Not that it made Bower handing her off okay, but Dean felt sick just thinking about what could have happened to her if she'd crossed the wrong Dom.

He gave Bower a curt nod and turned away. "Next time, bring her to me."

"Next time?" Bower laughed. "If there's ever a next time, you don't deserve her."

Dean didn't reply. Hell, he wanted to kill the man, but he agreed with him. Carrying Silver to a loveseat angled off the bar, he spoke softly as she stirred, glancing up just once to thank Chicklet for the blanket she laid over them both.

The second Chicklet moved out of hearing, Silver let out a broken sob. "I really fucked up."

"Silver, look at me." He locked one arm at the small of her back and curved his hand around the back of her head. "You were punished. It's over. Clean slate."

A little hiccup escaped her and the hope in her glistening eyes broke his heart. "Clean slate? Really?"

"Yes, baby." He kissed her forehead. "But you're going to be sore for a while. Let me take care of you. I know a way to make it bearable."

Burrowing her wet face into his shoulder, she nodded.

"Up with you." He stood and smiled as she wrapped her arms around his neck. "Have you had enough of the club for tonight? I'd like to take you upstairs."

"Upstairs is good." She wiggled a little and hissed in pain. "Soft bed. No more pain."

"No more pain." He gave her a little squeeze and lowered his face to her mussed up hair. "I'm proud of you though."

"Proud of me? But . . . I was bad."

His lips found her ear. He whispered, "You weren't bad. You made a mistake."

"I'm always bad. I don't want to be. Didn't want to be. Not this time."

"I know." He looked around, found his brother. Tim nodded,

letting him know he'd watch the club. Leaving Dean with no worries besides the contrite little bundle in his arms. "That's why I'm proud. You didn't run away. You faced what you did and accepted the consequences."

"He's still mad at me." Her tears soaked through his shirt and dampened his flesh. "I didn't make things better."

Carrying her up the stairs, he whispered all the right platitudes, telling her she'd done well, that she was a good girl, strong and brave, repeating again and again that he was proud of her.

But she hadn't taken the cane to please him. She'd taken it for Bower, and he wasn't here to say what she needed to hear.

Which meant he had to find a way to show her Bower's opinion didn't matter.

Laying her down on his bed, he tucked her under the blankets and stretched out beside her. With her nestled against his side, he spoke quietly, feeling her body relax as she absorbed his words. "What he thinks, how he feels, doesn't matter anymore. You've proved yourself to me and to anyone else watching. They all saw how strong you were."

"I don't care what *they* think." She chewed at her bottom lip and gazed up at him. "I'm . . . I'm surprised you're not mad at me too. I broke *your* rules."

"You paid for it. You more than paid for it. I deserve twice the beating you got for letting you come to the club all alone. I should never have left you alone. It won't happen again."

"Promise?"

Tomorrow, she wouldn't be asking him that. Tomorrow she'd likely curse him and Bower and every Dom in existence while wishing them a slow, bloody death in a pit full of broken glass. She'd be cold with Bower and likely stiff and professional with Dean.

If he let her.

Which he wouldn't.

"I promise." She was already asleep when he answered, but it didn't matter. Granted, tomorrow things would change. But not this.

Because tomorrow, he would still be the man who could keep that promise. And she would still be the woman who needed it.

* * * *

Everything changed as closing approached. Landon hunched over the bar, tipped back a vodka shot, then chased it with a few gulps of beer. Around him cracking whips and piercing screams became flesh slapping flesh and low moans. The lights dimmed, a subtle hint to wrap things up.

He should leave. There was no reason to stay. And he wanted this fucked-up night to end. But he had nowhere else he needed to be.

"Don't give up on me. Please."

He rolled his head from side to side, cracked his neck, and gestured for the bartender to refill his glass. The man didn't hit on him this time. Smart guy.

"If you weren't willing to finish this, you shouldn't have touched her."

He used his fingertips to massage his temples.

I shouldn't have touched her.

She hadn't given him a choice.

Before the willowy, submissive bartender—who'd likely leave the bottle if Landon asked—could pour, a tall woman slipped up behind him and said a few sharp words under her breath. The man bowed to her and scrambled out from behind the bar with a rag and a spray bottle.

"Hey, I'm Chicklet." She leaned across the bar and gave him a toothy smile. "And I know you're new here, so I won't make an issue of it, but there's a rule about getting shitfaced and driving home. Do it once and don't bother coming back. Want to throw me your keys?"

"I walked."

"Good man." She laughed and took out another shot glass, filling them both. "Guess you're smarter than you look."

One brow raised, Landon stared at her. "What's that supposed to mean?"

"Well . . ." Chicklet let out an appreciative sigh as she tossed back her shot. "You've been over here for a while, trying to erase the night with some eighty proof. And I've been over there trying to figure out why. Figured I might as well ask, but let me tell you, if you're beating yourself up over punishing that little girl, I'm going to knock you off that stool and make you look like you tried to stop a puck with your face."

Woman looks like she could do it too. He almost smiled as he shook his head. "No. It needed to be done."

"So what's the problem?"

He clenched his jaw and held up his shot glass in a mock salute. "Tell you as soon as I figure it out."

Liquid fire and a split second of numbness. Not nearly enough. Eyes closed, he let the buzzing in his head drown out the sound of Silver's sobs. The sight of her sweet submission as she handed him the cane . . .

Sacrament! It had taken every shred of discipline he had to keep going. To carry out the punishment. To step back when her defenses were down and she might have let him in. If Richter hadn't shown up when he did, she'd be in Landon's arms now, and this time he couldn't have pretended he didn't want more.

Chicklet snorted. "It's like that, is it?"

Definitely a Domme. And a bartender. Kill me now. "Like what?"

"Well, you're either friends with her or you're friends with him. And you've got it bad." Chicklet sloshed more vodka into both their glasses. "Noble and just a little stupid. I think I'm going to like you."

Landon's lips quirked. "Thanks, I guess. But you're wrong."

"I'm never wrong." She took his empty glass and washed it in the sink behind the bar. "Not about stuff like this. That girl flipped things on my baby Dom, but I can't see her pulling that with you. She didn't make you do anything you didn't want to."

"Like hell, she didn't!" He stood, rage searing from his scalp to his fingertips. "She forced me to punish her! He should have been watching her!"

"Yeah. *He* should have." Chicklet cocked her head. "But you're her 'friend' right. Why weren't *you* watching her?"

"It's not my place."

"So what's your place?"

He snatched up his bag and turned his back on the bar and the nosy Domme. "We're just friends."

"Uh huh. Well, just one problem with that."

He stopped and his spine went stiff. "Which is?"

"I can't remember the last time I beat a friend's ass."

Chapter Nineteen

Stinging pain woke Silver. Sharp, shocking, and abrupt like her first Brazilian wax, only this didn't fade. Light pressure, slickly coating her bottom with some kind of cream, lessened it. *So nice.*

She groaned and pressed her face into her pillow. Asher didn't usually wake her up for sex—jumping her in the heat of the moment was more his style, but she wasn't about to complain. As long as he took it easy on her ass because . . .

Because Landon had hit her with a cane. Fifteen times. At the club. She was still at the club.

And that *wasn't* Asher.

Rolling and scooting up, she came face-to-face with Dean.

"Sorry to wake you, sweetheart." His hooded eyes held a hint of amusement. "You snored right through the last coat; I figured you'd sleep through this one too."

Still at the club and in *his* bed. After the night she'd had, how the hell had she fallen asleep at all? He had to be lying. "I zoned out for a bit, that's all. And I don't snore."

"You're not loud. It's adorable actually, like sleeping next to a noisy kitten." Dean patted the bed beside him. "Now come here. I'm not finished."

Noisy kitten? Bite me! She pursed her lips. "What if I don't want to?"

Dean sat up and squared his shoulders. "Then I won't press the matter. It would be silly of you—this cream speeds up healing considerably—but you haven't agreed to be my sub yet—"

Wait. What? "'Yet?' As in I will?"

"As in, we will discuss it."

"Oh no, we won't." She pushed up with one hand. "With what happened last night—"

He pressed on her shoulder and forced her back down. "We *will* discuss it, Silver. After."

She didn't bother asking "After what?" She knew. But really,

217

why not discuss it now? Shouldn't take too long. "It's not happening. I've made my decision already. I don't want to be anyone's sub."

At first, he didn't comment. He held up the little glass jar. When she sighed and rolled over, he resumed spreading the clear creamy stuff over her sore bottom. His soft touch was almost as soothing as the cream itself.

Then he spoke, his tone rough and low. "It's actually not that bad. He didn't hold back much, but he didn't break the skin. The deeper bruises will be an unpleasant reminder for a few days—you might want a pillow for your office chair."

Tears sheened her vision. She hid them in the pillow. *Landon* hadn't held back, and she hadn't wanted him to. But it hadn't made a difference.

Screw him. If being a Dom is more important than being my friend, I don't need him.

Her throat locked and she let out a little cough. No better. Losing Landon hurt worse than every lash of the cane combined. It would be hard not to have him in her life.

You'll get over it.

"What is it, Silver? No, stop hiding your face." Dean's hand curved around her shoulder and he pulled until she lifted up enough to look at him. "Tell me what you're thinking."

Her chin quivered. She glared at the center of his chest.

Dean let out a slow exhale through his teeth. "Fine. How about this—tell me why you went to the club last night."

No harm in that. She shrugged and toyed with a loose thread on the black comforter. "I was curious. I figured maybe I just liked a bit of pain, and if I could get a man like Carter, a man who wasn't—"

His expression softened into a grin. "An 'über Dom'?"

"Yeah." She tugged at her bottom lip with her teeth. "If he could get me off with just a bit of pain, without all the other stuff, then that would explain why sex is better with you."

Most men would have gotten all puffed up and smirky. But Dean's brow furrowed as he came down to her level, his head braced on his hand. "So you went through all that because you didn't want to be with me?"

"No! It was to prove to myself that I didn't *need* to be with you.

Or someone like you." She shook her head, absolutely positive he wouldn't get it. "I've been on my own for years, doing whatever I wanted, not answering to anyone. I enjoy my independence. I don't want to give it up."

"Who says you have to?" He reached out and brushed her hair off her cheek. His hand hovered there for a while, then rested lightly on the curve of her jaw. His thumb smoothed over her bottom lip. "What if all you need to give up is a bit of control in moments like this. I already see you pulling back because you're afraid to let me get too close. What if you need me to stop letting you?"

What if . . . ? No. This wasn't him just asking to be her Dom. He wanted more. She drew back. "I can't—"

"But I can." He raked his fingers into her hair. "Don't. Move."

Pure liquid heat spilled. She panted. This was exactly the reaction she was afraid of.

He moved before she could react to her fear, grasping her wrists in one hand and drawing them high above her head. Fur-lined cuffs snapped around them. "I'm going to take you now, love, and you will let me. While I have you, your focus will be on feeling everything I'm doing to you." His fingers slid from her wrist, down her arms, slowly, so slowly, awakening every nerve with his soft touch. "You will demand nothing." He pushed the blanket away from her naked body. "And you will hold nothing back."

No, no, no! She couldn't do what he asked. This wasn't about sex. Sex she could do. Hot rough sex with no strings attached. This, with him, wouldn't have strings. No, it would have goddamn shackles.

He cut off her intended protest with a hand on her throat and his mouth over hers. The light pressure didn't cut of her air, but she gasped in the hot exhale from his lips and lost the will to fight. His tongue dipped in and she moaned as it teased a tender spot at the top of her mouth. He thrust deep, withdrew, and bit her bottom lip just hard enough to make her squirm. Tiny pain, the kind her body easily accepted as pleasure because it felt so fucking good.

"There we go." He smiled against her lips and kissed her again. "Are you still afraid?"

Yes. And no. Neither answer made any sense, so she simply gazed up at him, into his beautiful hazel eyes, at his tussled hair, at the tiny lines around his strong mouth. Everything about him was . . . familiar. Solid.

Safe.

Then she knew. Not in any way she could explain, but she arched up to kiss him and whispered, "No. I'm not afraid."

"That's my good, brave girl." He slid his lips along her throat, nibbling and sucking as his hand stroked her side, closer and closer to her breast, but never touching it. His free hand delved into her hair and he used it to arch her neck, leaving her vulnerable to his teeth as he explored a trigger along the corded muscle and bit down hard.

Her spine bowed and she whimpered. Her nipples ached with the need to be touched. Moisture slicked her pussy, so unbearably hot that she clenched her thighs for some shallow relief.

"Please . . ." She tossed her head from side to side as he licked and nipped the sharp angles of her collar bone. And moved lower at a languorous pace that was going to kill her. "Please just f—"

His fingers left her hair and covered her lips. "Shh."

He stroked down the center of her chest. Trailed the path with soft kisses. His stubble scraped the sides of her breasts.

Need grew into a desperate, living thing. Since he wouldn't touch her breasts or her pussy, they absorbed every sensation. The muscles of her stomach twitched under his lips and her cunt clenched. His tongue traced a circle around her belly button and lower . . . lower . . .

"It's easy to let a man fuck you, love. And I could have, several times this week. God knows I wanted to." His lips whispered over her flesh, and goose bumps spread as the impact of his words hit her. Wanted to, but hadn't? *Why?* He answered as though he'd read her mind. "But you weren't ready to give me what I need. You are now. And it was worth the wait, dragonfly."

Oh . . . oh! Her hips jutted up as he lapped over her smooth mound and slipped the tip of his tongue into the crease. Her mind scrambled for control and she rasped out, "Dragonfly? Why dragonfly?"

"The legends of the dragonfly mostly revolve around illusions, hovering over something deeper." His tongue dipped in again.

"Something more. I believe that fits you perfectly."

Absorbing his words through the erotic haze spreading over her was a challenge, but part of her managed. His little ways of making her feel special overwhelmed her need to keep fighting. This man knew her, heart and soul. She moved to spread her thighs to let him in, but he held them shut between his shoulder and his hand.

"Not yet, love." His tongue pressed in, almost reaching her clit before withdrawing. His mouth opened wide and he kissed her pussy lips like he'd kissed her mouth. His groan sent vibrations over her sensitized little nub, and he held her down as her hips bucked. "Sweet. So fucking sweet."

She closed her eyes and pressed her head back into the pillow as he released her. Her hands clawed at the sheets above her head, wanting to be free to tangle in his hair. He shifted until he was kneeling at the bottom of the bed. Curved his hands under her knees. And lowered as he drew them apart.

Mouth and tongue and teeth covered her a second before she came. She screamed as pleasure tore through her, violent, merciless, slamming into her all over again before she could catch her breath. His tongue filled her, dragging out several more spasms, leaving her completely drained.

Not the first time he'd used his mouth on her cunt or made her come. Not the first time he'd tied her up and taken control. But for some reason, this was very, very different. Which scared her to death. For the first time, she didn't even *consider* demanding he fuck her.

But she did have one last request.

* * * *

"Let me hold you. Please, just . . . just for a minute . . . ?"

Dean smiled and climbed up to the top of the bed to release her wrists. The restraints were good for getting past all her walls, but in time, he hoped to teach her what else they were good for. Not now, though. Now she needed something more than dominance and submission. More than pleasure.

She needed to know he wasn't going anywhere.

He lay still as she wrapped her arms around his neck and settled her head on his shoulder. His dick throbbed painfully, a result of denying himself any release all week, but he ignored it. The feeling of her warm breath on his skin, her messy hair tickling his neck and his cheek, of all her soft curves relaxed against him—hell, he'd ride out the pain for this.

A little shift and a deep sigh told him she'd likely fallen asleep again. His lips curved and he brought his head up to kiss her hair.

Her wide-open eyes stared up at him. "I'm afraid."

His brow furrowed and his stomach muscles clenched as he moved to sit up, but she pressed both hands down on his chest.

"Listen, because I'll probably tell you I hate you again tomorrow. You're good at pissing me off." She let out a hollow laugh and shook her head. "But I'm afraid, really afraid because I have *never* let myself feel this way about anyone. I usually make a run for it when a man looks at me the way you are right now. But you won't let me run away, will you?"

"No." He slipped his hand alongside her throat, digging his fingers into the nape of her neck as he drew her down to taste her lips. "I won't."

Her eyes fluttered shut. "Good. Because I can't promise I won't try."

"Try all you want." He raked his fingers through her hair, then wound it around his fist. "You won't get far."

"Mmm." She brought her lips down to his chin and nipped at his jaw with her tiny teeth. "So, if I agree to be your sub, does that mean I have to do whatever you say in the bedroom? I can't get . . ." Her fingernails lightly scratched his chest, and she sucked his earlobe between her lips. "Creative?"

He groaned, loosening his grip on her hair as her knee bent over his thigh and she pressed her wet pussy against him. "I won't object to creativity."

"Good." She crawled backward, dragging her nails over his abdomen, and gave him an impish grin as she gave the head of his cock a chaste kiss. "Because I feel like I've been very selfish. May I make it up to you by sucking your dick, Master?"

Cheeky little brat. He laced his fingers behind his head. "You may.

But next time—ah, fuck!"

His dick twitched as her hot lips covered it in one smooth motion. He ground his teeth and watched her take him in all the way and hold him there. The pressure from her throat almost set him off and his balls tightened.

"Yes! Ah!" He grunted as she lifted, swirling her tongue around and around before dropping again. The way her eyes rolled back as she savored him told him she enjoyed this almost as much as he did. He tried to distract himself by imagining scenes where he could use this to his advantage. A hard suck tore him from his thoughts of her kneeling, bound while he fucked her face. If he let this go on, he wouldn't last.

He needed to take control. Of her and himself.

"Slowly, Silver." He leaned up on one elbow and put his hand on the back of her head, holding her down when she took him in all the way. "Just like that. Fucking beautiful."

She didn't try to fight him, simply swallowed and moved up at a torturously slow pace when he let her. Her tongue flicked the tip of his dick, and she gazed up at him expectantly.

"Again, and use your teeth—gently, on the way down. There's my good girl."

Guiding her pace brought his pleasure to a tolerable level, and if her wiggling hips were anything to go by, ramped hers up. He thrust up once, surprising her, and held his breath against the urge to come.

"Enough now." He grinned when she automatically sat up and pouted at him. Time to rein her in a bit. "Is that pretty pussy still wet, baby?"

A blush spread over her cheeks as she nodded.

"I won't fuck you."

She scowled. "What the fuck is wrong with you?"

He arched a brow.

"Sorry, Sir." She rolled her eyes. "Why won't you fuck me?"

"Keep that up and I won't touch you again." He frowned until she lowered her eyes. "Now, go get a condom from your purse."

The confused look she gave him before scrambling off the bed made him smile. Silver wasn't spoiled, not really, but she was pampered and accustomed to instant gratification. Denying her that would keep her off balance. And likely keep things interesting.

She returned and perched on the edge of the bed, fidgeting with the small square package. Her rumpled hair covered her face, but he took note of the way she bit down on her swollen bottom lip, like she wanted to speak and was trying very hard not to.

"What is it, Silver?"

Her head shot up and her throat worked as she swallowed. "Why do we need this if you won't . . ."

"We will go together to get tested soon, but until then, I think it's a good idea to use protection when I'm inside you. Are you on birth control?"

Her lips parted in a wide O, then snapped shut. She nodded.

"Was there something else?"

"You will be inside me?" She cringed as though she'd said something stupid. "I mean, I thought you didn't want to . . ."

"I don't want to fuck you, sweetheart." He lifted his hand to cup her cheek. "You've been fucked enough. Not to say I won't take you hard, but I won't just be using your body or letting you use mine."

Her whole body shook. The concept seemed to frighten her. But all she said was "Oh."

"Cover me and come here." He let his hand drift down to her shoulder as she tore the package and rolled the condom over his dick. As soon as she stretched out on the bed, he pulled her against him so she lay on her side, in his arms, with no pressure on her poor bruised butt and no way to escape. His hands on her shoulders with his forearms braced against the length of her back caged her well, and by her rapid little pants, she knew it.

"Dean . . ." Her hands flattened on his chest as though she'd push him. Tears clung to her lashes. "Just do it. Just—"

"Running already, pet?" He bowed to kiss her eyes, her cheeks, her lips, spreading the salty moisture. "Open for me. Take me inside you. Carefully. The cream may have numbed you for a bit, but it won't last."

She gasped in a shaky breath and nodded. Her knee rose over his hip as she slid her hand down and took him in her fist. She shifted and brought him to her opening. Her eyes met his as she moved her hand and let him slide into her.

"There we go." His words came out husky as he filled her to the hilt. So fucking slick and hot. Consuming him. He groaned as her quivering body pressed closer, testing his endurance. Her feverish lips glided along his throat, right over his hammering pulse. He buried his face into her hair and inhaled the subtle fragrance of honey melon. He didn't speak again until he had himself in hand. "Now move with me, little one."

For the first time since he'd known her, Silver's movements were hesitant. Unsure. She tipped her hips toward his, accepting him, but froze before he could drag himself out. This was unfamiliar to her and she didn't seem to know what to do.

Transferring one hand to the opposite shoulder so his arm crossed her back, he dropped the other to her knee and drew it up to his waist. Grinding into her slowly, he bent down to whisper in her ear, "Just follow my lead."

She whimpered and clenched down on him. "Like a dance?"

He smiled. "Yes, just like a dance, my little dragonfly."

Chapter Twenty

Silver twirled around her office, laughing out loud. Perfect. Just perfect. All her plans for promoting the team had panned out so far. Already they'd sold more season tickets than any other season, and she could take full credit. Three days of working crazy hours had paid off.

Daddy is going to love this!

Flipping open her day planner, she picked up a pen and put it in her mouth, chewing thoughtfully. The Cobras had a week-long preseason road trip, so the photo shoot would have to be scheduled for next week . . .

A sound from the door brought her head up. Her face broke into a smile as Dean stepped into her office. Wearing the new tie she'd bought him. No more no-nonsense black and grey. Nothing extreme either, but forest green complemented his eyes. Which ran over her now with such raw desire she wanted to drag him into her office and get naked. They'd both been so busy they'd done nothing but talk on the phone since this past weekend.

She missed him. She missed talking about the game while snuggling in bed, missed their debates over everything from politics to the plots of the movies they watched—military dramas which she surprisingly enjoyed. And the way he shut her up with a kiss when she gloated about making a good point . . .

Never in her life had she felt this way about anyone. Connected to them as a *whole* person. The sex was amazing, and he aroused her by just looking at her, but she didn't curse at him anymore to do her on the closest available surface when he made her hot. Well, not *every time*. And a quickie wouldn't hurt . . .

Professional at work: Dean's Rules 101.

Fingering the pearl buttons high on her throat, she waved him over and pointed at her book. "You aren't going to believe what I pulled off."

His tongue traced his bottom lip as he approached her. "Remind me about the office policy?"

Her nose wrinkled. "*Your* office policy."

"Ah, yes. Mine." He let out a gruff laugh. "Show me what you pulled off before I forget why the policy is a good idea."

Oh, I could so torture you! Tempting—but no. She wanted to see what he thought of all her hard work more than she wanted to get off. Of course, maybe he'd think it was stupid. It wasn't his style. Or even Daddy's style.

"Hey, what happened to the woman who was so excited she danced around her office for about ten minutes?"

Heat rushed over her cheeks. She glared at him. "You were watching me!"

He shrugged. "Your door was open." He rested a hand on the edge of her desk and studied her book. "You've booked several meetings with a Canadian network. Are you getting the team more airtime?"

"Kinda." She circled her desk as she spoke, straightening her pencil holder and her files. Her purse lay open on the far corner and she fetched a lollipop. The second the candy was in her mouth she felt much better. *Here goes nothing.* "We're doing a reality show."

Shock? Outrage? Amusement? She prepared for any or all, but he simply nodded.

"Other teams have done it. Are you thinking of following certain players into their personal lives or a 'inside the locker room' type series?"

"Umm . . ." Those were actually good ideas too. She'd have to look into it—after they saw how the ratings went with her original idea. "Well, you see, I'm sorta going for sex appeal."

His brow lifted. "And . . . ?"

"Well—"

"Silver, if you don't get to the point, I am going to bend you over this desk and spank you." He picked up a long wooden ruler. "With this."

He was teasing and she knew it, but she couldn't help but wince. He'd been right about needing a pillow.

His forehead creased and he cursed under his breath. "I'm sorry, sweetheart."

"It's okay." She sighed and glanced down at her buzzing phone.

Landon. She pressed "end" and squared her shoulders. It took her a moment to remember what she wanted to tell Dean. *Oh, right. Sex appeal.* "We're going to have a competition to recruit ice girls."

"Ice girls."

"Yes."

"No."

No? No! She slammed her fist on the desk and broke her lollipop. "Yes! You don't get to veto this, Dean! It's happening, whether you like it or not!"

"I've seen these girls prancing around on the ice. They distract the players. Our men need to focus on the game and not the half naked women shaking their asses in their faces." He shook his head and slumped into her chair. "I understand how this might seem like a good idea to you, but we need to concentrate on getting the team to the playoffs."

"If we don't get viewership up, no one will care if they make it to the playoffs! Now get out of my chair!" As soon as he moved, she sat and pointed across the desk. "That's your place! Now you're going to fucking hear me out and stop thinking like an old-fashioned tight ass!"

His eyes narrowed. "Pet—"

"Don't you fucking *dare* 'pet' me!" The chair crashed to the floor as she thrust back up to her feet. "We can please the old farts who love old-school hockey, or we can appeal to a new generation and make this team into a real franchise!" Since he'd stopped glaring at her, she decided to stop screaming. "I've given the okay for the network to audition across the nation. I'm using my own money to bring the girls who make the cut here, and I've already found a nice place for them to stay. And just so you know, these aren't just hot, sleazy girls shaking their asses. They're figure skaters, speed skaters, women with real talent. They'll put on shows in between periods and do charity events with the team. Granted, the guys might drool a bit, but they'll have to deal with it and so will you."

Her breath came out in a huff. She turned around and righted her chair, then took a seat. Energy buzzed through her veins and she prepared to continue the argument, but one look at his face stole her breath. A flash of teeth, a glint in his eyes, and, *oh my God*, he was actually grinning.

His hands lifted in surrender. "You're right. It's not something I—or your father—would have come up with, but it just might work. And, more importantly, you are in charge of PR, not me. I'm guessing you didn't hire any of the agents from the list I gave you?"

"No." She toyed with the little red shards of candy scattered over her desk. "I talked to a few, but their ideas seemed . . . boring. And then I came up with some ideas and—"

"Good. This team needs something fresh, and I'm sorry I didn't see that." He sighed. "After what you did with the charity event, I should have."

She sat up straight and inclined her head. "You are forgiven."

He smirked. "How gracious of you, dragonfly."

Oh, so not fair! That special nickname he now had for her made her feel the silly warm fuzzies. How could she not forgive him?

"Yes, well just don't do it again." Thrumming her fingers on her planner, she tongued her bottom lip and tried to find somewhere else to put all her restless energy. Now that she wasn't mad at him anymore, make-up sex seemed as good a place as any, but that brought her back to his stupid rules. So . . . business . . . "I take it you didn't come here just 'cause you missed me?"

"I've been looking for an excuse to see you, but no, in all honesty, I have to discuss something with you." He leaned back in his chair. "The team is going on a road trip for the next week. We have one game scheduled in the Eastern Conference and four in the Western."

"I know that." She patted her book. "I spent Monday morning getting all organized. Every game is in here. Pink for away games, blue for home."

His lips quirked. "Red is typically home, while blue is away."

Childish, maybe, but she couldn't help but stick out her tongue at him. "It's my book."

He chuckled. "Very true."

"So what did we need to discuss?"

"I'm going with the team to see how my brother performs as head coach." He waited for her nod, then continued. "I'd like you to come with me."

"Oh!" Her mind went over the schedule. Buffalo, San Jose, Los Angeles, and Vancouver. She'd always loved traveling, and it would be nice to get away. With Dean. *For work.* A cruel voice in her head reminded her. She sighed. "That's a long time to go by your rules."

Dean stood, straightened his jacket, then strode around her desk before she had a chance to stand. He trapped her with his hands on her armrest and loomed over her. "Work hours are nine to five, pet. We will also attend games, but beyond that—" his lips curved into a positively evil smile "—the rules don't apply."

* * * *

Dean hesitated as Silver opened the door to her apartment and almost retreated. The place had fallen victim to a cotton candy explosion. He'd never been to her apartment, but he had a hard time believing any man, gay or not, had every set foot in the place.

Pink and powder blue everywhere. The walls were a pale raspberry color, the white sofa was buried in tiny cushions, the wood floors covered in a peacock feather printed carpet. He inched inside, warily avoiding getting too close to anything. A wet paint scent hung in the air, and he'd rather not wear that color on the plane.

And she wants to redecorate the VIP boxes?

"Oh my God! You should see your face!" Silver shut the door with her hip and let out a bubbly laugh. "Feeling less manly just being in here?"

He gave her a tight smile. "Where are your suitcases?"

"Dean." Sauntering up to his side, she gazed up at him, eyelashes fluttering. "I redecorated. Don't you like it?"

"It's . . ." He hated to lie, but no good would come of telling her the truth. So he settled for a diplomatic response. "Very interesting."

"It's hideous!" Silver smacked his arm. "I wanted to make some changes since Asher and Cedric moved out, so I hired a interior design student and told her she could sell everything inside the apartment—except my personal stuff of course—and use the money to give the place a face-lift. I didn't have the heart to tell her I hated it, so I'll have to put up with it until I have time to make it look less like Candyland."

He couldn't hold back his sigh of relief. He'd fully expected Silver to be high maintenance, maybe even messy—which would have irked him since he liked order in his life, but he could have dealt because he lived with a teenager who thrived in chaos. This, however, looked like something someone on an acid trip would find pretty.

Shaking his head, he pulled her against him and wrapped his arms around her in a straightjacket hold. "It's not nice to tease your Dom, Silver."

"Nice is boring." She looked over her shoulder at him and smirked. "Besides, if I don't keep you on your toes, you start acting like you have a stick up your ass. Or a great big butt plug."

"Hmm, speaking of great big butt plugs . . ."

Her cheeks went as hot pink as her throw pillows. A spoonful of arousal with a dash of fear. Utter perfection. If only they had time to play.

Why ruin the moment by reminding her we don't? He brought his lips to her ear. "I'm glad you chose a skirt today, sweetheart. All I have to do is bend you over and move the string of your thong aside to get access to your pretty little asshole."

She whimpered.

"Would you hold still while I slicked you up with lube and slowly worked it inside you, or would I have to tie you down?"

"No, no tying. No butt plugs." Her hips pressed back against his pelvis, and he groaned as her tight little bottom bumped his very hard cock. "I'll give you anything you want."

"You'll give me anything I want anyway, pet."

Her pulse pounded against his lips as he kissed her throat. She squirmed a bit, but not enough to convince him she really wanted to get away. "What do you want?"

"I want . . ." He rubbed his freshly shaved cheek against her neck, tightened his grip on her arms, and nipped her earlobe. When she gasped, he released her. "Your suitcase." He smacked her butt. "And hurry, dragonfly."

With a strangled scream, she stomped off, muttering something about an egg-sucking-ass-clown.

He chuckled and wandered into the kitchen. Which had a

strange poker slash chess theme in black and periwinkle. Wincing at the visual assault, he took a seat at the table and called out, "Either I help you redecorate when we come back, or you'll be spending a lot of time at my place."

"Both sound good to me!"

"We have thirty minutes to get to the airport!" He double-checked his watch. "Are you almost ready?"

"Almost!" She paused. "Sorry, I'm being rude! Would you like a drink or something? Help yourself!"

Choosing a shiny red apple from the fruit bowl on the table, he stood and idly paced from the kitchen and back while he ate the tart fruit, his mind going over all this trip would accomplish. Observing his brother's coaching style, the rookies who may be ready to join the team, and the performance of both Demyan and Bower. Having Silver along was a plus. They would learn how to work as a unit. He could teach her more about the game.

And more importantly, hold her in his arms every night.

A few last bites close to the core and he was done. He checked his watched again. Fifteen minutes.

"Silver?"

"Coming!"

Uh-huh. He sighed and went to toss the core in the trash. Maybe he should go back to giving her two hours to get ready.

The apple core hit the side of a hardcover book. Dean frowned and picked it up.

The Game by Ken Dryden. He had a copy of this book—only his was much older. This looked brand new. He glanced at the small white trash can and spotted two other books. Not ruined, since other than several takeout containers, they were the only things in the garbage. He fished them out, then took a cloth from the sink to clean some sauce from the dust jacket of *The Boys of Winter.*

Inside the cover, he spotted a short note: *Apprendre à surmonter tes obstacles, mignonne. Landon.*

"What are you doing?" Silver asked from behind him.

He closed the book and pressed his lips into a hard line. He'd figured Silver would be upset for a while about what had happened last weekend. Hell, *he* was still pretty pissed off. But not at Bower. At himself. If he hadn't put Silver in that position, things with her and Bower would still be . . .

Be what exactly?

Damn if he knew. He couldn't even say for sure how he felt about their "friendship," but he did know it bothered him more to see them at odds. Especially since it seemed like Bower was reaching out.

Picking up *The Game,* he turned to face her. "What was this doing in the trash?"

The color left her cheeks. Her bottom lip trembled but was held still by her teeth. And in a blink, her expression turned completely unreadable. If he hadn't been paying attention, he wouldn't have caught the telling slip.

"I don't want those books. I rarely buy paper books anymore. Such a waste of space—"

"These were a gift."

"So what? People get rid of gifts all the time." She fiddled with the grey scarf around her neck, then slid on some big, black sunglasses. "Let's go before we're late."

Dean nodded and carried the books to the kitchen table. He dropped the neat—and now clean—stack with a thunk. "Yes. Let's. After you put these in your carry-on."

"Dean, I—"

"Now, pet." His face remained still, even though he wanted to laugh at the way she ground her teeth. "I suggest you hurry. I'd hate to start off our trip with a punishment, but I will. And I guarantee you won't enjoy it."

She swallowed and picked up the books. Then hugged them to her chest. "You know who sent them."

"Yes." He walked by her to collect her suitcases from where she'd left them by the door. "He chose well."

* * * *

Are we flying to Buffalo or Hong Kong? Landon pressed a white-knuckled fist against the armrest, struggling, as he had for the goddamn everlasting flight, to stay put.

"Why don't you just go talk to her?"

Landon tore his eyes away from the back of Silver's head and scowled at Carter. "Why don't you continue your story about blowing kisses to the Bruins' bench after you won the shootout?"

Carter grinned. "That was something else, but I finished and you weren't really listening anyway. I added a naked ref doing the Macarena in the middle of the rink and you just grunted."

Fuck. The last thing he needed was the guys catching him staring at Silver. He'd done his best to distract himself, first by taking a nap with his ears plugged with hard-core music from his iPod—which lasted through the first three songs from AC/DC's greatest hits— then by engaging in conversation with Carter. He liked talking to the kid, but Silver was too close, and too distant, and he'd given up on looking away.

"You were with her Saturday." Landon recalled the way she'd stripped for the kid and clenched his jaw. *Not your business, Bower.* He had to ask. "I didn't stick around to watch, but you two seemed to be getting along pretty well. What happened?"

Rubbing his hands on his knees, Carter shrugged his bowed shoulders. "Hell, I can't Dom a woman like her. Actually, I'm not sure I can Dom anyone. She made me look like a real pussy. Worse, actually. I thought Dean was going to kill me until Chicklet stopped him."

"Kill you?"

"I slapped her."

I'm going to fucking kill you! Landon leaned forward and hissed through his teeth. "You. Did. *What?*"

The younger man paled, but he didn't back away. "See, that's how everyone's going to react when they find out. Doesn't matter that she told me it would get her in the mood, that she needed it to get into the scene. I was supposed to be in charge, and I let *her* top me."

Damn. Anger switched to pity as Landon sat back. Carter was right; most people wouldn't understand how slapping a woman would be okay in *any* situation. The kid was still growing into his Dom boots, wasn't even experienced enough to scene in the club without his mentor close by, and one mistake would have the subs he might be able to top avoiding him like the plague.

"You sure you're a Dom, Carter? Maybe Chicklet can show you—"

"She's tried. Nothing big, just some bondage and flogging when she first took me on. It was weird, taking orders from a woman, but kinda hot. I liked how the ropes felt." Carter's brow furrowed as though he was thinking hard. "We tried other stuff too. With . . ."

"With?" Landon's brow shot up when Carter shook his head. "Hey, don't go all secretive on me now. After the overshare with the two chicks and the tampon string—seriously?"

Carter laughed. "That was some awesome freakiness. Strippers rock!"

Landon rolled his eyes. All right, the kid didn't want to talk about it. Fine with him, so long as—

"So, what's going on with you and Silver?"

Dropping his head to his hand with a groan, Landon muttered, "You're a fucking pain in my ass. Let it go, man."

The kid went on as though he hadn't heard. "You should send her a present. Girls forget everything you done wrong when they get presents."

"It's not like that."

"What-fucking-ever! Just try it."

"I have."

"Oh." Carter frowned and scratched at the peach fuzz on his jaw. "Well, she was a model—or an actress? If you sent chocolates, maybe she thinks you don't understand that she's watching her weight. Try flowers. Chicks dig flowers."

Landon snorted. "Have you ever *had* a girlfriend?"

"Tons." Carter smirked. "But I thought it wasn't like that with you two?"

Asshole. "I sent her books, okay? Had a new one delivered every morning for three days. She's not ready to talk to me so—"

"Of course she's not! You sent her fucking books?" Carter barked a laugh. "Have *you* ever had a girlfriend?"

"Yeah." A trigger went off in his head, breaking the dam of memories. His jaw ticked. He had to move. Had to walk before he did or said something he'd regret. His tone went rough as he stood and sidled past Carter. "Just one."

Eyes straight, he strode down the aisle between the seats. A flash of golden waves stopped him short. Silver had her back to him as she climbed over Richter, giggling at his stern look. When she straightened, he blocked her path.

"Hey." He glanced at Richter, who inclined his head. "Can we talk?"

Her chin hiked up. "No."

He blinked. "No? Just like that? I thought we were friends?"

"I thought so too. Now I know better." She glared at him. "Can you please get out of my way, Mr. Bower?"

Why the hell didn't you leave her alone? Give her some space; she'll get over it.

If only that were true. He had a feeling, if he let her, she'd forget him.

But he still got out of her way.

* * * *

The bathroom door clicked shut. Silver leaned against it and covered her face with her hands. Being with Dean had gotten so easy lately. His intensity still scared her sometimes, but the balance between their relationship and their partnership in running the team, kept her from being overwhelmed. She had a feeling he was taking it easy on her, which made her lo-*like* him even more. Landon hardly ever crossed her mind.

Liar.

Okay, so she thought about him when he called, even though she never answered and erased his messages without listening to them. And for the past three mornings, she'd stared at the packages delivered to her doorstep for about an hour before opening them. Then held them for another few minutes before tossing them in the trash. But they were just books. They weren't *him*.

She missed him.

You don't need two Doms in your life, Silver.

Probably not. Hell, she wasn't sure she needed one. But she did know she needed one who'd take care of her after bringing her to that place where she felt exposed and fragile. She loved and hated feeling that way. Loved it because sex was fucking mind-blowing, mostly because it wasn't just a dick attached to some random man. It was Dean. And Dean looked at her like she was more than just a hot cunt.

Hated it because if she hadn't been so exposed, Landon couldn't have hurt her so badly. He'd reminded her that no matter how hard she tried, she'd always fuck up, so why bother trying?

All it would have taken was one word, one touch, hell, even if he'd *looked* at her the way he had all the other times she'd felt completely alone, in the way that said "You've still got me" . . . Out of everyone she knew, he was the only person she'd convinced herself would love her no matter *what* she did.

You've seriously got to drop that word from your vocabulary. Love is just a word people use when they're stupidly wrapped up in someone. Landon doesn't love you.

Not that she needed anyone to love her. Well, maybe Oriana, but that came with being sisters. And it would be nice if her kids loved her—no guarantees there, she was pretty sure out of the three kids, she'd been the only one who really loved her mother. And Daddy . . .

Daddy loves the game.

The game. Yes. If she focused on the game, she could ignore Landon.

Inhale. Exhale. She straightened and looked in the mirror. Damn, she was pale. One look at her and Dean would know something was wrong. She brought her hands up to her cheeks, pinching them for color. And noticed they were shaking. Bad.

Her purse hung on her arm. Inside was something that would calm her down and make the rest of the trip go real smooth. She'd have the strength to stare Landon down without saying a word.

She palmed the little vial and tipped it from side to side to watch the powder coat the glass.

No.

Before she could cave in and take the easy out, she stuffed the vial into the zipper compartment in her purse and zipped it out of sight. There were other ways to deal with this. Like talking to Dean.

Oh yeah, there's an idea. 'Sir, I'm having trouble with another man'.

She snickered and tried to picture Dean's expression. Her mind made it fierce, but then it changed into the one that made it okay for her to say she was scared. She bit her lip.

Maybe she could talk to him after all.

Chapter Twenty One

The plane shook with turbulence and the seat belt light flashed. Dean frowned at Silver as half her vodka spilled on the front of her shirt and she giggled. This was her third and she was obviously feeling it. Which made it her last.

"Silver, slow down." He put his hand over hers on the glass and helped her lower it to the cup holder. Then he buckled her in. "The men shouldn't see you like this."

"Like this? What? Drunk?" She giggled again. "Oh, Dean, you have no idea. I'm not even close."

Like hell, you're not. He cut off her grab for her glass. "You wanted to say something before Tim asked to speak to me. What is it?"

"Oh." Her gaze darted across the aisle. She started to turn but then held herself in place with her hands gripped to the armrests. "I—"

"Shut your fucking mouth, Carter! Seriously, you ever speak her name again, and you'll be breathing through a fucking tube!"

"Oh, chill out. I just said pregnant chicks are hot, and she's got that glowy thing going for her. You worried it's not yours? I would be."

Can't someone gag that kid? Dean glared at his brother, who shrugged. As long as they were stuck in their seats, Mason and Carter were on their own.

"Carter, seriously?" Bower let out a tight laugh. "Mason, relax. He's just jealous. If a chick doesn't strip for a living, he doesn't know what to do with her. Oriana's a fine woman and we all know it."

At Dean's side, Silver went perfectly still.

"Yeah, the Delgado women are something else." Demyan leaned over his center aisle seat and shot Silver a wink. "And they've got some brains. Or I wouldn't be here."

The men, scattered throughout the plane, grumbled, but none argued with him. Silver slid down as far as her seat belt would allow. For a woman who enjoyed the spotlight, she certainly didn't look like she wanted it now. Of course, with how hard she was working to come off as professional, Demyan's blatant flirting was bound to make her uncomfortable. Perhaps he and the man should have a little chat.

But not here. Actually, the plane wasn't really the place for any conversation that didn't directly relate to the game. Whatever Silver had to say would have to wait.

Dean sighed and took her hand. "We'll talk after we land."

She gave him a grateful smile. "I think that's a good idea."

He inclined his head and relaxed into his chair. As his eyes drifted shut, he heard her shuffling through her bag. Through slitted lids, he watched her take out a *Cosmo* magazine.

His lips quirked. "This is a business trip, Silver. You'll have plenty of time to catch up on the latest fashions at the hotel. If you're trying to make a good impression, you might want to find more appropriate reading material. Which is why I had you pack those books."

Her grip tightened on the magazine. "You don't get to dictate my reading material, Dean."

"It was a suggestion, sweetheart. Not an order."

"Calling me 'sweetheart' isn't appropriate for work either," she said through her teeth before slamming the magazine back into her bag. After pulling out *The Game,* she plopped it open on her lap and gave him a "happy now?" glare.

He smiled with his eyes closed. "You're right, Miss Delgado. I apologize."

"Good."

"Ken Dryden was a goalie, you know. Vital to his team and complex—as goalies tend to be. I think this will give you some good insight into our Mr. Bower. He's quite the fan."

"Dean?"

"Hmm?"

"Shut up."

Dean chuckled, then drifted off to sleep.

* * * *

242

Most of the men were paired up in standard rooms with two king-sized beds, but Dean had paid extra for a suite, wanting to make sure Silver was comfortable. If she'd objected to sharing with him, he would have left her the room and bunked with his brother, but thankfully, she simply walked in and plunked onto the sofa with a happy sigh.

"Oh, this is perfect!" Tucking her feet under her, she smiled at him. "Classy hotel, a suite with a hot tub. Honestly, I thought we'd be crashing at some sleazy motel. I was fully prepared to be 'roughing it' for the next week."

Dean tipped the porter and carted Silver's bags to the bedroom. "Sticking millionaires in a motel would be odd, don't you think?"

"Maybe, but they're jocks. I figured they wouldn't care."

"Some don't, but it's in our best interest to make sure they're reminded of their worth. We expect a certain level of conduct from them on the road—more than we'd expect from them at home. Having nice rooms to come back to before and after a hard game is a nice perk. Courtesy of the team. It gives us the right to come down on them if their behavior isn't above par, but it's not usually an issue." He went to the mini-fridge and took out two bottles of water. "The rookies may be a little overwhelmed by all this, but they've all been paired up with veterans. Trips like this bring the team closer."

"That's good." She thanked him for the water and patted the cushion beside her. When he sat, she leaned against his side. "I'm glad you asked me to come."

"I'm glad you agreed to." He kissed her hair and took a few gulps from his bottle, enjoying her presence and the companionable silence. But he only allowed himself a few moments. He still had to meet with the team, and he didn't want to waste the short time they had alone. "So, you were saying . . . ?"

She laughed and shrugged. "Oh, it was nothing really. I'm glad you made me read that book though. It—"

"I didn't make you."

"Whatever. The point is, I like it. Seeing that side of a player's life is interesting. And it's very well written. I used to think all jocks were stupid—no offense, but some seem like there's nothing more to them besides what they put into the game. This makes them seem more like normal people."

Dean shook his head and brought a handful of her hair to his lips. Her fruity shampoo scent had faded, but he could smell her, fresh and sweet, an essence that was hers alone. "I'm sure there are prejudices about pretty blond actresses."

"A few." She shrugged again. "But most of them are true when it comes to me. I dropped out of high school. I'm not that smart. And you'd be disgusted by some of the things I've done to get ahead in my career."

He frowned and tugged at her hair until she was forced to look up at him. "No. I'm disgusted that you were left in a position where you felt you had to do those things. You're a very intelligent and creative woman, Silver. I used to think you were stubborn, but most of that is determination."

Her face broke into a wide smile and her eyes glistened. "Thank you. That means a lot, coming from you."

His chest tightened as she glowed with his approval. Damn it, for such a confident woman, she was so insecure. She knew she was beautiful. She knew men wanted her. But she didn't expect to be appreciated for more than what people could see.

"You know how good it makes me feel that my opinion matters to you, love?" He took her face in his hands and pulled her up so he could kiss her. She melted into him and he gathered her into his arms, settling her on his lap. "We might not always agree, but I like that you challenge me and force me to accept that I'm not always right. I've been with many submissive women, and most, no matter how intelligent, how independent, are happy to take my lead. And I thought that was what I wanted until I met you."

"Really?" She pulled out his tie and traced her finger along the blue and green pattern. "Should I remind you of that the next time you tell me no?"

"Absolutely." He kissed her again and smoothed his hands down her back. She looked nice in her tailored skirt suit, but for the rest of their conversation, he needed her less buttoned-up. "Now, why don't you go slip into something comfortable? I don't have much time before the team gets together, but I'd like to cuddle for a bit."

She unfolded from his lap and stood but hesitated in front of him. "Shouldn't I come too?"

"I'll leave that up to you, but honestly, I think it would be better if you don't come to every meeting. You'll get a reputation as an intrusive owner, and that's never good. The media feeds off things like that, and the fans will start to blame you for everything that goes wrong with the team. It hasn't gotten out that I'm a partial owner, and I'd like to keep it that way. As the GM, I'll take most of the heat, and that's how it should be. I promise to discuss my decisions with you, but that's between us. As far as the press is concerned, all my decisions are made on my experience. They may question my every move, but not as much as they would if it came from you."

"Okay, I can handle that." She pulled the pins from her hair and grinned as she shook it free. "I had a director like that. If we made a suggestion for changes in dialogue, he'd act like it was all him. Some of the actors didn't like it, but I got what he was doing. If it was him calling the shots, it was considered his 'style.' If it was us, we were difficult to work with and any fallout could ruin us. Fine, he took all the credit, but he took all the risks too. And he was a good guy. If we made things better, he shared the spotlight."

He caught her hand before she could slip away. And studied her face as he spoke. "Do you miss it? The life you led in Hollywood is very different from the life you have now."

Her forehead creased as she turned her hand and laced her fingers with his. "Sometimes I do, but . . . I like this. I never felt real with all the cameras and the spotlight. All I had to do was smile pretty and read my lines. You expect more from me and . . . and it makes me want more from myself. On set I was someone who could be replaced. Here, I'm not."

"No. You're not." But damn, if she missed it, how long before an opportunity came up that would tempt her to go back? "I wish I could tell you to forget that part of your life, but you can't, can you? You still have an agent looking out for the right part, and if he or she finds one, you'll want to go."

She stared down at their clasped hands and shook her head. "I don't know if I could. I'd want to, but for the first time, leaving would be hard."

"Silver, if you're afraid to leave me, don't be. I'll always be here when you come back."

"So you'd let me go?"

He already felt her pulling away. Maybe she'd gotten an offer and hadn't taken it because of him. Or because of the team. It was good that she knew they needed her, but he wouldn't let anything hold her back. His little dragonfly, always skimming the surface of the pond. Damage her wings and she'd drown.

"I'd let you go." He released her hand to prove his point. "Just swear to me you won't forget what's waiting for you."

"I swear." She stared down at her hand, looking a little lost. "But . . . well, I haven't decided anything yet. So how about we not start saying goodbye. It's kinda depressing."

Dean chuckled. "It is, isn't it?"

"Yep." She put her hands on his knees and dipped down to kiss him. "Stay put. I'm going to get changed."

After she disappeared into the bedroom, he rose from the sofa and stepped up to the window to look out at the glowing city skyline. He couldn't remember the last time he'd taken a trip for longer than a day or two for meetings with the GMs from other teams. It had probably been with his wife, who had insisted on at least four vacations a year and always complained when it was time to go home. She'd never been the domestic type, but he made enough money to hire a nanny and housekeeper so she didn't have to be. He'd done everything in his power to give her the freedom she'd obviously desperately needed, but it hadn't been enough.

He wouldn't make that same mistake with Silver.

"I wish you didn't have to go." Silver came up behind him and hugged his waist. "I was looking forward to—"

"I won't be long." He turned and angled her chin up with a finger. "But there is one thing I need from you before I leave."

She gave him a sly smile. "Yes?"

"The truth. You wanted to speak to me about Bower, didn't you?" He frowned when she pulled away and shook her head. "Maybe I shouldn't go. I won't tolerate lies and making that clear is more important than anything I need to discuss with the team."

"Not talking isn't lying."

"And you think not talking is an option?" Without waiting for her answer, he hooked his arm around her waist and dragged her to the sofa. He sat with his thighs spread and pulled her between them, using his feet to open her legs wide. "Lace your fingers behind your neck, pet."

She quickly obeyed, which shocked the hell out of him. Chest rising and falling with her quick little breaths, she leaned into him and whispered, "I thought you had to go?"

"I do, but Tim can start without me." He slid one hand around her throat and dipped the other down the front of her bright pink boxer briefs to cup her pussy. "Talk to me, Silver."

"There's nothing to—Oh!" Her pussy clamped around his finger as he thrust it in deep. She fought to close her thighs as he forced them further apart. "What are you doing?"

"Interrogating my naughty little sub." He slicked her moisture over her clit, rubbing the little nub until the tip swelled from its tiny hood. Her hips jutted forward, and he tightened his grip on her throat until she gasped and went perfectly still. "Let's start with an easier question. Was Asher and Cedric your first ménage relationship?"

"My first . . . ? Ah! No!" She trembled as he gently massaged either side of her clit with his fingers. "I've only been in one monogamous relationship—when I was in high school. With a teacher."

Dean swallowed back the urge to curse. Reacting to her confession was no way to get her to share more. His tone remained surprisingly level. "What happened?"

"He was possessive. He hated it when I talked to boys my age. I felt smothered. I didn't want to leave him, but . . ." She made a mewling sound as his fingers glided down and curled into her. "But I needed to be able to make the choice!"

The choice. Yes, he could see that. Sometimes Silver needed her choices taken away from her, needed to be forced to surrender to her own desires—to actually *feel* something beyond shallow pleasure. But if she felt something for another man, being denied the opportunity to explore that would smother her.

And right now, he had a feeling she was getting in the way of her own happiness. He had a feeling he knew who she would choose—if she let herself.

Might as well be blunt. "Do you want Landon?"

"Landon? No!" She shook her head and whimpered as he slid his fingers up and over her clit. "We were friends. I didn't want to be more. I don't have many—okay, *any* friends, and I wanted to keep him."

"So what changed?"

"You know what changed." She tried to close her thighs and huffed. "Uck! Please, Dean! You're killing me!"

What he saw between Silver and Landon didn't look like friendship to him, but maybe he was wrong. Either way, she did need Landon in her life. He pinched her clit hard and whispered in her ear. "I may have an idea, but I will hear it from you. You have exactly fifteen minutes."

Lifting her head, she stared at the clock on the desk across the room. "What happens in fifteen minutes?"

"I leave and you will stay here, unsatisfied, until I return."

"I'm quite capable of satisfying myself."

He let out a gruff laugh as he slowly filled her with two fingers. "I'm sure you are, but you won't. Every time you touch yourself, you'll think of how it could be me, touching you, fucking you—"

"You said you wouldn't fuck me." She whimpered as he stroked her, her juices spilling around his fingers as he found the spot that would give her a fierce orgasm, fully aware that he wouldn't let her come until she gave him what he wanted. "Dean—Ah!"

Slipping out again, he toyed with her clit. Her cunt radiated heat, and he hardened as he thought about how it would feel wrapped around him. His jaw clenched as he tamped down his urges and focused on teasing her to the brink, over and over.

"I wouldn't fuck you when you still believed that was all I wanted from you." He pressed lightly on her windpipe, right under her chin. "But you know better now, don't you?"

"Yes, but . . ."

"I could be fucking you now." He thrust in and out until her muscles rippled, telling him she was almost there. And stopped. "But I won't. And you only have five minutes left to decide whether or not I will leave you hanging."

She groaned and dropped her head back onto his shoulder. "All right, you bastard, I'll tell you. Just please let me come!"

"Oh no, that's not how this game works, my love." He fisted his hand in her hair and let out a low growl against her throat before biting down. Her hips bucked as he stabbed his fingers into her. "You'll come after you tell me what I want to hear."

* * * *

Silver shook her head and twisted her body, desperately seeking what she'd been denied. The way Dean held her made it impossible to move enough to find relief. She was powerless. At his mercy. And fuck, being tortured by him was hot.

Part of her wanted to tell him to go to hell. She had all kinds of toys, and she didn't need him. But damn it, she could already picture herself trying and getting nowhere. She did need him. And, more importantly, she'd wanted to tell him anyway. This way made it easier because she didn't have a choice.

"I'll tell you!" She sobbed as his fingers left her, needing to get off so bad it hurt. And thinking of Landon hurt just as much—no worse, because pleasure wouldn't make that pain go away. Tears spilled down her cheeks as she forced the words out. "He hurt me! He just walked away . . . I don't even want to think about it! I know it's fucking pathetic, but I can't deal with him right now! I know I'll have to, eventually, but for now I just want him to leave me alone! I don't want to! Please don't make me!"

"Oh, sweetheart. Shh . . . it's okay. I won't make you." Dean's grip on her hair loosened and his kissed her cheek. "Fuck, I didn't realize—I wouldn't have—"

"Don't apologize!" She pressed her eyes shut and focused on the dwindling heat between her thighs. She'd told him. It was over. She just wanted her fucking reward. "Just finish it!"

His fingers plunged in and his thumb pressed down on her clit. Her core erupted, and she bit down on her tongue to hold back a scream. White flashed across her vision as her body shuddered uncontrollably, and only his arms around her kept her from collapsing to the floor in a boneless mass.

It seemed like hours passed before she could speak again, but one look at the clock showed her they'd just reached his fifteen minute mark. Her head lolled back into the crook of his shoulder as she peered up at him.

"You're mean, you know that?"

His forehead creased and he shook his head. "I wouldn't have pushed so hard if I'd known, Silver. I'm sorry."

"Don't be." She closed her eyes and sighed. "I'm glad you made me tell you. I just wish I knew what to do about it. I can't avoid him."

"Yes, you can. Let me speak to him—make him understand you both need time to sort this out."

"You're asking me?" She clung to him as he stood and carried her to the bedroom. So what if it made her look like a damsel in distress. It was nice to feel like someone wanted to take care of her. "I mean, I figured you might want to talk to him, but I didn't expect you to ask my permission."

"I'm not, little one. I was simply hoping I wouldn't have to force the issue."

All tucked in, she shook her head and smiled. "You don't. I surrender."

He laughed. "About time."

"For now."

His warm breath caressed her cheek as he bent down and kissed her. He stayed there, not moving until she opened her eyes. His lips curved slightly and his eyes crinkled. "For now is all I want, Silver."

The darkness weighed down on her after he left, but she couldn't sleep. For some reason, his words haunted her. He'd told her he'd let her go. He'd accepted her teasing "for now." As if . . . as if he didn't expect this thing between them to last.

Well, I've got news for you, Mr. Richter. She hugged a pillow to her chest and scowled at the door. *I'm not going anywhere.*

Chapter Twenty Two

Tipping his beer to his lips, Landon nodded for Richter to sit. As the man took the seat across from him, Landon's gaze locked on the smudge of lipstick on his collar, hardly noticeable with his jacket done up as it had been during the meeting, but now, with his jacket draped over his arm, the peach smear might as well have been a florescent sign.

Red flashed over his eyes and green rotted his insides until he got a grip. He refused to be jealous of Richter. At least he was taking care of Silver.

Carter cleared his throat and rose from the chair beside Landon. "I'm thinking I don't need to be here. If you don't mind, I'm going to see when the red skirt gets off." He wiggled his eyebrows as he finished off the last sip of his beer. Then he lightly punched Landon's shoulder. "Make it fast and I'll save you some."

"Don't bother." Landon ran his tongue over his teeth and focused on Richter, who'd gestured for the waitress to bring another beer. "See you in the room in a bit."

Shrugging, Carter turned away and crooked his finger to the barmaid with the red skirt. She ducked her head, then held up one hand, mouthing "Five minutes."

"I'm surprised you agreed to share a room with the kid." Richter watched Carter lean over the bar and shook his head as the barmaid moved in close to let him whisper in her ear. "He doesn't have many fans on the team."

Landon laughed. "I don't see why not. He's passionate and he plays practice games the same way he plays real ones. The guys shouldn't let him get under their skin."

"He asked Callahan if Oriana likes watching as much as Perron does."

"He was just messing with him."

"During a meeting. In front of all the men." Richter's brow shot up at Landon's chuckle. "You can't think it's appropriate for him to ask if Mason's ass is as tight as it looks?"

Inhaling deep to keep his beer from shooting out through his nose, Landon shook his head. "No, but it was fucking funny as hell."

"He's alienating himself from the team. That's not funny at all."

Right. Because they're such a welcoming bunch. Landon set down his beer and clenched his fist beside it. "They don't like the way he acts on the ice. I get that he's a dirty player, but that can work in our favor. Notice he doesn't have as many penalty minutes as Mason? Carter draws them by agitating the tough guys—"

"He's a rookie. He's got to learn to play the game properly before he goes out there and starts pissing everyone off."

"Why? He's getting the job done. You've got plenty of good little rookies who will do what they're told. He's talented and cocky, sure, but he can give us the edge we need. Tim doesn't have a problem with him."

"True. But Tim might not be the head coach for long."

Shit. If his own brother isn't safe, Carter certainly isn't. Landon drained his beer and inclined his head when the waitress rushed over to offer him another. *And neither am I.*

"You didn't come down here to talk to me about Carter's play, did you?" Landon braced himself for the inevitable. He was either going to be made backup or sent down. Only . . . shouldn't Tim be telling him? "Just spit it out. It's awfully good of you to take the time out of your busy schedule to speak to me yourself."

Richter rubbed his jaw and sighed. "Bower, you really should work on your confidence. From what I've seen, you are an excellent goaltender. *You* will likely give us the edge we need. Tim has nothing but good things to say about you. Actually, when I asked how the men were taking to you, he brought up the fact that goalies are a breed apart, and so long as your performance remains consistent, your relationship with the other players doesn't really matter."

Starting on his fresh beer, Landon nodded. "Well, there you go."

"But I'm not here to speak to you about you making friends on the team. Or your performance." Richter frowned and leaned back in his chair. "I'm here to speak to you about Silver."

"Ah . . ." Landon took a few more gulps and tried to make his face go blank. So far, since the plane, he'd done a pretty good job not thinking about Silver. Carter helped by cracking him up with his commentary on the other players, and the hotel staff, and his numerous ex-girlfriends. The kid wouldn't leave him alone, which had annoyed him at first, until he realized the jabbering started whenever he went quiet.

Carter knew something was bothering him. And had caught on that he didn't want to talk about it. Damn observant. *He'll make some lucky sub a good Dom one day.*

Just not Silver. Because the man for her was sitting across the table from Landon, about to lay down the fucking law.

"I shouldn't have spoken to her without your permission." Simple courtesy. Nothing Landon didn't know. But just saying it made him feel like he'd taken a rake to his guts. "I apologize. It won't happen again."

Dean's hands slammed on the table, and the waitress approaching them jumped and scurried away. "Damn it, Bower, it's not like that. At the club, yes, I'd appreciate it if you'd respect me as her Dom. But we're not at the club. I am asking you, as her friend, to understand that she needs some space."

"As her friend." Yeah, make that clear. "I do understand."

"Good." Dean eased back into his chair. "You'll both be very busy, so it shouldn't be difficult. She's trying very hard to prove herself and so are you. Neither of you needs the distraction."

"So noted." Landon held up his empty beer bottle in mock salute. "Now, if there's nothing else, there's an early practice and I should turn in." *Should, but won't.* "If you'll excuse me?"

Before he could walk away, Richter stood and blocked his path. His lips formed a hard line as their eyes met. "She misses you, Landon."

Landon? What the fuck? We friends now? He smirked. "Is that so?"

"Yes. It won't take long for her to get past this. Now is not the time."

"Can I ask you something?" He moved into Richter's space when he inclined his head. "Did she ask you to keep me away from her?"

"Not exactly, no. I pressed the matter—"

"Got it."

Richter let out a sound of disgust. "Don't be an asshole, Bower.

You hurt her."

"Yes, I did." He cocked his head, about ready to laugh at the way the man acted like he had a fucking clue about what was going on between him and Silver. *If I hadn't stepped aside, she'd be mine.* "How long before *you* hurt her? *Again.* I can't be what she needs, and I get that. Hopefully we can be friends again. But one way or another, you better step up. Prove that I made the right decision—that you're as good for her as I think you are. If I was in your place, I wouldn't have politely requested that you stay away."

"Really? So you'd choose her friends? I'm sure she'd take that well."

"I wouldn't choose them." Damn it, he was so done with this conversation. Richter just didn't get it. "I'd just make sure she had better friends than me."

"I see." Richter patted his shoulder and stepped past him, tossing back. "As I said before, you have to work on that confidence."

The bar, the halls in the hotel, went by in a blur as Landon made his way to the elevator. He found himself in his room, not quite sure how he'd gotten there. All he knew was he had a minibar full to bring him to the numbness he craved. He took the small bottles out by the handful, glancing over his shoulder as he heard movement behind him.

Carter held up a bottle of whiskey. "I come prepared."

Landon sat back on his heels. "Where's your date?"

"With her husband. Hopefully." Carter rolled his eyes. "Yep, I've got standards. She started bawling when I kissed her, and we sat for a bit and talked. I could have gotten her she's got a thing for hockey players, but when she mentioned her baby and how lonely she is when her man works overtime—hell, I'm a lot of things, but a home wrecker ain't one of them."

"Your parents divorced?"

"Uh-huh. Obvious much?"

"It's the only reason I see you turning away guaranteed pussy. You had a hard-on for that girl all night, and she looked ready to do you on the bar." Landon took the bottle from Carter and walked over to his bed to get comfortable. He took a few swallows, then handed the bottle back. "You do know if she wants attention, she'll find it."

"Tying her up and dumping her in a cab seemed a little excessive," Carter said. "I did consider it though."

Landon snorted. "You've been spending way too much time at the club."

Carter nodded. "Maybe. Hey, speaking of the club—"

"Let's not."

"Come on. I've gotta know." Carter took a swig of whiskey, capped it, then set the bottle between his feet. "Why did you choose a cane? If you'd spanked her and told her she was a bad, bad girl, she wouldn't be mad at you. You two could have—" He mimicked humping until Landon stood and took a swing at him. Falling off the bed, he burst out laughing. "Seriously, buddy, you know you want to!"

"If I didn't like you, I'd murder you. *Seriously.*" Landon retrieved the whiskey and went to the other side of the room where he'd be less tempted to crack it over Carter's head. "You could be fucking that barmaid now."

"But it would be wrong."

"Exactly. And if I'd punished Silver in a way that was at all sexual—if I'd taken advantage of her while she was vulnerable . . ." *And crying. You made her cry, you son of a bitch.* "I'm not the man for her, Carter, anymore than you are. It would have been wrong."

"She wouldn't have taken the punishment from me, Bower." Carter dropped on his bed with a groan. "She took it to please you."

Yeah, right. "She took it because she didn't want to be banned from the club."

Carter snorted. "You sure are a dumb shit. Fine, you didn't want to fuck her, but you had to know she wouldn't appreciate being passed off."

"I wasn't—" Landon's phone went off and he took it out of his pocket. He grinned, swaying a little as he answered. "Hey, sis!"

"Oh, Landon." Becky sighed loudly into the phone. "I knew you'd be drinking."

"You did?" When had his sister become psychic? He lifted the bottle and frowned at it. Empty. Damn. "You finished it all, you fucking lush!"

"What?"

"Not you, Becky. Carter," Landon said. "The rookie is wasted."

Carter gave him a one finger salute.

"Landon, tell me you're not getting plastered with one of the guys. It won't help." Becky went quiet. "You need to talk to someone."

"Ah, hell. Now you're going to tell me I need a shrink?"

"*I* think you need a shrink," Carter said.

"Go fuck yourself."

Nodding solemnly, Carter rolled off the bed and stumbled toward the bathroom. "Might as well. No one else is going to."

Becky sighed again, returning his attention to the phone pressed against his ear. "No, I don't think you need a shrink—not that it would hurt you to speak to a professional. I was thinking . . . well, your girlfriend. Silver. She went with you guys, didn't she?"

"She's not my girlfriend."

"Then what is she?"

Plopping down on his bed, Landon threw his arm over his face. Nosy big sisters were a pain in the ass. "She. Is. My. Friend."

"Fine. She's your friend. You can still talk to her about it, can't you?"

About it? What the hell is she talking about? He groaned as the room spun. "Becky, what are you talking about?"

"Oh . . ." She sucked in a harsh breath. "Nothing. Nothing at all. You should get some rest. From the sounds of you, you're going to need all day to sleep this off before the game."

"Nothing my ass. Why would you—" The reason for his sister's call hit him like a puck going 100 miles per hour. He sat up and swallowed. How the fuck could he have forgotten? Two years. Only two years and he was acting like it had never happened. "I have to go."

"Shit, Landon, I'm sorry!"

"Don't be." He thrust off the bed and tripped toward the minibar. He needed to burn the images out of his head, and liquor usually did the job. Not all the time, but tonight . . . "Just do me a favor?"

"Anything." Becky sounded on the verge of tears. "I'm so sorry, sweetie. I shouldn't have reminded you—"

"I shouldn't have needed reminding." He tossed back a mouthful of tequila. Then rum. "Just . . . just bring some flowers to the grave, okay? I'll pay you back."

"Don't worry about it." She paused. "Landon, I love you. And you know it wasn't your fau—"

He couldn't let her finish. But he wouldn't upset her by arguing with her. "I love you too, Becky. Goodnight."

Hanging up, he slumped against the wall. *Love you as much as I can love anyone.*

* * * *

The sun was way too bright, blazing over Landon's closed lids like the fireball that had flared up from his stove. A vise squeezed his brain and his stomach—

He lurched from the bed and practically knocked Carter over on the way to the bathroom. His strength spewed out from his guts as he knelt in front of the toilet. "Idiot." He mumbled between dry heaves. "You deserve to suffer, you fucking idiot."

"You and me both, pal." Carter shuffled into the bathroom, giving Landon a weak smile as he slapped his back. "You're probably in worse shape than I am, though. Had to help you in here a few times last night, but I got some water in you, which should help."

Landon didn't remember leaving the bed, or drinking anything other than beer, whiskey, and half a dozen tiny bottles of everything else. But his mouth didn't taste as acidic as it would have if he'd been puking up alcohol. The kid had taken care of him. Destined for sainthood, that one.

"Thanks, man." Landon let Carter help him up and inhaled deeply. It had been a long, long time since he'd let himself get this wasted—a year to be exact. Never happened on a game day, but he had a few tricks that would help him cope. "I'm gonna take a shower, then go for a jog. Usually gets me feeling almost human. You wanna come?"

Carter backed away, holding his hands out in front of him, his expression serious. "I like you. But not *that* much."

What the— Landon groaned and shoved Carter out of the bathroom. "For the jog, you asshole."

The kid's laughter sliced through the door Landon slammed in his face and stabbed into his skull. Despite his pain, Landon managed to chuckle. Under an ice-cold shower spray, he scrubbed quickly without letting his thoughts drift to anything depressing. He tipped his head back, filling his mouth with water and spitting it out until his mouth stopped tasting like rancid meat. Swallowed to rehydrate himself. Then went to the room to dress for his jog.

Without a word, Carter followed him outside the hotel and kept pace with him as he pushed his body beyond the dragged-behind-a-four-wheeler-through-the-woods sensation. Sweat soaked his tank top, his muscles burned, and his stomach took another lurch. This time, he managed to hold down the bit of water he'd drunk. But he needed to eat something.

"Hungry?" He asked Carter as they slowed in front of a grocery store.

Carter's skin took on a green tinge. "I'm starting to hate you. You go ahead. I'm going to keel over right here and die."

"We've got three hours to pull it together, kid. I'll pick us up some crackers and bananas. Some eggs would be good too if we can stomach them."

"Where the hell are we going to cook the eggs?"

"Who said anything about cooking them?"

Covering his mouth with his hand, Carter retreated to a bench and folded onto it. "You are a fucking sadist. Ever hear of salmonella? I'll pass on the side of food poisoning with my hangover, thanks."

"Organic eggs aren't likely to make you sick, you wuss." Landon shrugged when Carter made a gagging noise and headed into the store to get what he needed. At the checkout, he chatted with the cute Goth girl at the cash register, feeling almost normal. Just another game day after a few too many. No reason to dwell on things he couldn't change. He controlled what happened on the blue paint, between the pipes.

Narrowing life to those sixty minutes suited him just fine.

Grabbing his bag, he glanced over to the glass storefront and cursed. Apparently sixty minutes wasn't going to cut it. The game wasn't going to wait until they got to the rink.

"Hey, aren't you the guy who's with that hot singer? Mel-something? The one I loosened up for you?"

Landon groaned as he approached Carter and the three Sabres that surrounded him. The rookie didn't get the concept of keeping the trash talk on the ice. "The guy" was Dirk Nelson, the Sabres' captain. And "Mel-something" was his wife.

Anyone you haven't slept with, kid?

To his credit, Nelson just laughed. "Nice try, rookie. See you on the ice. Hopefully you can prove yourself there, because you didn't make much of an impact on my wife. Then again, she doesn't remember most of her past boy toys."

"Oh, she remembers me. I took her virginity," Carter said with a smirk.

"You were still eating cat shit out of the sandbox when she lost her virginity, kid."

"I'm talking about the back door, Einstein." Carter's mouth opened wide as Nelson's eyes narrowed. "Oh, fuck! You didn't know your ol' lady was an anal slut? You have no idea what you're missing!"

Landon yanked Carter out of reach just as Nelson went for his throat. The captain's teammates dragged him away, struggling and cursing all the way to a black SUV. Carter bent over, laughing so hard that Landon had to punch him in the arm to get him to stop.

Red-faced and gasping, Carter finally straightened. "Did you see—Oh my god, that was fucking classic!"

"What the fuck is wrong with you? He's going to be on you all night, you know that, right?"

"Let him fucking bring it." Carter squared his jaw and rolled his shoulders back. "I wouldn't have started on him if he didn't bring up my little sister."

"Ah . . ." Landon made a face, glancing over at Carter as they headed toward the hotel. "How old is your sister?"

"Sixteen."

"Shit."

"Yeah." Carter shrugged. "I don't think he'd touch her, he's just taking digs, but if he wants to throw down the gloves, I'm game."

Landon didn't know what to say. Nelson had at least fifty pounds and five inches on Carter. The kid had spunk, but he wouldn't win if it came to fists on the ice. Thankfully, with Mason out there, it wouldn't come to that.

An hour later, in the locker room, Landon pressed his fist to the wall beside the white board displaying the lineup and groaned.

Mason wasn't playing.

* * * *

The press box in the HSBC Arena wasn't as nice as the one in the Delgado Forum, but Silver noticed a few things she wanted to add during renovations. Earlier that day, she'd gotten a tour of everything from the offices to the wives' room—she hadn't even known there *was* a wives' room! Or that the forum had one too—and the Sabres' president had answered all her questions about the changes scheduled at the arena over the next two years. Silver absolutely *loved* the high-definition video displays they planned to add outside the building and brought up installing them outside the forum to Dean when they met again just before the game. As usual, he seemed unsure of the idea, but he agreed to look into it when they got home and get her in touch with the right people if that's what she wanted to do.

She peeked at him from under her lashes as he paced the other side of the room, speaking to some agent about a defenseman he really wanted to sign. The way his tone sharpened just a little as he went over numbers and contract details, made goose bumps rise all over her flesh. And down lower, her body recalled that tone when he'd woken her up early and she'd been grumpy with him. After saying "Do. Not. Move," he used his mouth and tongue to make her come twice and then taken her hard and fast.

A morning person, she was not. But if that's how mornings with him would be, she might just turn into one of those perky the-sun-is-out-and-the-birds-are-singing people!

Screaming orgasms at dawn beats coffee any day.

Dean paused and looked at her, his lips curving into a knowing smile. Her nipples hardened and she snapped her gaze to the ice, willing it to cool her down.

There, a black and gold jersey with the number 20 and Bower on the back. A chill prickled down her spine. She inched closer to the glass, watching him as he did a few laps around the far end of the rink. Seeing him out there, bigger than the other men in all his equipment, more important in his position, made him seem . . . untouchable somehow. Like the actors people had actually heard of in some of the movies she'd done. They might all be working together for a common goal, but her small part was nothing compared to his.

He's never made you feel like nothing, said a voice in her head that she didn't recognize. Too many voices. The freakin' pushover one could join the diva in the mental trash compactor.

"He made me feel like *less* than nothing," she said under her breath as she took a step back. "So shut up."

Dean held a hand over his phone and lifted his head. "Did you say something, Silver?"

"No." She smiled at him and took a seat in one of the swivel chairs. "I think the game is about to start."

He nodded, quickly ended his conversation, and came over to take the seat beside her. As the game got underway, Silver tried to follow the play, but through the corner of her eye noticed Dean fixated on the far end of ice.

"He looks stiff. Uncomfortable." Dean's lips drew into a hard line. "Tim said it looked like he'd been drinking last night. My idiot brother should have put in the backup."

If only I didn't know who you were talking about. "He looks fine to me. I wish you'd trust your brother. You said I might come off as an intrusive owner. Are there such things as intrusive GMs?"

His jaw clenched. Then he sighed. "You're right. I may be overanalyzing my brother's worth as a coach. I'll try to tone it down a notch."

"Good."

"But I still don't think Bower should be in nets."

Uck. Do I have to spell it out? He was a man, so probably. "I don't want to talk about him."

Dean angled his chair toward hers, spreading his feet apart as he leaned forward. His slight frown, the stillness about him, unnerved her. "I understand that you're upset. And that you're not speaking to him. But I asked you to come on this trip for a reason. Look at him." He nodded toward the ice below. "Tell me what you see."

Rising again, she folded her arms over her chest and glared down at Landon. He took his place in front of the net and slapped his stick against the pipes. His stance was stiff as he bent his knees and several of the forwards took shots at him. He stopped most, but the easy flow from the last time she'd seen him out there was gone.

His head just wasn't in it. She couldn't say how she knew, exactly, but he appeared to be somewhere else, leaving his body to go through the motions.

She dropped her head and sighed. "You're right. I don't think it's the drinking that got to him." *It's probably you, you coldhearted bitch.* She ground her teeth. "But whatever it is, he shouldn't be out there."

Dean nodded and stepped up to put his hand on her shoulder. His eyes said what he wouldn't.

Whatever it was, whatever would come of Landon stepping up to guard the fort, there was nothing they could do about it. It was too late.

Chapter Twenty Three

A big fist flew and Landon winced as Carter took a solid punch to the jaw. The fight lasted for seconds after Nelson and Carter dropped their gloves, midway through the first period—the refs had stayed close, ready to break the men apart as quickly as they could. Carter tried to hold on, but that hit threw him off his skates. Nelson lifted his fist, growling something Landon couldn't make out.

And Carter laughed, baring his blood-coated teeth.

Stupid little shit. Landon thought, grinning and shaking his head. At least he'd made it through the fight without needing a stretcher to cart him off the ice. Nelson had gotten his licks in. The game could continue without any more bullshit.

The puck remained in the offensive zone for most of the five minute fighting penalties, giving Landon plenty of time to take a drink and let his mind wander. He shifted from side to side to keep his muscles loose and kept his head down so he wouldn't be tempted to look for Silver. Not that he could see her from down here while she stood high above him in the press box, but somehow, he could feel her. Watching him. Damn it, he would give anything to have spent a moment with her before the game—to tell her . . .

Fuck, man. Get over it. Talk to Becky if you need to get it off your chest. Silver doesn't need to hear it. She hates you enough without knowing—

White, blue, and gold sweaters rushed him, and he dove as the puck came at him. He landed and lifted his head just in time to see the Sabres celebrating their goal. 1-0. He better snap the fuck out of it.

His defensemen glanced at him, then skated away. He pushed up to his knees and gave his head a hard shake. A stick bumped his arm.

Carter crouched down to eye level. "You good, buddy? They really left you hanging."

"I'm good. Just fell asleep." He let out a shallow laugh. "That woke me up."

"Fair enough." Carter stole Landon's water bottle to rinse out his mouth, then spit on the ice. "Don't worry about it. I got this."

Landon nodded and they bumped helmets. He managed to make his mind go blank and centered on the little black disk. Dropped. Swept up by Carter and passed to their youngest rookie, who fumbled and ducked as Nelson rushed him. He lost the puck and Nelson barreled down the rink. Landon came out to meet him.

Bent down low, Carter hip-checked Nelson and stole the puck. He paused and grinned. "Tell Mel butterflies look some nasty over dimples!"

Nelson roared and chased Carter across the ice. The kid moved like a jaguar, long strides and pure speed, feinting to the left and attacking from the right. The Sabres' goalie fell for the ruse and looked back as Carter tucked the puck into the empty net.

First period over. Landon met up with Carter as the team headed to the locker room. Slumped on a bench, he pulled off half his layers to let his body cool down. The rookies congratulated Carter on his goal, but the few veterans ignored him. Landon studied the men, taking note of the cliques that formed between the old and the new. He had to give Callahan credit. As a captain, he pulled the team together, and his alternate, Perron, worked as the glue. Unfortunately, neither of them were here. The excitable rookies really had no one to lead them. Except for Demyan who snubbed them all and Landon himself, who'd never been comfortable with team politics.

"You guys were real solid out there!" Tim grabbed the shoulders of two rookies and inclined his head to Carter. "That goal was highlight reel-worthy. But take care of those hands. We don't need them busted up in a fight."

"Got it, Coach." Carter pulled off his shirt, flexed, then laughed. "I need to beef up a bit before I take on that guy again anyway. He's got fists like a fucking sledgehammer!"

Tim nodded. "Yes, but so does Mason. Let him take care of the man."

"Mason's not here."

"With the way you chirped out there, Nelson will be on you all season. I like that you don't turtle, kid, but if you're going to run your mouth, let him take the penalty."

"Will do," Carter said.

Landon laughed as Carter approached. "So you've got it? Next time he takes a swing, you gonna stick your head in your shell?"

"Hell, I don't know." Carter scowled and dropped onto the bench beside him. "I should, shouldn't I?"

"He could have ended you out there."

"Yeah . . . not so sure about that." Scrubbing his face with a towel a trainer handed him, Carter mumbled. "I didn't even get in a punch. I looked like a damn pussy."

"Fuck that." Landon shoved the kid almost off the bench. "You made up for losing the fight by putting us on the scoreboard."

"I guess . . ."

The kid was damn competitive. Which was good. So long as he put that energy where it actually counted. But he didn't need a pep talk. "So . . . butterflies?"

Carter lifted his head and chuckled. "Yeah. Mel has one on each butt cheek. She's hot, but they're all gross and faded. Like she sat in something. And they're right over her dimples, so they look squished."

"Damn. So you really did fuck her?"

"Oh, yeah. She wouldn't take no for an answer. You know the type."

Landon nodded, even though he didn't. He'd been with a woman who knew him before he'd been drafted. Before he was someone. He hadn't let sex or women take away from his goal to be the best. And that mind-set had cost him too much for him to change it now.

Sweaty, smelly, and all suited up again, Landon followed the others out to the rink for the second period. The next twenty minutes were uneventful. The tie held well into the third period. Demyan, whose minutes had been limited so far, pulled a double shift and led a merciless strike against the Sabres' goalie. Not quite as fast as Carter, but the way he fluidly spun and dodged his opponents made them all look like toddlers learning to skate on two-bladed "cheese-cutters." He had the puck for most of his shift and played cat-and-mouse until, with only five minutes left on the clock, he walked up to the blue paint and surprised the Sabres goalie with a smooth five-hole shot.

The crowd booed as Demyan took a flamboyant bow. Bad enough he'd made asses of their entire team, but he had to rub it in.

Entertaining? Yes. But Demyan was proving to everyone—including his own team—that he had no class. Not one of the Cobras—except Carter—congratulated Demyan for the goal.

Of course, Demyan didn't look like he gave a shit. Slouched on the bench, he pushed his helmet over his brow and folded his arms over his chest. Looked like he was taking a nap. The rookie close to him scooted over as though afraid that whatever was wrong with him was contagious. The Sabres' bench grumbled and their goons leaned over the boards, shouting insults at Demyan.

A fresh lineup took the center ice face-off. Carter managed to sweep up the puck before the focus fully shifted from Demyan's antics. Weird, because the kid had riled up their captain . . .

Yeah, but Demyan disrespected the team and the fans.

Intentional? Hell, Landon doubted it. Scott Demyan was an arrogant, cocky fucker. Why would he care about taking the target off the kid's back?

No time to dwell. His fumbling defense had moved too far into the Sabres' zone. The eager rookies wanted some of Carter's spotlight, and he seemed happy to give it to them, saucering easy passes to the line for one-timers. Not a selfish player then. Good man.

The defenseman flanking the left missed his pass. Nelson picked it up for a breakaway.

Landon blocked out the rink. Blocked out the crowds. Saw nothing but the puck and the man charging him. And Carter, catching Nelson, and diving to knock the puck away from his blade.

Nelson cursed and slashed his stick into Carter's face as the kid tried to rise. Players crowded around them, fighting for possession. Carter dropped to his hands and knees. His blood splattered the ice beneath him.

The ref didn't see him. The linesmens' attention locked on the play as Nelson careened into the net. The puck left his stick. Landon grabbed it. And hacked his stick into Nelson's legs.

A harsh whistle. Shouting. Landon tossed his stick and skidded to Carter's side. The trainer joined him, knelt on the ice, and used a towel to hold the torn flesh of Carter's mouth together. Blood soaked the white cloth as the trainer helped the kid stand.

"That fucking bastard." Landon left Carter to the trainer's care and looked around for Nelson.

Demyan already had him. A swift uppercut sent the Sabres' captain flying. A ref grabbed Demyan from behind and hauled him back.

"You're fucking lucky, you pussy! This isn't over!" Demyan howled and gave the screaming crowd the finger. "Hope you enjoyed the show, you sick freaks!"

Fuck what people say about you, man. Landon grinned and shook his head. His whole body quivered with rage as Demyan was shoved toward the hall leading to the locker rooms. *You're quality.*

Someone was dragging Landon and he glanced back to see a ref glaring at him.

"You're out of here."

He snorted. "Yeah, well, that's a surprise."

"Shut it, Bower." Tim reached out and fisted his hand in Landon's jersey. "Get out of here. I'll talk to you later."

"Carter—" Landon shook his head and tried to turn. Blood. So much blood. "He—"

"We've got him. Just go."

Go. You can't help him. He'd been ejected from the game. Hell, he'd probably be suspended. The temporary satisfaction of lashing out at Nelson dwindled away, leaving him empty and cold. *Some fucking pro you are. Was it worth it?*

He snarled and punched the wall on his way down the walk of shame.

It damn well better be. This is all I've got.

****

"I can't speak for the league. There will be a review of what happened on the ice and both Scott Demyan and Landon Bower will accept whatever supplementary discipline is handed down."

Dean folded his arms over his chest, watching his brother

address the media, and grudgingly admitted he was handling the questions well. So far.

A familiar face in the crowd of reporters stepped forward and Dean cursed.

"Would you say you support your players' actions on the ice?" Rebecca Bower thrust her mike at Tim like a dagger she wanted to stab him with. "Rumor has it that Bower was in no condition to play tonight. No one is all that surprised by Demyan's actions, but perhaps you wouldn't have to worry about losing your starting goaltender for any amount of time if you'd sat him tonight."

"There are many rumors, Ms. . . ." Tim's brow shot up and he smiled. "Bower. I fully understand your concern, but if that was Landon playing at less than his best, I look forward to what he'll bring to the team this season. As for the players' actions, we have many passionate men on this team. Passion is shown in many ways, and while I cannot encourage retaliation in the manner it was displayed today, I expect my players to react when their teammates are targeted as our young Mr. Carter was."

"Didn't he ask for it?" Another reporter shouted out from the back of the crowd. "He made derogatory comments to the Sabres' captain about his wife."

"More rumors?" Tim shook his head. "Many things are said on the ice. Carter is having surgery to piece his mouth together as we speak. I don't believe anything he may have said warranted such a brutal attack."

"So you're claiming Nelson's actions were intentional?"

"Watch the replays and make your own judgments," Tim said evasively. "Thank you."

Well done, brother. Very PC, yet he'd managed to support the players and state his opinion. The previous coach, Paul, hadn't been comfortable with the media. He came off as brusque and had more than once thrown players he didn't like under the bus. Which Dean should have paid more attention to, but the man seemed so professional he hadn't questioned it. Only in hindsight did Dean realize the man had been wrong for the team.

Seeing Tim out there, confident and approachable, gave him a new outlook on the skills a coach needed to run a team like the

Cobras. He couldn't wait to see where his brother would bring them this season.

But first, he had to deal with Bower. Demyan, he would leave to Tim, but Bower . . . as a goalie—as a *Dom*—he should have shown more control.

Silver came to his side and slipped her hand into his. "Can we go now? I need to see if Carter is okay."

Carter or Landon? He almost asked but thought better of it and simply nodded and squeezed her hand. "Sure." He noticed Rebecca, off to the side of the conference room, glaring at him. "Just give me a minute."

Rebecca's lips twisted into a scowl as he approached. "I don't care what the coach says. Landon shouldn't have been out there."

"Rebecca." His brow furrowed as she stared at him expectantly. "Your brother is a grown man. You can't come running every time—"

"This time is different."

He studied her face. Maybe she wasn't overreacting. Bower had gotten drunk. And maybe not because of his problems with Silver. "Different how?"

She glanced over at the other reporters, at Silver, and shifted forward. "Can we talk somewhere private?"

Silver might not . . . He looked to Silver and she inclined her head. No jealousy in her eyes. Just concern. He gave Rebecca a stiff smile. "Yes. Follow me."

Another conference room, the one he'd used to speak to the players the night before. Smaller, but private. He took a seat and motioned for Rebecca to do the same.

"I shouldn't be telling you any of this, but I have to tell someone since Landon won't. Hockey is his life and if he doesn't let this go, he's going to lose that too." Rebecca covered her face with her hands and hunched over. "I can agree with one thing Tim said. Landon is passionate. He's played hockey since he was four years old and our parents supported him, even when he got older and threw away other opportunities for more training, more time at the gym. He didn't have much of a social life—except with the other players, and even then, only the serious ones. He had one girlfriend in high school. The only girl who could put up with seeing him only once or twice a month. He stayed with her through college."

Rebecca stopped talking. Looked torn, as though not sure she should continue.

Dean steepled his hands on the table. "Sounds like he had something special with her."

Shaking her head, Rebecca stood and started to pace. "That's the thing. It wasn't really special. She just fit with his lifestyle, even after . . ."

"After . . . ?"

"Landon had a college professor who was an old-school Dom. Strict leather. He saw something in Landon—a need . . ." Rebecca went to the window and placed her hands on the ledge. "He introduced Landon to D/s—he was attracted to my brother, but Landon is straight and not at all submissive. Somehow, it worked out anyway. Because Landon wanted to learn. They became very close friends. From what I understand, Tracy was totally into everything Landon wanted to try. She threw herself into a 24/7 with him— whenever he was around long enough—"

"She became everything he wanted."

"Yes and no. She played the perfect sub, but she started to come down on him about the time he spent with his mentor and his friends. Bitched about the time he spent with his family. He tried to accommodate her until one day she pushed him too far." She sighed. "Right in front of us all—Mom, Dad, our little brother—she lashed out and said she was tired of sharing him with his gay friends. Landon is nothing if not loyal. He ended things."

Her face was twisted in rage when she turned. Dean tensed, not sure if he should let her go on. This was too personal. Too painful.

But she continued before he could make up his mind to stop her. "He went on a road trip, came back, and found her waiting for him. She was pregnant! Wasn't it wonderful?"

"He went back to her."

"Of course he did. My brother isn't the type to turn away a woman carrying his child. But . . . the baby was stillborn." Her voice hitched. "He was so in love with the idea of being a father! It tore him apart. He tried to make it work after, but she hadn't changed.

She got worse and worse until he couldn't take it anymore. She was smothering him!"

"Rebecca, you don't have to—"

"She committed suicide a week before the second anniversary of their baby's death. She called him and begged him to come back to her. It was training camp; he couldn't just leave. And she'd been calling and calling . . ."

Jesus Christ. Dean stood and pulled Rebecca into his arms as she sobbed. "It's not his fault. I get it. Breathe, sweetie."

"He blames himself!" Her whole body trembled. "She slit her wrists in his bathtub and made sure he found her there! He hasn't been in a relationship since. I can't . . . I can't let her destroy him! I hate her! I fucking hate her!"

"Shh . . ." He stroked her arms and let his voice lower to a soothing, yet firm tone. "Thank you for telling me, Rebecca. I couldn't help him if I didn't know. You're an amazing sister. He's lucky to have you."

She sniffled, then groaned. "He's going to be so mad that I told you."

"I won't tell him you did. Here, clean yourself up." He took out the grey silk handkerchief from his suit pocket and handed it to her. "You go tell him off for playing hungover. He's probably at the hospital. Do you want a lift?"

"No." She dabbed her wet cheeks and took a deep breath. "I can get there on my own. Just . . . just make sure he knows he's worth something. I thought he and Silver were . . . but they're not. They're friends. And he could use a friend right now."

"He has several." He smiled. The woman pulled it together quick. If her face wasn't red, he wouldn't have guessed that she'd just bared her soul. "Do you mind if I tell Silver? I think he needs her more than anyone."

"Tell her." Rebecca's jaw went hard. "And tell her if she ever hurts my brother, friend or not, I'll turn her pretty face into roadkill."

"So noted." Dean gave her a moment to compose herself, then gently guided her to the door. "I really don't think you need to worry about Silver, though. I think she'll be good for him."

"So do I." Rebecca hesitated and frowned up at him. "But you—"

"Let me worry about that." Dean gave her a hard look when she opened her mouth to protest. "Rebecca, I don't appreciate subs questioning my actions."

Her cheeks reddened. Then she laughed. "Yes, Sir!"

"Good girl." He inhaled as she walked away, then spotted Silver and held out an arm, welcoming her into his embrace.

She snuggled against him and mumbled. "You've got something bad to tell me, don't you?"

"Yes, my love." He kissed her hair and sighed. What if he was wrong? What if believing her "Landon and I are friends" was an indulgent fantasy? Would she still want him? He had to believe she would. And make sure she made an informed decision. "But all you have to do is listen."

And not leave me in the dust once I'm done.

Chapter Twenty Four

Antiseptic and—Silver's nose wrinkled—blood. The scent didn't bother her as much as the length of stitches, piecing Carter's swollen mouth back together, marking a black track from the left side of his bottom lip almost down to his chin. As she watched, he laughed and leaned forward so Scott and Landon, who both stood by his temporary ER bed, could see the stitches inside his mouth.

The room spun like a tilt-a-whirl and Dean caught her elbow. "Breathe, sweetie. He's fine. Just showing off his 'war wounds.'"

Must he? Her concern stepped aside and common sense took over. She didn't need to be here. She needed to be . . . *In a nice hot bath with a bottle of tequila. Enough to completely blank out what I just saw.*

As her gaze flitted away from Carter, it locked with Landon's. He opened his mouth—then stood and lightly punched Carter's arm. "I'm going to go pick up a few things for you, patch-face. Demyan, you mind giving him a lift back to the hotel when he's cleared?"

"Sure thing," Scott said.

Landon shuffled past her and Dean, pausing when Carter called out to him.

"What?"

Carter pointed at his mangled lip and managed a painful-looking, lopsided grin. "Few more of these and I might be as ugly as you!"

Chuckling, Landon gave him the finger and walked out.

Wow, not even a nod? A smile? Nothing? She chewed on the inside of her cheek, confused by how much it bothered her that Landon hadn't even acknowledged her presence. Fine, she wanted some space, but . . .

On the drive here, Dean had told her all about the shit Landon had been through with his ex. Part of her—a big part—wanted to talk to him. To get him to tell her himself. They were supposed to be friends, and if he was having a rough time of it, he needed to know she was there for him.

But she wasn't. Which made her feel guilty and pissed off all at once. It was his fault they weren't speaking. Should she just forget he'd hurt her because he'd had a rough life?

No. Forgetting it wasn't an option. They had a long way to go before they could be friends again.

Still, she couldn't just let him leave. And anyway, she *was* his boss. It made perfect sense for her to remind him of that after what had gone down on the ice. They had some things to discuss.

Even though he obviously wanted nothing to do with her.

Doesn't work that way. Silver squared her shoulders. *I'm the one who's mad. If I have something to say, he's damn well going to listen to me.*

Following him out to the exit, she cleared her throat and folded her arms over her chest. "Mr. Bower."

He stopped short. His back muscles tensed under his snug grey T-shirt. "Yes, Miss Delgado?"

"Don't get all pissed off and go on another bender. You'll still be expected to show up for practice."

With a gruff laugh, he turned to face her. "Is that so?"

"Yes. And you don't have to run away the second I walk into a room."

His brow arched. "Run away? Is that what you think I'm doing, *mignonne*?" His lips curved into a dark smile. "You wanted me to stay away. I'm staying away. Don't push me."

She dug her nails into her palm to stifle a shudder. "Is that a threat, Mr. Bower?"

"Landon." He moved closer, his grey eyes holding the heat of molten steel. His tone took on a knife's edge as he backed her into a wall. "Say my name, Silver."

There wasn't enough air to say his name. She gasped as her lips formed it, and that appeared to be enough. His hands delved into her hair, tearing it free from her loose updo. Her scalp tingled. Her heart forgot to beat. His lips came down on hers, and she lost herself to the taste of him. Mint and salt. Brutal, bruising pressure. Pain, so fucking sweet. The smooth thrust of his tongue, possessing her mouth until she whimpered because it was all too much.

His kiss gentled, massaging her lips as the tip of his tongue teased hers. He eased his hands from her hair and curved them around her face. "I'm sorry. I had to."

Her brain snapped back into her skull. She shoved him and her hand whipped out, catching his cheek with a loud, satisfying *Smack!*

"No. *I'm* sorry." Her eyes teared and her whole body quivered. "I'm sorry bad things happened to you, but you don't get to do that. You don't get to hurt me, then leave me, then do that."

Landon gave her a curt nod, then lifted his head. "I'm afraid I must apologize again for trespassing, Sir. I swear this is the *last* time it will ever happen."

He walked away and she locked her legs against the insane urge to follow him again. To scream at him. To give him a few more slaps.

To demand another kiss.

Strong arms came around her and she stiffened, then relaxed into the familiar embrace. Hot and musky. Solid. Her man. Dean.

Dean . . . she glanced over her shoulder and held her breath. Was he mad? He smiled and shook his head, as though answering her thoughts.

And then he did. "I'm not angry. Actually, I've been expecting this."

"You have?" She let out a bitter laugh. "Of course you have. I'm a slut and—"

"Enough." He turned her and hugged her tight. "*He* kissed you, pet. That doesn't make you a slut. What I'd like to know is what exactly were you hoping to accomplish?" Dean whispered into her hair. "I'm assuming that wasn't it?"

"No." She groaned, miserably. "I don't know. I guess . . . I don't want him to forget about me. I won't pretend I'm not mad, but I want him to know . . . I'm still here."

"He's not likely to forget, my love." Dean's pulse beat slow and steady against her cheek. "You know how he feels about you."

"I do not. And it doesn't matter how he feels." Fisting her hands in Dean's shirt, she glared up at him. "I'm with you. And you need to stop acting like I'm going to leave, because I'm not going anywhere. I . . ."

Dean shook his head and sighed. "Silver, you don't have to say—"

"Shut up." She smacked his chest and grinned when he frowned at her. "Interrupting is rude, *Sir*."

"And smacking your Dom is not very smart."

Oh shit. She let him go and backed up. "We're still at work."

"Work hours are over, little one. But we'll discuss this at the hotel." His eyes crinkled as he looked her over. "I do believe we'll have to try out the new gag I bought for you. Your screams may disturb the staff."

Heat flashed over her cheeks. "Umm . . ."

He smiled. "Now. You were saying?"

What was I saying? She nibbled on her bottom lip and shrugged. "I'm not going anywhere. I'm with you. So Landon—"

"We'll figure out how to deal with Landon when the time comes." He took her hand and kissed her forehead. "Just keep one thing in mind." He tipped her chin up. "I will never make you choose."

Won't make me choose?

The night air stirred her mussed up hair as they made their way to Dean's rental. She stared at the side of Dean's face all the way there, then again when she got inside the car and he climbed in behind the wheel. He didn't say another word on the drive to the hotel, which was good, because her mind was racing and she probably wouldn't have heard him anyway.

He won't make me choose. She stared out the window and chewed the inside of her cheek in thought. *What the hell does that mean?*

* * * *

Dean closed the door to the hotel room and leaned against it, thumbs hooked to his pockets as he observed Silver, aimlessly wandering around the room as though not sure what to do with herself. Likely overthinking things.

We can't have that.

"I mentioned punishment, didn't I?" He smiled slowly as she spun around and tripped backward into the sofa. "Oh no, pet. I'm not chasing you. Strip. Then kneel by the sofa."

Her skin paled even as she peeled off her shirt. "But—"

"Ten, my love." He held up a hand before she could get herself in more trouble without a fair warning. "You're getting off easy. Consider that before you say another word. And know I will add five for each one."

She finished stripping and dropped hard to her knees with a wince. "You can't—"

"That's twenty. You were saying?"

She pressed her lips together and scowled.

"I should add five for that look. Be a good girl. The seats in the LA press boxes are rather hard." His lips curved into a smirk. "And I don't think they provide pillows."

The scowl disappeared. Her teeth grazed her bottom lip, so damn distracting he almost lost his train of thought as he recalled how that mouth felt sliding all the way down his cock. Fortunately, his sense of responsibility took over before he went to her and abandoned all thoughts of discipline. She needed this. Tonight, more than ever. If he let her get away with hitting him, she would expect him to let her get away with everything. He'd shown her respect as a partner. He'd earned the same as her Dom.

Lucky for her, he was taking into account her inexperience. He had a whole arsenal of creative punishments for naughty little subs. But he would save those. For now, they would stick with something a bit more traditional.

"I'm going to our room to collect a few things." He moved in close to her and nudged her knees apart with his foot so her glistening pussy was fully exposed. Much better. "Don't move."

A quick nod as her lips parted.

"Let's not forget ourselves, pet."

Her throat worked. She shut her mouth and nodded again.

He let his approval show in a soft smile. Then went to the bedroom to get what he needed.

Silver hadn't moved in his absence, which earned her another smile. He stepped up to her side and petted her hair before dropping his small black toy bag and his walking stick on the coffee table in front of her.

Eyes wide, she groaned and stared at the long, thick, polished wood. "Oh . . ."

"Not exactly a word, so I'll let it go." That got him a dirty look.

He chuckled. "I rarely use this for punishments, but I keep it with me at all times in case my knee acts up."

Lips pursed, she looked at his knee. Concern. Very nice.

"An old sports injury which ended my military career, unfortunately." Her snort brought a roar of laughter from deep in his chest. "Not surprised that I was in the military, I see."

She rolled her eyes.

"Bad girl." His eyes narrowed as he caught her chin and held it in a firm grasp. "I've slacked in training you. That. Ends. Now. I'm trying to be patient, pet, but stop testing me."

There. His heart warmed as she lowered her eyes, showing the first sign of submission in a long time. Too long. He finally had her exactly where they both needed her to be.

Caressing her cheek with his fingertips, he moved away to open his bag and take out several "toys." Some she would recognize. Others she wouldn't. He spread them out on the table, then took a seat to let her take them in.

"We are going to try something—something I don't do with most of the subs I've had because they know what they like, and it ruins the effect of the punishment." He reached out to play with her hair, loving the way she struggled not to lean into him as he did. Most women enjoyed having their hair petted and stroked. Silver was no exception. "I've noticed something about you. Much as you talk back and protest, once you understand the reason behind a punishment, you accept it. Your body still responds, but you're truly sorry after. And not just because you're sore."

She glanced over her shoulder, eyes glistening. She was already sorry.

For a moment, he wanted to toss the punishment and just tell her all was forgiven. But that would teach her nothing, and she had to understand that forgiveness came with accepting the punishment. She's been denied that with Bower, and he wondered if it wasn't a trigger. Delgado didn't seem the type to let an infraction go after doling out punishments. And if he was right, she needed to see Dean was always consistent with his discipline and his love.

"This is what you're going to do." He sat forward and held out his hand to the table. "You will either choose one of the implements

I've provided, or, if you'd like, I will use my hand. Show me your choice. You will not speak. And once the punishment starts, you will not be able to. I mentioned the gag?"

Her tongue flicked over her top lip, and she looked at the bit gag that lay at the far end of the table.

"Yes. That's it. It should fit comfortably and prevent noises loud enough to bring the police. I got the leather straps in pink just for you."

She barely managed not to give him another dirty look.

"Quick save, sweetheart. Now make your choice."

It took her longer than he'd expected to choose. She fingered the tawse, flicked the strands of the flogger, and avoided the riding crop and his walking stick as though they were living things with sharp teeth. The paddle drew her attention for quite a bit. She traced the words embedded in the wood. Brat.

Shifting on her knees to face him, she wrapped her fingers around his wrist, brought his hand up to her mouth, and kissed his knuckles.

"My hand?" He held back a grin at her nod. For some reason, her decision pleased him very much. He reached over and picked up the bit gag. "Open wide, my love."

The soft silicone fit nicely in her mouth. Her nose wrinkled as she got used to the sensation. The pale pink leather straps looked lovely against her pale cheeks. He did up the buckle, then slid back a little and patted his thigh. She rose gracefully, her expression . . . peaceful. As she laid herself over his lap, he stroked her back, reminding her that, even though this would hurt, he still cared about her. Deeply.

"Brace yourself, love."

So small. So fragile. But he didn't hold back. Every strike sounded through the room, along with her silent sobs. And it broke his heart just a little to carry out the punishment.

She'll learn. He reminded himself, holding her as she repeated again and again, words obstructed by the gag, but not too difficult to figure out, how sorry she was. *And so will you.*

* * * *

Silver calmed and peeked up at Dean. And damn, he didn't look like he had enjoyed that at all. Which was so wrong. She was the one who'd screwed up. Again. Why should he have to pay for it?

Drool spilled down her chin, and she brought her hand up to wipe some away. So gross. He didn't need to see her like this, all wet and sniffly.

He stopped her and used his sleeve to dry her face. "Shall we take it out for a little while, love?"

She blushed. Hell, she wanted it out just so she could tell him how much she liked him calling her "love." But she could only nod until he did.

And once the gag was gone, all she could think about was getting that miserable look off his face. "I'm sorry. Don't be upset anymore. I promise I'll never hit you again."

His lips slanted into a dry smile. "Don't make promises you can't keep."

Uck. I'm tempted to hit you now! "Hey, are you saying I can't be taught?"

"No. Not at all." His jaw clenched. "But I haven't been teaching you, have I?"

Idiot! Thankfully, she kept that one to herself. "What was the first spanking then, or the orgasms you refused to give me, or the flogger—need I go on? If I make you feel like less of a Dom—"

"Oh, baby." He hugged her and kissed her hair. "If anything, you make me feel like more of one. And you remind me of all that I should be doing. But you're so new—"

"I can take it." She sat up and folded her arms over her breasts. "I'm tougher than I look."

He threw back his head and laughed. Before she could get insulted, he rasped out. "Then I'm in trouble."

She smirked and straddled him. After scraping her teeth along his rough jaw, she whispered, "If all you're going to do tonight is spank me, you're damn right you are."

He growled and lifted her up, dropping her on the sofa and grabbing her wrists in one hand before she could react. He reached between them and undid his pants. His hot, throbbing dick pressed against her entrance. She thrust up to take him in.

Wait!

"Wait!" She gasped, hating her stupid brain for stopping him. But she'd forgotten something. "Condom. I'm clean, I swear, but I might have missed my pill. I can't remember . . ."

"Ah." He gave her a sheepish smile and pushed off her. Reached into his back pocket. "Let's not take any chances."

His dick beckoned and she couldn't help bending up to take it in her mouth. She watched his face as he fumbled with the condom wrapper. He tasted better than candy, all hot and salty. Come to think of it—she swallowed him and came up slowly—she hadn't needed any sugar since . . .

Dean. Here. Now.

"Stop." Dean tugged her hair and quickly covered himself. "I don't know what that thought was, but you will tell me." He shoved her onto the sofa, trapping her with his heavy body, and drawing her arms over her head again as he shoved deep inside her. "Later."

Fast. Hard. Pounding into her without leaving her a second to let her mind wander. His dick speared her almost painfully but filled her so completely she didn't miss having a functioning brain. Sweat slicked their bodies as they slid together, hers rising as he slammed in. She gasped as the first climax erupted, spreading lava through her core and her veins, so fucking hot. He forced her to bathe in the heat until it took her again and again. She ignited and screamed. He covered her mouth and grunted as he collapsed on top of her.

"Mmm." The inside of her eyelids flickered red and black. She panted against his hand. Her back tightened and a sharp pain robbed her of the lingering pleasure. "Mmmphff!"

Dean pushed off her. "Did I hurt you?"

"Oww!" She whimpered. Then giggled. "I have a cramp in my back!"

Smart man. He didn't laugh at her. Gathering her in his arms, he carried her to the bedroom, his tone gruff with the strain to hold in his obvious amusement. "I know just the cure for that."

He abandoned her in the bed for just a second before returning with some oil from the fucking gods. She sighed as his fingers worked her muscles loose.

"Damn it, Dean." *Say it! Just say it!* "I love you."

He went still. Then bent down to kiss the small of her back. "Silver." He paused and kissed her again before saying, very quietly. "I love you too."

Chapter Twenty Five

H alf a day to lounge around and enjoy one another. To whisper those sweet words a few more times as their eyes locked and the urge overwhelmed them. For the first time, Dean was able to look into Silver's eyes, the same golden shade as her sister's without the contacts, and see her come out of hiding without any force involved. His heart sputtered as he took her in, this young, beautiful woman so obviously in love. Glowing, almost shy with the emotions coming off her in waves. He hadn't really noticed before how quickly she'd rushed to primp herself when she got out of bed every other time she woke up in his bed. But now that she hadn't, now that she lounged around in nothing but his T-shirt and boxers, with her hair tangled and her feet bare, all he could think was "I want more of *this*."

But he'd bought them all the time he could. And it was ruined.

"Daddy—" Silver shook her head and slid to the other side of the sofa when Dean put his hand on her shoulder to comfort her. Hugging her knees to her chest, she curled into herself like a small, wounded animal. "Did you see the way he handled the puck? Acquiring Scott wasn't stupid—no, I'm not arguing with you. Please don't get upset, Daddy. Your heart . . ."

She winced and blinked fast. Near tears. Enough was enough.

"Miss Delgado, please tell your father I'd like to speak with him when you're done." He did his best to keep his anger out of his tone, but by the way Silver's eyes widened, he'd failed. As she say goodbye and passed him the phone, he laid his hand over hers and stroked her knuckles with his thumb. Hopefully she'd understand that he wasn't angry with her.

"So, you're fucking her."

The crudeness of Delgado's words completely threw Dean off. He gritted his teeth and inhaled very, very slowly. "Excuse me, sir? I think I must have heard you wrong."

"I'm not an idiot, Dean. Don't treat me like one." Delgado rasped in a labored breath. "My daughter obviously has no business sense, but she knows how to work a man. She'll ruin this team if you let her."

"I find that hard to believe, Anthony." A cold smile slashed across his lips. "She knows people, and that knowledge has come in handy. Take Demyan, for example. I'm sure you'd agree that he turned out to be a better acquisition than either of us expected."

"Are we speaking of the man who just received a ten-game suspension for leaving the bench and assaulting another player?"

"He was defending a teammate! Surely you remember how important that is?"

"And the goalie? We've lost him for five games because of his reckless behavior."

And how the hell is that Silver's fault? "I chose the goaltender. And signed him *after* discussing it with you, at your insistence. I don't believe it was a mistake, but if it was, the blame rests on my shoulders."

"Damn it, Richter!" Delgado gasped and wheezed. The way he switched from Dean's first name to last made it seem as though he was trying to come at him from another angle. His next words confirmed it. "You know I respect you. After the mess with Stanton last year—I could have fired you. But the man fooled us all. I know my daughter. She'll give you anything you want to get her own way. You should ask her how she got her first A in high school. I'm positive you'll be as disgusted as I was."

"With all due respect, sir, the time your daughter spent on her own in Hollywood changed her a great deal. Perhaps you don't know her as well as you think."

Silver's head shot up. She stared at him, either shocked that he'd contradicted her father, or surprised that Dean thought she'd changed. He'd find out which—even if it took another interrogation. *After* he was done with this nonsense.

"Don't say I didn't warn you." Delgado wheezed again, then moaned. "This is exhausting. Tell Silver I will call her tomorrow. And she better pick up."

The dial tone sounded. Dean put the phone in his pocket and slouched back into the sofa. He patted his thigh. "Come here, love."

She pursed her lips, sighed, then stretched out and rested her head on his thigh. "I'm sorry."

"For what?"

"He liked you. *Respected* you." She pressed her face into his pants and mumbled. "He won't anymore."

"I liked and respected Paul Stanton," Dean said as he smoothed her hair away from her face. "I was wrong about him. Your father was wrong about me. And *is* wrong about you."

"Whatever."

He fisted his hand in her hair. "Speaking of respect, 'Whatever' never qualifies as a respectful response to your Dom. I'd like a 'Yes, Sir' in this instance."

Snorting out a laugh, she turned to look up at him. "You don't get automatic 'Yes, Sir's when we're discussing business or my family. Haven't you learned that yet, you dumb ape?"

Laughing at naughty little subs taught them nothing. But he had a hard time containing his amusement. "Cheeky brat. I believe we've discussed you calling me names?"

"Yep. You love it."

Well, at least she didn't seem on the verge of tears anymore. Doing what he was about to do to her when she was still upset would be unethical. He stood and loomed over her, letting his tone drop to the one she understood on a baser level. "I think punishments will become part of our daily routine—at least until you learn how to behave yourself."

She squeaked like a little mouse popping out of her hole and straight into a cat's paws. Scrambling sideways, she made a halfhearted attempt to escape him. Her breath whooshed out when he caught her with an arm across her stomach.

"Dean!" She giggled. "You don't want to punish me! You hate punishing me!"

"No. I hated punishing you last night." He bit her earlobe hard enough to draw another squeak. "I'm going to enjoy this."

* * * *

Blueprints covered the desk in the new hotel room. Silver had brought them along so she'd be prepared for the meeting when she got home, figuring she'd have plenty of time to go over the designer's suggestions. She hadn't planned to need anything to keep her busy when they reached LA—seriously, this had been her home for years! She had friends to visit and beloved sights to see!

But this wasn't home anymore. Dean was right. She *had* changed. And she didn't feel like she belonged here anymore.

Not that I really belong anywhere.

"Stop that." Sucking her teeth, she set down her pink highlighter and pushed away from the desk. Her phone sat on top of her files like an ugly black bug—a cockroach, buzzing in a way that filled her with dread. Oriana had already called once today, just to make sure she was doing okay, so it wasn't her. And Landon wouldn't call—not that she wanted him to.

Only one person could be calling her now. Daddy.

Three days in a row—a new record. Not that it should surprise her that he was showing interest. He wanted to make sure she wasn't doing anything else that would jeopardize his team.

Bracing herself, she picked up her phone and answered. "Hello, Daddy."

"Tell me you're not with Dean."

She cringed. Every time he'd called, Dean had been nearby to cut the call short. She didn't need him to protect her from her father, but the way he supported her made her feel—well, whole again. A few short words from her father could shatter her, but a single touch, a look, from Dean built her right back up.

He can't be with you all the time, wimp.

Her eyes pressed shut. "No. He's not here."

"Good. He's finalizing a trade for a new defenseman. I don't need you distracting him."

"I know, Daddy. He told me. And we've already agreed he'd handle that side of the business." She glanced at the blueprints. "Actually, I'm working on some of those renovations you asked me to look into—"

"Good. That's what you should be doing." He actually sounded pleased. "Make everything pretty, my little doll. Just not too pretty. You can do that, right?"

"Yes, Daddy."

"Wonderful." He paused. "And when you get home, I'd like you to end things with Richter. I'm not sure why you'd even want to mess around with a man like him—he's not interested in your party life, and you can't pretend to be his type of woman for long, can you, my dear?"

Her eyes stung. "I'm not pretending."

"Of course you are. It took me a while to realize it, but you do have some skill as an actress. He'll see through you soon enough. Imagine the damage it will do to the team if you drag this out."

He's wrong, he's wrong, he's wrong! She hit her thigh with her fist. "I love him!"

"I seriously doubt that. You're like your mother, Silver. You love his power. His money. Not that you need either, I've given you more than enough, but your mother was the same way. Always wanting more. The only person she ever loved was herself."

"That's not true! She loved us. Antoine, Oriana, me, and you!" A lead ball lodged in her throat, heavy, hard, impossible to swallow. "You didn't know her, and you don't know me!"

He laughed and she swore she could hear him clapping. "Emmy worthy, my little doll—"

Doll. That's what he always called me. How he always saw me. And Mom. Something inside her snapped. "I'm not a fucking doll!"

"Watch your tone, young lady," he said, his tone cold. "You will show me the respect I deserve."

"Fine." She held up the phone and pressed end. Her eyes widened and she tripped backward, dropping the phone as she fell. *Oh my God! I just hung up on Daddy.*

But he deserved it. He shouldn't have said those things about her mother. He could be so . . .so . . .

She couldn't find a word for it. But she did know one thing.

That was the last call she'd be accepting from her *father* for a very long time.

The decision made her feel a little stronger, but she couldn't seem to stop shaking. She crawled to the desk and grabbed her purse. Took out a pack of Twizzlers and a lollipop. Then her vial.

I don't want this. I don't need it.

It took all her candy and five packets of sugar from the coffee tray on the little buffet, but she finally regained control of her body and her cravings. Decided to take a little nap.

And fell asleep to the images of white powder coating glass.

* * * *

Harsh charcoal grey suit and a stark white shirt. Dean's welcoming smile froze on his face as Silver approached. Too controlled. Too well put together. She did professional well, but this was more. Her fake green eyes shimmered. Delicate armor that fit so well, that wouldn't shatter, but that probably should before she got too comfortable in it.

But until he figured out why she'd pulled it on, he had to tread carefully. He moved away from the agent, extending his hand to her. "Miss Delgado. I was hoping you'd join us."

Silver took his hand and smiled her transparent, crimson-lipped smile. "Silver, please, Dean. I hope you don't mind, but it's too late in the evening for formalities."

Good. At least she isn't pulling away from me. He held onto her hand a moment longer than necessary, searching her face for a clue to how to best proceed. Nothing. She was looking at the man he'd been speaking to in the lobby outside the bar with polite interest.

"This is John Keeton. The agent to the player I signed tonight." Dean drew Silver to his side before releasing her hand so she could shake hands with Keeton. "John, this is Silver Delgado."

"A pleasure," Keeton said, clasping her fingers and grinning. "I like the direction the team is taking with you at the helm. It gives players like Ramos the opportunity to get the exposure they deserve. I'm sure you'll be pleased to know he'll agree to any publicity or charity work you come up with. He's very committed to his job."

"That's good to know." Silver withdrew her hand and glanced over at Dean. "I hope you were about to go into the bar to celebrate our latest acquisition. I'd love a drink."

There, just a slight tension around her eyes. He'd rather speak to her about whatever was bothering her than let her drown it, but a drink or two to help her relax wouldn't hurt.

"We were." He held out his arm and she put her hand in the

crook of his elbow. "Martini or beer?"

She let out a twinkling laugh and shook her head. "Champagne is more appropriate, but I was thinking bourbon."

Bourbon? Dean frowned. His little sub certainly wasn't a light drinker.

John chuckled, looking absolutely charmed. "A lady after my own heart. Let's find a booth near the door so Ramos can find us when he's done speaking to the coach."

They took their seats in the booth and waited for their drinks, chatting about the recent suspensions and some of Silver's plans for the team's exposure. The magazine spread she mentioned spurred a fierce debate in which John took her side, but despite Dean's need to defend his team's integrity, he loved the fire he saw in her eyes as she brought up all her points like parries in swordplay. He argued fiercely until she stood and pointed at him as though about to make the killing thrust.

"Know your role and shut your mouth!" Her eyes sparkled with amusement. "I don't need your permission. Most aren't nude photos. Get over it!"

"Most?" She's joking. Or she better be. "I can't see you getting any players—except Demyan perhaps—to pose naked."

"They'd be artistic shots. And you have no idea what men with big egos will do." She paused and smirked. "Scratch that. Actually, I was thinking a shot or two of you might—"

"Silver, that is *not* funny." Actually, it was. But he wasn't about to encourage her. "There's absolutely no need to promote me."

"Well . . ." John smirked and leaned across the table with his tumbler between his hands. "With a team as new as the Cobras, it makes sense to use every asset you have. You're a good looking man, Richter. Why not exploit your virtues? I know *I'd* enjoy seeing you in a centerfold."

An uncomfortable silence followed John's words. His sexual leanings were no secret. And he was fairly aggressive in his pursuits. To the point that he'd lost several players because of his advances. From the little Dean knew about him, the man considered a straight man one who hadn't met him.

Dean arched a brow when Silver leaned into him and ran her

hand up his thigh.

"Are you hitting on my man, John?" She brought her glass to her lips and licked the rim. "Because if you are, I have to warn you, I don't care what sex you are. I'll slap you down like a bitch."

John lifted his glass and inclined his head. "I apologize. I didn't realize you'd staked a claim."

"I have." Silver held her glass out to chime it with John's. "Just don't do it again."

The whole thing seemed very backward. Dean shook his head and grunted as Silver's hand slid up to his crotch. Damn if he didn't feel like a piece of meat being claimed by an alpha wolf. Shouldn't it be him guarding his territory, rather than the other way around?

Then again, Silver never made him feel like he had to fight for her. She made him feel like here and now, she belonged to him. But how long would that last? What they had between them was new and exciting. If he didn't keep it fresh, she'd get bored. And he'd lose her.

Then step it up, Richter. His lips curved in a slow smile as he brought his lips to Silver's throat. "I'm afraid you offer nothing that this woman can't give me, John. But I'm flattered."

"You should be." John chuckled and set his glass on the table. "Ah. Finally. Sebastian Ramos, I would like you to meet your new GM and owner. Dean Richter and Silver Delgado."

A large man with sleek, long black hair and dark brown eyes stood by Silver and gave her a hooded look. "Silver. I was hoping to speak with you this evening. I was taken aback by your offer, but once I considered, I realized you needed time to accept that part of yourself. And now that you have, I am eager to continue where we left off."

The man had a thick accent, as though English wasn't his first language. Dean observed him, taking in the smooth, alluring tone of his voice and matching it with the Latino appeal. Big, buff, and attractive. Silver's pulse quickened against his fingers. She knew this man. Very well. And something about him either frightened or aroused her.

By her expression, he figured the mind-numbing, raw attraction likely scared her. And the dominance the man wielded so easily. Bower would be his first choice for exploring her clear desire for a ménage. Being with two gay men wasn't an accident—perhaps a miscalculation on her part, but Silver wasn't a one-man woman. Dean had accepted that, but perhaps he'd been too closed-minded. Maybe the other man wouldn't be her dear friend. Maybe it could be Ramos.

"I've been looking forward to meeting you in person, Ramos." Dean smiled, trying to keep his face relaxed even though he didn't know this man and something inside him objected to letting him anywhere near Silver. "Please join us."

* * * *

"Sebastian," Silver whispered as her mouth went dry. Hair rose on the nape of her neck, and she found herself leaning forward slightly, though she managed to keep one hand in Dean's and the other fisted at her side. Even though her fingers tingled with the memory of his soft hair which still spilled in dark brown waves past his massive shoulders. Even though the way he looked at her made her want to lay her wrist in his palm.

Sebastian looked over her, to Dean. "May I?"

Dean must have nodded, because Sebastian moved even closer to her.

"I would like to say hello to you properly. Come to me, *muñeca*." The smooth, dark olive flesh of his face creased around his lips and eyes as he held out his hand. "Do not be afraid."

Her lips tingled. She knew exactly how he wanted to say hello. And shamefully, parts of her were heating up, eager to greet him. All she had to do was stand and let him take control. She'd bolted once, but she wouldn't this time. Not with Dean right there to keep her safe.

"It's okay, my love," Dean said softly, his lips brushing her ear. "Do whatever feels right."

Giving in felt right. It had the first time she met him, until he cuffed her wrists together and she realized if she didn't get away, she'd completely surrender.

No. I don't want to. She swallowed and the grip on her hand tightened a little.

"Silver, speak to me." Dean curved his hand under her chin and turned her to face him. "Ah, I see. Why don't you go for a walk, sweetie? I'll meet you outside by the fountain in a few minutes."

Don't need to tell me twice. Sebastian had already stepped aside, so there was nothing keeping her from making a beeline straight for the terrace. She skirted by a waitress and a group of businessmen who moved after she quietly said "Excuse me." None leered at her, which was weird until she realized she wasn't dressed sexy at all. She looked presentable. Mature. Like a woman who could run a franchise like the Dartmouth Cobras.

She'd felt strong when she'd left the hotel room. Power suits usually gave her the confidence to face all those people who thought she had no business playing owner. She wasn't the Silver Delgado who flirted and slept around, she was . . . she was the one Dean had come to respect. The one Dean treated like a partner. The one Dean loved.

And all Sebastian had to do was look at her and she didn't know who the hell she was anymore. Dean said she was submissive. He'd proved it. But she'd never thought she was *that* submissive.

Lemon trees surrounded her as she ambled along the garden paths, heading for the fountain with the cool dancing statue and all the stone birds. There was another fountain right in front of the hotel with bright lights shooting out of the rippling pool of water, but she didn't want to be around people right now. As long as they were in LA, people might recognize her. And she'd had quite enough of "old friends" for the evening, thank you very much.

In front of the fountain, breathing in the warm air, all flowers and green things lingering in the heat that still rose from the stone path, she managed to regain her center and stopped picturing herself kneeling to any Dom that glanced her way. Actually, for a moment she pictured Sloan trying to pull off "The Look" with her and snickered. Maybe she hadn't turned into a hopeless doormat after all.

"I take it the walk helped?"

Silver closed her eyes and relaxed into Dean as he came up behind her and wrapped her up in his arms. "Yes, the walk helped very much. But . . . I didn't embarrass you, did I?"

"Embarrass me?" Dean let her go and spun her around. "What

in the world gave you that idea?"

"You're a Dom. He's a Dom. He probably thinks you haven't trained me very well."

Dean shook his head as he pulled off his jacket and laid it on the grass by the fountain. "I *haven't* trained you very well, but there's no rush. We'll decide how far you'll go together." He sat on the jacket and patted the space he'd left beside him. He waited until she sat before he continued. "I'm just sorry I let him make you feel uncomfortable. I thought you were attracted to him, and I needed you to know—"

"Yes, you told me you wouldn't make me choose. I thought that was just with . . . anyway, it doesn't matter. I don't want to—I'm not interested in Sebastian. Conversation over."

"Oh no, you don't. Talk to me, Silver." Dean's tone took on that edge that told her he wasn't beyond making her speak. And she knew very well that he was capable. His hard eyes bored into hers as he reached out and stabbed his fingers into her bun, using it as a handle to tip her head back. "You're attracted to Sebastian."

"Yes." It came out as a whisper, but she was sure he heard her.

"He's the 'über Dom' you told me about."

"Yes."

He nodded slowly, his gaze fixed on the water trickling steadily into the fountain. "What happened between you two?"

Damn. He had to ask. Well, the story should amuse him, if nothing else. "I went to an elite BDSM club Asher's friends were raving about. Found myself a hot guy pretty quick who would give me a bit of kinky fun. Not too dominant, of course, still pretty new to 'the scene.' He tried to top me and got all aggravated when I wouldn't submit for real. I laughed at him and he grabbed my arm real hard— so a dungeon monitor came over." She shivered as she recalled the cold look Sebastian had given the man. His power oozed off him in waves and her body seemed to absorb it. "The guy took off and Sebastian pulled me aside. He told me I was cheating myself of the experience, that I needed someone who could 'handle me.'" She squirmed as she realized Dean had told her pretty much the same thing. "I got all sassy and said 'Someone like you?' and . . . all he said was 'Yes.' He latched onto my cuffs and clipped them together, and I freaked out because I could feel myself surrender. A few words. A look. And I was a goner."

Dean nodded slowly. "Did you tell him you were afraid? Did he notice?"

"Oh, he noticed. He whispered in my ear 'This ends only when you say your safeword.' So I said it. He unclipped my wrists and hugged me. Told me I wasn't ready. Told me to come back to him when I was."

"You're ready now, Silver."

"I know."

"Then . . . ?"

"Then what? Why not go for it? Just because I'm attracted to a man doesn't mean I need to fuck him. I love being with you. You don't make me feel cheap or slutty. Like you're using me or I'm using you. It's more! What's between us is more, and I would never consider being with another man unless—" What the hell was she saying? "No. There's no 'unless.' I'm with you. You're stuck with me."

"I don't consider that a hardship, precious." He released her hair, then shifted positions, pulling her inward to sit between his thighs. The tension left her scalp as he took her bun apart. "But I'm sorry that I read you wrong. I don't ever want you to feel trapped with me."

She groaned, caged between his legs, forced to endure the blissful massage that made the roots of her hair tingle while forming coherent words. "I don't feel trapped."

"But you may crave the attentions of another man in the future. If Sebastian was something you wanted—"

"Wanted. Needed. I have no idea what you're trying to give me anymore, Dean."

"I'm trying to make you happy."

"Well, handing me off to a guy who scares the crap out of me isn't going to make me happy." *Handing me off to anyone won't make me happy.* Why couldn't he understand that she needed more than the lust she felt with Sebastian? That she needed something deeper from a man. Something real. She pursed her lips and latched onto his wrists to still his hands. Then she looked up at him. "And what makes you think I'm not happy anyway?"

"I'm not blind, Silver. You were doing the ice princess act again." He pinched her chin and gave her a hard kiss. "Was it your father or—"

"Yes. My father." *What else could possibly be bothering me? The stupid suspensions? The fact that I don't have to worry about seeing Landon anymore?* A great big fist clenched in her chest, and she gasped to breathe past it. And spoke quickly before Mister Observant thought she was hiding something. "My father pissed me off, okay? And I hung up on him. Very rude. You should definitely punish me."

Dean's eyes widened. Then he threw his head back and laughed. "Punish you? I'd rather reward you! How about breakfast in bed? Champagne and strawberries. And crepes."

Mmm, that sounds nice. She rested her head on his shoulder and smiled. "Only if you make the crepes. You spoiled me from eating the ones anyone else makes."

"Deal."

The fountain gurgled as they sat there for what seemed like hours, just enjoying the peace and quiet, Dean taking in the sights and Silver watching him. Her fingers traced the fine lines in his white shirt. It smelled a bit like ironing and starch—thanks to her—and he smelled like the light, woodsy soap he'd brought along because he preferred his own to the hotel brands. She loved that about him. No matter where they were, he was, well, Dean. He didn't have a thousand different faces like the people she'd known. Or like her. Or like Landon.

She frowned at that last thought. Landon didn't have a thousand different faces. Just two.

"We've got two more days before we head home, Silver." Dean kissed the top of her head. "I won't push you. Not this time, but—"

"That's good to know." She stuck her fingers between his shirt buttons to toy with his chest hair. "I hate it when you're pushy and bossy and—"

He pushed her onto her back, and she stared up at him as his teeth flashed in a grin. His hands framed her shoulders as he leaned over her. "You hate it, do you?"

"Mmmhmm." She squirmed as he lowered one hand to undo

her pants. "Oh! Not out here!"

"Yes. Right here." He made a rough sound in his throat as his fingers delved into her panties and slicked through her folds. "As I was saying." He shoved his fingers deep inside her and curved them forward. "You have until we get home to tell me what the 'unless' was."

She panted as he stroked her up to climax and groaned as she considered his words. "Do I have to?"

His head titled to one side and he smiled. "Yes. But shall I take a guess?"

"Only—" she gasped as he pressed in further. "—if you—" her thighs trembled as he stroked that spot and red hot coils wound tighter and tighter inside her "—don't stop."

"I won't." He stretched out, half on her, half above her, his fingers still stirring and thrusting. Then he said softly, "You've only ever truly submitted to one other man, Silver."

"I don't want to talk about him! Oh!" One last, lingering stroke and she couldn't have managed another word if she'd wanted to. Her hips bucked as she rode the sensation to the shuddering end.

"All right, my little dragonfly." Dean gave her a hooded look as he brought his fingers to his lips and sucked them clean. "You can consider this conversation over."

Why is that not at all reassuring?

He didn't give her time to dwell.

Chapter Twenty Six

In the graveyard, Cimetière de Grande-Rivière in Gaspé, kneeling in the damp earth, Landon swept the dead grass away from the small, white marble plaque and brushed his fingers over the engraved words. "Landon Bower Jr." The birth date and the date of death were the same. His brow furrowed as he read the poem he'd had carved beneath it. *A Dream Within a Dream* by Edgar Allen Poe. His parents had tried to talk him out of using it, but—he lifted his head and smiled at his grandfather's tombstone, right beside his son's, where he could watch over him forever. His grandfather had read Landon the poem when he was too young to understand the meaning. He would have approved.

"I never thought I wanted kids, LJ." His eyes stung and he coughed to clear the tightness from his throat. "But I wanted you."

He clung to the only memories he had of his son. The ultrasounds he made sure were scheduled when he wasn't on the road. The kicks against his cheek when he sang to a swollen belly. And the day his son was born.

The young nurse had tears in her eyes as she shook her head and reached out to touch his arm. "I'm so sorry. Would you . . . would you like a moment to say goodbye?"

No air to speak, he'd just nodded, cradled the tiny blue bundle she placed in his arms, and pressed a soft kiss on the cold brow. If not for the color of his son's skin, he could have convinced himself he was sleeping.

He'd managed to hold it together until the nurse took his son away. Then something inside him shattered. Right there, in the hall, his knees gave out. His father, who'd stayed close through the difficult labor, caught him. Embraced him tightly before telling him firmly that he needed to be strong. That his baby's mother needed him.

A tear escaped and he let it fall. He focused on the phoenix at the top of the plaque, rising into flames straight from its shell. He couldn't say whether he believed in heaven, or something else, but he knew, without a doubt, that his son had gone on to something more.

"Daddy was really stupid, kid." He shook his head and laughed.

"I always imagine you're watching me play, cheering me on from wherever you are. But I went and got myself suspended." His lips curved into a rueful smile. "Then again, you're my kid. You probably didn't mind me going after that guy. Your great-grandfather would have said I did the right thing too. I'll just have to make up for being gone next time I get on the ice."

"I agree."

He'd been so focused on speaking to his son that he hadn't heard Richter approach. They hadn't had a chance to speak since before the league had handed down his suspension. Tim was the one who told him to go home and get his head on straight. He had no idea how Richter had found him—*probably Becky*—but he didn't want him here. This was something he did alone, at least once a year. Even Becky and his parents wouldn't intrude on his time with his son.

"What do you want, Richter?"

"Why didn't you tell me? Or better yet, Silver." Richter took a step back as Landon rose. "You could have taken some time off to come down here and—"

"I wanted him to see me play. He—" Damn it, the man was going to think there was something wrong with him. Not that he had to explain it, but for some insane reason he needed Richter to understand. He respected the son of a bitch more than he could say. "This was my dream—playing pro. I gave up everything to get where I am today. If he'd lived, I would—" *Shit, he's not going to think I'm insane. He's going to think I'm an asshole.* "I would have had to play on his birthdays. But he'd be okay with that, because he'd be so proud to see his daddy out there."

Richter put a hand on Landon's shoulder and squeezed. "I'm sure he's very proud of you. And if it counts for anything, even though I hated not having you out there for the last few games, I'm damn proud of you too."

"Shit, man." Landon's throat locked and he tried to pull away. Richter jerked him forward and barred an arm across the back of his shoulders. Landon snarled over a sob. "No one comes here when I visit. I don't want anyone to see me like this."

"Too fucking bad." Richter thumped his back hard, then moved away. "You *need* someone to stop giving you what you want."

"You're a pushy bastard." Landon rubbed his suit sleeve over his eyes, then shoved his hands in his pockets. "So, I take it you didn't come to give me shit about getting suspended?"

"No. I came to see if you were all right." Richter had the grace to look away as Landon composed himself. "I love Silver and she cares about you very much. It would destroy her if something happened to you after she pushed you away."

It should bother him that Richter had come because of Silver, but strangely enough, it didn't. He got it. He would have done the same in Richter's position. Besides the game, Silver was the one thing they had in common.

"How is she?" His forehead creased as he thought back on the rag magazine his sister had shown him this morning. "The Delgado princess—Torn between two lovers". "Are you sharing her with that asshole? I saw the pictures of you guys in LA. He was standing over her, and she looked pretty freaked out. And you were just sitting there—"

"I wouldn't share her with just anyone, Bower." Richter began to walk, then paused. "Do you need more time? I can meet you at your place later so we can discuss this."

"Just give me a minute." Landon turned away and took a knee beside his son's plaque. He bent down and kissed the cool marble. "Bye, LJ. I'll come back as soon as I can. I hope you know Daddy loves you so, so much."

He joined Richter and they made their way down the long path to the parking lot. Halfway there, he gave Richter a sideways glance.

"Whatever you wanted to discuss must be pretty important to take you away from preparing for the season," Landon said. "So have at it."

"I came for the reasons I said, Bower." Richter jaw tensed. "Silver needs to know you're okay. She needs you."

"She has you."

"So you're just going to let her go? Does she mean so little to you?"

Landon really wanted to knock the man down a fucking peg or two. Who the hell did he think he was? "I'll never let her go. I'm giving her the space she needs—that you asked me to give her. But after that, I'm sticking around. So you better get used to it."

Richter chuckled. "I wouldn't have it any other way. As I said, I won't share her with just anyone. But I will share her with someone who's got half of her heart, who cares enough about her to show her how special she is. Someone willing to fight for her. Someone willing to stick around."

The man had to be bat-shit fucking crazy. Landon stopped at the edge of the parking lot. "You want to share her with me? How do you know I won't take her away from you?"

"Because you love her as much as I do, you stupid asshole." Richter grabbed the lapel of Landon's jacket and let out a low, feral sound. "You wouldn't do that to her. At least you better not."

"I gave her to you." Landon wrenched free and his lips curled away from his teeth. "What is it? You're not enough for her?"

"Coming from the man who decided, without even asking, that he couldn't be enough, that's pretty fucking rich," Richter said. "Silver and I could be happy together, but I can't bear looking at her and seeing the regret. Who knows how long it will last—she's not the type to be tied down—but while she's mine, I will see her truly whole and cherished as she deserves to be. If I'm only a memory, it will be a good one."

Landon shook his head, confused. "So you're asking me to stick around, but you're ready to let her go in the end."

"Yes."

"Well, I'm not." He inhaled as some weight inside him lightened a bit. Then he groaned and rubbed his hand over his face. "Why are we even discussing this? She's not even speaking to me."

"She will." Richter slapped his shoulder. "You're doing a scene with her Saturday night. You promised to teach me how to use the wand."

"She won't submit to me. Not after—"

"She doesn't need to." Richter smiled. "She'll submit to me. Besides, I agreed to teach you too."

Pulling out his keys, Landon stared down at his shoes. "I won't use the whip on her. I've hurt her enough."

"Yes. You have," Richter said. "But I have other things to teach you."

"Like what?"

"Lesson one. A good Dom never stops learning. Keep that in mind. I won't let you touch her if you think you're above improving yourself."

"You're telling me things I already know." Landon ground his teeth together, hating the feeling that this man could give him the opportunity to get close to Silver, and take it away on a whim. "I'm not above learning."

"Good." Richter smiled. "I'll see you Saturday."

I'll see her Saturday. Landon watched Richter walk away, then turned to his own car. As the engine purred, he held on to the steering wheel. Why or how didn't matter. He'd see her.

I'm getting a chance to set things right. He glanced back at the graveyard and steeled his resolve. Sometimes, people didn't get a second chance. But now he was getting one.

And damn it, he'd make it count.

Chapter Twenty Seven

The chair creaked as Silver slumped forward on her desk. Finally home, but there had been so much to do she hadn't even unpacked. A Post-it note stuck to her cheek as she lifted her head just enough to see the clock hanging over the door in her office. Quarter after six. Her meetings were done for the day. She could leave.

Uck, I don't want to move.

Maybe she should just sleep here.

A soft rap at the door and Dean appeared. He took one look at her and practically growled. "That's quite enough. You're taking tomorrow off."

She plucked the Post-it off her cheek and crumpled it into a tiny ball. Tossed it. It landed on the edge of her desk. "First of all, Mr. Richter, we're still at work. So stuff your orders up your shit hole. Second—" A yawn cut of her words. "I was just about to leave. But I'm not taking tomorrow off. Friday, then the weekend. I can manage one more day."

"Stubborn." Dean shook his head. "Fine. Can I walk you to your car, *Miss Delgado?*"

"Certainly." She gave him a tight smile and stood, holding onto the edge of the desk when the weight of her head threatened to tip her over. "Oh, stop looking at me like that. I'm younger than you are." She stuck out her tongue. "I can take it."

His lips curved into a spine-chilling smile. "Can you? We'll see."

The tiny bite of fear woke her up enough to get down the hall and into the elevator. Trapped in there with him, she kept close to the wall and eyed him warily. But the smile was gone and he hadn't made a move. When the elevator doors opened to the garage, she stepped off and let out the breath she'd been holding.

Then screamed as he hefted her up and threw her over his shoulder.

"Put me down!"

"Work hours are over, pet." He smacked her ass twice, hard, on the way to her car, then sat her on the hood. "Be good and stay there."

She hopped of her car. "Like hell, I will!"

"Silver." His sharp tone locked her in place. "Strip. Then kneel."

Here? She glanced around nervously, but didn't even consider disobeying. Her mind had gone to *that* place, the one where she didn't really need to think, where she could just do. Good things happened when she went to that place.

Naked. On her knees. She waited.

He went to his car, parked beside hers, and opened the trunk. Her pulse quickened, but she kept waiting. And was rewarded with a smile when he returned.

She almost melted into a puddle right there on the pavement. Moisture slicked the insides of her clenched thighs.

"You get one choice, then not another word." He continued as she nodded. "My place or yours."

Her big cushy bed or his firm one in the house he shared with his daughter? Easy enough. "Mine."

"All right." He held up what he'd gotten from his car. Duct tape. He shook his head as she sputtered. "No. It's time for quiet now, little dragonfly." He ripped off a piece and covered her mouth with it. "Stand up."

The tape went around her wrists. Another length bound her ankles.

He observed her with a satisfied smile. "You do realize I can do *anything* I want to you now, don't you?"

A muffled whimper escaped. She nodded.

"Do you trust me?"

Another nod.

"Good. Very good, Silver." He picked her up and put her in the backseat of his car. After climbing in behind the wheel, he leaned over the seat and studied her. "You know, you're beautiful like that, but I don't think we'll be using gags often. You'd be begging me to take you now if you could. I miss hearing that."

Need reached a boiling point in her veins as he drove, and she glared at the back of his head. It was good that he'd restrained her. She really wanted to hurt him right now.

Shortly after, he carried her into her condo, unlocking the door with the key she'd given him the day before. He brought her right to her bed and then set her down gently. Before ripping the duct tape off her lips.

"Ow! Damn you!" She wiggled into a sitting position. "What happened to the nice guy I met on the trip?"

"You won't listen to 'the nice guy.'"

"But I'll listen to the fucking sadistic bastard?"

"Maybe." He grinned and patted her cheek. "Sleep in. Go hang out with your sister tomorrow. Take it easy." He chuckled when she scowled. "Stop that, pet. I'm too tired to punish you. And I want us both well rested for the club on Saturday."

"You should have just said so." She pouted, not really giving a damn about looking childish. The whole kidnapping scenario had almost been fun. But he'd ruined it by pulling her back into independent woman versus head case mode. "What if someone had seen us?"

"Someone did." He smirked. "Callahan and your sister were in the parking lot."

"Asshole! You had me strip in front of them? I swear you've got mouse turds for brains."

His hand latched on to her chin. "Next time you speak to me like that, I'll stick something nasty in your mouth."

"Promises, promises."

He snorted. "You're going to keep pushing me until I punish you, aren't you?"

Suddenly exhausted, she shook her head. "No."

"Good. Then let me ask you something." He moved away from the bed and crossed his arms over his chest. "How far do you want to go with this? Are you willing to truly submit to me? Fully?"

"All the time?"

"Not all the time. But when we're alone, or at the club. Do you trust me enough to explore that side of yourself with me?"

There was that intensity again. But it didn't scare her anymore. She answered without hesitating. "Right now, I hate you almost as much as I love you. But I do trust you. So . . . yes."

"All right." He climbed onto the bed behind her and freed her wrists. "Between now and Saturday night, you are going to do exactly as I say. Pamper yourself. Relax. But don't forget, your pleasure is mine."

"What?"

"You don't come unless I allow it. And if I'm not around, you can assume you do not have my permission."

"But . . ." She pressed her thighs together and groaned as her core throbbed. "Tonight . . . ?"

"Tonight I'm going to tuck you in, and you are going to go to sleep. If I stay, you're going to tempt me to either punish you, or make love to you. For the first time in my life, I don't trust my own restraint. I'm actually relieved that you chose your place." He put his hand flat between her breasts and pushed her onto the bed. Then he tugged the blanket up to her chin. "Tomorrow you will tell me about your day when I call you. Saturday, I will pick you up, bring you to my house, cook you the best meal you've ever had, then prepare you for the club."

"Prepare me?"

"The only answer I need is . . . ?" He arched a brow.

She sighed. "Yes, Sir."

"Sleep tight, my love." He kissed her forehead and reached over to turn off the lamp by the bed. "I swear to you, this will all be worth what I have planned."

Staring at the ceiling, she heard the door close softly and the lock click. He fingers twitched as she brought her hand to her belly, letting it inch lower and lower until the tips of her fingers found moisture. But she couldn't go any further.

Curled up on her side, she willed herself to sleep and watched the minutes turn to hours on her digital clock. By the time darkness took over, her lips were sore from frowning.

Worth this? She clenched her thighs and pressed her erect nipples into the cool side of the sheets. *Mister, it better be.*

* * * *

Heat and steam, scented with some delicate flower like baby's breath. Silver sighed and let herself slip a little farther into the bath as Dean massaged her scalp and lathered her hair with the fragrant shampoo. His fingers pressed and rubbed, and she felt herself relax from where he touched down to the soles of her feet. The only tension that remained was sexual, but he'd already made it clear she'd have to wait for that relief.

Her eyes slitted open and she watched the tea candles around the bath flicker, the only light in the darkness. Dean had an old-fashioned iron tub on lion feet, so deep and wide she could picture them both fitting in here quite comfortably. As he moved down to mold the muscles at the base of her skull, she moaned. The pleasure was decadent, wonderful—but desire burned a constant flame, almost painful, almost too much.

"Soon, my love." Dean used the extendable showerhead to rinse her hair. "All right. All done. You can get out now."

Shaking hard, even though the room wasn't cold, she rose and closed her eyes as droplets dripped from her hair and teased her sensitized skin. She stepped out of the bath and gave Dean a grateful smile as he wrapped her up in a big fluffy towel. He kept an arm around her as he led her to his bedroom. He sat her on the bed and used another towel to dry her hair. Then he sat behind her and used a wide bristle brush to smooth out her damp tresses.

"I think we'll leave it loose tonight." He moved in front of her and smiled. "Yes. Absolutely beautiful. Stand up so I can dress you."

Silent as she'd been since dinner, when he'd informed her she wouldn't speak again until he told her she could, she watched him take out a pale pink lace baby-doll and a matching G-string. His fingers grazed her neck and her sides as he put it on her, causing tiny flames to lick her flesh. When he had her step into the panties and began sliding them up her thighs, she tensed and gasped.

Oh, God! She whimpered as the soft lace covered her. *I can't do this anymore. I can't!*

"Silver, look at me." Dean cupped her cheeks and held her gaze until she regained control. "There. That's better." He stroked her bottom lip with his thumb. "I won't let you spoil this for yourself by taking the easy way out. Two days may seem like a long time, but a week would be worse. Think about that before you let yourself slip."

She nodded and his smile returned, broad and full of the

approval she craved. He was right. She *could* do this.

You better. She thought as she smiled back at him. *You couldn't survive a week.*

Dean brought her a pair of strappy white sandals, slipped them on her feet, then covered her with a large leather jacket. He was already dressed in leather pants and a snug black T-shirt. They were both ready for the night.

Almost.

His toy bag sat by the door and he reached inside it, pulling out a leather collar and matching wrist cuffs. He held out the collar for her to see the words engraved in it: "Master Dean's Dragonfly."

"Tha—" Her eyes widened and she snapped her lips shut. No talking.

"Nice save, sweetie." Dean grinned as he buckled the collar around her throat. "And you're very welcome."

Strangely enough, the collar and cuffs steadied her, made her feel more controlled. Not by herself of course, but being under Dean's control always felt safe. Even though some small, irritated voice in her head objected to giving in. Objected to being denied. If she'd been permitted to speak, she would have cursed him out. Not having that option left her free to go where he was taking her. Not just to the club, but to something more. She didn't have to argue or fight.

He'd take her where she needed to be.

* * * *

Landon wiped his sweaty palms on his leathers as he caught sight of Richter. The man had called him earlier to let him know about the scene he wanted for Silver. It irked to have another Dom telling him what to do—no, not just another Dom. He got instructions from the Doms he scened with all the time: limits for their subs, tips on sweet spots, all that good stuff. It never bothered him; those Doms had the right to control the scenes.

Richter had the right to control the scene with Silver. And *that* was the problem. Landon could have had that right if he'd . . .

Drop it, Bower. You don't know that, not really. A large, coarse rope wound around his throat as he watched Richter take Silver's coat and saw the worship in her eyes as she stared up at him. Something was different about her. The way she moved, slowly, as though in a trance. The way she seemed comfortable wearing Richter's collar. The way she tilted her head as he spoke, giving him all her attention.

She's submissive. You knew that. He took a deep breath and went back to setting up for the scene. Richter had reserved the bondage frame for them—something Landon didn't use often. It left the sub fully exposed, with eight eyebolts lined up along the inside of the frame to secure wrists and ankle cuffs, and one overhead. A beautiful piece, really, in polished mahogany, solid enough for him to do chin ups on the upper bar without it even shaking—which he'd done earlier to make sure it was safe.

Of course, safety wouldn't be a problem; he knew what he was doing. The problem was Silver would likely bolt the second she spotted him. And there was no way she'd agree to the scene.

You don't know that. She might stay because . . .

Because Richter would command it. And she'd feel compelled to obey.

Tough shit. If she's not okay with it, it's not happening.

As Richter approached with Silver a step behind him, Landon's heart tripped a beat. His blood rushed downward. He hadn't gotten a good look at her outfit before, but it was impossible not to notice—and react—to it now. Delicate lace covered the gentle swell of her breasts, the almost translucent fabric the same pale pink of the sweet pea flowers on the vines his mother had grown when he was little. The lace parted beneath her ribs and flowed down to the tops of her thighs. A tiny swatch of cloth in the same color covered her pussy, though he could still see the smooth flesh beneath it.

He brought his gaze up to her face to find her eyes cast downward. Her hair, the color of the winter sun, fell forward, covering her cheeks.

For a second, only divine intervention could have stopped him from taking her and giving her all the pleasure he was capable of, but he leashed his urges and focused on Richter.

Richter took her wrist and pulled her forward until she stood right in front of Landon. "Eyes up, pet."

She looked up. Her bright green eyes narrowed. She pressed her lips together.

"None of that, dragonfly." Richter's tone was gruff and he kept his gaze locked on Landon as he spoke. "Master Landon is going to do a violet wand session with you. Thank him for being so generous with his time."

The muscles in her jaw twitched.

Richter frowned at her. "Silver—"

"No." Landon held up a hand to Richter and reached out to frame Silver's chin with the other. "We won't do this unless you want to. I agreed to teach your Master"—*damn it, he hated giving that title to another man*—"but I can do so with another sub. You can watch. I refuse to do anything that will make you feel uncomfortable."

Her throat worked as she swallowed. She glanced at Richter, then faced Landon. Her chin jutted up. "Thank you for your time, Master Landon. And for your considerate offer." Her lips curled slightly. "But I will do this for my *Master.*"

Not for you. Landon nodded. "I guess that's how it should be."

"You guess?" Her words snapped like the whip in a scene across the room. Her eyes went wide. She looked at Richter again. "I'm sorry."

"Don't apologize to me." Richter folded his arms over his chest. "Bower is in charge of you now. I would suggest not *forcing* him to punish you again though, my dear."

Fuck that. All his training, all his experience, rejected the idea, but he'd rather be skinned than punish her tonight. Still holding her chin, he moved in until their bodies almost touched. "I don't need you to apologize. And feel free to speak your mind. I won't punish you."

"I have nothing to say." She held out her wrists. "Let's do this."

Submissive, yes. But her spirit hadn't gone anywhere. He'd always thought his ideal sub would be docile, perfectly obedient, but *that* sub wouldn't be Silver. No one could be Silver.

And he didn't want her to be perfect. He wanted *her*, just like this.

The edge of his lip hiked up as he took her wrists and pulled her against him. She let out a cock-hardening gasp.

"Yes, *mon petit chaton.*" He slid his lips along her jaw and whispered in her ear. "Let's."

* * * *

This, this was what all the preparations had been for. Silver bit into her tongue to keep from whimpering as Landon's body pressed against hers. Her nipples jutted out, poking his solid chest, so hard he had to feel it. Her clit pulsed in a tattoo of pure lust.

Lust. That all it was. Dean had gotten her so worked up she'd do just about anyone.

But this was Landon. And damn it she missed him holding her, laughing with her, just being close to her. She inhaled and that familiar scent, sweat and some kind of soap that smelled like spring, filled her. Her skin tingled and she scowled.

All physical reactions. No big deal. *Just another demonstration, like the one he did with that nasty couple. Nothing special.*

But one of those stupid little voices she'd locked up after he'd proved how *very* much she meant to him objected, and she had to move away from Landon. Put some space between them before that voice reminded her how much she needed to mean something to him.

He didn't let her get far. His grip on her wrists wasn't tight, but he held on when she tugged. "No, Silver. There's only one way to stop this scene." His jaw hardened. "What's your safeword?"

"Red," she said, rolling her eyes. "And I'll use it if I have to."

"Good. And you may use yellow if you're overwhelmed but don't want to end the scene."

"Got it. Not that I'll have a reason to. Dean is here and I trust *him* to keep me safe." She sneered at his wince, but his reaction didn't satisfy her. She wanted to hurt him like he'd hurt her. She wanted to slap him like she had when he'd kissed her. She wanted to scream at him. But if she did that here, Dean would have to punish her. And that wouldn't help her . . . situation. But one last little jab would feel damn good. "Please get on with it, Master Landon. Unless you think another Dom could do a better job with me than you can. Doesn't make a damn bit of difference to me."

Since "My Master" has decided to let me play with another man. It almost hurt, but they'd discussed this. Better Landon than Sebastian . . . maybe. Better anyone than Landon really. But she trusted Dean's motives. And she would prove to him that she didn't need anyone else. No matter who he marched in front of her. Be it Landon or the whole damn team. *It doesn't matter.*

"Doesn't it?" Landon's lips twitched. "Fine. Hey, Demyan! Nice of you to stop by. How you liking the place so far?"

A masculine chuckle, right behind her. Then Scott stepped up to her side. "I wasn't sure at first. Seen some things that creeped me out a bit, but . . ." His gaze ran over her, stripping her, one inch of lace at a time. Looking at her like men had since she'd gotten old enough to be worth looking at. "Silver, my brain just went blank. You—"

"*Went* blank?" Silver let out a light, airy laugh. "Scott, I'd be flattered if I didn't know there wasn't much there to begin with."

Scott frowned and looked over at Dean who'd propped his shoulder against the side of the frame. "Isn't she supposed to respect me or something?"

"You're not a Dom here yet, Demyan." Dean shrugged. "Besides, Bower is in charge of the scene, and he's given her permission to speak her mind." Dean's gaze fixed on her. "I'll step in if she goes too far."

Aren't you fucking sweet?

"Speaking of becoming a Dom, Demyan, how would you like to give me a hand strapping her to the frame?" Landon took one of her wrists and held it out to Scott. "Clip her wrist cuffs to the top bolts. I'll get her ankle cuffs."

Scott nodded and moved in, forcing her back into the frame. He spoke low as he clipped one wrist. "You really into all this kinky stuff, Silver? You know you and I could have some fun without this."

"I—" She bit her lip and took him in, still freaking hot, still the type of guy she'd have fucked in a heartbeat back in Hollywood. No-strings-attached sex. She'd enjoyed it before; why should now be any different? "I don't know."

"Let me help you decide." Scott whispered before brushing his lips over hers. Out of the corner of her eye, she saw Dean push away from the frame. Landon moved to her other side as Scott tasted her lips with his tongue and curved his hand under her breast. "All you have to do is tell them you want me."

Want you? She blinked and assessed her body with detached interest. She wasn't dead, so yeah, he turned her on, but wanting him didn't seem to be enough. *I want a drink. I want to get fucking stoned. And I want you. But I don't need any of it.*

"Scott . . ." Her flesh craved touch as though the heat within would split it open without. But *not* from just anyone. "Don't . . ."

"Oh, sorry, Demyan. I forgot." Landon stepped up behind Scott. "She needs to be naked."

No! The blood left her face and washed cold through her veins. As Scott reached around to undo the halter top of the baby-doll, her eyes sought Dean's. He mouthed something.

"Yellow"

"Yellow! Damn you, Landon!" She jerked back as far as her one trapped wrist would allow. "Yellow!"

Landon put his hand on Scott's shoulder. "That means stop and renegotiate, man."

"Ah." Scott retreated. "Doesn't take a genius to figure out why. I don't get to play, do I?"

"No," Dean said before Landon could answer. Then he grinned. "But two of my waitresses have been eyeing you since you walked in. They've been together for a long time, but they like to use a man on occasion—you don't mind being used, do you?"

Scott threw his head back and laughed. "You need to ask? Just point me in the right direction, boss."

Silver did her best to ignore them. And Landon, who stood in front of her, silently, waiting for something.

Letting out a huff, she reached up to unclip her wrist. "You said you weren't going to punish me."

"Yes. I did." Landon's tone told her nothing. Leaving her only his words to go on. "That wasn't a punishment. That was a lesson. Bad things can happen when you lie to your Dom."

"You're not my Dom."

"Why did you lie to me, Silver?"

Her bottom lip quivered. "You're not my Dom."

"I am right now. So answer me." He blocked her attempt to slip by him and pulled her into his arms, holding her. Warm, solid strength chasing away the chill of how wrong Scott's hands had felt on her. Landon had always felt right. And he always would, damn him! She couldn't take it anymore. She stopped struggling and collapsed into him, thumping his chest weakly with her fist even as he whispered, "Why would you pretend just any man would do? You have two men that love you very much."

"Love me?" *Are you fucking kidding me?* She sniffed, hating how pathetic she must look. Runny nose, probably all red. Tears in her eyes. All his fault! "You pushed me away. I took the punishment because I knew I fucked up. I needed you to know I got it. That I was sorry! But then you left me there like I was nothing!"

"You had a good man—a better man! I hated punishing you!" He raked his fingers into her hair and kissed her forehead. "What we had was perfect. I didn't want to ruin it. But I did anyway."

"All you had to do was tell me you weren't mad anymore. Maybe give me a hug." *Why did he have to make things seem so complicated?* She shoved at his chest. "Was that really too much to ask?"

"Would that have been enough?" His eyes held pain, the pain she'd wanted him to feel, the pain she'd seen on the plane, that she'd seen every time he'd looked at her since. But she didn't want it anymore. "I would have held you, told you everything was okay . . . then I would have made love to you. And I couldn't have let you go. I'm not good enough for you."

She had the crazy urge to laugh. *Not good enough for me?*

"Oh, shut up, you dumbass." She slipped her hand behind his neck and dug her fingers into the tense muscles. "How 'bout you let me decide that?"

Slamming her lips into his, she drank him in, still angry and damn frustrated, but for a split second, it didn't matter. She had him, right here, right now. After all that thinking she meant nothing to him, only to learn he wanted her as much as she wanted him. And now he was all hers, this stupid man who didn't think he deserved her. She'd make him pay for that. What he'd done to her was nothing compared to what he'd done to himself.

She nipped his bottom lips, then drew away. "Can I ask you something?"

He looked a little dazed. "I told you already. Speak your mind."

With a smug smile, she poked him in between his ribs. "How does a sub punish their Dom? Because you promised to come to me when you needed me."

"You wouldn't accept my phone calls."

"You could have found a way. We're going to have a chat about what was bugging you before you got yourself suspended."

"Yes, ma'am."

"And . . ." Hell, she might as well take advantage while she had the upper hand. "I want penance for what you pulled at the club. Foot rubs every morning for a week."

His brow shot up. "You planning to spend a lot of time at Max's place?"

She shrugged. "We have a lot of time to make up for."

Dean cleared his throat. "You called yellow, pet. If you've negotiated enough, it's time for the scene to continue."

Raking her bottom lip with her teeth, she looked over at him, wondering if this bothered him. Maybe there was still some negotiating to do. "You said you wouldn't make me choose. Is this what you meant? I can be a selfish bitch and keep you both?"

He chuckled. "Well, you're certainly not getting rid of me." He cocked his head. "And you may keep him if it pleases you."

"It pleases me." She smiled up at Landon. "If that's okay with you?"

Landon gave her a lazy grin. "I think you've forgotten yourself, pet." His grin widened when she shuddered at the familiar endearment. "You may keep me. But it's my—*our*—" he inclined his head to Dean "—pleasure you should concern yourself with. I think you've said all you need to say. Silence now. I'd like to enjoy my new little sub without all this chatter."

Our. She couldn't think beyond that wonderful word. She wanted to dance and sing! Only she wasn't even allowed to talk. Of course, she wasn't all that good at the obedience thing yet.

So she ignored his last request. "But—"

He put his finger over his lips. "I told you to speak your mind. I told you I wouldn't punish you tonight. But if Dean and I are going to share you, I believe he'll have no problem doing so in my stead if you disobey. Are we clear?"

A freakin' catch. Why am I not surprised? She wrinkled her nose and nodded.

"That's my girl." He slid his hand down her cheek, to her throat, then hooked his hand to the front of her nightie. "Now, as I told Demyan, you really do need to be naked for this. So do not move."

Her breath whooshed out of her as he pulled her baby-doll over her head. The flames within reignited.

Her eyes locked on Dean. She mouthed "Thank you."

And he smiled.

* * * *

All that emotion: pain, regret, love—Dean shook his head as he stood back and watched Bower strip Silver—he could almost lose himself to it. Could almost believe that this could last.

His gaze followed Bower's motions as the man clipped Silver's wrists to the upper corners of the frame, then attached her ankle cuffs to the bottom corners. Other than the odd touch to her side or her thigh for comfort, he seemed to avoid contact. A glance at the insides of Silver's spread thighs showed Dean why. The soft, pale flesh glistened, damp with her arousal.

Dean grinned. Bower didn't want her to come yet. The right touch would set her off. So he was being very careful. *We're going to play our needy pet for all she's worth.*

Since Bower was in charge of the scene, Dean caught his eye as he approached Silver and waited for his nod before touching her. It felt odd, asking for permission to touch the woman that had been his alone for so long, but a relationship like the one he'd instigated demanded mutual respect.

"My poor baby, this is hard for you, isn't it?" He pinched Silver's chin between his thumb and finger, making her look into his eyes as he stroked up her slick inner thigh and smoothed his hand over her pussy. Two fingers moistened in her juices sank into her feverishly hot slit. "But you're going to show Bo—Master Landon how eager you are to please him. You're going to make me proud." He gently fucked her with his fingers until she whimpered and her eyes widened with the effort she made not to give in to the sensation. "No matter what he does to you, you won't come until he allows it, will you?"

Her tiny teeth dented her bottom lip. She shook her head. The metal clips holding her wrist cuffs rattled against the eyebolts. Her nostrils flared. But she managed to pull herself away from the edge.

Landon came up behind her, swiftly braided her hair, then pinned it out of the way. He kissed her throat and pressed his body against her back. "You have more control than I thought you did, *mignonne*. I'm impressed." He brought his hard gaze to Dean's as he slid his hands up her sides and cupped her breasts. His fingers scissored over her nipples. "You enjoy being here, between us. Your pulse has sped up; your skin is damp with sweat. You love knowing we can, and will, do anything we want to you."

Her pupils dilated. She nodded as much as she could with Dean still holding her chin.

"You're right, *mon petit chaton*. We've have a lot of time to make up for." Landon's grey eyes softened slightly as he continued to study Dean, as though he'd confirmed something to himself. Most likely that they were on the same page. "Shall we get started?"

Dean withdrew his fingers and inclined his head as he used them to moisten Silver's lips. "I think that's a very good idea."

Chapter Twenty Eight

Landon made sure the wire attached to the base of the long, black wand circled wide from the unit, giving him plenty of space to move around Silver's body, and attached the most basic electrode. A hot rush of power flowed through him—not from the wand, he hadn't turned it on yet. No, it was a feeling of control. Electricity was his element. The one thing besides guarding the net that he had full confidence in.

He glanced over at Richter as the man dimmed the lights over their roped-off section. Far off screams and leather slapping flesh, as well as flesh slapping flesh, came to him, along with the dark, violent thrum of Lazarus AD's "Lust." Damn, he hadn't heard that song in awhile. A cool song, but he blocked it out with everything else. Found his center. And opened it to include Silver, and, to a lesser extent, Richter.

"This is the Mushroom." He held up the wand so both Silver and Richter could see it. He circled the flat base with his finger. "The width lessens the intensity. I like using it to wake up the nerves and warm the flesh. I'll start on the lowest setting."

That had to be the shortest intro he'd ever given. But Richter could learn more later. Landon had Silver watching him with nervous anticipation, her sleek, naked body bound and available to him.

He turned the knob at the base of the wand and smiled over the pink glow. "I thought you'd like this color."

She giggled and the pulse at her throat sped up.

Moving in, he held the wand over her arm, then ran it smoothly from her elbow down to the base of her breast. He pulled the wand away and took her mouth hard to taste her little gasp. Putting a breath of distance between them, he stroked the wand under her breasts, up the other arm, and smiled as she began to pull on her restraints.

"It probably feels a little strange, tingly and warm." He lowered the wand and followed the path he'd taken with his other hand, pausing to tease her nipples. "This is nothing, *mon amour*. Just—" he bent down and flicked his tongue over a rosy little nub, already nice and erect "—a little—" he sucked hard until she jerked and tried to twist away from him "—taste."

Panting, she stared at him as he knelt before her. She twitched, making helpless little sounds as he kissed just above her knee, then worked his way down with his lips. And back up with the wand. When he reached her inner thigh, she threw her head back and swallowed back a scream.

"Silver." Richter took a step forward, then stopped himself and gave Landon a tight smile. "I apologize. I've never tested her limits. I don't know how readily she'll use her safeword if she needs to."

We'll have to work on that. But Landon understood Richter's concern. "I make a habit of reminding a sub several times during a scene what their safeword is. I don't think she needs it yet . . ." He cocked his head. "Silver, tell me your safeword."

"Yellow. Red." She shook her head as though to clear it. "Red. It's red."

"Good girl." He arched a brow at Richter who nodded, satisfied. Looking back up at Silver, he stroked her leg and smiled. Her lips were pressed tight together, but he had a feeling it was from impatience more than anything else. He decided to test her. "We've only just begun, *chaton*, but I don't want to overwhelm you. Would you like me to continue?"

She lifted her head and whispered something to the ceiling. Her narrow gaze came down, fixed on him, dark and downright deadly.

Damn. That look could light me on fire. He stared her down, his cock hardening as he watched her struggle with herself. Finally, she lowered her eyes.

"Yes I'd like you to continue." Her tone was sharp, but her jaw worked as though she was chewing on what else she wanted to say to him. Her lush lips curved slightly and amusement lightened her features. She shook her head and sighed. "I'll get better at this, I promise. But . . . please. Please continue, Sir."

Hard-won submission. The best fucking kind.

He turned up the wand until the soft buzz became a loud hum. "Very good, Silver. I know that wasn't easy for you. I think you've earned a reward."

"I—"

"Shh." He smirked when she frowned. "Not another word, or I'll change my mind." He pressed his palm to her belly, slipping lower and lower as she shivered and pushed against him. He spoke just as the wand took the place of his hand. "You may come. Whenever you're ready." He drove his fingers into her cunt, all wet and ready for him, then withdrew them and let the wand touch her flesh. "As often as you like."

* * * *

More and more heat. A stingy bite of pain. It went away and Silver shook as Landon's fingers pushed into her one again. She convulsed as they slipped away. The bite returned, along the crease between her pussy and thigh. Her orgasm raged through her, so fierce a scream ripped from her throat before she could stop it. The aftershocks reverberated through her body like the earth under a stampede, coming closer and closer until she was sure she'd come again if the fucking man blew on her.

"Oh, oh, oh!" Her eyes teared as he teased a sensitive spot along her side with sharp electric bites. So good, yet almost too much. Then . . . not. Her head felt airy and the pain was gone. She moaned as a pink glow hovered over her breast, snapping at first one nipple, then the other, such a sweet, sweet sensation. Tiny lightning bolts shot downward, and her clit ached as it absorbed them. Like when Dean pinched them, only without the pressure.

Dean . . . She spotted him, still close, his eyes hooded as he watched her. Slightly dazed, she smiled at him and he smiled back. His lips moved, but she couldn't make out what he said.

"Silver." Landon filled her vision, his grey eyes sparkling as though filled with the electricity he used on her. He grazed her cheek with his knuckles. "You in a good place, precious? Does anything hurt?"

She laughed. "Hurt? Oh, no. Nothing hurts. Nothing at all."

He nodded and moved away, returned, and reached up. His fingers slid around her wrists. His hand ran down her arms and massaged her shoulders. "All good."

"All good." She giggled as a bit of loose hair tickled her neck. "Very good, Sir."

"Hmm." He studied her like she was one of those funny pictures that changed when stared at long enough. "If we're careful, we can keep you here for a bit longer, *mon amour.* Would you like that?"

Staying here sounds perfect. Swaying a little, she nodded.

"This is the indirect method," Landon said. "I'll go into more detail next time, but for now I'll just show you the effects."

Landon flowed by her, blurry around the edges. She heard him behind her. His fingers skittered down her spine, and her back bowed as tiny shocks leapt from his fingertips. Alternating heated petting and a lighter, teasing touch, stirring the charge over her flesh as though he was painting her with it. Then something hit her and she jumped. Widespread, stinging strikes, almost painful. She whimpered and arched away.

It stopped. She panted and whipped her head from side to side. Now Landon was in front of her. Holding a shiny flogger. He gently brushed the strands of the flogger over her breasts. The pain intensified. A snap and she drifted away from it, higher than she'd been before. He hit her stomach. Her pussy.

Oh God! Her clit burst and she sobbed as she came again. Heat and mind-numbing ecstasy. Her body couldn't take anymore. Her legs didn't want to hold her up. But she needed more. Just a little more . . .

Dean appeared, close to her side. "Landon—"

"Yes, I see."

Her ankles and wrists came loose. She fell, but not far. She pressed her eyes shut as the fuzzy, dark room tipped sideways.

"That's enough for tonight, *mignonne.*" Landon held her close, settling down somewhere far away from the frame where he'd played with her. "You did very well."

"Is it over?" She frowned when he nodded. "Not yet! It can't be over!"

A hand brushed her hair away from her face. Dean looked down at her. "Pet—"

"The last time was too short! I need—" She pressed her thighs together and swallowed against the urge to sob again. "I-I . . .oh please!"

"Shh." Dean knelt by her side. "Open her for me, Bower. I know what she needs."

Landon turned her in his lap, letting her rest her head against his shoulder as he spread her thighs. He kissed her cheek. "Next time we play this way, pet, you won't be denied first. I think, together, it was a bit too much."

She agreed. But she wasn't given a chance to say so. Dean cupped her pussy and slowly slid two—no, three—fingers deep inside her. He pumped at a steady pace. Then something started buzzing. Vibrations pressed against her clit and she squirmed. Landon held her arms to her sides. Dean forced her legs open wider. Restraints, ropes, chains—they didn't need any of that to keep her exactly where they wanted her—the buzzing sped up and she hissed through her teeth—to take her however they chose. She imagined the things they would do to her and . . .

"Ah! I'm going to—" *So full. So wonderfully full.* "Landon! Mmm . . . Dean . . ."

"Now, Silver." Dean let out a gruff sound and rose up to kiss her. He growled into her mouth. "Come now."

A burst of flame erupted in her core and spread until all her strength evaporated in wisps of erotic smoke. Tendrils of pleasure lingered as a heaviness came over her, weighing down her limbs, leaving her draped limp on Landon, gazing up at Dean as sleepiness dragged her toward darkness.

His lips curved into a satisfied grin. "I think she's had enough."

Oh yeah. She smiled into the cozy black. *I'm done.*

Chapter Twenty Nine

Landon shifted restlessly on the bed as he watched Silver sleep. She looked relaxed. Peaceful even. But he didn't like leaving those red marks on her breasts and back untended. Unfortunately, Richter had gone downstairs to close up the club, and Landon hadn't gotten a chance to grab his toy bag.

The front door to Richter's small apartment above the club creaked open. Landon sat up and sighed with relief as Richter came into the room, carrying his bag. "Thanks, man. I wanted to get some aloe on her. And I have something else for her in there."

Richter nodded and dropped the bag by the bed. "No problem. Wish I could have come up sooner, but Demyan . . . hell, if he or either of the waitresses can walk after tonight, I'll be shocked."

Snorting, Landon slid off the bed and bent down to dig into his bag as Richter took his place on the bed.

"Dean?" Silver groaned. Then sat up fast. "He left again, didn't he? That fucking—"

"I'm right here, Silver." He sat up on his heels and showed her the tube of aloe. "Your skin might feel a little tight, like you have a sunburn. This should help."

"Oh." She bit her lip and her cheeks flushed. "I just thought—"

"I know." Landon sighed as he stood. He hated that she thought he'd abandoned her, but he had to regain her trust. "I won't ever do that to you again, Silver. I promise."

"I believe you."

"No, you don't. Not really. But that's okay." He forced a smile and gestured vaguely at the bed. "Lie on your front so I can take care of your back."

She spread herself out and Richter moved to her other side, playing with her hair as Landon climbed onto the bed and straddled her thighs. After squirting some aloe in his hand, he warmed it between his palms and gently coated her reddened flesh with the clear green gel.

"Fuck, Landon. That feels good."

Her moan tightened his balls. He clenched his jaw and added another coat to a bright red spot below her shoulder blade. "Language, pet."

"Oh, stop being so uptight." She turned her head and smirked at him. "Are you going to bitch if I ask you to fuck me?"

Shit. He bit the inside of his cheek as his dick pressed against the inside of his leathers. *She doesn't need any more tonight, Bower. She's just being a brat.* "Behave yourself."

Her eyes widened in mock fear. "Or what? Are you going to punish me?"

"*Silver—*"

"My back is fine now, Landon," she said, sweetly. "Can you do my front?"

He groaned and shifted away from her, glancing at Richter. "Is she always like this?"

Richter chuckled. "You didn't think you were taking on an easy sub, did you?"

"No, but . . ." He shook his head. She'd top him if he let her. Which would happen when he joined the fucking Leafs. He lightly smacked her thigh, right over a small burn. "Turn over."

She hissed and flopped over, glaring at him. "Jerk."

"Do you have a gag, Richter?"

"Several." Richter stood. "Any preferences?"

Silver tried to scramble up to the headboard, but Landon dragged her back down by the ankles. She sputtered and held up her hands. "No gags. I'll be good."

"Clasp your hands behind your neck and don't move." Landon waited until she obeyed, then squirted a glob of cold gel right on her breast. He smirked when she hissed. "I was trying to be nice, but it's difficult when you insist on testing me."

"That's not what I was—Oh! Mmmm." She thunked her head into the pillows as he molded his slick palms over her breasts and squeezed. "Damn it, three times should have been enough."

Three times . . . ? Ah, so she thought coming would sate her. Maybe she needed more after all. He flattened his hands over her belly and worked his way down. "I think I've given you all I care to tonight, *mon amour.*"

Her bottom lip stuck out in a charming pout.

"But—" he sat up and pulled off his shirt "—I have needs as well. And I think I'm going to use your sweet little body to satisfy them."

He pushed her legs apart and lowered his head.

"Landon?"

"Quiet, Silver." He parted her glistening folds with his fingers and laid a gentle kiss right on her clit. "I've been fucking dying to do this since we met."

* * * *

Silver's brain took a while to catch up to her body. Her hips jutted up as Landon's wicked tongue delved into her, tasting her, torturing her all over again. She stroked his close shaved head, torn between being devoured by pleasure, and the enormity of having him, here, all hers to love and enjoy.

You love two men, you crazy bitch? Her nails dug into his scalp as he sucked on her clit. And it felt too damn good for doubt to touch her. So she shoved the voice of doubt aside and simply allowed the tender emotions flow through her. *Yeah. I do. And it's fucking awesome.*

Before long, she felt herself tipping over the brink of climax, but she forced herself away from it and sought out Dean. Neither of the men had gotten much out of the scene. She needed to give something back.

Dean smiled as though he understood and rose from the bed to strip. Landon kissed her inner thigh and waited while her gaze raked over Dean's solid muscles, not as large as Landon's, but nicely defined. Fine brown hair dusted with a bit of grey formed a V from his chest down to the thick white elastic of his black boxer briefs. Just the right amount of hair to be sexy, and God, she *loved* touching it. Not many of the men she'd known before had chest hair, and she'd never realized how much she missed the feel of it until she'd gotten herself stuck with two guys who waxed more often than she did. She even missed seeing pubes. Dean kept his trimmed and fuck, the texture when she held his balls in her hand while sucking on his dick . . . her mouth watered and she snapped her eyes back up to his face as he laughed.

"Go ahead, sweetheart." Dean moved closer, took her hand, and ran it down his chest. "I love it when you touch me while you have that look in your eyes. Like you're starving."

She gave him a sly smile as she pulled his boxers over his dick and let them fall. His erection was dark at the crown with thick veins along the length that beckoned for her to stroke them with her tongue. A bead of pre-cum on the tip for her to taste. Her lips parted as he knelt beside her on the bed. He helped her up enough so she could take him in. And held her there as he languorously thrust into her mouth.

Salt and clean, rich musk. She swallowed as he pressed deep, hitting the back of her throat. Her lips slid easily over his smooth, hot flesh. Her own heat spilled over Landon's tongue as he thrust it in and out of her, matching her pace with Dean. Being between them was utter perfection. She'd been in ménages before, she'd always preferred it, but it had never felt like this.

"Silver." Landon lifted his head and his breath rushed out over her. "I need you."

She glanced up at Dean and let his slip from her lips when he nodded. "I need you too."

Landon pushed off the bed and peeled off his leather pants. He paused just long enough to don a condom, then crawled over her, curving his hands under her hips to lift her up. He tipped his dick downward and eased into her, watching as their bodies came together.

The stretching, the slick glide, opened her up as she took him inside her, but not as much as the raw emotion in his eyes. She reached up and pulled him down, wrapping her arms around him as he drove all the way in.

"Let it go, Landon." She kissed him, then lowered her head to the crook between his shoulder and his neck. "Whatever it is, let it go. Just for now."

He pushed up and nodded, sliding out and grinding back in. She focused on tensing and releasing, determined to make sure he found the pleasure he'd given her.

After a few hard thrusts, he lifted his head and grinned at her.

"*Non, mignonne.* I see what you're trying to do, and it's not happening."

"What—"

He slammed into her and her breath escaped her in a gasp. Hand on her hips, he rolled over. He pulled her up until the tip of him threatened to slip from her clutching pussy.

"Richter, would you join us?"

"Gladly." Dean fisted his hand in her hair and pressed slick fingers against her back hole, spreading cool, slippery lube. "You didn't really think you had any control over this, did you, dragonfly?"

She whimpered as his fingers speared her. He fucked her with them, adding more lube as Landon pressed up into her pussy. Dark embers of desire came to life deep in her core as Dean removed his fingers and pushed the head of his dick against that snug entrance that had been used before, but never in a way she enjoyed. And Dean was quite a bit bigger than Asher. Which meant more stretching. More burning. But she knew how to make it easier, so she relaxed the tight ring of muscles and let him in.

"Pet, you will listen to me." Dean tugged her hair, fully seated in her ass, but perfectly still. "I'm not fucking your ass like Asher did. I'm taking you, while Landon takes you, because we both need you too much to take turns. Every part of you belongs to us."

"I know." Her vision blurred as tears spilled over her lashes. "It's just—"

"Silver." Landon took her face in his hands and gave her a hard look. "You asked me to let it go. You have to do the same. Be here with us. This is ours. No matter what others did in the past, they can't ruin this for us."

"No." She sniffed and smiled at him. He was right. "No one will ruin this."

"That's my girl." Landon took hold of her wrists and drew them behind his neck. "This will be rough. I'm ready to lose control, and I don't know if I can be gentle."

"Don't be." She bent down and nipped his chin. "I can take it."

Dean's fingers dug into her hips as he hammered into her. He bit her shoulder and growled. "Yes, you can."

The abrupt filling burned, all around both men, stretching her.

She cried out as they both pounded into her. Dean's dick stirred as Landon gave a few shallow thrusts. The discordant pleasure threw her off her perch of control, and she clawed at the back of Landon's neck as they rode her hard. Sweat beaded on her brow and trickled down her back as she struggled to keep up with them. Dean lapped up her spine even as Landon pressed his teeth into her throat and bit down. Carnal flames burst within.

You selfish cunt! She inhaled deep and did her best to bury her pleasure. *You've taken enough! Give them something!*

"I can't stop!" She cried out as Dean pistoned in and out. "Please come with me."

Landon bowed up as Dean dropped down.

"I'm with you, *mignonne*."

"*We're* with you."

She felt them burst within and accepted her own release as they enfolded her in muscle and heat. Her whole body split open, and her head struck Dean's shoulder as she threw it back and screamed. The violent quakes inside her came over and over, tensing until all her muscles were locked into the throes of pleasure.

Perfectly still, she held her breath and waded into tranquility, afraid it would toss her into oblivion. Neither man moved.

"Silver?" Landon rose up on his elbows and stared at her. "Tell me you're okay."

Easy enough. "I'm okay."

"Like you mean it."

Uck, since you put it that way . . . Was she okay? She winced as Dean pulled out. Well, for one, she was a little sore, but not bad sore. And the sex had been fucking awesome. But . . .

She swallowed and slid her hips upward, off Landon. Her thoughts flew into a vicious storm, wildly assessing what she had just done. She'd fucked him. All that time she'd just wanted her friend back, and now that she had him, the first thing she'd done was fucked him.

It wasn't like that. You didn't fuck him.

Then what *had* she done? Had she finally managed to completely ruin one of the best things she'd ever had?

"*Mignonne*." Landon tugged her down, facing him, and whispered in her ear. "Talk to me."

She groaned at the sudden urge to break down and cry. "It's going to sound stupid, but I still want us to be friends."

"*Tu me rends fou.*" Landon nipped her earlobe and laughed. "We can still be friends, but we both need more."

"I know, but I'm going to miss that fun stuff."

"So you think I'm going to be boring now?"

Still a bit sniffly, she buried her face in the pillow. Uncontrollable giggles overtook her and she did her best to muffle them before gasping out. "Well, you are a Dom."

The *smack!* Dean laid on her ass echoed over Landon's laughter. She sat up with a yelp.

Dean shoved her back down. "Are you comfortable being shared by us, dragonfly?"

"Yes . . ." She rested on her side, looking from Landon to Dean. "If you are?"

"Sweetheart, if I wasn't okay with this, Landon wouldn't be here." Dean punched Landon's shoulder, then plopped onto his back and rolled Silver against his side. "What's that look for, goalie?"

"I'm not used to you calling me Landon." Landon shrugged and stretched out on her other side. "But I am grateful that you included me. You didn't have to."

"Yes. I did." Dean wounded a strand of her hair around his fingers and smiled at her. "I promised I wouldn't make her choose. I'm just happy she didn't decide she liked Demyan better. I don't think I could stomach sharing a bed with him."

Her skin crawled as she pictured Demyan in Landon's place. He wasn't a bad guy, really, but he didn't look at her like Landon did. Like she was special. Her nose wrinkled as something occurred to her. "You would have let me choose him?"

"Honestly?" Dean shifted over a bit. Elbow on the bed, he settled his head in his hand. "I don't know. If I thought you needed him, maybe. But it became pretty clear tonight that you don't."

"Am I that easy to read?"

"I wish you were." Dean touched her cheek and sighed. "This would have happened sooner."

"Put the blame where it belongs." Landon shook his head and

grinned. "Then again, maybe it's better things turned out the way they did. I wouldn't have been as generous as Dean is."

"That can change any time, asshole." Dean gave Landon a lazy smile. "Leave her again like you did, and you'll see what happens."

Landon inclined his head. "So noted." His eyes widened. "Oh, speaking of which, I have something for you, Silver."

Like she needed anything else? What she had already was more than she could possibly have hoped for. "What is it?"

He leaned over the bed and came up with a folded blanket. "I got this for you . . . I figured you could use it when we watch movies or . . ." His brow furrowed. "During aftercare."

As he spread the blanket over her, she fingered the extremely soft fabric and admired the brilliant colors. A southwestern pattern with simple geometric shapes in red and blue, split by a rich tan length.

"I know it probably won't go with anything at your place, but—"

"Landon, I love it." She patted the bed beside her. "And anyway, nothing goes with my place right now, including my own stuff. Dean said he'd come over and help me fix it. This blanket gives me some ideas, so thank you."

Dean curved against her back and stroked the blanket over her shoulder. "Yes, I think I could work with these colors. Anything is better than your Pepto Bismol decor."

"Pepto Bismol?" The mattress groaned as Landon laid down, and for the first time, Silver got a chance to really take in how big he was. His arms were thicker than her thighs and everything about him was hard as molded steel. Except for his eyes and his lips.

They could be though. She ducked her head as his lips formed a tender smile and resumed exploring him. He had a large tattoo on his right side, over his ribs. A tribal style phoenix rising from broken glass—no, from a shattered shell. A ribbon above the phoenix bore a date in Roman numerals, and part of a familiar poem was written across the center of the phoenix where the dark lines faded.

She read the words in a whisper. "Take this kiss upon the brow, and, in parting from you now, thus much let me avow—You are not wrong, who deem that my days have been a dream. Yet if hope has flown away, in a night, or in a day. In a vision, or in none, is it therefore the less gone? All that we see or seem, is but a dream within a dream."

Landon silently watched her.

"Tell me about it, Landon." She trailed her fingers over the ribbon. "I need to know."

"Do you?" He extended his hand and slipped his fingers into her hair to touch her scar. "And when will you tell me about this?"

"Soon."

He nodded slowly. "All right. Well, I'll tell you about this soon too."

"Like tomorrow?"

"Sure." He pressed her head down to his chest and spoke over her. "You sure it's okay for me to crash here tonight?"

"Yeah. It's fine." Dean murmured into her hair. "Place is usually empty. You can stay here as long as you need to."

"What if I want him to stay at my place?" Silver moved to turn and face Dean, but Landon trapped her hand on his chest and Dean dropped his arm over her hip. "Uck! You guys don't get to decide everything!"

"While we're still in the bedroom, pet, yes, we do," Dean said.

Him and his rules. She rolled her eyes, glad neither of them could see her doing it. "Fine. But we will discuss this when we're not in the bedroom."

"We'll discuss whatever you want, *mon petit chaton*." Landon yawned. "In the morning. *Tais toi maintenant*."

Dean snorted.

"You understand French?" Strands of hair spilled into her mouth as she turned her head as far as she could. She stopped glaring when Dean pulled her hair away from her face. "Thanks."

"You're welcome."

"So what did he say?"

"Be quiet."

How fucking rude. "Why—"

"That's what he said." Dean grinned and kissed her nose. "And I think it's an excellent idea."

"All right, but I'm making a new rule." She pursed her lips. "No more saying things I can't understand."

"You don't make the rules, pet."

"You're such a—"

"Careful."

"Arg! Fine!" She pressed her face into Landon's shoulder to hold back a laugh. Sometimes, the whole sub thing felt like walking a tightrope, arousing to try and stay in line, even more so dreading what would happen if she slipped. Then there were times like this when it was just plain fun. With Dean anyway. So far Landon wasn't much of a *fun* Dom.

"Actually, *'Tranquilles'* is 'be quiet.'" Landon eased away from her and his eyes shone with mirth. "I told you to shut up."

"Oh, you—!" She snatched up a pillow and swung it at him. He caught it, pulling as she lunged forward.

They both fell off the side of the bed. Landon let out a loud grunt.

"Mind not breaking my goalie?" Dean called out.

"*Your* goalie?" Silver folded her hands over Landon's chest and bent down to kiss him. "Screw that. He's all mine."

Chapter Thirty

Dull grey fog hovered outside the bedroom window and a chill crept under the blanket. Dean rolled onto his side and opened his eyes in slits to take in the empty bed. Light laughter broke out from beyond the partially closed door. He caught the scent of bacon and cursed.

His first step speared pain from his knee straight up into his thigh. He staggered forward and glanced at his cane, propped against the wall by the closet.

Oh, hell no. He drew himself up to his full height and strode as steadily as he could from the bedroom to the kitchen. Folding his arms over his chest, he leaned on the doorframe and grinned.

"Got yourself in trouble already this morning, dragonfly?"

Sitting naked in the middle of the small round wooden table, Silver had her arms bound behind her back in a simple, yet efficient arm tie. A quick bit of rope work, the kind he often used in capture fantasy.

Silver pouted at him, but didn't answer.

"Hungry, boss?" Landon brought two plates to the table. Eggs, bacon, beans—the works. He snickered when Dean eyed his unscorched kitchen. "I picked this up from the diner down the street. I've learned my lesson."

"Good man." Dean pulled up a chair and dug right in. He thanked Landon for the coffee he set before him, then eyed Silver. "So what's with the table ornament?"

Landon shrugged. "I don't like grumpy subs first thing in the morning. She snapped at me when I asked her what she'd like for breakfast and then told me to just 'get some fucking coffee.'"

Dean shook his head as he chewed on a nice greasy piece of bacon. His brow furrowed as he looked Silver over. She mustn't have been there very long, but—

"Don't worry, I didn't leave her here like this while I was gone." A muscle in Landon's cheek twitched. "Actually, I tried to take it easy on her. Asked her to set the table. Came back to find her still

335

sitting here, sulking."

"Well, she's certainly not a morning person." He smiled at her over his cup as he recalled the last time she'd been moody with him in the morning. "Not usually anyway."

Silver ducked her head as she blushed.

"I don't expect Little Miss Sunshine at the crack of dawn, but I won't tolerate nastiness." Landon held a forkful of eggs up to Silver. "And we've spoken about her eating habits."

"I see." Dean watched the younger man feed Silver, wondering whether or not he should interfere. Landon's strict training might come in handy during a scene, but Silver wouldn't enjoy being micromanaged. "She's always had a healthy appetite with me."

Landon sat back and frowned. "If you've got a problem with how I'm handling things, just say so."

"Landon, if I had a problem, I would. The two of you will have to negotiate your relationship." Dean shoved some beans into his mouth. The pain in his knee hiked up to a level that couldn't be ignored any longer. His stomach turned as he pictured either going through the day with his cane and some painkillers, or toughing it out. The dampness of fall near the ocean made the latter almost laughable. But his pride didn't see it that way. He pushed his plate away from him and braced to stand with his face as blank as possible. "I'm going to take a shower. I won't be long if either of you need a lift."

"Wait." Silver inhaled and looked from him to Landon. "Please untie me, Sir."

"Silver, I told you—"

"Red."

Landon's colored dropped. He shot out of his seat and went around behind her to untie the knots. "Why didn't you tell me you were hurting? I asked you—"

"This isn't about me." Silver hopped off the table and brushed by Landon, coming up to kneel in front of Dean. "What's wrong?"

Dean smiled down at her and grazed his knuckles down her cheek. "Nothing, pet."

"Don't fucking lie to me." She stood and held her hand up toward Landon when he made an angry sound. "Look, I want this, with both of you. It's kinda exciting to know I can get punished for being naughty, even if I rarely enjoy the punishment. And sometimes it just makes me feel like you know I can do better. But I think I have the right to expect things from you too. Like some goddamn honesty."

"I'm sorry." Landon rubbed his hand over his face. "If I went too far—"

"I'm not mad at you!" She jabbed her finger into Dean's chest. "I'm mad at you! I'm supposed to tell you when something's wrong, right? Or is that just during a scene?"

"I think we have more than the scenes, my love." Holy shit, she was sexy all fired up with concern for him. And she was right. He sighed and took her hands between his. "The weather makes my knee act up. It's damp and cold and—"

"And . . . ?"

Pushy little thing. But again, he would be pissed if she hid her pain from him. He sighed. "And it hurts like a motherfucker."

"Do you have anything for it?" She blinked. "Your cane! Oh my God, how could I have forgotten? Why aren't you using it?"

He frowned. "Because I hate the stupid thing." His lips quirked. "Unless I'm using it on a mouthy little sub's butt."

"Can't see you doing that if you can't stand up straight. You'd get in what? One hit? Maybe two?" Silver folded her arms over her bare breasts. "If you're going to beat me, at least make it worth my while. Now please tell me you have pain meds."

"I'll get the cane," Landon said.

The young Dom, such a stickler for protocol and discipline, with just enough experience to know what he was doing but not enough to bend into a full time relationship, had surrendered. What hope did Dean have?

He brought Silver's hands up to his lips and kissed her fingers. "They're in the cabinet above the stove."

Her expression softened. She quickly went to get him his meds and a bottle of water from the fridge. Then she sat across from him, watching him as though she didn't trust him to take the painkillers if she looked away.

After popping the pills into his mouth, he washed them down

with a few gulps of water. Smiled at her.

She frowned at him. "Don't ever do that again."

"I won't." He held still, then exhaled heavily when she grinned. "You're quite a force, little one." He accepted his cane from Landon and laughed. "Little piece of advice, goalie. Don't piss her off."

Landon pulled Silver to her feet and hugged her from behind. "Don't I know it."

Silver shot an impish grin at Landon over her shoulder, then back at Dean. "So long as you two know your place."

Dean barked out a laugh. Oh, he knew it. And for once, he saw Silver not as a woman he'd eventually have to let go, but as a woman who wouldn't let go of him.

Funny how she'd flipped things on him. He didn't know how things would be a year from now, or ten years from now. But he had a very good feeling all three of them would be there to find out.

* * * *

Silver drove Dean to work, but Landon decided he needed some exercise and ran the distance. Crazy man. Still, she couldn't help but wonder if he'd done that to give her and Dean some time alone.

"So what do you have planned for the day?" Dean asked as he walked her to her office, leaning heavily on his cane. He'd ignored her suggestion to go to his own office and take the weight off his knee.

And *she* was stubborn? She wrinkled her nose as she answered his question. "I've got to convince five more guys to pose for the magazine I hooked up with. I've already got Scott and . . . "

His brow shot up. "Sebastian? He really makes you uncomfortable, doesn't he?"

"Not as much as before. It's just . . . the way he talks . . ." She rubbed her arms as a chill skittered along her flesh. "He was the first man I even considered submitting to. It was almost like I couldn't help it."

"Oh, sweetheart." He opened his arms and she leaned into him, feeling safe as she always did when he was around. He stroked her back and spoke softly. "It will be different now. Trust me. He's a good Dom, and he knows you're with me. If his reputation is anything to go by, he'll keep a respectful distance. At work, you're the team's owner. At the club, he'll expect you to treat him like any other Dom. But not like *your* Dom." He tipped her chin up with a finger. "Understand?"

"I think so." For a split second, she wanted to ask him to come with her to lay siege on the men. It would be easier for him to convince them to get in front of the cameras. But she wouldn't. This was her job and she'd manage just fine on her own. "See you around lunch?"

"I look forward to it." He kissed her and slowly moved away, his spine stiff as he made his way down the hall, obviously trying not to limp.

It took everything she had to leave him and go into her office to collect her things. She wanted to stay with him, make sure he was okay, but he wouldn't appreciate that any more than she would in his position. So she grabbed her files and checked the clock. Then groaned.

The players wouldn't show up for practice until nine. Which meant she had an hour with nothing to do but sit here and try to figure out how the hell she'd handle them. She slumped into her chair and flipped open the file. The magazine had requested certain players, not including Scott and Sebastian, which made things a bit easier because the editor had faxed her Friday to tell her either, or both, would be perfect.

Which left her with five players who'd refused to commit. Carter had been all for it at first but had pulled out after he healed enough to face that his scars wouldn't fade much more. Christ, he was still a damn good-looking guy, but he'd turned down all interviews and still wore a full cage mask on the ice.

Of course, there was one other man on the list, one who was quite comfortable with his own scars, who could convince Carter he had nothing to be ashamed of.

There's no way he'll do it if I ask.

But . . . she smirked and pulled out her phone. *He* wouldn't do it for her. However, she did know who he *would* do it for.

"Hey, sis." She let out a heavy, dramatic sigh. "I need your help."

* * * *

"Holy shit, Oriana!" Silver pounced on her sister in the lobby, hugging her, then holding her at arm's length. "I *love* this outfit. Seriously! And you have to promise to let me borrow those boots!"

"You don't have to suck up." Oriana pulled her long black blazer jacket, double breasted and classy vintage, closed and gave her a tight smile. "I already said I'd do it."

Damn it woman, do you ever look in a mirror? You're gorgeous! Silver wanted to tell her Oriana exactly that but didn't bother, because she wouldn't listen. Of course, Silver had a new method of attacking her sister's lack of confidence that she had no problem using.

Besides, she really *did* want to borrow those boots! New Rock, leather stilettos with red flames. She had to dab the corner of her lip to make sure she wasn't drooling.

"I'm not sucking up. To be honest, I'm not used to you looking this stylish. That white shirt is really cute over those tights, and that jacket . . . but maybe I'm giving the wrong person credit." Her lips curved slightly. "Are you letting Max dress you now? Or . . . oh! Dominik! I can see him picking out your clothes for you. He's got that Daddy Dom vibe."

"Fuck off, Silver!" Oriana laughed and shoved her toward the elevator. "The men only dress me when we go to the club."

"I never see you at the club."

"Of course you don't. Dominik and Richter discussed it a while ago and agreed it was best if we went on different nights. I figured it would be a little weird . . ."

"They talked to *you* about it?" Silver frowned as they got on the elevator and headed down to the level with the locker room, gym, training room, and coaching staff offices. "Nobody mentioned anything to me."

"Dominik brought it up after you attacked Sloan."

Silver made a face. "I gave him a friendly little 'Welcome to the Family' tap. No big deal."

Oriana snickered. "Right. Well, I have a feeling you won't be doing that again. What did you get, twenty?"

"Something like that." Her cheeks heated up as she avoided her sister's amused look. "He's fucking strict."

"You're a brat."

"There's that too."

Her sister grinned and glanced down the hall when the elevator door opened. It was empty, but she spoke softly anyway. "Do you get punished often?"

What was this? Oriana used to hate it when Silver told her about her sex life. Then again, punishments didn't always involve sex. She ran her tongue over her bottom lip. "Sometimes . . ."

"When was the last time?"

Silver's face was on fire. She'd rather talk about sex—which didn't make any sense. "This morning. You?"

"Last weekend." Oriana shrugged. "Don't forget, I've been with them a lot longer. And Dominik's the only one with rituals and rules that took any getting used to."

"Rituals?"

"Yes. Like how I greet him at the door, or things I do when we're eating together." Oriana shot her a quick look, as though needing to make sure she wouldn't be judged—as if Silver, of all people, would even *consider* judging her sister. Finally, Oriana exhaled and smiled. "Different Doms expect different things, and it feels nice once you get it right. I didn't at first."

"But you were trying?" Silver thought over some of the books she'd read and vaguely remembered skimming over something about rituals. Kneeling or standing in a certain way. Sounded boring. "Did he punish you anyway?"

"No, he just made me repeat it a few times. Five the first time. Then he added five times every time I got it wrong after." Giggling the way she had when they were very young, she leaned close and whispered, "I had to pick up my fork fifty times before I could eat once."

"*Fifty?*" Silver stared at her sister. "What's so complicated about picking up a fork?"

"Well." Oriana cleared her throat and dropped her tone to a decent impersonation of Dominik's. "You do not touch the fork until you are given permission. And that's after you are fed the first bite. Lifting your hand to pick up the fork is a mistake." Her full lips formed a hard line. "Try again, pet."

Silver threw her head back and laughed. "You are awesome at that! Wow!"

Oriana bowed. "Why, thank you."

"So why did you keep lifting your hand? I mean, getting to fifty times—"

Heavy footsteps sounded right behind them. Dominik stepped out of the men's bathroom. "She was bored of the ritual and decided to act out." He slid his hand around the back of Oriana's neck and pulled her toward him. "But she quickly learned that doing those small things to please me is much more pleasant than being a brat and trying to get a reaction."

Rather than looking scared or embarrassed, Oriana leaned into him, content as a well-fed kitten. She winked at Silver. "I also much prefer eating *at* the table."

"Please don't share any of this with Landon." Silver could already picture him making her sit on the floor and eat out of his hand. Of course, sitting on the table, all tied up, wasn't much better. "He doesn't need any more ideas from you." *Polite might help.* "Sir."

Dominik grinned and shook his head. "Call me Dominik or Mason here, Silver. And don't worry about me giving him ideas. I hear he was trained 'Old Guard' style. He'll have you doing High Protocol whenever he's not on the road."

You've got to be kidding me. "Isn't High Protocol the really intense stuff?"

"Yes. For example, a slave should never look her Master in the eye."

"*Slave?*"

"Oh, you hadn't discussed that yet?" Dominik guided Oriana along with him, toward the locker room. "He must be taking it easy on you."

Oriana twisted away from Dominik and poked him in the ribs. "Will you stop teasing her!"

Dominik caught her wrists and gave her a lazy half smile. "Who says I'm teasing? And what have I told you about poking me?"

Silver swallowed as her sister's eyes widened.

"Now?" Oriana asked in a whisper.

The big man nodded and jerked his chin toward the bathroom. He folded his arms over his chest and arched a brow when Oriana hesitated. "Would you like me to help you?"

"But then you won't—"

"No. I won't."

"Then I'll manage on my own, *Sir*." Oriana stalked off.

Shuffling her feet, Silver glanced over at Dominik. "Do I want to know?"

"Probably not." He made a dismissive motion in the direction of the player's lounge. "Most of the guys should be in there."

Chewing hard on the inside of her cheek, she squared her shoulders. "Thank you."

"Oh, and, Silver?"

She glanced back at him. "Yes?"

"I agreed to do the photo shoot. Oriana got a hold of me right after you called her. I told her it might be better for her to speak to Sloan in person."

"Then maybe I should wait for her."

"Sloan will respect you more if you ask him yourself," Dominik said shrewdly. "If that doesn't work, let Oriana try. But I wouldn't hold my breath either way."

"Well, gee, that's encouraging," she mumbled before turning away from him and striding up to the door. She inhaled and pushed the door open.

About twenty men lounged around, drinking Gatorade or coffee either at the bistro style tables or on the big leather coaches. Landon wasn't there. Scott spotted her first and sat forward, a crooked grin on his face. The towel wrapped around his waist looked ready to flop open. Droplets of water covered his chest and his pecs tightened as she fought to tear her eyes away from him. Movement to the left made her jump.

Sebastian held up his hands in a I-am-harmless gesture. "Would you care for coffee, *muñeca*?"

Inching away from him, she nodded. His accented words still drizzled within like liquid caramel but lacked the power he'd used before. Maybe Dean was right. Maybe he would keep a respectful distance.

"We have practice, so let's make this quick." Sloan, who sat on a sofa beside Max, leaned forward and propped his elbows on his knees. "You need how many guys for the photo shoots?"

All the men in the room went silent.

Silver started when Sebastian appeared at her side again, then whispered "Thank you" as he calmly held out a cup of coffee. Her mouth had gone dry, so she took a sip before speaking. "The magazine has requested seven men. I have two—now three since Dominik has agreed."

"Which leaves four," Sloan said. "Are there alternates if the players aren't interested in posing for the damn pictures?"

"Yes."

"Good. Well if I'm on that list, you might as well choose an alternate." Sloan stood and strode around the table. "Who are the other men?"

She'd completely lost control of the conversation. Not that she'd had control in the first place. Her gaze swept over the room and she couldn't find one friendly face. Well, Scott, if the look Scott was giving her could be considered friendly. And she wouldn't look at Sebastian, who'd mercifully moved to the other side of the room. Carter stared at his bottle of Gatorade and Max . . . actually, Max was frowning at the other men.

"She's doing this for the team, guys." His smooth southern drawl took on a sharp edge. He scowled at Sloan who glanced back at him. "I'm thinking you all should cut her some slack."

"I got everyone here to hear her out," Sloan said. He gave her a hard look. "It's not a difficult question, Silver. Who. Are. The. Other. Men?"

"Carter. Max and . . ."

The door to the locker room opened and she bit her lip. Landon's smile faded as he studied the other players. He tossed the towel he'd been using to dry his face over his shoulder.

"What's going on?"

Before she could answer, Oriana and Dominik entered the room with a woman Silver didn't recognize. A badge on her chest identified her as Scarlet Patterson.

The photographer for the photo spread. The "professional" the editor had promised to send, who apparently handled all kinds of sports stars.

Redheaded, perky, with her green jewel toned blouse unbuttoned enough to reveal her generous cleavage and a skirt short enough to guarantee full ass exposure if she bent over, the woman immediately got all the men's attention. Except for Landon whose narrowed eyes were fixed on Silver.

Silver put her hand on his forearm, squeezed the taut muscle, and spoke low. "Let me handle this. Then I'll explain, I promise."

Landon gave her a curt nod. "Yes. You will."

Scarlet slinked forward, offering her hand first to Silver, then to Sloan. "I know I wasn't scheduled for today, but something came up." She looked over the men and stared at Scott as she continued. "Your secretary—Anne?—told me I could come in."

Silver pursed her lips. *That woman is so fired.* "We're still discussing who is willing to pose."

"Oh! But you've had weeks and everyone's here." Scarlet shot a shy smile at Scott and simpered. "You've posed for magazines before, Mr. Demyan—"

Scott gave her a slow, assessing look. "Call me Scott. And yeah, I have no problem posing for you."

The twit let out a breathless little laugh. "Perfect! And of course we have the captain—"

"You do not have the captain."

All around the room, the men started muttering. By the sounds of it, the magazine would have to do a spotlight on Scott alone. Even Sebastian looked pretty disgusted.

Scarlet pouted at Sloan. "Oriana already said she didn't mind!"

Oriana shook her head and paled a little. "That's not what I said!"

"You said Silver was speaking to him. And that he'd help Luke get over his misgivings." Scarlet approached Carter and cocked her head. "It doesn't look *that* bad, Luke. And we can angle the shot to get your good side."

Landon tensed beside Silver. Carter stared at the floor and

hunched his shoulders.

Enough was enough.

"I'm afraid there's been a mistake." Silver stepped away from Landon and slipped between Scarlet and Carter. "I was assured the magazine was sending a professional."

Crimson lips pursed, Scarlet looked her over. "Silver, I understand that you're new at this, so I won't take offense, but unlike you, *I* have years of experience. Let me handle the boys. All you need to do is cash the nice big check the magazine will send you when I'm done."

Smiling sweetly, Silver nodded and spoke low. "Can I ask you something, woman to woman?"

"Yes . . . ?"

"How much cum did you have to swallow to become this stupid? I just want to make sure I'm not nearing my quota."

Scarlet's face turned the color of her lips. Her hand came up. "Why you little bitch. I'll—"

Oriana stepped forward. "Try it."

Taking a deep breath, Scarlet glanced from Oriana to Silver and let out an airy laugh. "I apologize. It slipped my mind that you're both involved with several of the players. I'm accustomed to simply making sure the men I photograph are . . . comfortable. But if you'll give me a list, I'll make sure to take a more hands off approach."

"I'd rather they send someone else." Silver inclined her head to her sister, grateful for her support, but needing the men to see *she* could stand up for them all on her own. "I'm sorry you wasted both our time—"

"There is no one else." Scarlet put her hands on her hips. "Perhaps I should just tell the magazine you're no longer interested in reaching our extensive readership."

Damn it. It had taken weeks to convince the editor to even *consider* showcasing the team. They desperately needed the exposure. But with this woman, she'd likely lose what little respect she'd managed to gain from them.

Sloan cleared his throat. "If we can agree to some boundaries, I'm sure we can find seven men who would be willing to pose."

"There are boundaries in place." Silver hugged herself to stifle the urge to hug Sloan. When had he turned into a decent guy? "Only Scott and Sebastian have agreed to nude shots. And those must be tasteful. The other men will take off their shirts. Whether they're okay posing in boxers or not is up to them."

"Of course." Scarlet straightened her skirt and visually stripped each and every player. She spent the longest time staring at Landon. "I must use the goaltender, of course. Can I do you, Mr. Bower? I mean—"

"Stop talking before I strangle you with your cheap-ass extensions." Silver gouged her palms with her nails and let ice seep into her tone. "I can see you came here thinking this team wasn't well known enough for you to bother approaching with some fucking class. But *my* team reached the playoffs last year, and they've earned some goddamn respect. Maybe you've hit a dry spell and you can't help throwing yourself at every available male. There's obviously at least one man—" she cast a dirty look at Scott "— whose standards are low enough to accept your blatant offer. My other players are either family men or just not that desperate. If they agree, you may take *pictures* of them. Try more and I'll have you charged with sexual harassment."

Scarlet rolled her eyes. "Oh, please."

"You really are as dumb as you look." Silver inched closer to Scarlet and spoke low enough so only she could hear. "You have no idea what kinds of connections I have." She took her phone out of her purse and held it up. "One phone call and I could ruin your magazine."

It was a bluff. If she could actually bury the magazine, she wouldn't be dealing with this woman at all. But the woman didn't seem bright enough to figure that out.

"Should I assume you're not making that phone call?" Scarlet asked, glancing nervously at Silver's phone as it buzzed.

"Are you capable of doing your job?" Silver checked her phone. The building contractor. She let voice mail pick up. *One thing at a time.* "With your clothes on, Miss Patterson?"

Scarlet sneered. "Yes. I can do that, Miss Delgado."

"You can 'do me' first." Scott called out, breaking the tension in the room.

All the men laughed.

"Well, since that's settled, I've got to get back to the office." Silver bit the edge of her lip and glanced at Sloan. *Do I dare ask?* "Can you take it from here, Captain?"

"Yes." Sloan's lips curved slightly. "And thank you for looking out for the team's interests, Silver. I appreciate that."

Wow. A thank you? Silver stared at Sloan as he held a finger up for Scarlet to wait and gestured for the team to join him. Hell, maybe he wasn't half bad after all. And she'd never seen Oriana so happy—her sister glowed every time she glanced his way. Maybe it was about time to admit he was good for her sister.

A heavy hand dropped on her shoulder, and she swallowed as Landon spoke low in her ear. "Why am I only hearing about this photo shoot now?"

"I forgot. Kinda." The last time she'd gone over the list, they hadn't been speaking. But that wasn't why she'd automatically skipped his name and started considering alternates. She just couldn't see him stripping for a camera. Hadn't wanted to ask. "There was so much going on—"

"I won't do this if you're not comfortable with it."

"That wouldn't be fair, would it? I mean . . ." She glanced at her sister who eyed Scarlet like the woman might pounce on one of her men. "I didn't think twice before asking Oriana to help me get Sloan in on it."

"Did you think it would bother her?"

"No. Not really."

"So, as I said." His fingers loosened on her shoulder and he sighed. "I need to know if it bothers you."

It did, a little. But knowing that he wouldn't do it if she asked him not to helped. And she had to be professional about this. Women would swoon when they saw his picture. They'd buy his jersey and watch games just to see him.

Besides, they would never have anything more than the pictures. This man was off the market.

She just had to make sure little Miss Bimbo with the camera didn't forget.

Landon swung Silver around to face him. "Listen to me,

mignonne. You don't have to trust her. You have to trust me. Do you?"

As long as you don't have a cane in your hand . . . ? She nodded.

"That's my girl." He grinned and put his arm around her shoulders. "I'll go after Demyan. I want to get this over with."

Ignoring Scarlet's breathless thanks, Landon pulled Silver from the player's lounge, into the locker room, and slammed her against the wall. He ravished her mouth, sucking, biting, thrusting with his tongue. Then he slid her up the wall with one arm around her waist and slipped his hand under her skirt.

"I didn't touch another woman while we weren't speaking. I didn't want anyone else." He bit her throat as he slid his fingers into her panties. "I don't want anyone else. And don't you fucking forget it."

His fingers pushed into her and she gasped. "Landon! We're at work!"

He chuckled, stroking her clit with his thumb as he pumped his fingers in and out, faster and faster. "Like I give a shit."

"Someone could come in—"

"You're right." He took his fingers from her and held her when her knees gave out. "So how about after the photo shoot, we go somewhere where we won't be interrupted."

Uck, I should have kept my mouth shut. Her insides throbbed and the heat he'd stroked simmered. She glared at him. "That was mean."

He kissed her nose. "But you still love me, don't you?"

"If I didn't, I'd make you eat your nuts." She stiffened as the door opened, and groaned when Sloan appeared. "I've got to go."

Landon moved away from her, shielding her as she fixed her skirt.

"Bower, I think you and I should have a talk about what's appropriate in the locker room," Sloan said.

"Stuff it, Callahan. I've seen Mason groping Oriana in the hallway." Landon blocked her escape and gave her another slow, deep kiss. His forehead pressed against hers, he whispered, "I'll meet you in your office after practice. Around two."

All she could do was nod. And make a quick getaway.

Two o'clock couldn't come soon enough.

* * * *

Landon checked his watch and rolled his eyes. He'd gotten in two hours of practice before Callahan suggested he go check if Demyan was finished. But the freakin' door to the office that Scarlet had set up for the shoot was locked. And no one answered when he knocked.

What a fucking waste of time. He crossed his arms over his chest and leaned against the wall. If Silver didn't need this photo spread to prove she could get the team more attention . . . but she did. At that was the *only* reason he'd agree to it. Whatever Silver said, he could tell she didn't want him doing this. But she was torn between jealousy—which Scarlet hadn't helped with—and her dedication to the team. She could deal with her jealousy. Failure with what her father had entrusted to her was another matter entirely.

Carter shuffled down the hall and Landon ground his teeth as he saw how miserable the kid looked. That bitch had made him feel even more insecure about his scars.

"Callahan agreed to do the shoot." Landon didn't phrase it as a question. Carter had said he'd do it if the captain would. He wouldn't be here otherwise.

"Everyone did. Perron's right. Silver's trying to get the team out there, you know?" Carter leaned his shoulder on the wall and hid the damaged side of his face against it. "And like that chick said . . . they can take pictures of my good side."

Bitterness scalded Landon's guts. "That chick" had no goddamn class. "If they're going to shoot your good side, you better show off that scar. All the greats have them. You got that playing the game, man. It's nothing to be ashamed of."

"Bite me, okay?" Carter scowled. "You're still pretty."

"Hey, a black eye won't improve your looks. I'm not fucking pretty."

"People don't take one look at you and look away fast, like they don't want to offend you." Carter's hand shook as he brought it up to his lips. "You know the last puck bunny that came on to me was afraid to kiss me? She offered to suck my cock, but she cringed whenever my lips came anywhere near hers. That's just messed up."

"They get over it." Callahan strode toward them, his lips curled in a sneer. "You're a hot shot and you're worth some decent cash already. They still come after me, and look at my face."

"You're the captain. And you're worth ten times what I am." Carter stared down at his worn sneakers. "Besides, you've got Oriana. If I had a woman like that." His lips twisted. "Or like Silver, I wouldn't be . . ."

"Kid, you've got to stop fucking puck bunnies and strippers." Callahan slapped Carter's shoulder. "Find a woman at the club. Richter has some quality subs, and all they want is a good man to top them. Demyan's been bragging about the two he had this weekend."

"Demyan knows shit about being a Dom, and he can still top a sub." Carter glanced up at Landon, then made a face. "I . . . well you know what happened. The subs are fucking scared of me."

"Of you?" Callahan eyed Landon. "What happened?"

Landon shook his head. "That's for him to tell you."

Carter let out a sharp laugh and dropped his head back. "I'm surprised you don't know. I slapped Silver. She asked me to, but it doesn't matter. I let her top me. I went back once and . . . shit, I had to leave. Everyone knows."

"Come with me on Friday." Sloan rolled his shoulder and grinned. "I'll find you someone."

"Thanks, Captain, but I'm good." Carter glared at the door. "What the fuck is Demyan doing anyway? Is it going to take this long for all of us?"

Sloan snorted and reached out to pound on the door. "Make it quick, Miss Patterson, or you'll be three players short. I need to get my men back on the ice where they belong."

Seconds later, Demyan emerged, zipping his pants and grinning like a fool. He smirked at Landon. "Your turn. Enjoy."

Landon left the men in the hall and stepped into the office. Scarlet spun around to face him, holding a tissue to her lips.

"I need you to take your clothes off." She moved toward him, her gaze eating over his body like she could chew his clothes off with that alone.

He pulled off his shirt and tossed it aside. "That's all you're getting, Miss Patterson. Tell me where you want me."

"Honestly." She licked her lips and smoothed her hands over her breasts. Her shirt was undone and her bra was on the desk behind her. "Right here is good."

Sleazy and pathetic. Even if he didn't have a woman like Silver, he wouldn't be interested.

"Pick up your damn camera."

He went to the faux stone wall, faced her, and put his hands on his hips.

She scurried to grab her camera and blinded him with the flash.

Chapter Thirty One

A colorful sight greeted Silver as she stepped into her office. Candy rosebuds in red, pink, and yellow, rock candy lilacs, jujube tulips, and her very favorite, cake pops covered in chocolate sprinkles. The huge, tasty bouquet sat in the center of her desk, brightening the whole room which otherwise seemed as grey and gloomy as the weather outside. She spotted a man in a well tailored suit standing by the window, and her face broke into a huge smile.

"Dean, this is . . ." *Not like you at all.* So far he hadn't been big on gifts, and whatever he got for her, he gave her in person. Actually, that man wasn't big enough to be Dean. "Who are you and what are you doing in my office?"

The man's shoulders hunched forward slightly, but he didn't answer.

"You have five second to give me a fucking name before I call security."

He turned slowly, his handsome face shadowed and lined with exhaustion. "So if I give you a name, does that mean you won't kick me out?"

"Asher." She slammed her fist on the edge of her desk and tried not to wince as pain ricocheted up her arm. "You need to leave. Right now."

"Silver, please just hear me out." He nodded toward the bouquet. "That's got to get me at least a few minutes of your time."

Her hand convulsed as she fought the urge to throw the damn thing at him. But she wouldn't waste good candy. She sneered as she stalked across the room. "A few minutes? You mean like the amount of time it would have taken you to tell me you and Cedric were getting married? To break up with me like I wasn't just an inconvenience you had to get rid of?"

Asher cringed and nodded. "I admit, I could have handled that better."

"Ya think?"

"You weren't happy with us. And Cedric was miserable." He hung his head and raked his fingers through his hair. "I had no business getting involved with you, but I liked the glamorous lifestyle. I never made any secret of that. I thought we were both getting what we wanted. You, a man who'd never ask you to commit, and me, connections I never could have gotten on my own. I got in the habit of treating it like a business, and that was just messed up. I did—I *do*—care about you. Just not half as much as you deserve. And I'm sorry."

"Why are you telling me this now?" Silver hugged herself, hating that she wanted to believe he'd actually cared. Looking back made her feel sick. All the times he'd fucked her had been like a payment for what she'd given him. It made her feel like a worn rag a man used to jerk off in. "You've moved on and so have I. This might have meant something the next day, but it's too late for me to give a shit about how sorry you are."

He shook his head and reached down to pick up the briefcase sitting by his feet. "Sorry wouldn't have meant anything, no matter when I said it. I wanted to call you, or see you, but I had to have something to offer to earn your forgiveness."

"The candy?" She laughed bitterly. "If you think *that* makes up for anything—"

"No, the candy was just to . . . break the ice, I guess. I thought that would be enough for you to at least listen. I've worked my ass off getting what I really thought would make a difference." He approached the desk, keeping a wide berth from her, and opened the briefcase. "I know it probably doesn't mean much, but I've been looking out for you. I found out that the investors that paid to rig games tried to approach you once, but they haven't come back and I figured they wouldn't just give up. So I thought, maybe, if I could dig into it a little, and get you something you could use to protect yourself against them, you'd *consider* forgiving me."

Her brow shot up. "And you did this pro bono? Asher, I know you better than that. Someone else must be paying you or you wouldn't bother."

"I swear on my life, I got this just for you. I've been working shit jobs just to cover the rent over the past few weeks. Cedric's been doing the same. We're barely managing." He made a face. "You didn't notice I'm wearing a last season suit? I'm handling divorce cases for God's sake! And not even big ones. My last three cases didn't make me enough to buy new shoes!"

Ah, so that's it. Maybe Asher did want her forgiveness, but as always, he had another agenda. "You're looking for a job."

"Well . . ." He had the grace to look away. "I wouldn't turn one down."

He hadn't changed. But then again, this was the man she'd . . . kinda loved because he was exactly what everyone thought she was. And he'd never judged her. When she'd met him, she really needed that. For old time's sakes, she'd hear him out.

"I'm not making any promises." She jerked her chin at his briefcase. "But show me what you've got."

He pulled out a file, flipped it open, and picked up an envelope. Withdrawing several pictures, he laid them out on the desk.

Her eyes went wide. Jami, Dean's daughter, was in all of them. With her boyfriend . . . Ford, yes, that was his name. They were kissing, smoking joints, drinking. But Silver had done all of that at Jami's age. These weren't candid shots of nefarious activities, they were pictures of a fairly normal eighteen-year-old girl.

"Why are you showing me this?" She gathered the photos and stuffed them in the envelope. She felt like she was spying on the kid, and no matter how nasty the girl had been last time she'd seen her, she'd respect her privacy. "I'm not going to rat her out to her dad if that's what you're thinking."

"Do you recognize the man in the photo?" Asher took the envelope and pulled out one photo. "Ford Kingsley."

"I met him once."

"*Kingsley*, Silver! Please tell me you've read up on those dirty investors that screwed the team last year!"

She shrugged. The fat representative had gone away. She hadn't really thought much more about it. "They approached me once, but Dean scared them off."

"I doubt that. Kingsley Enterprises has their hands in just about everything. Ford is the only heir." He groaned when Silver gave him a blank look. "Think about it! It's no coincidence that he's dating the daughter of the Dartmouth Cobra's GM. You wouldn't cooperate, so he's going to use her. I bet even Mr. Richter would forget the integrity of the game to keep his daughter safe. Do you know she's been practically living with Ford? She's a kid in lust, and he'll fuck with her to get what he wants. Which is games his family can make money from."

"That fucking piece of shit." Silver pictured Jami, so much like her at that age, defying Daddy to get her freedom. Only Dean wasn't trying to keep her in a gilded cage to protect his image. As hard as it was on him, he let her live her own life and did his best to support her. And in return, she'd put him in a position that jeopardized everything he'd worked for. But she wasn't to blame. "Where is this bar Ford works at? I guess his daddy owns it?"

"He does. And I know exactly where it is. He's there now." Asher took in a noisy breath. "I figured you'd want to go talk to him, but you've got to be smart about this. Get something you can use on him. Get him to spell out what he wants you to do."

"And I'm assuming this conversation will be recorded? So we can use it against him in court?"

"Sexy and smart." Asher grinned. "If you weren't a chick, I've had told Cedric to suck it up. I seriously love that you've got brains in that blond head of yours."

"Quit rimming my ass, you idiot. This is good. Enough for me to consider putting you on my payroll." Silver punched his shoulder. "And I *might* forgive you for using me if we can get Ford to back off Jami. Just tell me what you need me to do."

"It shouldn't be hard. Just be your charming self." Lips twisted into an evil smile, Asher leaned close to her. "From what I hear, Ford is as much of a dog as our stud Demyan."

Silver cocked her head. "Our stud?"

"You wouldn't have him if it wasn't for me. And if you *do* hire me as the team's new lawyer—and you need one, by the way, since the last one worked for Kingsley . . ." Asher's licked his lips. "Let's just say Cedric and I have fantasized about Scott a few times, and he'd be fun to play with, if he's willing."

Silver thought on how Scott had flirted with Scarlet. "I'm starting to think that man will fuck anything with a hole. So go for it.

But for now, how to we trap Ford?"

"He won't be shy about telling you what he wants from you. The whole family is arrogant as hell." Asher grabbed her purse and dumped the contents on her desk. He eyed her as he opened the zipper pocket and pulled out the vial. "How have you been doing with this, anyway? Sweet stuff still takes the edge off?"

"You know it does. Now put that shit away and stop going through my stuff, we're not together anymore and you know I don't lend out my lip gloss." She plucked a rose from the bouquet, stripped off the plastic, and stuck it in her mouth. *Mmm. Strawberry.* "I'm handling it. You were saying?"

Asher picked up her phone. "Call me just before you go into the bar. I'll record the conversation. We can use it against them. Much as they want to make money off the team, they won't risk their reputation."

"So should I tell them I've got them when I'm done? Or should I save it for when they come at me again?"

"Tell them. If they know killing you won't keep them clean, you'll be safe."

"So going there isn't safe?"

"No, but neither is sniffing coke. You've never played it safe, Silver. Don't start now."

Yeah, heaven forbid. She rolled her eyes and sucked hard on the lollipop. "I'll give you one thing, Asher. You know me."

"So you'll do it?"

"Yeah, I'll do it." She picked up the picture of Ford and Jami and frowned. Jami looked so happy. Finding out she was nothing but a pawn would hurt her so bad. But it had to be done. "I guess we keep this between us?"

"Your dad doesn't know I got you shot, does he?" Asher rubbed his fingers over his eyes. "Fuck it, Dean is a better father than yours ever was. Do you really think he needs to know about the trouble his daughter's gotten herself in? If you do, then tell him, but I think this will get a lot more complicated than it needs to be."

"Dean would freak. He wouldn't let me do this." Hopefully *he'd* forgive her if he ever found out. "Let's save the kid, and me, a big headache and get this over with."

"That's exactly what I hope you'd say. The bar should be pretty empty now."

Great. She grabbed her jacket from the back of the chair and pulled it on. *No witnesses. Ford will like that.*

She'd be lucky if she got off with a caning if either Dean or Landon ever found out.

But she'd take the pain if she made it out of there alive.

* * * *

Silver sucked hard on her rose lollipop and tongued the hard petals. Her heart throbbed in her ears as she stepped off the elevator and checked the main floor. All clear. She'd made it this far without anyone questioning where she was going. Her staff wouldn't; her leaving wasn't a big deal. She'd taken off for the road trip on a whim. Nobody took her seriously. Including her secretary who now had two weeks to find another job.

No need to worry about that now. This didn't involve the team. Or it shouldn't anyway.

Out on the sidewalk, she plucked the lollipop from her mouth and let out a sigh of relief. Then giggled. Sneaking out as a teen had been less nerve-racking.

Sneaker soles slapping pavement pulled her away from her internal fist-pump of success. She stopped and turned.

A dark smile and a flash of very white teeth spelled out utter failure. Dominik jogged up to her side and put his hand on her shoulder. "What's your hurry?"

Further down the sidewalk she saw Oriana and Max. Oriana gave her the big sister I-know-you're-up-to-something look before hooking her arm with Max's and heading to her favorite café.

"I expect an answer, little sister." Dominik's tone made her shiver. He'd never used *that* tone on her, the one that made her want to kneel and apologize for even considering misbehaving.

Thanks for siccing the scary one on me, sis. Clasping her small studded leather purse in her hands like a pathetic little shield, she gave him her most innocent smile. "Oh, I'm just running late for a meeting Asher set up—"

Dominik frowned. "Asher?"

Brilliant, Silver. She wrinkled her nose and shrugged. "We've worked out a professional relationship. He really is a good lawyer."

"Perhaps. But why would you need a lawyer?" His hand left her shoulder, and he folded his arms over his extremely wide chest. In that position, he *looked* like a damn enforcer. "Are you in some kind of trouble?"

"I'm not in trouble" —*yet*— "I'm just . . . helping a friend."

"I see. Is this friend in trouble with the law? Are you going to speak to the police?"

"No! The cops *really* don't need to be involved." *ShutupShutupShutup!*

"Ah. And what about Richter and Bower?" His brow arched. "Do they know that you're getting *yourself* involved?"

"They will."

"When?"

"After."

"I see." He rubbed his chin and glanced up at the forum. "You passed Richter's office and didn't think to mention it to him. I have a feeling you know he wouldn't approve of whatever it is you're doing."

"He's busy." She ran her tongue over her teeth and sighed. "I swear I'll tell him—I'll tell them both. This is just something I need to do."

"Something potentially dangerous, I gather?"

"Umm . . ."

"Umm is not an answer. I can't allow you to put yourself in danger, Silver."

Damn it. I am so going to get you for this, Oriana. She had to hurry, or she'd miss her meeting with Landon and that would *definitely* let him know something was up. Which left only one way out.

"Come with me then." Actually, having him along was a damn good idea. Ford was less likely to try and intimidate her with someone like Dominik watching over her. Dean and Landon would be less pissed if they knew she'd been careful. A total win-win. "It shouldn't take long. And you are the enforcer."

Dominik chuckled. "On the ice, little one."

"Well, consider this me adding to your duties. It's just a meeting, but if you're there, you can assure my dear sister and everyone else that I was perfectly safe."

"Very well." He put his hand on the small of her back and redirected her to his SUV. "But you will tell me *exactly* who your friend is and who we're dealing with on the way there."

Her heels scraped the sidewalk as she tried to pull away. "I wanted to take my car."

"I'm sure you did." Dominik unlocked the driver's side door. "Get in."

* * * *

The Office sat between a boarded-up bakery and a used boat lot in a fairly rundown part of the older port district. The bar itself looked well kept enough, with clean whitewashed brick and a large sign over the spotless reflective glass front, featuring the name in bold, black metallic print.

Not the dingy, creepy joint she'd expected.

A light laugh breezed out with her exhale as Dominik joined her on the sidewalk. "I can honestly tell Dean and Landon I was at 'The Office' this whole time."

Dominik didn't seem to find that funny. He strode forward and held the door open for her. "Make it quick."

Snapping her suit jacket straight by the hem, she walked past him and stepped into the bar. The hovering smoke cloud appeared to be a thinned version of the fog outside. Off to one side, plain high tables with black padded stools lined the wall. A long, half oval counter in red polished wood took up the other side of the room. Two men leaned on the counter, one the pudgy guy that Dean had scared out of her office, the other a middle-aged biker all darned up in leather.

Behind the bar, Ford uncapped two bottles of Heineken. He laughed at something the biker said and scratched the center of his hairless, bare chest. The entrance to the bar stood wide open, giving her a clear view of the rest of him. Low riding jeans, showing off his trim waist and the sharp cut of his pelvis, accented by a metal studded belt. He wasn't that muscular compared to, say, Landon, but it wasn't hard to see why Jami had been attracted to him. Something about his smile hinted at an invitation for a reckless ride.

Silver had been on a few of those. They'd lost their appeal along with the last fad of animal print.

Her heels snicked loudly on the old wood floor as she approached the bar. She smacked her best bitch-on-a-mission expression on her face. "Hello, Ford."

"Hey, Silver." Ford faced her and smirked. "I was wondering how long it would take before you stopped ogling me and remembered your manners."

"Ogling?" She snorted indelicately. "Oh, I get it, you're one of those."

Ford brought his beer to his slanted lips. "One of those?"

She tossed her head and shrugged as she slid onto a stool at the end of the bar. "If a woman looks at you, she *must* want you." She batted her eyelashes. "If I'd met you a year ago, I'd have played with you for one night. You're not utterly revolting."

"I guess it's a good thing we didn't meet last year." He held up his beer. "Thirsty?"

"No. And I don't plan to be here long."

"You're the kind of girl that's unbuckling a guy's belt before you get his name, aren't you?" He exchanged a look with the biker and chuckled before turning back to her. "All right, let's do this. How can I help you, princess?"

Her eyes narrowed. "Don't call me, princess, you cocky stump dick."

"Since my dick is officially off the table, how about we stay on track? Unless you want to start trading insults?" He took a swig. "You've been around. Shall we discuss your floppy pussy lips?"

Lips parted, she stared at him. *Oh, you didn't just fucking go there.* "I should slap you."

He rolled his eyes and sighed. "You're boring me, Silver. I've heard a lot about you but never that you were boring."

"I'm not here to entertain you—"

"You're *here* to entertain everyone. Are you getting to a point?"

"Yes. I want to know why you're using Jami. If you want

something from me, just say so."

Nodding slowly, he took another swig. "What is it you think I want from you?"

You're supposed to call Asher before you get him talking, dummy. Shoving her hand in her purse, she pressed send on her phone and snatched a stick of red licorice from an open mini-pack. After snapping her purse shut, she stuck the licorice in her mouth and chewed hard.

"You tell me. I know dough boy there works for your family. And your family is invested in the team." She swallowed and dropped her gaze to the bar top. "Daddy says I have to keep the investors happy. I can't be doing a good job if you're going after the GM's daughter rather than coming directly to me. We don't need to play games."

"I like playing games. I like playing them even more when I know the outcome." He gave her a shrewd look. "Are you hearing me?"

She nibbled on her bottom lip, glanced toward Dominik—who stood by the door like a bodyguard—and leaned forward. "I'm new at this, so no, I don't think I'm hearing you. Are you talking about the Cobras?"

"What else would I be talking about?"

"But . . ." She shook her head and made her eyes go wide with confusion. "All we can do is put together the best possible team. You probably know the sport better than I do. We've got a pretty good lineup . . ."

"Yes, but a good lineup isn't enough. You can't make money off games when *everyone* can guess the outcome. You make money when you *know* the outcome."

"But how could anyone know the outcome?"

"You're smarter than that, Silver. I'm sure you know the goalie last year was throwing games. The team was good enough to win several despite him, but they remained the underdog. Most people bet for the opposition." Ford eyed Dominik. "You have no idea how much money can be made when you bet against the odds—but aren't really betting against the odds."

Her hand hovered over her mouth. "Is that even legal?"

"Of course not. But neither is buying coke." Ford held up his beer in mock cheers. "I've done my homework too, sweetheart."

"So you want me to . . ." She shook her head. "What does Jami have to do with this?"

"Nothing anymore. I don't need her." He straightened and rolled his shoulders. "She's more immature than I thought she was and more trouble than she's worth. She broke up with me this morning."

"Oh." Silver bit into her licorice and ground it to pulp between her teeth. "So . . . you thought *I* would . . . fix the games for you?"

"As if you could. Your fuck friend is the goalie; he's too clean to go for it." Ford's hand shot out and he wrapped his fingers around her wrist. "He might do it for you though—"

Dominik crossed the room, and she looked up to see his eyes darkening to the color of wood freshly beaten by a storm. "Silver?"

"I'm okay." She twisted free of Ford's grip and glared at him. "I won't ask Landon to throw games. They mean too much to him."

Ford laid his forearms on the bar and lifted his shoulders in a careless shrug. "Well, I don't really need you either. But I won't share the profit unless you make this easier for me. Who else are you fucking? The GM's too uptight to work with. What about that new guy? Sebastian? He's a defenseman. He could be useful."

Her throat locked. "I'm not fucking him."

"And Scott? Actually, I considered approaching him myself. He seems the type."

"I think Scott would surprise you."

"Are you doing him? I'm sure it wouldn't take much for you to find out." Ford's lips twisted slightly. "And you came here with your sister's boyfriend. He could be useful."

Dominik must have heard that; he was close enough. But he didn't say a word.

"He came here to make sure you didn't try anything." She sat up and her chin jutted out. "And he's loyal to my sister."

"But you trusted him enough to come here and discuss this with me?" Ford set down his beer and flattened his hands on the bar. "How do you know he won't say anything?"

"He doesn't need to. You've said enough." Smiling sweetly, she picked up her purse. "The team needs your family's money, so I won't go to the cops. Unless I have to—"

Ford grabbed the collar of her blouse. "You're not involving the cops."

"I suggest—" Dominik reached out and latched onto Ford's wrist "—you let her go right now."

A click from the far end of the bar made Silver's heart skip a beat. She knew that sound. From the corner of her eye, she could see the black metal gleam of the gun in the biker's hand. He motioned with it for Dominik to move away.

Dominik snarled and fisted his hands at his sides. "She's got someone on the phone, listening to all this. I suggest you let her go before he calls the police."

"Chill, Cort, they were just leaving." Ford released her and held up his hands. "The drama isn't necessary, but I must say, well played, Silver. I just hope you don't forget that you *do* need my family's money. Your daddy dumped everything he has into this team. You know that, right?"

"I know that." Silver rubbed her throat and retreated to Dominik's side. "Just stay away from my family—and that includes Jami—and we'll be fine. Otherwise, I'll expose you and let the league cover the loses. I've got other ways to put this team back on track. We won't need you for long."

"We'll see." Ford thrummed his fingers on the bar. "Maybe Kingsley Enterprises will tighten their purse strings a little, just to remind you how much you *do* need us. But either way, I wouldn't count on me leaving your family alone, princess."

"If you touch Jami—"

"Jami will be fine. She was a good time, that's it. I don't threaten kids." He inclined his head toward Cort, who still had his gun out. "But, as I said, you're leaving."

Dominik latched onto her arm and dragged her toward the door. "Yes. We're leaving."

Outside, Silver stumbled away from Dominik as the world did a lopsided spin and she almost pitched herself face-first into the sidewalk. Dominik hauled her up and practically carried her to his car. After sitting her in the passenger seat, he dug his fingers into her shoulder.

"You tell Dean—and Landon—today." His jaw went hard. "Or I will."

"I'll tell them." She gasped and pressed her hands into her stomach. *Shitshitshit. I am so fucking screwed.*

As Dominik drove, she stared out the window, her eyes burning with unshed tears. Landon and Dean could punish her all they wanted. It would change nothing.

She'd royally fucked the team. And she had no idea how to fix this.

Chapter Thirty Two

Landon pushed open the door to Silver's office, a broad smile on his lips, and her gift draped over his arm. One look at her blotchy face and his excitement drowned under concern. With long strides, he cut across the room and pulled her up against him.

"What happened?"

"Just hug me for minute." She buried her face under his arm. "You're going to be too mad to hug me after I tell you."

He stiffened, but stroked her back until she stopped shaking. "I'll never be too mad to hug you. Tell me what it is—it can't be any worse than signing Demyan."

"Oh, it's worse."

Fuck, why do I have a feeling you're not exaggerating? He put his hands on her shoulders and eased her back so he could look into her teary, bloodshot eyes. "How about you tell me and let me decide?"

His whole body trembled with rage as she finished telling him what she'd done. Not at her—hell, he grabbed her and held her tight, sick with the idea that he could have lost her. His rage was at that man, Ford, who'd been stupid enough to threaten her. If that bastard was here right now, Landon would rip his head off and beat his body to a bloody pulp.

Burying his hands into Silver's hair, he tugged her head back and kissed her forehead. "I'm proud of you for bringing Dominik. This could have turned out so much worse if you'd gone alone. Who knows what that son of a bitch would have—" Fear clogged up his throat and cut off his words. He inhaled and kissed her cheeks, her eyes, then groaned into her mouth. "Don't *ever* do anything like that again. I know your heart was in the right place, but you risking yourself like that is inexcusable."

"I know."

"And you know I will have to punish you."

"Yes." She sniffed and stared at his chest. Her fingers curled into his T-shirt. "Dean will too. But I'm okay with that. It's better being punished than having you both decide I'm more trouble than I'm worth."

"Get that thought out of your head right now. You're worth all kinds of trouble." He cuffed her chin lightly with his fist. "I got you something. Actually, it was a gift for you, Dean, and myself. Unfortunately, it's going to become part of your punishment."

She raked her bottom lip with her teeth and glanced at what he'd left on the desk. "Can I see it?"

"In a moment." He undid the buttons of her suit jacket, pulled it off, then went to work on the buttons of her blouse. "Humor me. I need to touch you. See for myself that you're really okay."

"I'm sorry, Landon." She trembled, whispering, "I didn't even think . . . after what *she* did to you—"

He paused on the last button. "So you know."

"I need to hear it from you."

Fair enough. Hearing about any of her past pains from anyone else wouldn't be enough for him either. He stripped off her blouse, then unzipped her skirt. "We got together in high school. I wasn't big on dating, nothing long-term anyway, but she didn't take me away from training, didn't bitch about my crazy schedule. It was perfect. As a stupid teen, I saw her as the type of girl who could become the perfect hockey wife. She never came between me and the game. But as we got older, she expected all my free time to be hers. She tried to come between me and my family, which should have been a big red fucking flag. I felt too guilty about leaving her on her own all the time to see it."

He removed her bra and sucked in a breath as Silver stood before him, practically naked, and whispered for him to continue, the understanding in her eyes more than he'd ever hoped to have from anyone who wasn't family.

But he had it from her—*and* Dean. *You're one lucky bastard, Bower.*

He ran his hands up and down Silver's arms and forced himself to keep talking. "After I got into the lifestyle, well, she made herself seem even more perfect. She wanted it all. We had fun . . . but she hated that I had new friends. Gay friends. She knew I was straight, that they weren't a threat to our relationship. That wasn't the problem. She couldn't accept that they were gay." He shook his head. "I realized I didn't know her at all. Her prejudices became a serious issue. She said nasty things about them, and *that* was when I ended it. It probably sounds stupid—"

"It doesn't sound stupid to me. Like you said, you didn't know her." Silver laced her fingers with his. "It obviously wasn't the only issue, but as far as I'm concerned, it was a pretty big one."

"Yes, well I had to get over it. She showed up at my door one day and told me she was pregnant. She'd been on the pill, but I guess she forgot to take it. We'd only ever been with each other, so we didn't use any other protection. Which is no excuse. I mean, I didn't want kids, so I should have done my share to make sure it didn't happen." He lifted one hand to rake his short nails over his scalp. "But it did, and I wasn't about to abandon my kid. My family's always been close. My parents had their issues, but they made it work. I figured I could do the same. And . . . things weren't too bad while she was pregnant. Of course, I spent all my time with her, but I wanted to be involved with everything. I wanted my son to know my voice, even before he was born."

"You wanted to be a good father."

"I wanted to be at least half the father mine was. I couldn't be more without giving up the game, but I couldn't do that." A thick ball of acid curled up in the back of his throat. He rolled his eyes toward the ceiling and blinked against the burning in his eyes. "He died as she was giving birth to him. I made it there just in time for the nurse to tell me—for her to let me hold him. We mourned him together, and I tried to be there for her after. But without the baby, we had nothing. Almost a year later, I told her we would always have him, but we would never have us."

"I guess she didn't take that well?" Silver touched his cheek, her eyes full of pain. Pain for him. Which he didn't deserve. She frowned. "You felt guilty about leaving her."

"Of course I did."

"You have a right to be happy. You weren't happy with her."

"She wasn't happy either! She wanted another baby! I couldn't . . ." He swallowed. "She told me nothing would fill the hole he'd left unless I gave her another baby. I wouldn't even consider it. She told me she was going to lose it if I didn't come back to her. But she had been telling me that every day. Usually after asking me if I was hanging out with my gay friends again. I'd just gotten drafted and I was trying to move on with my life. I'd had enough. Before we hung up, she told me she'd be waiting for me at my place. And she was. She was in the bath and . . ."

You should have done something. You took the easy way out.

Silver's hand covered her lips. "Landon—"

"She'd slit her wrists with one of my razors. There was so much blood." He curved his hand around his throat. "I didn't know. She'd never talked about suicide. I would have done something—"

"I know you would have."

"No, you don't know. She obviously had issues. She needed help. And I wasn't there for her."

"You were there for her as much as you could be. She made that decision and that's on her. No one else." She jerked on his shirt collar, magnificent in all her naked glory. "What would you say to me if I told you I blame myself for my mother's death? For the fact that she got in that car and killed my brother?"

"You were a little girl. How the hell could you possibly think that was your fault?"

"I won second place. I wasn't good enough for her. That's why she was in the car. To get me a second chance."

There was no way could Silver possibly blame herself for that. "Her own stupidity."

"Exactly."

"It's not the same."

"It's exactly the same. They both made choices. and there's nothing either of us could have done to stop them." She dropped her gaze as though thinking it over. And accepting her own words as she looked up, her eyes hard. "Blaming ourselves is pretty arrogant, don't you think? As if we had the power to change them. To control them. We didn't."

What an odd way to look at it. But she was right. He bowed his head. "No. We didn't."

"Now." Silver scowled. "Would it be horrible of me to tell you I want to go back to how mad at me you are? Either that or we can sit down and have a few drinks and get all depressed."

"None of that." He shoveled mental dirt over the part of him that clung to the past and focused on the woman in front of him. The one who held his heart in her delicate little fists. "I still want you to see your present. I want to see it on you before we go speak to Dean."

"Damn." Silver's lips twisted as she looked at the clothes bag on her desk. "You're going to make me wear whatever it is to go see him, aren't you?"

He chuckled and patted her cheek. "Part of your punishment. You've been a very bad girl."

And I'll do anything to make sure you never forget that this will not happen again. I won't lose you.

He had to say it out loud. "I won't lose you. I won't let you do anything that could take you away from me. I love you too fucking much."

"And I love you too. But don't expect me to thank you for this."

Grinning, he bent down to pull off her panties. "I think that would be going a bit too far. Just accept it. That's more than enough for me."

* * * *

Three players off waivers and four rookies with new long-term contracts. Not a bad day so far. Dean absently rubbed his knee and smiled as the door opened. Bolleau had gone home early, and other than his assistant, there was only one—all right, perhaps two people who would come to his office without an appointment.

Both came in and his jaw nearly hit the floor.

Silver dropped to her knees, crawling toward him with a flirty smile on her lips. Her long, silky pigtails slipped back and forth over her shoulders with each sensuous motion. Her white shirt, completely unbuttoned, held together by only the part tied over her belly, gave him a lovely view of her breasts in a red plaid push up bra. The short red tie around her neck didn't hide a thing. She knelt in front of him, assuming the position as gracefully as any well-trained slave. Knees apart, hands resting on her thighs, palms up. Her short, red plaid skirt rose all the way and his lips curved as he took in her bare little pussy. No panties. Very nice.

Leaning forward, he set his elbow on his knee and his chin in his hand. "What's this?"

Silver batted her eyelashes. "I wanted to show you how submissive I can be."

"By disobeying me?" Dean chuckled. "Oh yes. Now, I'm convinced."

Landon stepped up to her side and wrapped one pigtail around his hand. "Disobeying him? Am I missing something?"

She tipped her head back. "We're not allowed to play at work."

"Ah. Well, extenuating circumstances." Landon's lips thinned. "Would you care to tell him why we're really here, or should I?"

Her throat worked as she gulped. Long black lashes fluttering, she pouted. "I'm here to get a spanking."

"A spanking?" Dean glanced at Landon, who shook his head. Apparently Silver would be answering his questions. "Have you been naughty, pet?"

A flush spread over her cheeks. "Not exactly. I kinda did something stupid."

Okay, enough with the fucking games. He pushed off his chair and scowled. "Someone better start talking."

She did. In a rush. "I brought Dominik, so I was safe. I was worried about Jami—but don't worry, she broke up with him. But I thought he was using her. He's the son of one of our investors, the ones that rigged games. I got him to tell me everything. It's recorded. I think that will help."

"Wait a damn second! What? Jami is in trouble?"

"I thought she was. She dumped the asshole."

"What asshole?"

"The one she was dating."

Dean slammed his fist on the corner of his desk. "I didn't even know she had a boyfriend! And you decided to deal with this without telling me? I told you not to meet with the investors."

"Actually, you told me not to meet with Mr. Lee." She looked up and winced. "Sir."

"Calling me 'Sir' doesn't make this all right, Silver. She is my daughter. You come to *me* if she's in trouble. And you . . ." He threw his hands up in the air. "You have no idea how dangerous these people are!"

"She does now," Landon said.

A dead calm washed through him. He waved Landon away and stared at Silver. "Stand up."

She stood.

"Look. At. Me."

Her wide, glistening eyes met his.

"What did they do to you? Tell me everything."

"Nothing." She reached out, and when he didn't stop her, pressed her body into his. "Ford grabbed my shirt and . . ." She took a deep breath. "Dominik stepped in and told Ford Asher was on the phone—"

"Asher?" His calm was sizzling. "Did he put you up to this?"

"He told me about Ford. That he was Kingsley's son and was probably using Jami. But that's over. It's over." She straightened and took a step back. "I fucked up and I'm sorry. Let me make it up to you."

"Make it up to me? How could anything—" He caught Landon shaking his head and cut himself off. Going on and on about this wouldn't change anything. She was here. Safe. And she knew she'd made a mistake. That was enough for him, but not for her.

Part of him was tempted to tell her to go so he could process it all, but that would make her feel like she couldn't be forgiven. And as much as he hated punishing her—no, this time, he wouldn't. This time he would feel like the punishment just might discourage her from doing anything so foolish every again.

"Has Master Landon decided on a fitting punishment?"

She screwed up her face and shuffled her Mary Janes. "He bought this outfit for us to have fun together. He made me wear it to come here—only the janitor saw me, but that was bad enough. And he said . . ." She glanced at Landon and he nodded. "Five swats from each of you, every day for a week, with any implement you choose, should teach me a 'lesson.'"

Ah, so the punishment won't ruin the scene. I like that idea. Of course, there was a chance that the scene itself would lessen the impact of the punishment, but one look at Silver dashed those concerns. She wouldn't forget why she was getting "spanked." Landon had mentioned an "implement" to her, so this wouldn't be an intimate hand whacking that could be misconstrued.

Very well. Ten to show her they meant it, and then some fun. Which meant, after giving her his five, and reminding her why she needed them, he couldn't bring it up again. Until the next five. But in a way, that worked for him. It was straightforward. And once it was over, they could all move on.

"All right, well since Master Landon was given the information first, I think it's only fair that I should make the first marks on that pretty ass." He opened his desk drawer and pulled out a long wooden ruler. "I think this fits our little scenario, don't you?"

"Yes, Sir." She pressed her lips together, hiding a smile. "This is going to hurt, isn't it?"

"Yes, it is."

"Am I allowed to call you names?"

It was very, very hard not to laugh. *Impertinent little brat.* "I wouldn't suggest it. Hands on the desk."

She slapped her hands on the desk and wiggled her butt. "I'm ready."

"Good." He flipped her skirt up and cracked the ruler over her ass hard enough to draw an automatic yelp. A nice red welt crossed her pale cheeks. *Perfect.* "Don't bother counting yet, that was just for warm up."

"You mother—"

Crack.

"And so was that."

* * * *

I want to go down to the rink and plant my ass on the ice. Silver shifted from knee to knee, unable to sit fully back on her heels because her butt stung like iodine on skinned flesh. She couldn't get comfortable. Dean had gotten in a few extra—*the bastard*—and Landon had kept his strikes to the undercurve of her ass. *That man is positively fucking evil.*

"How are you feeling, Silver?" Landon leaned his hip on the

edge of the desk, close to her side, and reached down to tuck her hair behind her ear. "We can stop now. All you have to do is ask."

She kept her head down, more out of self-preservation than anything else. Dean *might* let her get away with giving him her sharpest fuck-you look, but Landon certainly wouldn't. They had given her the choice to snuggle and then carry on with the day, or prove to them that she didn't hurt too bad to play.

As if kneeling for ten minutes proves anything. "I don't need to stop, Sir."

"Is there a reason you won't look at me?"

"No, Sir." She pressed her lips together and hung her head until her chin almost touched her chest. If it wouldn't get her another few whacks, she'd have a few choice words for him. Why though? Not the punishment. Not even the pain. For some reason, she just felt irritated and had to fight not to lash out. Her nostrils flared as Landon studied her quietly. Her nails bit into her palms as Dean watched them both.

"Is there something you'd like to say, Silver?" Dean rested his elbows on his knees and bent forward from his office chair. "Are you uncomfortable?"

"Aren't I supposed to be?" *Why are you both staring at me?* The silence changed and she glanced up, catching herself at Dean's hard look. "Sir. No, I'm not uncomfortable, Sir."

"Better. Do you need to use your safeword?"

For the pain? No way. But if something doesn't happen soon . . . "No, *Sir.* I'm perfectly fine."

"That's good," Landon said.

"Yes." Dean nodded and sat back. "Very good."

Screw this. She shot to her feet and slammed her fists into her hips. "You know what, I don't know what kind of game you two are playing, but I'm fucking done. You're both—"

Landon's hand covered her mouth. "That's enough. Let's not earn ourself another punishment." His breath rasped into her hair as he pulled her back against his hard chest. "I stopped while I was still having fun."

She shivered and peeked at Dean. The bastard folded his arms behind his head and smiled at her.

Her eyes narrowed. "Punishments aren't supposed to be fun."

"For you." Landon fisted his hand in her hair and jerked it to one side. He bit her earlobe, then let out a deep, spine-chilling laugh. "I like marking your flesh, Silver. Does that scare you?"

"Landon, I don't –"

"Dean will be teaching me how to use a whip soon. Who do you think I'll be practicing on?"

Her core clenched even as she trembled like a kitten just brought in from the cold. The reaction confused the hell out of her. Landon was scaring her, but . . . but not in a way that made her want to get away from him. More the way a horror movie scared her. Freaked even though she was safe, peeking out at the danger between her fingers.

"Would you let me whip you, *mignonne?*"

A quick breath. She held it in, closed her eyes. And nodded.

"But it scares you?"

"Yes."

"Then why would you want to do it?"

She frowned. That was a weird question. "The same reason I want to—no, *need* to—" That got her a smile of approval from Dean which warmed her, calmed her. She stopped shaking. "Do any of this. It excites me. And . . . and part of me needs to do it for you. It feels good when I can give you something that makes you happy."

"Thank you. I appreciate your honesty." Landon kissed the hollow behind her ear. "That makes me happy. I need your submission too, but only if it's real. If you're really not feeling it, then don't pretend. Make me earn it."

"You'll spank me or—"

"Not always. Sometimes I'll find other ways to show you who's in control." He used her hair to expose her throat and grazed his teeth along the length. "Like I am now."

Her pulse quickened. For a split second, she felt ready to submit for real, to melt into him and whisper Sir in a way that meant something. But her hands were still free. Hitting him was out of the question, but prying at his fingers in her hair wasn't breaking any rules. She worked her fingers into his hand and twisted her body away from his.

His arm barred across her belly and air whooshed out of her. "Do I need to tie you?"

Energy buzzed in her veins as she smiled through her teeth. "If it pleases you, Sir."

"But you won't hold still."

Trick question? Well, he hadn't "commanded" it. "No, Sir."

"It'll be rather difficult to tie you while I'm holding you, won't it?"

She bit back a smirk and nodded.

Dean let out a dark chuckle and hooked his fingers to her skirt to draw her between his thighs. "It's a good thing there's two of us then, isn't it, pet?"

He closed his thighs tight against her hips and grabbed her wrists.

Trapped. Her heart thumped hard into the cage of her ribs as Dean forced her to her knees. Her nipples tingled and her breasts felt swollen, heavy. The air she gasped in tasted like the men and pure, hot sex.

Landon knelt behind her, biting down on the nape of her neck until she whimpered and stopped struggling. Then he laughed breathlessly and pressed his solid length against the small of her back. "Now we've got you."

He left her and returned seconds later, crouching down next to Dean to undo her shirt. He flipped her bra off her breasts and used the folded cups to push her breasts up. Then he rolled her nipples between his fingers and thumbs. Jolts of pleasure heated her whole chest as he tugged hard. He released her nipples, reached into his pocket, then pulled out a small package.

Nipple clamps. She shook her head and tried to throw herself backward. "No way. No fucking way."

"Yes." Landon cupped one breast and applied the clamp. Her eyes teared as the pain rode over the preceding pleasure. He didn't give her a chance to adjust to the fierce pressure before applying the other. "Breathe, Silver."

She didn't want to breathe. She wanted to kick him.

"I need to tightened them a bit."

Tighten them? She shook her head. "Please, no!"

He watched her face as he tightened the clamps, not stopping until tears spilled over her cheeks. Then he frowned. "What do we say when it's getting to be too much?"

"Yellow."

"Shouldn't you be saying that now?"

She inhaled and shook her head. Damn it, something inside her needed him to keep pushing. Didn't want him to hold back. If he took it easy on her, or if she used that word and got him to back off, she would lose . . . this helpless feeling. Fuck it hurt. Bad. But he wouldn't have gone even this far if he didn't think she could take it.

"She's fine, Landon." Dean bent down and kissed her forehead. "Please continue. I'm curious to see what you're going to do with that thin rope. It's not to bind her?"

"No." Landon undid her tie and held it up. "I think this will suffice."

Landon took her wrists from Dean and used her tie to bind them at the small of her back. Then he draped the rope around the back of her neck, letting the ends dangle as he folded the middle part under her collar so it didn't touch her flesh. He came in front of her again and strung one end of the rope through a clamp.

"Take your dick out, Dean. I need her to take you in deep so I can adjust the length."

Adjust the length?

Dean didn't ask any questions. He simply undid his suit pants and pulled out his engorged cock. He gently guided her down, stroking her cheek with his knuckles as she opened her mouth and took him in.

"A little deeper—there. Can you breathe around him okay, pet?"

The swollen head of Dean's dick almost hit the back of her throat. But if she opened her mouth wide enough, air passed around it. She gave Landon a little nod as she stared up at him, then Dean.

"Fuck, Silver, you feel damn good around me. Move your tongue a little." Dean groaned as she moved her tongue as much as she was able, stroking back and forth against the base of his cock. "Yes. Just like that, pet."

Okay, this was good. She loved the way a man's cock felt in her mouth, his pulse, his pleasure, all hers to control. It made her feel special because she was damn good at this, and men had been telling her so since long before she should have had any idea what a blowjob was. The clamps putting a slight weight on her nipples changed things a little, but not enough to tear her away from her practiced motions.

Until Landon attached the other end of the rope to the second clamp. Rising tightened the rope and her breasts stretched painfully. Lowering eased the tension, but got her stuck with Dean's dick almost lodged in her throat.

Her breaths came hard and fast through her nose. She peered up at Dean, pleading with her eyes.

"Let her up for a minute, Landon," Dean said.

Landon undid one side of the rope and helped her sit up.

Dean traced her bottom lip with his thumb. "Yellow or red, pet?"

"Re—" She shook her head and swallowed. "Yellow. I don't think I can do this."

"Why not? Are you having trouble breathing?"

"No."

Nodding, Dean touched her cheek and smiled. "You were scared and panicked a bit. This is called predicament bondage. I've never seen it done quite like this, but it's fucking hot. I think you'll enjoy being trapped, pleasuring me, while Landon plays with you. Shall we try again?"

I don't want to. She pursed her lips and glanced from him to Landon. Their expressions were unreadable. She could either give in or refuse. If she refused, well, she doubted there would be any consequences. But she would miss out on whatever they had planned.

Mentally putting herself back in that position, trapped, available, her focus entirely on her body between both men . . . Maybe she could do this after all.

"Okay." She smiled at Dean but gave Landon a dirty look. "I don't suppose you could loosen the clamps, Sir?"

"*Mon petit chaton,* if they were too tight, you wouldn't be giving me that look. You'd be crying and begging." He cocked his head and gave the rope a sharp tug. Pain flared out and she squeaked. And the crazy man grinned. "Not even a whimper. I'd test your limits a little more if you weren't so new, but I think this will do for today."

"You make pond scum look good, you know that? I—" She stopped talking when Dean took hold of her jaw. "Umm . . ."

"Yes. Umm." Dean frowned. "You know better. Apologize."

"I'm sorry." She rolled her eyes. "Sir."

Dean tapped her cheek. *Very* lightly, but it still surprised her. Her head snapped right out of the defiant mode, and she gazed up at Dean with her lips slightly parted.

His lips quirked. "Don't think I forgot you telling Carter to slap you. Don't ever expect me to hit you as hard as he did—in the face, anyway—but I do believe a love tap will get you into the right headspace quite efficiently."

"Yes, Sir." Her eyes were teary again, but something about it was almost refreshing. She could finally let go. She sucked on her bottom lip and turned to Landon. "I really am sorry."

"Good girl." He smiled and took a knee, kissing her long and hard. "I know this isn't easy. But I promise, it will be worth it."

He maneuvered her back over Dean's cock, and she stayed in position as he reattached the rope to the clamp. And this time she didn't go for cock-sucking pro. She simply let Dean inside without resistance.

Behind her, Landon lifted her skirt. Her insides clenched as his fingers slipped inside her pussy. His thumb passed over her clit, and her body jerked at the shock of pleasure. White-hot pain glazed her nerves as her breasts swung. His free hand spread her ass cheeks, and she winced as he pressed on a sore spot. Saliva gathered in her mouth, and she did her best to gulp around the dick in her mouth.

Another finger, wet with her own juices, pushed into her back hole. Once it was fully inserted, Landon placed his knees between hers and opened her thighs. And thrust his fingers into her pussy and her ass all at once.

Erotic sparks lit within as he fucked her with his fingers, moving her over Dean at his own pace, giving her no choice but to receive them both. They rocked together, back and forth, a little faster, a little rougher, lost to passion. Dean groaned as her chin bumped his balls and gathered her hair in his hands as his dick swelled. He came in her throat in hot spurts. Landon bent down and bit her ass cheek right over a welt. The sharp sensation wound with everything pitched her into a violent orgasm. Ecstasy shredded her into a million pieces. She forgot about the strings and threw her head back to scream. Agony burst through her breasts.

"Ah—!"

Dean covered her mouth and dropped down to help her slack the ropes. "Not here, love. I won't have people judging you because of this. You were perfect."

She shook her head. Something was missing. Then she knew. "Landon?"

"Do you want more, Silver?" Landon's fingers slipped from her as he kissed the small of her back. "I can wait."

"No. I need you to . . ."

"Then brace yourself, *ma chérie.*"

A rap at the door froze them all.

"Shit." Dean stood and did up his pants. "One minute!"

Landon pulled her into his lap and under the desk. As he undid the ropes, she giggled.

"It's not funny." He smirked. "Don't make a sound."

Before she could tell him she wouldn't, he removed a clamp. She bit into her cheek as pain exploded in her breast. When he took off the other, she slumped into him and sobbed into his chest.

He covered her breasts with his hands. "I know, *mignonne.* It will pass."

"Come in," Dean said.

Footsteps. Then a deep sigh. "Hey, bro."

"What's wrong, Tim?"

"It's Jami." Shoes scuffed on the carpet. Tim cleared his throat. "She's in the hospital. She overdosed."

"What?" Dean's chair hit the floor and Silver winced. He moved out of sight. "Overdosed? On what?"

"Cocaine."

Her heart beat so hard, it almost drowned out the sound of the door slamming. She pressed her eyes shut and curled into Landon's arms.

No. Anything but that.

Chapter Thirty Three

Dean took his daughter's hand and sat beside her on the bed. Her face was drawn and—damn him, how had he not noticed how much weight she'd lost? She was old enough to make her own decisions, yes, but she still lived under his roof. He should have used what little control he still had over her to . . .

What control, Richter? She doesn't listen to you anymore.

But he should have tried harder.

"Daddy." Tears streaked down Jami's pale face, and for a moment, she was his baby again. Six years old and asking him to check for monsters in the closet. Twelve and writing him tearstained letters from summer camp, begging for him to come get her. Which of course he had. "I'm so sorry. I didn't mean to—"

"Shh. It's okay, baby. You made a mistake." He kissed her cheek and spoke low. "Did that boy you were with—?"

"I don't want to talk about Ford. He's such a loser."

"What did he do to you?" He actually managed to sound calm. Not at all like he was tempted to commit murder.

"What . . . oh! Nothing, really. He just didn't like my friends and—okay, maybe he was right about them." She sighed. "But seriously, I don't need a guy telling me what to do."

"No. You don't." *Hypocrite.* He shut down the mocking, internal laughter and squared his jaw. "But you do need to stay away from the drugs. Is this the first time you ever . . ."

She fiddled with the sheets covering her and stared at her hands. "First time with coke."

"Oh, Jami—"

"I knew it. You're mad." Scowling, she pulled away from him and sat up. "Why do you think I had them call Uncle Tim? I knew you'd freak out."

"I'm not freaking out. I'm trying to help you. You're drinking and doing drugs." He shook his head and closed his eyes, reminding himself that his daughter needed his support. Anything else would be taken as a challenge to defy him. Like when he'd tried to talk to her about her drinking. "What about school? You seemed so excited—"

"I dropped out. It was boring and I haven't decided what I want to do yet. I enrolled to make you happy."

"Well, what will make you happy?"

"I don't know yet."

"Maybe I can get you an internship at the forum. What are you interested in?"

"Jeez, Dad, seriously?" She slumped onto the pile of pillows. "I'd rather pick up trash for a living than have anything to do with fucking hockey."

He grinned despite her scowl. "Trash collectors make a decent living."

"That's *so* lame." A snort escaped her as she gave him her patented "get real" look. "Besides, I'm not worried about a job right now. I'm really messed up."

"Okay, I get that." His brow furrowed when she laughed. He pulled her blankets up to her chin. "Get some rest, sweetie. We'll figure this out together. I'll take some time off work—"

"You never take time off work."

"But I will. All I care about right now is making sure you're okay." He paused as a nurse opened the door to Jami's private room and nodded when she held up a blood sampling kit. "I'll be right outside the door if you need me. And when I come back, we're going to discuss rehab."

"*Dad!*" Jami blushed and glanced at the nurse. "I don't need rehab."

"Jami, you do." He moved aside to let the nurse pass. "We'll talk more when you're done."

Out in the hall, he took a deep breath and pressed his fist into the wall. Silver came up behind him and wrapped her arms around his waist.

She was quiet for a bit, then whispered, "How is she?"

"Lucky." His throat locked. He blinked fast. "What have I done to her? She needed me and—"

"She's a big girl, Dean."

"So what? She's my daughter and I failed her. I'm all she has." He tugged on his tie and undid the top button of his shirt. "I don't know how to help her."

"Can I try?" Silver held onto the sides of his suit jacket as she stepped back. "Maybe she'll listen to me."

"You're her father's girlfriend, Silver. Right now she resents you. I don't see how—"

"I've been where she is, Dean. She might learn from my experience."

"I'd agree if it was trouble with a man—"

"I'm not talking about men." Silver pressed her lips together and let her hands fall to her sides. "I've done some messed up shit. We haven't talked about my past much."

"No. We haven't." He smiled wanly and reached out to take her hand. "And I'd like to, but now isn't the time."

"Now is the perfect time. I can help her because . . ." Her throat worked as she dropped her gaze to her feet. Normal black heels— thankfully she'd changed out of the schoolgirl outfit in time to come with him to the hospital. He didn't need a reminder of what he'd been doing while his daughter was being rushed to the ER.

Since Silver didn't finish her sentence, he squeezed her hand and sighed. "Please, love. Whatever you have to tell me, make it quick. I don't want to leave her alone."

She inclined her head. "Okay. There's no good way to tell you this. But I've been clean for about nine months."

"Been clean?"

"I did coke in Hollywood. It got pretty bad. But I quit."

"No." *Fuck no.* He didn't need to hear this now. "Silver, what did I tell you about lying? This isn't helping."

"I'm not lying. You have no idea how many stupid things I did out there. Drugs are at the top of a long list." Her eyes looked almost glassy as she peered up at him. "But like I said, I quit."

"I would have heard if you went to rehab."

"I didn't."

"So then how did you quit?"

She held up her purse, opened it, and pulled out a small vial of white powder. "I kept this on me so I knew I could start up again whenever I wanted to. And constantly reminded myself why I didn't. I ruined the life I built getting stoned. I still have cravings, but I use candy to stave them off. It's not easy, but it works. If she doesn't want to go to rehab—"

"She *is* going to rehab." His vision narrowed to that vial. How had he missed this? Silver did drugs? Okay, she said she'd quit. But she had the shit that had poisoned his daughter in her hand. And he had a feeling it had been on her this entire time while they were together. Every time she'd stuck a lollipop in her mouth, it was because she wanted to use.

What am I supposed to do with that? He took a big step back. "You need to go. I don't know what to do with what you've just told me." Restraining his urge to shout made his tone sound lifeless. "I could have lost her. I could lose you. I can't handle this right now."

"I'm not trying to upset you, Dean." She hid the vial in her purse. "I just wanted to let you know you didn't have to deal with this alone. Give me a call if you need anything. I'll swing by later."

"Please don't." Dean looked over as the nurse came out of his daughter's room. "I'll call you."

Silver's hands locked around her purse in a stranglehold. Her chin jutted up. "Okay. You know my number."

"Silver, don't be upset—this isn't coming out right. I—"

Inhaling through her nose, Silver shook her head and jabbed her thumb over her shoulder in the direction of Jami's room. "Don't worry about me. Worry about her. I was strong enough to get past this on my own, but I didn't have a choice. She's lucky to have you."

She slipped away and he cursed under his breath. She'd gone completely unreadable there, and he couldn't tell how much damage he'd done asking her to leave. Not that he could do anything about it. In any other situation, he'd go after her and make her talk to him, but he wouldn't leave Jami.

He covered his face with his hands and did his best to plaster a blank expression on his face before returning to his daughter's side. Where he belonged.

* * * *

Silver let out a blissful sigh as she sank into the bath and soaked all her senses in the rich cinnamon scent. Dean had bought the bath oil for her, told her to use it in a hot bath when she was stressed or . . . sore. Right now she was a little of both, but she wouldn't let it bring her down. Jami's doctor had assured her that Jami would be fine, though he couldn't tell her anything else. She was worried: she hated what the kid was going through—but Dean could take care of his daughter. Jami had gotten a bad scare. She might listen to him now.

And if not, well, she'd made the offer to talk to Jami, and hopefully Dean would consider it once he'd calmed down. It hurt that he hadn't wanted her around, but she got it. His baby was lying in a hospital bed and expecting him to be rational was pushing it.

What if he can't get over you being a cokehead? What if he wants nothing to do with you?

Dean wouldn't do that. He loved her.

You should have told him.

Maybe she should have—she sank deeper into the tub—but she hadn't. There was no use second guessing herself. She didn't use anymore. Rarely wanted to even, come to think of it. She'd stocked up on candy only once in the last couple of weeks. A new record. She used to do it daily.

The bathroom door creaked open and she turned her head, smiling as Landon stepped in. Dean must have called him to check on her.

See, he still cares.

But one look at Landon's face tightened her gut. He stared at her in the bath as though seeing something else, his face pale and tight. She sloshed out of the water and almost did a face-plant as she tried to get to him.

"Landon!" She yelped as her hip hit the sink. "Landon, look at me."

He blinked and yanked her into his arms. "Sorry. I just—"

"I know."

"Your door wasn't locked. I heard the water, and when I came in here I saw . . ." He shook his head hard and kissed her forehead. "Forget it. You're obviously fine and you're too strong to . . . to do anything stupid." He bent down and sniffed at her throat. "Mmm. You smell good."

"Do I?"

"Fuck, yeah." He crowded her back toward the bath and lifted her by the hips to set her bruised butt on the ledge. "Hold on tight. I don't want you to slip."

She winced at the throb of pain, clinging to the edge of the bath as he dropped to his knees and pulled her legs over his shoulders. His tongue speared her and she threw her head back. He gave her no time to prepare before licking and thrusting, but the oil slicking her body made it easy for him. Her body caught up quickly, and he moaned against her as he lapped up the spilling moisture.

"I could eat you all fucking night."

"Damn it, Landon, what about you?" She tried to close her legs, but in that position, didn't get far. "I won't let you get me off without taking anything yourself."

"You won't 'let' me?" His chuckle sent vibrations deep into her cunt as he nibbled lightly on her rapidly swelling clit. "I'd like to see you try to stop me."

He teased her mercilessly, using his teeth and his tongue, driving her up to the peak and easing her down before adding his fingers and tossing her over the edge. He picked her up just as her arms gave out, milking the last spasms from her with several shallow thrusts. She squirmed as he watched her face and curved his fingers inside her, his lips slanted in a wicked smile.

"You're not trying very hard. What happened to not letting me get you off?"

"You dick." She smacked his chest without thinking. "That wasn't fair."

His jaw ticked as he stood her up and turned her around. Her hands latched onto the tub as he gave her three solid slaps on the ass. Right over the ruler welts, waking each and every one like he'd lit a fuse of agony. She choked back a howl of pain as one last, stinging smack on fiery wet flesh bowed her spine.

"What did you call me?"

"Nothing!"

"Get in the bath." He released her after making sure she could stand on her own. "I've decided I'm ready to 'get off' now."

She scrambled into the bath, slowing as she slipped, and sat up to watch him strip. Her pussy throbbed, both from use and from need. His cock jutted out, dark at the tip as he rolled on a condom. He climbed into the bath and put his hand on her throat.

Her eyes widened. "Landon?"

"Dean says you like this, but he's been careful not to push you too far. You trust him." His fingers put more pressure on her windpipe, right under her chin. "Do you trust me?"

The humid air didn't fill her lungs properly, and wasting the bit she had on words didn't seem smart. So she simply nodded.

"Good girl." He knelt between her legs and guided his dick to her entrance. He slammed in and shook his head when she reached for him. "Fingers laced behind your neck. I'll move you. You will focus on what I give you. Air." He lifted her with one arm around her waist, sliding her up the end of the bath and following with short dips keeping him just barely inside. "Pain." His forearm crossed her abused butt, and he smiled when she hissed. "Pleasure."

He drove in so hard, the sensation echoed up her spine, and down again in a rush like water crashing from a broken dam. Each brutal slam sent her floating on the current, swaying, dipping under, her mind lost to the uncontrollable carnal flood. No holding back, she had nothing to hold on to.

Changing the angle of his thrusts, Landon watched her, his misty grey eyes filled with heat. Water sloshed on the floor as he hammered in and out, gritting through his teeth. "Don't come."

Don't . . . She scrambled inwardly away from the beckoning climax and clenched down to hold it at bay. His smile of approval almost did her in. She whimpered as his grip on her throat tightened a little more.

"I want this to last, Silver. I love being inside you." His jaw muscles tensed. "I don't know if it helps, but I'm holding back too. I would love to let go, but not . . . yet."

The room spun. Her lips moved. She needed to breathe. Maybe she should say her safeword—Only, Landon wasn't holding her throat hard enough to choke her. She gulped in as much hot air as she could and realized she'd stopped breathing, all on her own. *Stupid.*

"There we go." Landon moved her over him, his hips rising and falling as his breaths matched hers. His hand rested slack against her throat. "Another big one. One more. Good. Keep going, just like that as I increase the pressure."

Again the squeezing, but not so much that air couldn't pass.

"Perfect. Now comes the hard part." He leaned forward, buried to the hilt inside her, and covered her mouth with his. He kissed her dizzy, then pressed his forehead against hers, exhaling on her inhale. Again and again, until every part of her fell in sync with him, all the way down to the rhythm of her pulse, deep in her core.

Complete surrender and it was . . . amazing. In a daze she stared into his eyes and melted at what she saw there. He knew he had her completely in his power.

"Come with me, *mon coeur*." His pace quickened and the corded muscles running up the sides of his throat tensed. "Arg!"

A white haze wisped over her vision as she convulsed, clenching and unclenching around his cock, torn away by a tidal wave that crashed over and over, never releasing her from its violent pull. She screamed and slumped forward, twitching when his dick shifted inside her.

"Fuck, I hope you came," she whispered with her lips on his slippery, cinnamon-scented chest. She flicked out her tongue to taste him and giggled. "It doesn't taste as good as it smells."

"Mmm." He kissed the top of her head and hefted her up, turning so he could rest against the back of the tub with her in his lap. "Either that or the tip of my dick just exploded."

"I'm that good, am I?"

"If I say yes, will your ego get even bigger?"

She lifted her hand to smack him.

He grabbed it and groaned. "How about you not do that? I'm too worn out to spank you again."

She smirked and sat back on her heels. The pain in her ass spurred her on. "I should take advantage of you."

"You'll regret it tomorrow. I got a new cane."

Yikes. "Okay. I'll be good."

"Ha." His lips curled. "I doubt it."

She stuck out her tongue, but his eyes had drifted shut, so he didn't see it. So she relaxed with her head on her chest. Or tried to. He looked like he wanted to take a nap, but she was wide awake.

"Feel like watching a few more westerns?"

"*Now?*"

"Yes, now. Do you have something better to do?"

"Sleep." His arm plopped over her shoulder. "Be a good girl and shut up so I can, okay?"

Rolling her eyes, she pushed to her feet and stepped out of the bath. Then pulled the plug. "Listen, pal. First of all, you can't sleep in the bath. Second, I'm putting you telling me to shut up on my limit list. Got it?"

He arched a brow without opening his eyes. "Are you really? So is that just during scenes? Because, with how rude you're being, if we're still in a scene, I should . . ." He yawned. "Damn, my brain isn't working anymore. Between practice and those photo shoots . . . you have no idea the positions that woman put me in."

Red sparks flashed in her eyes. How had she forgotten Scarlet? "I'm going to kill that bitch! Did she touch you?"

"Do you honestly think I'd let her?" Landon's eyes were open now. "She came out from her session with Demyan wiping her mouth. I'm not into sloppy seconds, thanks."

"But you'll share me with Dean?"

He frowned at her and sat up. "That's not the same, and you know it. I'm sharing you with another man who loves you as much as I do."

Some people wouldn't see the difference, but those people didn't matter. Her sister was with three men, and no one would *dare* call her sloppy seconds. Besides, hearing Landon tell her, again, that he loved her . . . damn, it was impossible to feel worthless and disgusting.

"Okay, you're right, Sir." She grinned as she pulled out two towels, then wrapped one around herself. "I should give you more credit anyway. You managed to snag yourself a chick like me. What would you want with her?"

"Exactly." Landon slipped out of the tub and took the towel she handed him to dry his face. "Now—"

He cut himself off so abruptly, Silver froze. And bit her lip as he stared down at his naked cock with the ring of useless rubber around the base. *No. Oh God, no.*

"Silver." Landon rubbed his lips with his hand. "Tell me you're on birth control."

She didn't hesitate. "I'm on birth control."

The relief in his eyes wrung her stomach like an old rag in his big fists. Which made it impossible to elaborate. All she could do was fucking *pray* she didn't get caught telling a half-truth.

No way did I miss more than once or twice.

Chapter Thirty Four

Silver nibbled on a jujube petal and put away the little pack of pills. Her friends back in Hollywood wouldn't see this as a big deal. At least once a week she'd seen a couple doing damage control. Two now and two tomorrow. She took them back out and tapped the edge of the pack on her desk. Four pills and she'd have nothing to worry about.

She had *plenty* to spare.

Idiot.

Not that she'd never forgotten before, being drunk or stoned made it easy to forget, but she'd been with Asher and Cedric and the risk had been negligible. Except when she slept around. But she'd always used condoms. Never had a problem with them.

Well, there's a first time for everything. Just get it over with. Landon won't have to pay for your mistake.

"Silver?" Asher knocked on the door as he entered her office. His brow lifted as he caught her hiding her pills under some files. "You're taking them early today? You used to take them at nine o'clock every night."

"I'm not taking them early. Just checking . . ."

"Ah. Did that again, did you? Guess sticking to anal for a few weeks isn't an option?" Asher gave her his most superior look, which tempted her to bitch slap him with her shoe. And, naturally, he couldn't just drop it. "Any reason it's an issue this time?"

"Why the fuck would I tell you?"

"I'll take that as a yes?"

"Do you want this job or not?" She crossed her arms over her breasts when he nodded and tried to turn on the charm, not giving him a second to sweet-talk her before continuing. "Sit down and shut up then while I make one thing perfectly clear." He sat in the chair in front of her desk, and his briefcase hit the floor with a dull *thud*. "I *know* you, Asher. I understand how you operate, and I didn't care when you were handling jobs for my 'friends' out in Hollywood, but things are going to be different here. You try to use anything you have on me, or learn about me, to get more money or anything else, and we're going to have a serious problem."

Tiny lines showed on Asher's smooth cheeks as he gave her an amused half-smile. "Are you going to sic your boyfriends on me?"

Head tilted to one side, Silver tapped her chin and smiled back at him. "You think I need them to hurt you? If we start sharing, some uncomfortable truths might come out about me, but the things *you* don't want anyone to know could get you killed."

Asher paled slightly, but his expression didn't change. He actually laughed. "You'd do it too, wouldn't you? I forgot what a coldhearted bitch you could be."

"Very bad idea if you want to work for me."

"I'll keep that in mind."

"Good." She put her hands on the desk and grinned. "So, you write up the contract? I'd like you to get to work on a few things right away, if you're not too busy."

He scowled. "You know I'm not busy. I let Cedric take the rest of my cases and cleared my schedule. Just like you asked."

"I hope you remembered to include in the contract that you work for me. Not the team."

"I did, but I don't get why—"

"You don't have to. Now hand it over. I'd like to read over the fine print before we go any further." She bit back a smirk as Asher dug into his briefcase, grumbling under his breath. "You didn't *seriously* think I'd just sign it, did you?"

"I figured you might be a bit distracted . . ." He shook his head and laughed again. "Then again, considering you got spanked after signing something without reading it, I should have guessed you'd be more careful."

"You taught me not to trust anyone too quickly, Asher. One of the few things I can actually thank you for."

He dropped his gaze to the papers he set before her and sighed. "So you don't trust anyone?"

"Not until they've earned it."

"And your men?"

My men. Just thinking about them gave her the silly warm fuzzies. She took the contract and shrugged because she didn't want to share too much with Asher. But she had to say one thing. "They've earned it."

It took about an hour to go over all the details of the contract, and to Asher's credit, he hadn't tried to slip in anything over the top. His retainer was higher than they'd agreed on, but he was worth it. She signed and handed him his copy.

Asher looked a little surprised but didn't comment. He sat back and folded his ankle over his knee. "So, where do I start, boss?"

She patted a stack of files on the corner of her desk. "I'd like you to look over the proposal for the renovations. They have to be in today." She pulled out a set of keys from her top drawer and tossed them to him. "Enjoy your new office. You're going to be spending a lot of time in there."

"Gee. Thanks." He stood and stuffed the keys in his pocket before grabbing the folders. "Anything else?"

Her lips slanted. "I'll let you know."

The door to her office opened just as he approached it. Asher made a strangled sound and tripped backward as Dean strode in and reached for him.

Dean let out a feral sound. "You son of a bitch. You've got some nerve—"

"Dean!" For some odd reason, she wanted to giggle as Asher scampered across the office to put her desk between him and Dean. She cut in front of Dean before he could follow. "I just had the carpets cleaned. Don't kill him in here, please."

The solid chest under her hand rose and fell with Dean's measured breaths. "What is he doing here? He almost got you killed!"

Asher sidestepped behind her. "I almost did what? What are you talking about?"

"Ford Kingsley threatened her! After you sent her to him! Getting her shot once wasn't enough?"

"That was an accident. I wasn't expecting—"

"I don't want to hear it." Dean's lip curled away from his teeth. "Get your pathetic ass out of here before I pitch you out that fucking window."

"Dean." Silver hooked her finger to his collar and tugged.

395

"Look. At. Me. Asher isn't responsible for what happened with Ford. He couldn't have known—"

"Bullshit. He's fucking dirty enough to have figured out who you were dealing with. I don't want him anywhere near you." Dean cupped her cheek and bent down to kiss her. "Maybe I didn't act like it yesterday, but I care about you. If you're still . . . if that shit is still a problem, I'll help you however I can."

"It's not." She wanted to ask him about Jami but not in front of Asher. So she focused on what they both already knew. "I told you; I've been clean for nine months."

"But you keep that vial in your purse . . ." He sighed and shook his head. "I need you to know I believe you. You're not doing that shit anymore, and I'm damn proud of you for quitting on your own. It's just a bad idea for you to have that crap on you. I understand why you do, but—"

"Her little vial?" Asher laughed. "So she finally told you about that?"

Dean dropped a fisted hand to his side. "You can leave now."

"Actually, I can't. My new boss gave me tons of work." Asher sidled around the desk. "I wouldn't worry too much about her 'stash' though. It's not coke."

Silver spun around and she and Dean spoke as one. "What?"

"I tossed it about a month after you quit. Just in case. Replaced it with icing sugar." Asher shrugged as he inched closer to the door. "You fucked up your life when you were on that shit. Hell, I'm no fucking saint. You were my meal ticket, but I also considered you a friend. I knew you wouldn't tell me if you slipped up, so I made damn sure I'd find out if you did."

"You didn't trust me."

"*You* hadn't earned it." Asher glanced at the door. "I'm gonna head to my office now, if that's okay?"

"Go ahead." Silver stared after him as he hustled out. *Damn. Just . . . damn.* All this time, that was all she'd wanted from him. To know he cared. And maybe he hadn't in any romantic sense, but he'd still looked out for her in his own way. She bit the tip of her tongue and peered up at Dean. "So . . . are we good?"

Dean inhaled and nodded slowly. "I don't like that you've got him working for you."

"I know."

"But, so long as you don't let him get you involved in anything dangerous, I'll accept it." He groaned and dropped a hard kiss on her lips. "I'm sorry about yesterday. I was . . . cruel."

"No, you weren't. You were a father, scared for his little girl."

"And you were trying to help."

"I made things worse."

"No, actually, you didn't." He drew her toward her desk and sat her on the edge. "I hope you don't mind, but I discussed what you went through with Jami. Not that I know much—it didn't seem to matter though. I think it made her feel better that I still loved you, even though you've made some mistakes. She agreed to go to rehab . . . there's a place in Halifax, close to my mother. She said she wants to stay with her grandmother for a bit and get away from the people she was hanging out with here. I offered to take some time off, to help her through this . . ." He closed his eyes. "She said that would make things worse. Knowing she was taking me away from my job, from you . . . we argued about it for awhile, until she broke down and made me promise not to let her ruin my life like she'd ruined hers."

Silver stroked his darkly scruffed jaw. "She hasn't ruined her life though. She's young. She'll get past this."

His lips hardened and he shrugged. "Yes, but she insisted that she could only do that if I let her go. By herself."

"She won't be by herself. She'll be with your mother."

Dean laughed. "That's the only reason I agreed. She knows my mother is stricter than I ever was. I'll have to tell you about her one day, but for now, let's just say she handled two 'husbands,' their three wives, and ten kids. Without any drama. I didn't have a traditional upbringing, but all my brothers and sisters turned into good, strong people. Because of her."

"Ten kids?" She had to stop herself from putting her hand over her stomach. *It's been a day. Seriously, don't get all panicky.* But the words escaped her before she could stop them. "Damn. I can't even picture myself dealing with one."

His brow furrowed. "Do you want kids?"

"Maybe." She moved away from him and went back to her chair. "When I'm not so busy."

"We'll talk again in ten years then." He moved closer when she shuffled through the papers on her desk. "Hey, is everything all right? Or am I just keeping you from your work?"

"You're not mad at me anymore?"

"I never was."

"All right, then everything is perfect." She patted her cluttered desk. "But yeah, you're very distracting. I've got half a mind to throw all this stuff on the floor and—"

"Bad girl." He chuckled and leaned over to kiss her forehead. "I have a few things to deal with before the Cobras go back on the road. I wish we could have gotten more home games. Are you going to be okay with Landon being gone so much?"

"I'm going to have to be." And maybe it was for the best. By the time he got back for his first home game, she'd know for sure if . . .

Just take the fucking pills!

But she couldn't. Some part of her had already decided to let the cards fall where they were meant to. And hopefully Landon wouldn't hate her for it. Not that she'd blame him if he did.

"Something's bothering you."

Her head shot up. Dean was way too attentive. What if he figured it out?

He's not a damn mind reader. Relax!

She smiled and ducked her head. "Not really. You guys have just been spoiling me. I don't know *what* I'm going to do if I go more than a day without a sore butt."

"I won't be far, Silver." He gave her a heavy lidded grin. "If you want, we can call Landon every night so I can dole out punishments on his behalf."

"Umm, how about no freakin' way?"

"We'll see." He straightened and tugged on his belt. "Okay, if I don't leave now, we will be using this desk and my rules won't count for anything. Spend the night at my place?"

"Gladly. Mine needs help."

"Maybe this weekend." Dean loosened his tie and took a big step back. "Just promise me one thing before I go."

She cocked her head and waited.

"Promise you'll come to me when you need me. Don't ever be afraid that I'll judge you. I wasn't yesterday; I just—"

"Let's forget yesterday." She looked into his eyes and saw that he sensed something. She *would* have to tell him. But not yet. "But I promise."

After he left, she did her best to get into her work. But she couldn't focus. Something was off. Dean read her well, but she had a feeling he wasn't just guessing.

Her heart lodged in her throat when she reached for a file and realized her pills were still there, half hidden, but not enough for anyone to wonder what they were. Dean knew she'd missed at least a day.

He hadn't guessed anything. He knew.

Chapter Thirty Five

D ean checked the roast in the oven and smiled as Silver came up behind him to whisper in his ear. "Give me something to do. I can't deal with Becky anymore."

Three weeks without Landon, and he knew Silver wanted him all to herself. And she would've had him, if his flight hadn't been delayed. Silver had actually gotten on her knees and begged him to come with her to Landon's newly restored apartment. Not that he hadn't planned to come anyway, even if he had to invite himself. Losing his best goalie and the woman he loved to a kitchen fire was *not* an option. It had been awkward, explaining his presence— Landon's subtlety left much to be desired, and Dean didn't know what to do with the cold looks from his father, but after hours on the plane, the very idea of a good meal seemed to compose the man. He'd come into the kitchen once to thank Dean for not letting his son and the "pampered chick" he'd gotten involved with poison his family.

Flattering. Really. The man wasn't much older than he was. It was hard not to lash out when he criticized Silver. But his mother had always told him extended family was something you dealt with when you chose this kind of lifestyle. She had dealt with too many "in-laws" to count. If all he had to deal with was Delgado, Oriana, and Landon's brood . . .

He smiled at Silver and pointed to the lettuce on the counter. "Chop that up and toss everything in the small bowls into the salad. If you cut yourself because you get distracted, I'll use the cane on you tonight. Deal?"

Her lips twisted. "Are you a sadist?"

"No. But if you wanted one, you should have been nicer to Callahan."

"Yeah. Fuck you."

"That's one, Silver. I'm not Landon. We don't have 'off time.'"

"You're such a dick. Really? Are we sticking with office hours?" She pouted and moved away to chop the lettuce. "No time out?"

"No. And that's two."

"Why not skip straight to five so I can have some fun?" She attacked the lettuce with the knife as though it needed to be murdered before consumption. "If you wanted me to be scared of the cane, you shouldn't have spent the last two weeks showing me how much I can enjoy it."

The sound that left him was something between a laugh and a growl. "Keep it up and I'll let Landon cane you."

"You never hand punishments to Landon." She crunched on a piece of lettuce. "But I suppose the appropriate response is 'Oh, please, Master, don't!'"

"Ten. With the tawse." That got her attention. And wiped the smile from her face. "Are you done yet?"

Lips pursed, she studied his face and shook her head. "You're joking, aren't you?"

"What makes you think that?"

"You didn't use the 'Me Dom, you Jane' voice.'" She yelped and jumped out of reach when he took a swipe at her butt with a wooden spoon. "I'm going to see if anyone wants some pickles."

"Pickles?" He looked her over. No, it was too soon for cravings.

She gave him a curious glance before taking a tray out of the fridge. "Yes. Pickles. With little onions and cheese. Appetizers, caveman."

"Silver." He let his tone drop to the one she took very seriously. "I'm done counting. I expect you to do so for the rest of the night. I enjoy spending time with you, and joking with you, but I won't tolerate insults, even in fun. That is how you play with Landon. Not with me."

Muttering, her expression a little sulky, she carried the tray to the door, "Yes, Sir."

Shaking his head, he went to finish making the salad. Sometimes he wondered if he should just let her take her little verbal jabs, but he didn't like the idea of a relationship where they were continuously cursing at each other and calling each other names. It wasn't as if she wasn't capable of speaking to him with the same amount of respect he gave her.

Actually, he couldn't remember the last time she'd gotten

mouthy with him. Before Landon went on the road trip, perhaps. It was entirely possible that she was acting out because she was nervous.

Dean put on some vegetables to steam and went to slice some bread for the table. He heard laughter from the dining room and set down the knife. Standing in the doorway, he watched Landon's family, enjoying their comfortable interactions, wondering, briefly, where Silver had disappeared to.

Adam Bower, Landon's father, raised his beer to his lips and grinned at his daughter. "Relax, Becky. Casey can't hear, she's teaching Silver all about *The Little Mermaid*. We're all adults." He turned to his son. "I ever tell you about the couple fooling around in the woods, Landon?"

"Dad!" Becky let out a huff and looked to her mother. "Can't you stop him? I hate it when he tells dirty jokes at the table!"

"Becky, you know very well I can't stop him once he gets going. And besides, I don't want to." Erin Bower patted her daughter's hand. "It never bothered you until you got married. You're divorced now, and we do not have to deal with that stuck up bastard anymore. Let your father have some fun."

"Can't we discuss something normal? Like politics?" Becky glanced over at Dean and turned red. "The weather?"

"We can always discuss your interview with Scott Demyan." Dean moved into the room to take a seat beside Landon. "I never did get any details. I hope he was . . . cooperative?"

The red spread from Becky's cheeks right up to her hairline and down her throat. "He was fine. So you were saying, Dad—about the couple—"

"Scott Demyan is a *fine* looking man." Erin sighed dreamily, no hint on her face that she was concerned of her husband's reaction. "I would hope that his reputation is exaggerated if you're interested in him, though."

"I'm *not*." Rebecca glared at her brother when he laughed, and out of the corner of his eye, saw her kick Landon under the table. "We came to meet your new woman. Shouldn't she be in here with the grown-ups?"

"Tell me you weren't grateful that she took Casey out of your hair for a bit. You were doing the zombie-mom thing." Landon smirked at his sister, cutting her off before she could protest. "But I *really* don't want to talk about Demyan. He comes near you, I'll kill him. Point final. I'm curious about the joke, Dad."

"That bad, eh?" Adam frowned over his beer bottle at his daughter and nodded. Then a broad grin broke over his face. "All right, so the couple are getting it on in the woods. After about fifteen minutes, the man curses and says 'I wish I had a flashlight.' The woman pulls away and says, 'Me too! You've been eating grass for ten minutes!'"

Landon snorted. Rebecca groaned.

Dean chuckled. "All right, supper is almost ready."

"You did all the cooking, let me serve." Rebecca bounded from the table before he could reply and called back. "Get Silver and Casey!"

Exchanging a look with Landon, Dean headed to the living room. Landon followed him and they both stood just in the entrance, grinning like fools as they watched her applying bright red lipstick to the little girl's lips.

She held up a compact mirror for Casey to take a look. "You like?"

"Perfect!" The child pursed her lips, then giggled. "Do you think the hockey guys will think I'm pretty?"

"For sure! But don't worry about impressing them, they'll all be old men by the time you're old enough to date." Silver leaned close and spoke in a stage whisper. "If I were you, I'd hold out for their sons."

Casey nodded, her face suddenly serious. "Gotcha."

"Silver, how about you come eat before you corrupt my niece." Landon stepped forward and held out his hand. "We've got about an hour before I have to hit the ice for warm up."

"Okay." Silver latched onto his hand and hopped to her feet, pulling Casey along with her. "You know, I was a little nervous about tonight, but your family is awesome. I'm glad I came."

I'm glad you met his before mine. Dean followed the trio back to the dining room, his lips twitching up as they let Casey take a seat between them. Landon served Casey's plate while Silver spread a napkin over the little girl's lap. For a moment he wondered at his lack of resentment. If his suspicions were correct, how much of this aspect of their lives could he really share with them? Would he always be on the outside, looking in?

Maybe, but he wanted Silver happy. And he would find his place with them.

He pulled out the chair at Silver's other side, sat, then covered her hand with his under the table. She gave him a hesitant smile.

"Guess what, Mommy!" Casey stuffed a big piece of roast in her mouth and spoke around it. "Remember the mean girl in day care?"

Rebecca circled the table, laying out the salad and bread basket. "We don't speak with our mouth full, Casey."

"Sorry, Mommy." Casey quickly swallowed and continued, obviously excited. "Silver told me how to deal with her!"

"Oh?" Rebecca paused at her daughter's side. "How?"

"Put gum in her hair!"

Adam barked out a laugh and his wife used her napkin to smother her own. Landon coughed.

Dean watched Silver's face. And smiled at the calm look she gave Rebecca.

"It worked for me."

"Casey, Silver was joking." Rebecca frowned at Silver. "*Weren't* you?"

Silver's brow furrowed. "No. Why should she have to put up with the nasty brat?"

Rebecca sputtered.

"Casey, honey." Erin composed herself and smiled at her granddaughter. "What do you think your teacher would do if you put gum in someone's hair?"

Casey pouted and scooted closer to Silver. "She'd put me in the naughty corner."

"You don't want that, do you?"

"No."

"Well, then, maybe you can just speak to your teacher." Erin sat back and arched a brow at Rebecca. "And if Mommy doesn't have time to go with you, I will."

"Thank you, Mother." Rebecca shuffled to the other end of the table and picked up the bottle of wine she'd opened earlier to let breathe. "I can handle it."

Dean thanked Rebecca after she filled his glass, then watched with interest as she moved to fill Silver's.

Silver put her hand over her glass and shook her head. "No, thank you. I'm fine with water."

Landon choked. His fork hit his plate.

That answers that. Dean eyed Landon as his father thumped his back hard. *Congratulations, buddy.*

Chapter Thirty Six

Titanium cage bars disappeared from Landon's vision as the puck dropped. Warm-up scarred ice spread out before him, and his mind locked on the play as Callahan swept the puck toward Mason. The puck thumped into Mason's dropped glove.

Fuck yeah. Landon pushed his mask up and grinned at Ramos, who'd circled back to guard his left flank. "That didn't take long."

"Yeah, the fucker." Ramos jerked his chin toward Mason as he rounded the Sabres' captain, Nelson, his bared teeth flashing white as the snow on the ice in his dark face. "We flipped for it. I get the next one."

Considering the way the last game had ended against the Sabres, Landon had no doubt there would be a few fights. The first one would dictate the tone for the rest of the night.

"He's a clean fighter." Ramos remarked as Mason tossed his helmet. "This is good."

"Not sure about that." Landon sprayed some water into his mouth and scowled as Nelson spun out of reach, his own helmet still secured on his head. "Not against that dirty asshole."

Then again, Landon hadn't seen Mason fight. And a lot of people would say his taking off his helmet was cocky and stupid. But Mason was a big guy. Maybe he was just evening things out.

Not that Nelson stands a chance of beating Mason. Landon smirked as Nelson took a wide swing, then danced out of reach. The man would be lucky to get in a single punch.

The refs inched closer, speaking to the men, obviously ready to end the "fight" since nothing had happened. Before Nelson could evade him again, Mason lurched forward and snatched a handful of his jersey. His fist clipped Nelson's jaw. Nelson bowed his head and drove into Mason's chest, taking away Mason's advantage of a wide swing. Mason's feral smile practically invited the swift uppercut from Nelson. A fucking gift.

Mason ended the fight with two quick jabs and pulled Nelson's jersey over his head. The refs wrenched them apart and directed them both to the penalty boxes.

Back to center ice. The players took their positions and Landon slapped his helmet into place. He skidded from side to side, then bent his knees and centered himself. *Here we go. Now it starts for real.*

Unfortunately, Ramos proved to be a goddamn wall and didn't let the opposition get anywhere near the net. Landon kept himself sharp for the first five minutes, reading the plays, calling out warnings when his teammates left themselves vulnerable for nasty hits, but hell, the net could have been empty and it wouldn't have made a difference.

He moved just to keep his blood pumping. But his mind wandered.

Water. Did you seriously freak because she asked for water?

This was the girl he'd caught having rum for breakfast.

Doesn't mean anything.

Like hell it didn't. He and Silver needed to have a little chat.

A full line change. Landon hardly noticed.

You've been gone for weeks. She didn't say anything when you called. She would have if . . .

The rookie defenseman, Owen Stills, missed a pass. The Sabres attacked, smoothly snapping the puck back and forth. The Cobras scrambled to recover.

Shot. Rebound. Landon dived to cover the puck and it slipped out from under his pad.

And was tucked into the net behind him.

Face-off. As soon as the puck hit the ice, the Sabres forward skipped it to his defense. Stills managed to intercept a pass, but then he iced the puck, trapping his line on the ice.

Maybe she's trying to clean up. She did tell you about the coke. Dean's reaction was enough to set her straight.

Landon hunched down and clenched his jaw.

Get your head in the fucking game, Bower!

The Cobras won the face-off. Too cleanly. Landon cracked his stick into the pipes when he found the puck behind him, gliding over the goal line.

"Shit, sorry about that." Another rookie, Swedish center Erik Hjalmar, skated over to pat Landon's pads with his stick. "Was trying to get it to Stills."

"Not your fault, man." Landon forced a smile. "I'm good. But you guys must be tired. Switch it up, eh?"

"Penalty's almost done."

Like I'm going to admit I need Mason out here. Still, he sighed with relief when the newbie line got traded for a fresh, more experienced one. With Ramos in front of him, he had time to catch his breath. Once Mason came out of the box, the puck spent a bit more time at the other end. Demyan skirted around the Sabres' defense and easily slid a pass to Carter who was practically sitting in the lap of the Sabres' goalie. A backhand shot made the sirens wail.

2-1. How about you do your job and give your team a chance to pull ahead?

Right. He cleaned the snow from the blue ice with his stick blade and his chin jutted up. The press box drew his attention. He couldn't see Silver, but he knew she was up there. Probably wondering what the hell was wrong with him.

She's fine. Dean's with her.

The next play happened so fast, he didn't have a chance to react.

3-1.

"Hey, Bower." Callahan slid up to his side as the game stopped for a commercial break. "We're not playing fucking dodgeball. Got it?"

I got it. Landon nodded and cleaned the ice again with his stick. "I'm good."

"I hope so." Callahan's eyes narrowed. "One more and you'll be pulled. Which might be good, since apparently there's something on your mind more important than the game."

"I said I'm good."

"We'll see."

"Hey, Captain!" Carter slowly back skated to Landon's side. "Since we've got a sec to chat, I was wondering if you could show me how to tie up a woman with tits as big as Oriana's next time we go to the club. Is it possible?"

"Carter, seriously . . ." Callahan shook his head. "Fuck off."

"I'm *being* serious!"

"After your stint with Silver? Kid, you're not touching my woman." Callahan slid backward, his hand wrapped around his stick in a choke hold. "Chicklet will teach you what you need to know."

"Your woman, but . . ." Carter cocked his head as though confused. "You know what, never mind. I'll ask Perron. I'm sure he'll get off watching her play with someone new."

"I'll do what?" Perron moved from the bench and stretched his legs. "You being a pain again, Carter?"

"Who me?" Carter shook his head. "Fuck, no. We're a team. I respect you guys."

"You have a strange way of showing it." Callahan grumbled.

Carter nodded. "So do you."

Shit. Landon sighed and grabbed Carter before he could skate away. Out of hearing, he spoke low. "I get what you're trying to do, and I appreciate it. But fuck, man, I'm not all here. Callahan's right to tell me off. You guys need me on my game."

"Yeah, we do." Carter frowned in the shadows of his own cage. "What's up with you?"

"I may have made the Delgado family . . . a bit bigger."

"May have?"

"Yeah."

"Cool. How about we sit down for beers and cigars when you know for sure?" Carter punched his shoulder. "Until then, give the woman something to cheer for, okay? The stress of watching you play like shit can't be good for her."

"Damn it." Landon laughed and punched Carter back. "You're right, you little fuck. I'm on this."

"Good. I'll go tie things up. You just do your thing."

"We're behind by two."

"I kinda noticed, buddy. Like I said, I'm gonna tie things up. Then I might let someone else get one in." Carter took Landon's water bottle and sent a spray into his open mouth. "We'll see."

Landon shook his head. "Generous of you."

"Hey." Carter winked. "We're all team players."

"Callahan was right. Fuck off."

Carter saluted. "Be glad to fuck on. Just say the word."

"Sure. You top her, and she says yes . . ."

"Really?"

"No. And even if I was okay with it, you'd have to go through

Richter."

"Ha! No thanks, pal." Carter took a few strides toward center ice, then glided back. "I bet you anything Callahan will be thrown out of the face-off. I'll take over and snap the puck to the defense. Probably Mason. He's solid, but you good if he misses?"

"I already told you. I'm good." Landon tightened his grip on his stick. "Get out there."

"Sure. Just one thing." Carter tapped his gloved hand on his chin. "Luke Bower has a ring to it, don't you think?"

"Carter."

"Yeah?"

"You score now and I'll make you my next kid's goddaddy. Make it reel-worthy."

"Reel-worthy?" Carter said with a chuckle. "Don't make it hard or anything."

Seconds later, Carter scored a pretty, twisting, snap shot. He threw his hands up, urging the crowd to keep cheering. Then he held up one finger. Not the middle one.

Perron cupped a smooth pass, feinted toward Callahan, then sent a bullet of a pass to Carter. Carter caught his own rebound and redirected the puck into the open net.

Tied. And that is how it's done. Landon's blood sizzled in his veins. If the kid could put them back into the game that easy, Landon would damn well keep them there.

This is for you, Silver. Nothing else gets past me.

The third line gave him a chance to prove it. Tired from a long shift, they fumbled and dragged their skates as though slogging through sludge. Big bodies crashed the net. Landon slapped a snap shot away from the top corner of the net. Cleared his crease with a few shoves and threw himself over the goal line as his own defense kicked the puck in the wrong direction. He couldn't trap it. It skidded right onto Nelson's stick.

Springing up, Landon put his head in the path of the bullet fast shot. A *clunk!* on his helmet.

He gloved the puck as it fell.

Ears ringing with the cheers from the crowd, Landon grinned at his teammates as they surrounded him, thumping his helmet and smacking his pads with their sticks.

"Now *that* was reel-worthy!" Carter gave him a one arm hug, then whooped loud enough to get the crowd going again.

That was what he was capable of. What the team deserved from him. His goddamned best. Whatever was thrown at him, whether it be the puck or something far more important, he could handle it. Now he just had to make Silver believe it.

* * * *

The phone was on silent, but Silver felt it buzzing in her purse. No way would she take her eyes off the game long enough to answer—now that she'd stopped covering them every time the puck came anywhere near Landon—but as soon as thing were tied up and he looked a little more solid, she touched Dean's arm and told him she needed to . . . go.

He gave her a knowing smile before turning back to watch the fight. Sebastian and Dominik both going at it now with the Sabres' tough guys.

"This rivalry is going to be great for ratings," Dean said to Mr. Bolleau just as she walked out.

Damn, why didn't I think of that? She rolled her eyes as she made her way down the hall, pulling out her phone. *All this work on promoting the team, and I just had to tell them to turn the rink into the UFC!*

Her urge to laugh dropped dead in her gut as she checked her missed calls. All but one from her father. The last from Anne.

She played Anne's message. "Silver, your father needs to see you. *Please.* He's not doing well. The doctors are saying . . . " Anne's words cut off with a sob. "I know you hate me, but I hope you'll come anyway. You know I wouldn't call if it wasn't important. He had a visitor and—you know he isn't supposed to have any stress! Maybe he'll feel better, seeing you. For once in your life, don't be selfish, he—"

Silver deleted the message and slammed her phone into her purse. Who the hell did that woman think she was? As if saying her father needed her wouldn't be enough? Just the numerous calls, after a week without any, would have gotten her to at least call back to see what was going on.

Screw her. Who cares what she thinks? She hit the button to the elevator with the side of her fist and leaned against the wall beside it. Her father had to be okay. If he wasn't—damn it, she'd hung up on him! And she hadn't called or seen him since. The updates she'd gotten from his doctor told her he was doing well, but rather fragile. Apparently the doctor fully supported Anne's decision to keep *everyone* away from him.

Except Anne of course.

Her palm itched with the need to grab a lollipop or—she breathed out a laugh—her vial of icing sugar? She delved back into her purse as the elevator doors opened, took out the candy and the vial, and tossed it all into the nearby trash, then ducked into the elevator just in time. Her purse seemed crazy light, but that was okay. Peering inside, she bit back a smile when she realized she'd accidentally tossed her two favorite shades of lipstick out with the candy.

"So, no more drugs or candy. No more alcohol." She ran her tongue over her teeth and cocked her head, looking at her reflection in the gold wall. "Guess I'll just have to shop to relieve stress. I'm going to need a few things."

Yeah, try to fit in a size two in another month.

Wrinkling her nose, she smoothed her hands over her flat stomach. Just over the last week, eating three meals a day—*because of Dean*—had gained her a pound or two. But she couldn't find it in her to care. Her body didn't belong to the spotlight anymore. And for some reason, that made her feel damn good.

Everything else though—well, that scared her to death. She had to talk to Landon.

Right after I talk to Daddy. She stepped off the elevator and into the parking garage. Her heels scraped concrete all the way to her car. *Uck, or, better idea, I could go home and crawl into bed. Hide under the covers for the next year. Sounds like a lot more fun to me.*

Only, hiding wasn't an option. She'd put off dealing with her father, and speaking to Landon, long enough.

Welcome to adulthood, Silver.

No sending her regrets for the RSVP on that one.

For the first half of the drive, a weight seemed to have wrapped around her chest, like a big heavy chain with the ends dangling over her limbs. She flicked on the radio and quietly hummed along to a familiar dance tune. Another had her singing along. "Domino," by Jessie J, came on. She turned it all the way up and sang at the top of her lungs.

Things weren't all bad. She was in love with two men who loved her back. Whatever happened, that wouldn't change. She had to believe that.

She *did* believe that.

Anne met Silver at Daddy's front door and clasped her hands, staring at her with bloodshot eyes as she drew her inside. "I'm so glad you came. He keeps asking for you and . . ."

Please say Oriana. Silver sighed when Anne didn't say anything. "*And?*"

"And your mother."

Fuck. "How bad is he, Anne? Honestly?"

"You would know if you'd visited." Anne blinked fast and her hands fluttered up to her throat. "Some days, he's himself. The same strong man he's always been. Other days . . . he rambles about the past. As though he's still there."

Nodding, Silver strode past Anne and up the stairs. She didn't stop until she reached the foot of Daddy's bed. And once there, couldn't take another step.

Her jaw locked. Her eyes stung. Pain welled in her throat and she had to look away.

This man couldn't be her father.

Dry, yellowed flesh covered the sharp bones of his face and sunk into hollow cheeks. His eyes were wet with tears, and drool slicked the edges of the mask covering his mouth. His hands shook as he lifted them to remove the mask.

"My little doll." He gasped as though every word took more oxygen than he could spare. "You came."

"I'm here, Daddy." She stumbled forward, hitting her knees on the floor by his side as she took his hand. She choked on a sob and pressed her lips to his cold fingers. "I'm sorry. I should have come sooner. I didn't know."

"It doesn't matter. You're here now." His lips twisted into a painful looking smile. "So beautiful. So like your mother. I had to see you—had to find a way to remember her face. You are the only thing we had together that was worth anything."

"But Oriana—"

"Isn't mine. I hoped I wouldn't have to tell you, but she wants the team. She wants what should have been Antoine's." His eyes narrowed and the tears fell. "It should have been her, you know that? She should have gotten in the car with your mother. Then we would still have him."

Her stomach turned. She shook her head. "You don't know what you're saying—"

"Yes, I do!" He rasped in a breath. "I do. She tried to replace him, but she was nothing to me! It took me a while to see it. To see her for who she is. She's another man's daughter. A man who always wanted what I had. We were friends once and we . . . we did things, shared things. I let him use your mother. I used his wife. And it destroyed both our marriages."

"Oriana looks just like Antoine. Like you." Rubbing her free hand over her face, she leaned closer and spoke fast. "Whatever you and Mom did, it doesn't change the fact that she's your daughter."

"She's not." His face reddened and he yanked his hand away. "Swear to me you won't let her take what's ours!" His chest collapsed and his eyes widened. "Swear it!"

"Daddy, let me get your nurse." She wanted to cover her ears as the machines attached to him started screaming. "She can—"

"Silver, Silver, you're all I have." He wheezed and reached around blindly. "Unless . . ."

"Unless?"

"He claims to be my son. I don't believe it, but if he is—"

He? "Who, Daddy?"

The door opened and the nurse rushed in.

Daddy held up his hand. "If he is—"

"You have to go." The nurse waved Silver away from the bed. "Don't worry, this has happened before. The doctor will be here shortly."

"Let me finish!" Daddy fell back and gagged. His body

convulsed.

The nurse injected something in his IV. She checked her father's pulse.

Silver covered her mouth with her hand.

"Hey." The nurse came to her and put her hand on Silver's shoulder. "It's not as bad as it looks. He gets like this when he's overexcited. It's not pretty, but he's not going anywhere. I'm sorry you had to see him like this."

"So he's not . . ." Silver hugged herself and stared at her father. He looked dead. But the heart monitor showed his pulse, a steady rhythm, never slowing though it had sped up for a bit. "The doctor hasn't said how much time he has?"

"No. But the heart attacks seemed to have affected his mind. He has episodes, but his body is strong, considering. You could come back tomorrow and he'll look much better."

"He's lost so much weight!"

"Well . . ." The nurse winced. "That's because he refused to eat until your mother came to see him. I put in an IV, but it's hardly enough to keep a man of his size in top shape."

"Maybe I should stay." She didn't want to. Not if she had to hear him talking about Oriana like that. But she would if it would help. "Maybe, if he sees me when he wakes up, he'll eat."

"I would agree, but he curses you out about as often as he asks for you." The nurse's look was apologetic. "The only person that keeps him calm is Anne. I think the only reason she called you is because his last visitor upset him."

"Who was his last visitor?"

"A young man. He's still downstairs if you'd like to speak to him." The nurse patted her shoulder. "After that, I think you should go home. There's nothing else you can do for your father tonight."

Silver nodded and stood. She backed out of the room, a photo of her parents catching her eye somehow just the thing she needed to take that last step. They looked happy. She knew it was fake, she was old enough to see their marriage for what it had been, a man who wanted to own a beautiful woman and a woman who wanted a man who could give her an easy life. But there must have been a time where they'd had more. Where they'd had something real.

At least, she hoped so. Her father must have loved her mother in some way if he still asked for her.

The house seemed bigger than she remembered as she walked down the long staircase. So empty. She tried to recall laughter and joy within these walls, but the closest she came was when it was just her and Oriana, playing when their father wasn't around. When he was home, they'd had to be quiet. She couldn't remember much from back when Antoine was alive. Maybe a couple of times before he headed out with his sports bag, when she ran to the door to wish him luck and he'd ruffled her hair.

He'd called her a little doll too.

Movement to her side brought her back to the present and she stopped on the bottom step. For a split second, she saw Antoine and her blood ran cold.

Ford smirked. "You look like you've seen a ghost."

Shitshitshit. She shook her head and grabbed the railing. "No fucking way. No. You fucking fraud! Get the fuck out of my father's house! Get out!"

"*Our* father's house, sis." He lifted his tumbler of what looked like brandy in mock cheers. "And soon to be mine. I *am* the boy after all, and he's got some old fashioned ideas. Soon as the DNA tests come in, I get everything. The house. The money." He took a gulp of liquor and laughed. "And the team."

"Like hell you will." She trembled as she strode toward him and slapped the glass out of his hand. It exploded against the floor. "That's why he's so messed up. You came here and made your bullshit claim and—"

"It's not bullshit. My dad finally told me everything. Why do you think I gave up on Jami? I didn't need her."

"You pathetic piece of shit. Do you seriously think you can con your way into my family?"

"I don't need to. And you know it, don't you?" He shook his head. "You saw it when you came down here. Face it, Silver. You're going to have to share."

"With my sister."

"Anthony says she isn't his. He doesn't have to give her fuck all."

"She looks just as much like our brother as you do." *I did not just say that.* She pressed her eyes shut. Trying to erase the image. Trying to deny what she'd seen. But she couldn't. "None of this matters. Daddy gave the team to me."

"And now he's giving it to me."

"He's not in his right mind."

"Prove it."

Silver sucked her teeth and smiled. Inclined her head and headed for the door. "I plan to."

Ford's laughter trailed after her. "Good luck, sis!"

She slammed the door to cut it off and stumbled toward her car. Her hand smacked the door and her stomach heaved. Vomit splashed the pavement and she choked on acidic bile.

Weak, as though she'd taken a beating, she climbed into her car and rested her head on the steering wheel.

And just think. The night's not over yet.

Chapter Thirty Seven

That last save looked like it had to hurt, but Dean spared only a moment to make sure Landon got up on his own before he resumed pacing and checked his watch. Almost an hour and a half. Where the hell was Silver?

Not where she said she'd be.

To be fair, she hadn't specified where she was going, he'd just assumed that she'd meant the bathroom. And she wasn't a child. She didn't need permission to go wherever she pleased.

Without calling. Or answering his calls.

Damn it, it's called respect. I wouldn't do this to her.

Silver didn't have much experience with relationships. Maybe she didn't realize he'd worry.

Bullshit. She's a smart girl.

Maybe something had happened to her. Maybe she'd gone outside to get some air and . . .

The buzzer sounded. The game went into overtime. Dean didn't give a damn. It might be too soon to put out a missing person's report, but there was no way he could stay and focus on the game without knowing where she was. Hopefully he'd find her at home, preferably just tired, more likely nauseous, and he could take care of her for tonight and save the lecture for the morning.

Dean turned his back on the rink and nodded to Bolleau. "Take some notes for me. I have to—"

Silver slipped into the press box, a shaky smile on her lips. Her makeup looked freshly done, but it couldn't hide the fact that she'd been crying. And her tone wasn't as light as she tried to make it. "Sorry I took so long."

He pulled her into his arms and kissed her hair. "What happened?"

"Ah . . .we'll talk about it later."

"Or now. Something upset you." He tipped her chin up to study her face. "You've been gone quite awhile."

Her gaze shifted away from his. "Something came up."

A muscle in his jaw twitched. "Something came up."

"Yeah." Silver glanced nervously at Bolleau. "What's the score?"

Bolleau looked at Dean. "If you won't be needing those notes . . . ?"

"Please stay, Bolleau. We'll finish watching the game." Dean caught Silver's elbow before she could take a seat. He kept his voice level. Calm. Every word measured and articulate so she couldn't claim any misunderstanding. "Give me your shoes."

"My shoes?"

He didn't even pause. "Then you may sit at my feet, close enough for me to feel you right there. That should give you time to think about what you'd like to say to me when the game is over."

"But—"

"There's no need to talk until then, Silver." He held out his hand and gave her a curt nod when she stepped out of her heels and handed them to him. "And just to give you a clue, I don't want to hear another 'sorry.'"

Her eyes narrowed and her nostrils flared. Her jaw shifted as she ground her teeth.

The overtime period started. Dean returned to his seat near the glass, not so much angry as disappointed. Her apology meant nothing if she thought that goddamn word would make things all better. She might not get why he was upset right now, but once she did, he knew very well submitting to a small punishment—and he was taking it pretty damn easy on her—would go a long way in making her feel that her actions were unacceptable, not unforgiveable.

Seconds later, Silver stepped up to his side. She took his hand, kissed his knuckles, and lowered gracefully to her knees.

Dean quietly let out the breath he'd been holding and stroked her hair as she laid her head against his thigh. They were all right. *She* was all right.

They won the game in the last seconds of overtime, and the crowds erupted in a cacophony of victory cheers for the Cobras and boos for the Sabres as the players left the ice. Dean stood and shook Bolleau's hand with a brief, "See you Monday."

Silver fiddled with a loose string on her blouse cuff as he

watched her from a few feet away. She bit the tip of her tongue and seemed to struggle not to look up at him. Obviously a little nervous about what was coming next.

Time to put her at ease. He approached with quiet steps, touched her cheek, then helped her to her feet. "Are you ready to talk to me?"

"Yes, but first . . ." She frowned down at her bare feet, and he was certain she'd ask for her shoes. But then she shook her head. "I'm sor—I mean . . . I probably wouldn't be too happy with you if you disappeared without telling me. I should have called or something. I promise I'll never do it again."

"Thank you, Silver. I'd appreciate that." He took a knee and helped her slip back into her shoes. After straightening, he hugged her to his side and kissed her forehead. "Would you like to speak to me about what 'came up'?"

"Da—My father wanted to see me. Anne left a message and it sounded pretty serious. I had to go."

"Yes, you did." Dean rubbed her arm as they left the press box. "Is he all right?"

"Good as can be expected, I guess." Her brow furrowed. "That bothered me, but there was more . . . remember that guy who was dating Jami?"

"Ford Kingsley?"

"Yeah, only, he's not a Kingsley. Apparently, he's a Delgado."

"A Delgado." *Fuck.* This could get messy. "As in your father's son?"

"I take it you know what that means? My father will give him everything. I don't care about the money and the house, I've got my own money, but the Kingsleys are behind the whole mess last season!" She pressed closer to his side, redirecting him away from the elevator to the stairs. "I need more exercise, I swear, the way you're feeding me is like you're trying to fatten me up or something!" She laughed, then shook her head and sobered right up. "Anyway, Ford's going to destroy this team if we let him."

"Oh, I doubt that very much." Dean ground his teeth and did his best to stay close to her side as she practically skipped down the steps. "Can you please walk normally? You're making me very nervous in those heels."

"Do you want to take them off me again?" She hopped to the second floor landing and gave him a cheeky grin. "Would that make you feel better?"

"Don't tempt me, Silver."

She rolled her eyes. "Fine. I'll be careful. But can you please tell me why you don't think Ford will be bad for the team?"

"I didn't say that. But I'm not overly concerned. *If* Ford is your brother and your father gives him the team, you are in a very good position to fight the transfer in court. Your father gave the team to *you* and he's obviously unstable. I don't think it would be difficult for Asher to prove—you might as well make use of the man since you've decided to keep him around."

"Okay, that I can do." She chewed on the edge of her bottom lip. "But what if I lose?"

"I still hold controlling interest in the team, Silver. Only by proxy, but as long as your father is alive, Ford can't override my decisions any more than you can. And I'm willing to bet he knows that. He'll be in a better position to try to bribe players himself, but I don't see him trying that." He smiled at her confused look. "I managed to avoid any serious issues with the league over what happened last season, but they will be watching us for awhile. The guys are also a bit gun-shy—which is why they aren't welcoming the new players with open arms. There's a lot of tension in the locker room. Ford won't get far with any of them, not for any amount of money."

"What if Ford doesn't use money? What if he tries—"

"With who, Silver?" Dean put a hand on her shoulder before she could step out onto the main floor. "He needs an impact player. We both know he'll never get Landon. Demyan's dealt with assholes like Kingsley before; I don't see him going for it. Your sister's men struggled through having a two-faced goalie and having one of their friends sell out, and they're all dedicated to the team. Who else could he get to that could actually decide entire games, Silver? Think about it."

She nodded and exhaled noisily. "I guess . . ."

"Sweetheart, Ford is young and ambitious. He gloated and it

made you nervous; I can understand that. But what you need to understand is that he doesn't have as much power as he thinks he does. Don't give him any more by letting him get to you, okay?"

"Okay." She dug in her heels as he turned her toward the last flight of stairs. "Umm . . . but what about my father? He's not doing good."

"You said he was doing as well as could be expected. Did his nurse give you any reason to doubt that? Do you feel like you should have stayed?"

"No. She told me there was nothing I could do."

"Do you believe her?"

Silver frowned and shrugged. "She's a nurse. I guess I have to."

"And the stress really isn't good for you, is it?" He chuckled as she blushed and hid her face against his shoulder. "I think it's about time we have a conversation with Landon."

She peeked up at him. "We?"

"Unless you'd rather speak to him alone."

"No! No, I want you with me. With us. You know that right? And, I mean, he might decide he doesn't want anything to do with me, and that will be a lot easier to deal with if—"

He covered her lips with a finger. "Silver, don't assume anything. Just tell him. I'll stay with you."

That look, that utter trust in her eyes, made his chest swell as if his heart had somehow gotten bigger, filled up, expanded, and damn, it felt good.

"I finally see what Landon meant." He bent down to kiss her and smiled against her lips. "I can't let you go. Not anymore."

"Stupid man." Her breath came sweet and hot as she deepened the kiss. "How many times do I have to tell you? I'm not going anywhere."

"Just one more time."

Giggling, she nipped at his bottom lip, then rose up on her tiptoes as she tugged him down to whisper in his ear. "I'm not going anywhere."

He groaned and picked her up, carrying her down the last few steps, kissing her, hardening as he forgot where they were going and why. He wanted her. Here. Now.

She gasped as he bit the side of her throat. "Landon . . ."

"I know we share you, dragonfly." He nibbled along her jaw, then teased the hollow behind her ear with his tongue. "But it would be nice if you could remember who you're with."

"Did you hit your head this morning, dumbass?" She pursed her lips and gave him a little shove. "Did you not tell me I should talk to Landon?"

Ah, yes. That. He nodded. Let her turn. Then latched onto the nape of her neck, hauling her back to speak quietly into her ear. "Once you're done with him, we will discuss you calling me names. Privately. With a bar of soap, some rubber elastics, and a pair of chopsticks."

"Chopsticks?"

"Mmmhmm." He smacked her butt and laughed when she scampered forward. "Now let's go congratulate our goalie."

She shot him a look over her shoulder.

"For the win." Dean winked. "He played well."

* * * *

Steam filled the large, dark blue tiled shower, but Silver's mouth went dry. Water cascaded over long muscular planes, drizzled down smooth, hard curves, washing away green-tinged, ocean-fresh foam. Landon tipped his head back under the shower, and her pussy clenched as his pecs and abs bulged. He looked huge, all the way from his wide shoulders down to his thick, well defined thighs. And his dick, hanging mostly soft under the warm spill of water, was impressive.

Dean had stayed behind to empty out the locker room and give them some privacy. She'd flushed as she'd passed the half dressed men, all fucking big and strong, and most so damn hot she wondered if the hockey gene gave them an unfair advantage. But none of them affected her the way this man did.

She kicked off her shoes and padded silently toward him, wanting to touch, to taste, just once before things got all serious. His eyes met hers just as she reached him, and his lips curved as he latched onto her wrists and pulled her under the spray.

The shower soaked through her blouse as their lips came together, their kiss slick and hot and wet. Hands on his chest, she pushed him back into the tiles and bent down to lick a nipple. She brought her eyes up to his as she lowered, teasing him with her teeth. He groaned and fisted his hands in her hair.

"Silver, we shouldn't." His grip tightened and her nipples twinged in response to the slight pain in her scalp. His hips jutted forward despite his protest. "Not here."

"Yes. Here." She flicked her tongue over the slit at the tip of his hardening dick. "Then we need to talk."

He went still and gave her a hard look. "No. We talk first."

"Landon—"

Yanking her up, he changed their positions, trapping her against the wall, tearing at her shirt as he shook his head and rasped out a harsh breath. "Talk. And make it quick because I want you right fucking now."

Her drenched blouse slapped the floor. Her bra followed, half torn from her body. Landon's large hands covered her breasts as he claimed her mouth once again. The painful throb of her nipples flattened under his palm made her breaths shallow. He stole the rest with his hungry lips, taking her mouth, his tongue snaking in and out over and over.

"Tell me." He bit her bottom lip, and his hot gaze lit a fire deep within. "Tell me, Silver."

Any willpower she had to hold back evaporated in the mist around them. She stared up at him and tears joined the droplets of water on her cheeks. *Please don't hate me.* "I'm having your baby."

His gaze grew even hotter as he smiled, laying a softer kiss on her before whispering. "I know."

"You do?"

"I do. I figured it out when you turned down the wine at dinner." He went to work on removing her skirt, cursed when the wet material stuck to her hips, and cast a glance toward the shower entrance, using one hand to swipe the water from his face. "You want to help me out with this, Dean?

"Gladly." Dean approached her from behind as Landon pulled her away from the wall. Dean pressed his bare chest against her back as he unstuck her zipper and rolled her skirt down. Water gathered where their flesh touched, spilling as he shifted to kiss between her shoulder blades. "Do you want me to stay, dragonfly?"

"You confuse the hell out of me when you ask." She tongued her bottom lip. Landon sucked on the side of her throat and she moaned. She fought to stay on track "And you—you're not mad?"

Landon shook his head and grazed his teeth over her collarbone. "Why would I be mad?"

"I forgot my pill."

"You weren't expecting the condom to break. And neither was I. It happened." He dropped down to his knees and kissed her belly, hovering there for a moment before whispering, "I'm scared to death, but happy. Are you?"

"Scared? Happy?" A gasping laugh of relief escaped her. "Yes to both! But are you sure we should still—?"

"Yes, we should." Landon gave her a lust-filled grin as he kissed the top of her mound with his moist lips. "We'll just have to be a little more careful." He nudged her thighs apart, forcing her to lean on Dean as he spread her folds and closed his lips over her clit. His tongue circled the tip and her knees shook as a soft electric pulse rode up her nerves, causing her cunt to clench with need. "And very, very gentle."

You're going to drive me insane for the next nine months? She thunked her head back into Dean's shoulder, grateful for his support, because she couldn't have stood on her own. His muscles rippled as he drew her arms up so she could hold on to his neck. Then he molded her breast in one hand and curved the other around her throat. His fingers dug into her jaw, turning her head to the side so he could kiss her.

Landon licked around her clit, the tip of his tongue putting pressure on first one side, then the other. He avoided the tip, lapping between her parted labia, exploring her with long strokes, stirring a pool of heat that flowed from his mouth up to the hand on her breast, the fingers pinching her nipple, and Dean's tongue plunging between her lips.

The sensations rushed together as Landon slid one finger inside her. Pleasure flared in her core and Dean swallowed her tiny whimpers, twisting her nipple so pain skidded along the edge of everything she felt. Another finger and Landon pressed his tongue down hard on her clit.

Close, so close . . . she panted into Dean's mouth.

The corner of his lip slanted up. "Don't come."

"I can't stop! I can't . . ."

Suddenly empty. Everything stimulating her gone.

Landon rose up and caught her chin, pulling her away from Dean to brush his lips over hers. "We've proved otherwise. I want to be inside you. I want him inside you. Then you may come."

Asshole! If you don't—but he did. Picking her up, he held her while she wrapped her legs around his waist. As she clung to him, he filled her and she threw her head back. Ready to burst, ready to let go. Behind her a condom wrapper tore and soon the pressure of Dean against her back hole grounded her, forcing her to relax and let him in. Snug, burning, carnal pleasure. In this position, she had no power. No control.

Their strength enveloped her as they lifted her together, thrusting up in a smooth, steady rhythm. Never too hard, but faster and faster, holding her right on the brink until the ground gave out beneath her. She came, trembling, biting into Landon's shoulder to hold back her screams. He grunted and jerked inside her, almost losing his balance. But Dean held steady and braced Landon with a solid grip on his shoulder.

Dean growled out his own release, his free hand on her hip jerking her down hard. She heard his back slap the wall as he used it to keep them all from collapsing to the floor.

Pinned between the men, Silver had no choice but to wait until they regained their bearings. Landon moved first, easing out of her with a wince. He cupped her cheek, kissed her, then pulled her away from Dean.

She smiled at him, glanced back at Dean, and frowned. He was favoring one knee.

"Damn it, why didn't you say something?" She reached for him.

Landon pulled her back again and shook his head. "I've got him."

Ignoring Dean's grumbled protests, Landon threw the other

man's arm over his shoulder and helped him into the locker room. Silver bit back a smile. The men didn't seem to notice that they were both still naked, but she certainly did. She took a minute to enjoy the view, her mind wandering to all kinds of naughty things that would probably never happen.

"What was that look?" Landon asked as he took three towels from a table by the lockers. He handed one to Dean and brought the other to her.

"Oh, nothing." She batted her eyelashes, then yelped when Dean grabbed her wrist. She tried to look innocent as he studied her face, but let out a sigh at his I-don't-buy-it look. "Fine. You sure you want to know?"

"Yes," Landon said.

Dean rolled his eyes and shook his head. "No."

Scrubbing his face with his towel, Landon arched a brow at Dean. "Why not?"

"Trust me. You don't want to know."

Since her clothes were drenched—*you thought that out real well, Silver*—she had to borrow a spare jogging suit and T-shirt from Landon. Her heels hurt her waterlogged feet as they made their way to their cars, but his smelly old runners would have looked like big old clown shoes on her. They all drove to her place so she could change, then decided to take Dean's car to the harbor.

Sipping a decaf iced latte, Silver rested her elbow on the railing and absorbed the peaceful darkness of the dark ocean, spread out endlessly before her. Dean stood at one side with his arm around her shoulders, Landon at the other with his arm around her waist. Utter perfection.

Dean gave her a little squeeze. "We have a lot to discuss, love."

"Yeah, but do we have to do it now?" Discussing anything might ruin the moment. "There's nothing that can't wait until tomorrow."

"There's one thing." Landon stepped back and squared his shoulders. "I'd like to marry you."

Her heart skipped a beat. Her stomach flipped. And all her blood washed cool as the ocean below. Marriage? A baby freaked her out less. Marriage meant living together, which meant seeing each other all the time, which meant he'd see her at her worst. Grumpy in the morning, probably moody from hormones . . .

"Breathe, Silver." Dean squeezed her again. "Marrying Landon isn't the only decision you have to make. I want you both to move in with me."

Breathe. Yeah, it would be swell if I could. She covered her mouth with her hand. "Move in with you? But . . ." There were a million excellent reasons why it was a bad idea. No doubt about it. But she could only think of one. "Jami—"

"Will be living with her grandmother. My house is bigger than either of yours. There's an extra room that can be fixed up as a nursery." Dean massaged her shoulder. "I can help you while Landon's away on road games."

Away . . . her bottom lip quivered. Hell, one second, she was panicking about the thought of living with Landon, and the next she was ready to cry because he would be gone. If this was how the baby was affecting her already, she was seriously not looking forward to the next nine months.

Calm down. Use your brain, woman! Your condo is no place for a baby.

True. But was she ready to give up her independence? To live full time with a man who made her want to hand over control with a great big bow on top? And another who would find whatever she held back? Did she want to make a life with them?

The answer to the latter came without a second thought. Absolutely. But the rest? It was too much, too fast.

She put her hand on her stomach and looked from Dean to Landon. "Do I have to answer now?"

Dean grinned. "I'd rather you didn't. There's no rush."

"Right." Landon brushed her still damp hair away from her face. "I want you to be sure when you give your answer. And I want to do this right. I didn't mean to blurt it out like that. Next time I'll have a ring and take a knee—"

"Good things usually happen when you're on your knees." Silver giggled when he tugged her hair. Then she leaned into him as he took his place at her side. "Let me get used to the idea of the baby first. Then we'll talk some more. I've just got to warn you, I'm not easy to live with."

Landon grinned and glanced over at Dean. "Neither am I."

"I am well aware of that." Dean smirked. "I'm thinking of putting a lock on the kitchen door."

They all laughed and went back to staring out at the ocean. Like her, the men were probably thinking of the future. But did they see what she did? Something vast as all that water, filled with the unknown? Children hadn't been in her short-term—or long-term plans. She had no idea what a normal family was supposed to be like. Not that they'd have one, exactly . . .

But they'd be able to give her baby something she'd never had from the adults in her life. And damn it, as much as both men drove her crazy, she loved them. They made her happy, made her feel like she was worth something.

What more do you need?

Time. Just a bit of time to make sure this was real.

Chapter Thirty Eight

February

Landon dropped his suitcase by the door and rolled his shoulders, still sore from the long plane ride from Florida. The sound of meat sizzling came from the kitchen and his stomach growled. After three weeks of room service and takeout, he could use some of Dean's cooking.

"Don't leave your shit by the door, Silver's liable to trip over it when she comes in." Dean called out.

Frowning, Landon left his things and went to the kitchen, resting his shoulder on the doorframe and folding his arms over his chest. He smothered a grin as he took in the sight of Dean, bent over the stove with an apron covering his suit.

"Need some help?"

"Thanks, I'm good," Dean said dryly. "And not a fucking word. I got back late. Ford fired the new PR person and I had to find a replacement. Silver won't be happy when she finds out. She liked the woman."

"Ford's still making trouble?"

"Of course he is. The old man is still hanging on, which means all Ford can do is make life difficult for the rest of us. I get a pile of folders on my desk every day for players the team doesn't need, who he's approached with crazy offers." Dean slammed a wooden spoon down on the table, and a glob of gravy soaked into the soft yellow placemat beside it. "Which means I'll have a hard time getting anyone to take any offers I make seriously when the deadline comes. We need defensemen, Mason's injured, and Ramos is playing hurt. The rookies won't carry us to the playoffs."

"Why don't you talk to Delgado?" Landon took a bun from the bread basket in the center of the table and took a big bite. He chewed, swallowed, then gestured vaguely with his empty hand. "He'd stop the little shit if he knew what he was doing."

"If only." Dean shook his head and went back to the stove to turn the steaks. "Last time I tried to talk to him, he went on about how his son is the future of the team. How he's a *true* Delgado."

"He still won't acknowledge Oriana, even after the DNA test?"

"No." Dean's brow furrowed. "It makes me sick that she had to do that. That she *agreed* to do that. She still wants him to accept her. Silver hasn't told her what he said . . ." His face broke into a smile. "But she gave the old man hell the last time she visited. Told him if she had to put up with Ford, then he better let Oriana get involved with the team. He finally gave in. And damn, Oriana is a fucking godsend. She's gotten Silver to back off some of her more . . . ambitious projects. And she's the only one Ford listens to. Not always, mind you, but she's gotten him to put more Kingsley money into the team. Silver would have had to cancel the last renovations otherwise, and she'd worked so hard on them—"

Landon went still. "She's not stressing too much, is she?"

"No. I got her to cut down on her work hours. She's good."

Yeah, I'll believe that when I see it. Remembering what Dean had said about his bags, he went back to the hallway and brought them up to the room he shared with Silver and Dean. Took some time to put everything away so Dean wouldn't nag, then returned to the kitchen and grabbed a beer from the fridge. He checked his watch and thrummed his fingers on the table.

Where is she?

Finally, he heard her at the door and practically knocked his chair over as he shoved away from the table. He froze in the hall as she came in, her arms full of bags, Oriana right behind her with more.

All he could see was her stomach, straining against the buttons of her long, pale pink coat. She'd hardly had a belly when he'd left, but now . . .

"What were you thinking?" He strode toward her and snatched the bags from her hands. "I asked you to be careful!"

Silver sighed and looked back at her sister. "I told you. He's lost his mind."

"This is why I'm waiting." Oriana moved around them and went to drop the rest of the bags on the sofa in the living room. "I am *not* looking forward to dealing with either Sloan or Dominik when I decide to have a baby." She sidled past Landon and rubbed her sister's stomach. "But I'm looking forward to spoiling this one."

"You staying for supper, Oriana?" Dean asked, joining them. "I can put on another steak."

Oriana shook her head. "Thank you, but no. Sloan told me he has . . . plans for tonight."

Dean grinned. "I'm sure he does. Enjoy your evening."

"You too!" Oriana kissed Silver's cheek, then gave Landon a hard look. "Pregnant, not disabled. Can you remember that?"

"Oriana . . ." Landon took a deep breath. She was right, of course, but it irked him that any sub would speak to him that way. Even though he should be used to it. Silver was worse.

Slapping his shoulder, Dean moved between him and Oriana. "I do believe Dominik planned to speak with you about meddling. Maybe he and I should have another chat."

Oriana paled. "No, Sir. I remember the last one."

"Very good." Dean inclined his head. "Good night, Oriana."

"Good night." Oriana shot her sister an apologetic look, then darted out.

Silver shook her head at Dean. "You're horrible. Do you have any idea what Dominik did to her last time?"

Dean removed his apron and gave her a slow smile. "No. Why don't you tell me? The man is quite creative, and I'm always looking for new ideas."

"Umm, no. That's okay." Silver bit her lip and reached out to grab Landon's hand. "Come on, I got something for you."

Halfway to the living room, Silver stopped and gasped. Her hand went to her stomach.

Landon's throat locked. "What's wrong?"

"Nothing! Shit!" Silver laughed and put his hand on her stomach. "Can you feel that?"

He couldn't feel anything, but he almost sagged with relief. "Is she moving?"

"He's kicking!"

"He?"

"I don't know! You can't feel it?" She giggled. "It feels weird. Uck, just trust me on this. The baby is fine. I'm fine. But you drive me nuts every time you come home. Like I said, I've got something for you."

Dean sat on the arm of the sofa as Silver dug into a bag, but Landon stayed where he was. What more could she give him? What more would she want to give him considering he was "driving her nuts"? He tried not to crowd her too much, but it happened, far too often.

She took out a box and bent down to one knee.

His eyes widened. He glanced over at Dean, who shrugged.

"Give me your hand." Silver's whole body trembled as she opened the box. She waved away his right hand and reached for his left. Then slipped a solid gold ring on his finger. "I couldn't think of a better way to tell you. But I'm ready."

"Ready?" It wasn't supposed to go like this. He should be the one kneeling. But . . . he shook his head and knelt in front of her. "Are you sure?"

"Absolutely." She held up her hand and drew Dean down beside them. "This . . . this is real."

After staring at the ring, at Dean, then at Silver, Landon nodded and pulled her in for a kiss. "*Oui, mon amour.* It doesn't get any more real than this."

Epilogue

Celebrity Dish

by Hayley Turner

Dartmouth Cobras are making headlines again! Are they serious Cup contenders? Who knows or cares! So, OK, they have four players among the top scorers in the league, and their goalie clenched the #3 spot, but that doesn't really matter to most of us. What we care about is the dirt!!

Scott Demyan's antics on and off the ice have made him a household name. There's even a fan website where puck bunnies can submit pictures they've taken in his hotel room to see who can get the biggest bragging rights. My question is, what bragging rights? Obviously, he's not too picky, but he is hot.

When you're on a team full of headline makers, perhaps the biggest surprise is the lack of news from Sebastian Ramos. Over the past few years, several starlets have been seen on his arm but the most anyone is willing to dish is that he's a perfect gentleman! Now rumor has it that the Dartmouth Cobras are known for being open-minded about "alternative lifestyles," but what secret is Sebastian really hiding up there in the frozen North? I suspect there will be some significant melting when I finally find out, and you can believe I will!

But we cannot forget about my favorite ex-starlet, Silver Delgado! Is she really off the market? Rumor has it that the aforementioned star goalie, Landon Bower, is her baby daddy. The couple will be tying the knot this summer, so all signs point to that being the winning bet. However, she's been seen acting awfully friendly with General Manager Dean Richter. They did have a relationship before Silver hooked up with Landon. Perhaps she's just following in big sister's footsteps. The more the merrier!

Cross-legged on the living room sofa, Silver read over the article Asher had scanned, emailed, and texted her about. A slight fluttering in her belly drew her attention. She rubbed the small bump over the top of her pale pink pajama pants and chewed on the inside of her cheek, trying to decide if the article bothered her as much as Asher had warned it would.

It really didn't. *She* knew who her baby's biological father was.

And who his daddies would be.

The stuff about Scott wasn't news, but the stuff about Sebastian . . . He was a good guy. Now that she wasn't scared of him anymore, she could actually kinda call him a friend. She didn't like Hayley digging into his personal life.

Unfortunately, she hadn't said anything that counted as slander. So Silver couldn't sic Asher on her. *Yet.*

Silver closed the laptop and set it aside. Time to sneak back in bed before Dean or Landon noticed her missing. She didn't need to be reminded again that her butt wasn't pregnant. Landon still fussed about her lifting anything heavier than her purse, but he had no problem picking up the tawse when she got mouthy. And Dean had been brainstorming on new punishments that would be safe for the baby.

Half an hour kneeling on uncooked rice had her thinking twice before insulting him *ever.*

Tiptoeing into the bedroom, she took in the both of them, sprawled over the bed. Landon, facedown, his arm draped over Dean's chest. Dean flat on his back, hands under his head, looking more like he was lounging in the sun than sleeping.

The light from the hallway made his open eyes shimmer. He smiled at her, gently moved Landon's arm, then shifted over to give her some space between them. "I hope you weren't up working, my little dragonfly."

Careful not to disturb Landon—though with the way he slept, she could jump on the bed without waking him—Silver crawled up to Dean and snuggled against his side. "I wasn't working—just reading something."

"Hmm." Dean studied her face in the dark, then nodded and adjusted her so he could cover her belly with his hand. "Anything interesting?"

"Not really." Reaching down, she fingered the gold ring on his left hand, given to him only days after Landon got his.

"I know I can't legally marry you too, and I know I already wear your collar at the club, but . . ." She'd almost dropped the ring twice before getting it on his finger. "The whole "til death do us part' . . . it goes for both of you, okay?"

Dean had lifted her up off her knees and held her tight. "Yes, my love."
He'd clasped her face between his hands and whispered against her lips. "And he
won't be the only one saying 'I do.'"

Another fluttering within—more like a birds wings than the tiny ones she'd felt the first few times—made her giggle. Dean chuckled and sat up.

"He's a lively one, just like his mother." Dean considered Landon for a moment. His hand remained on her stomach as he reached behind him to grab a glass of water off the night table. "He'll probably keep the three of us up all night for the first few months."

Winking at her, he tossed the water right over Landon's head.

"Fuck!" Landon shot up, and Silver winced as he hit the floor with a thud. He rebounded to his feet quick as he did between the pipes and shot her a panicked look. "What is it? Is it the baby? Is something wrong?"

"It's the baby," Dean said dryly, shaking his head. "But there's nothing wrong. He's wide awake and I thought you should be too."

Landon shook the water from his hair and climbed onto the bed so carefully it looked like he was avoiding land mines. His hand hovered over her stomach. His throat worked as he swallowed.

Silver bit her lip and looked at Dean. They both knew it bothered Landon that he hadn't been able to feel the baby yet. What if he didn't this time either?

Sighing, Dean put his hand over Landon's and lightly pushed it down. "Trust me. You can't miss this. I think he's getting ready to take your place on the blue ice."

A nice hard kick. Silver watched Landon and . . . there. His eyes widened with wonder, and he lowered to kiss right over the spot where their baby was still doing his "stretches" as Dean called it. He whispered something she couldn't make out. She could feel him trembling a little—he was still scared. But in just a few more months, he wouldn't have to be anymore. He would look into his son's eyes—she hoped they would be grey just like his—and he'd be able to let himself picture the life they'd have together.

Dean kissed her cheek and held her hand. And damn, he made everything perfect. He dealt with Landon's fear—and hers—with the same steady calm he dealt with everything else. He was with her when Landon couldn't be, and that slowly eased away the shadows of guilt she saw on Landon's face every time he had to miss a checkup.

Without Dean, she'd be hesitant to hope for the future, to imagine the wonderful life they'd give their child.

But with him, it was all she could see.

THE END

Visit the Dartmouth Cobras
www.thedartmouthcobras.com

BREAKAWAY

The Dartmouth Cobras

Sneak Peek

Pink and blue flashing lights. The sweet, slick perfume of sex. Two pairs of naked breasts pressed together as red lips met in a passionate kiss. A stage full of lust for a handful of cash.

Luke leaned forward and slipped a hundred dollar bill into the curvy blonde's G-string. She glanced down and gave him a sultry smile before bending down to suck on her "dance" partner's nice big nipples, one after the other. His dick jabbed at the inside of his zipper, throbbing with the kind of pain he craved when he needed to feel enough for his brain to shut the fuck up.

Not enough though. Not yet. He shifted as the women resumed fondling one another.

And I gave this up for her? His lips curled away from his teeth in a sneer. Good thing he'd come to the club on a night when the ladies were scheduled to put on a show. Something Silver Delgado, the club owner's girlfriend and partial owner of the Dartmouth Cobras, had come up with a few months back to up the club's income. And he'd missed out on all this while trying to be the relationship kind of guy.

Not because he suddenly wanted to settle down. No, it was for his mom. She'd just found out she had an inoperable brain tumor. Since his dad left them, all they'd had was each other. She was scared that she'd die and he'd be alone. His father's daughter and all the rest from that side didn't count as family. So she'd asked the impossible of him. She desperately needed to live to see him get married, and her doctors said she only had a year or two left. His shock had changed her tone pretty fast, and before he had a chance to say a word she'd whispered "Can you at least find a girl who you might want to marry, one day?"

He'd thought he could. He'd thought he had. It hadn't been horrible either; Teresa had been cool to have around when he wasn't on the road. She'd met his mom who absolutely loved her.

I loved her.

His stupid brain was going into overdrive. He shook as he pictured her all over Demyan, as he heard her telling him his fucked-up face disgusted her—fine, not in exactly those words, but—

Shut up!

He smashed the bottle in his hand against the side of the stage. The neck snapped off in his fist, cutting his palm. He drew in air and pain and shoveled the depressing thoughts into the back of his head. Teresa didn't matter. All that mattered was his mom, what she expected from him.

Sitting on the edge of her hospital bed at the end of the All-Star break in January, Luke had held her cold hands between his. "I don't have to go, Mom. They can bring up someone else to—"

"They need you. You won't do any good hanging around here while I'm getting tests. I'm not going to stop living, and I don't want you to either." She brought her hand up before he could argue. "My sister is coming to stay with me. I'll be fine."

"I ain't gonna be able to play good."

"Lucas Isaiah Carter, you better play well." She laughed when he winced at her use of his full name. Then she touched his cheek and whispered, "Don't dwell on this. Give me a reason to cheer each and every game. I'll be watching you."

His mom didn't ask him for much, and this was something he could do. At first he'd felt guilty, acting all normal with her still in the hospital, but every time he called, she seemed stronger, and finally she got to go home. And the act became real. Hell, people lived longer than doctors said they would all the time. Maybe she'd get better.

She still wants to see me happily married though.

Well, she didn't need to know he wasn't with Teresa. Not yet anyway. He could do that much for her, let her live with the illusion that her only child would one day give her grandbabies.

The heat from the cut on his palm spread, and he frowned as blood dripped on his shoe. Then glared at Demyan who was shaking him, snapping out nonsensical words.

Fingers raked into Luke's hair and his head was jerked back. Hot, minty breath flowed over his face as Chicklet, his mentor at the club, moved in close. "Come with me. Now."

He didn't even consider arguing with her. Then again, no one argued with Chicklet—not even Dean Richter, the Cobras general manager and owner of the club. She was the kind of Domme that could make even the most dominant man submit to some extent.

Not that Luke would *ever* submit to *anyone*.

She shoved him onto a leather sofa near the bar and went to the bar for a towel. After wrapping his hand tight, she straightened and put her hands on her hips. "What's up with you? You wanna hurt, you know I'll hurt you." She jutted her chin at his hand. "And I won't fuck up your stick handling when I do it."

Luke clenched his fist around the towel and shrugged. "It was an accident."

"Maybe so. But you took your sweet time taking care of it. And you weren't hearing Demyan when he told you you were bleeding all over the place." Her eyes narrowed as she studied him. "Where's your head at, kid? You completely zoned out."

"Just broke up with my girlfriend—no big deal." He gave Chicklet his most charming smile, even though he knew it wouldn't work on her. She had two subs—one of them his roommate, Tyler Vanek, and even that angel-faced SOB got the Full Metal Jacket treatment when he pissed Chicklet off. But he had to try. "You wanna know what I was thinking? Tyler's gone for a little while, trying to get his brain fixed." Wiggling his eyebrows, he let his gaze roam over her curvy, leather-clad body. "He won't mind if we have some fun while he's gone, will he?"

Chicklet's lips drew into a hard, mean line. "No, I don't think he'll mind at all. Stand up, boy."

Boy? He rolled his eyes and stood. "Chicklet, I ain't a sub—you know that, right?"

She smirked and glanced over to the right. "Wayne, you mind holding him for me?"

"Not at all." The huge bouncer came up behind Luke and shackled his wrists in big, beefy hands, jerking them back until his shoulders ached from the strain. "Where do you want him?"

441

"Get him in the upright stocks. The steel ones."

Twisting his wrists, Luke stared at Chicklet. "Whoa, wait a second—"

"You know the club safeword, boy." Chicklet arched a brow. "Ready to use it already?"

"No I'm not ready to use it. I'm also not letting you put me in the fucking stocks."

"Not letting me?" Chuckling, Chicklet motioned for Wayne to go. "Try to stop me. It'll be fun to watch."

Ignoring Luke's snarling protests, Wayne dragged him to the stocks, twisting his arm when he refused to bend down to them. The stocks were T-shaped, with metal cuffs built in at the ends which were quickly snapped around Luke's wrists, spreading his arms wide. At the end of the V base, shackles on short chains welded into the steel were set up to restrain his ankles. He fought harder to keep Wayne from getting them on him, but the man muscled him into position easily and slapped his thigh when he tried to kick him.

"Behave, boy," Wayne said in the same tone he used with his slave.

Rage pooled up from Luke's guts to his throat, lava hot and thick enough to choke on. "Don't call me boy, you big ugly gorilla."

The brisk click of Chicklet's boot heels drew his attention just long enough for Wayne to lock the last shackle. Chicklet used the end of a riding crop to tip Luke's chin up. "Wayne gets five in for the insult, *boy*. I suggest you think before you open your mouth again."

Eyes narrowed, Luke watched Chicklet set a big white medical kit on the floor. "What the hell do you think you're doing, woman?"

Chicklet straightened. "Mistress."

"Are you serious? You've never made me call you Mistress before."

"Very observant."

How the hell was he supposed to have a reasonable conversation in this ridiculous position? He tugged until his wounded hand, still wrapped in the towel, pulsed as though he had his heart in his fist. "So why now?"

Lips pursed, Chicklet paced in front of him, checking his

restrained wrists, running her hands over his shoulders and testing the muscles with her fingertips. Finally she stopped in front of him and squared her shoulders. "Because you need it. I feel like an idiot for not seeing it before, for easing off after giving you a little taste of submission."

"I'm not a submissive." He closed his eyes after another tug and took a deep breath. "Let me go, Chicklet. I get that you're trying to help, but you're wrong about me. I don't need this."

"Don't you?" Leaving one hand on his shoulder, Chicklet leaned close enough for her lips to brush his ear. "Let go for a moment and let yourself feel the restraints. Stop thinking about being a Dom. About what you *should* need. You don't get to decide that now."

Her soft tone soothed him, and he almost relaxed, almost admitted that not having to decide anything felt kinda good. But then he opened his eyes and saw people staring. Demyan, who'd given up watching the dancers. Wayne's slave who distractedly served the people at the bar. Laura, Chicklet's sub, who knelt by a bar stool with a calm expression on her face as though she saw her Mistress handle men like this all the time.

Which she did. She saw Chicklet handle Tyler like this.

But Tyler *was* a sub.

Gritting his teeth, Luke glared at Chicklet. "Let. Me. Go."

Chicklet clucked her tongue. "You worry too much about what others see when they look at you. Use the safeword, or shut up and let me take care of you."

He continued to glare at her, but didn't say a word.

"That's my boy." She looked over his shoulder. "Master Wayne, please take care of his hand. I'm going to fetch a few things from behind the bar."

As she walked away, Wayne came to his side and unwound the towel from his hand. He took out a flat gauze and covered the slowly oozing cut with it, then wrapped a bandage around Luke's hand. After taping it in place, he rose and folded his arms over his chest.

"What's eating at you, boy?" He took hold of Luke's chin when he tried to look away. Somehow he looked less ugly and more . . . powerful, standing over him. "You know, most good Doms submit at one point just to see what it's like. I've done it."

Luke's brow shot up and he lifted his chest off the bar as much as he could to face the man. "*You?*"

"Yes. Me." Wayne grinned. "Wasn't my thing, but I gave it a shot. Won't hurt you to do the same."

Snorting, Luke looked over to where Chicklet was approaching with her whole toy bag. "With Chicklet? I'd be disappointed if it *didn't* hurt."

Chicklet smiled. "That's the most honest thing you've said tonight. Don't worry, boy, I'll hurt you."

Luke's eyes went wide. He shook his head. "That isn't what I meant."

"That's exactly what you meant. You're not fooling anyone, Carter." She knelt, unzipped her toy bag, and pulled out a blindfold. "What you felt when you cut your hand is nothing compared to what you'll feel when I'm done with you. You wanna negotiate, you better do it now, because after I put this on you, I don't want to hear another word."

"Negotiate?" Luke let out a nervous laugh. "Come near me with a strap-on, *Mistress,* and you better never take these restraints off."

"So noted. I planned to keep this scene non-sexual anyway."

He swallowed and went still as she put the blindfold on him. Non-sexual. Which could only mean one thing as far as he knew.

Darkness stole the last of his resistance. He couldn't see anyone staring, so it was like they weren't there. "You *are* going to hurt me."

He heard Chicklet, and possibly Wayne, moving around him. Someone rolled his shirt up to his shoulders. Someone else undid his belt and slid his jeans and boxers down enough to bare his ass.

"I will, but only after Wayne does." Chicklet—it must have been Chicklet, because the lips were soft and her voice sounded close— kissed his cheek. "Count for me."

The *Snap!* came with a hot lick of fire across his ass. He clenched his butt and sucked in air as the sensation travelled down to his balls. *Holy shit!*

He groaned and whispered. "One."

Four more, harder, without pause, and he was panting against the urge to come. Forcing himself to count helped him hold back, but when smooth hands caressed his burning flesh he shuddered as the tip of his dick moistened with pre-cum.

"You're doing good, boy. Very good." Chicklet's approval made him feel bigger somehow. Stronger. Like he wasn't completely pathetic for letting her do this to him. "I'm going to play with you for a bit, put you in a good place. And you will not come."

"This won't make me come." He almost added "bitch" because being told what to do irked him, but he knew what kinds of toys she had in that bag. And he liked his nuts just as they were, thank you very much.

Clicking heels. A long body, both soft and hard in all the right places, pressed against his back. "You're so close, pet. I can tell. But if you're good, I'll let you go with your buddy, Demyan, and fuck one of those strippers. The redhead on stage now is an old favorite of Sloan's. She'll take good care of you both."

Luke groaned. And nodded. That sounded like a good reward. Not that he needed her permission to fuck anyone, but somehow, getting it, made it seem more . . . appealing.

Chicklet moved away from him. He heard a familiar *Whoosh* and braced himself. A sharp biting pain spread over his ass, snapping at the end. He grunted as the pain flared out, and his eyes watered as she hit him again and again. His balls ached with the need to come, but he focused on the heat, absorbing it, allowing it to consume him.

A woman's screams pierced his skull. The kind of screams he got off on drawing from a woman using the exact same tools Chicklet was using on him.

The steady strokes eased off. And his brain snapped back into place and everything that had brought him here came to him at once. He couldn't be a good boyfriend. He was a lousy Dom. Maybe all he was good for was getting beaten on. He was so fucking weak.

The blindfold was torn away, and he blinked as the dim lights of the club blinded him.

"Carter, look at me." Chicklet held his face between his hands. "You stiffened up. What's wrong?"

"What's wrong?" He laughed and clenched his wounded hand over the bandage until he could feel the moisture of fresh blood. But it didn't hurt. Nothing hurt, and goddamn it, he wanted it to. "I'm weak. You wouldn't have me here like this if I wasn't. I'm disgusted with myself, okay?"

"Damn." Chicklet shook her head. "I've never had a sub drop *during* a scene."

"This isn't a fucking drop! I need more! It felt good. Too good. And it shouldn't."

"It shouldn't? Is that what you're going to tell your next sub? That she shouldn't enjoy what you're doing to her?"

Luke blinked. "My next sub? But I thought you'd decided I was—"

"Take him down, Wayne." Chicklet massaged her temples with her fingers. "Honestly, I can't figure out what you are, Carter. You don't have the confidence to be a good Dom. You enjoy receiving pain, but you can't submit completely. And since you don't know what you want, you obviously can't tell me. I'm not a fucking mind reader. I just hope this helped you a little."

"It helped." His legs felt rubbery as Wayne freed him and helped him stand. But nausea almost floored him. He was such a loser. At least Tyler knew what he wanted. He embraced it. No one could call him pathetic for kneeling to Chicklet because it seemed so natual. And the Doms on the team all welded their power with unwavering confidence. Chicklet was right; Luke didn't have that. Not as a Dom, not even as a fucking man.

His eyes burned and he wrenched away from Wayne.

"Can I go now?"

"Not yet." Chicklet nodded to Wayne, and the man latched an arm around Luke's neck and wrestled him across the room to a sofa. He held Luke until he stopped struggling. Chicklet brought him a bottle of water from the bar. And a piece of chocolate. "We'll let you go when you're stable again."

"Chocolate?" Luke let out a rough laugh and took the water bottle. He gulped it all down and eyed the chocolate. "You gotta treat me like a chick now, too?"

"You think only chicks like chocolate?" Chicklet asked.

"I know they love it when they're on the rag. Are Domme's like that too?"

"Just eat the fucking chocolate, Carter." Chicklet shoved the brown chunk at him and glared at him until he ate it. "This didn't turn out the way I wanted it to. You're too stubborn. If you need a Dom, man or woman, I hope they're up to the challenge. You're a pain in the ass."

"Thank you." Luke grinned, actually feeling a bit better—not that he'd admit it. He was the good kinda sore, like after a hard workout. And that put everything in perspective. Wayne was an honest guy. If he said some Doms did this, then they did. And either way, he'd earned his reward. When Wayne let him go, he stood and did a seductive dance to the stripper music to prove to Chicklet he was good. "You ready to let me off the leash now, *Mistress?*"

"I'd be an idiot to put you on my leash, kid. But yeah, you can go." Her lips twisted as she studied him. "I like how quick you pop back though. But it might not last. Give me a call if you start feeling shitty again."

"Will do." Luke tugged the sweaty clumps of hair over his brow like a cowboy tipping his hat and sauntered away, He slapped Demyan's shoulder when he stepped up to his side. "You into sharing? Apparently the redheaded stripper likes it."

"Yeah, I don't mind sharing." Demyan scratched the golden scruff on his jaw. "Hey, you okay? That was—"

"Hey, you wanna be a Dom here?" Luke laughed at Demyan's hesitant nod. The man had been coming to the club for months but hadn't committed to anything. "Well, you might want to keep this in mind. Apparently a 'good Dom' learns about submission before he learns about control."

"All of a sudden, being vanilla doesn't seem all that bad." Demyan eyed the redhead who stood to the side of the stage, talking to Chicklet, as though wondering if vanilla would be enough for the woman. "I'm cool with fucking her if she wants it, but besides that . . ."

Luke chuckled and made a come hither gesture with his hand when the redhead glanced over at him. "Why make things complicated? She's hot. She's willing. You need more than that?"

Demyan paused, then shook his head. "Nope. That works for me."

They took the woman, whose name was Roxy, back to their apartment. And enjoyed her all night long. In every way possible.

And Luke almost managed to convince himself *he* didn't need more. After the third time, driving deep into her cunt while Demyan rammed into her ass, he almost believe it.

Almost.

* * * *

The metallic grind of the skate sharpener sliced through the chattering and giggling about the "drool-worthy" Dartmouth Cobras. Mission accomplished. Jami Richter clicked off the power to the machine and glanced over her shoulder at the crowd of perky blonds and busty brunettes sitting on the benches in the locker room, gawking. "Sorry about that." Damn, she almost sounded like she meant it! "Just got one more."

Ignoring the irritated muttering, Jami let her dark blue hair fall over her face and focused on getting just the right edge. She'd need it here, and not just at the bottom of her skate blades. All those girls knew she had no business trying out to be a Dartmouth Cobra Ice Girl—and worse, that she'd been given an unfair advantage by being bumped into the top 100.

"Hey." A petite Asian girl, one of the few girls who hadn't been giving her dirty looks all morning, slipped up to her side and picked up the skate Jami had just finished with. "I like your skates."

Bullshit. Jami tongued her upper lip and stifled the urge to snatch her skate back. Her skates were black vintage with yellow happy face laces. Everyone turned their noses up at them, but they'd been her grandmother's—they made her feel lucky. Like her grandma was still around instead of back in Halifax. And with Grandma around, she was less likely to fall on her ass.

Not that she'd admit that to this cutsy little dollface. But she *would* be polite until the girl gave her a reason not to be. "Thank you."

"You're great on the ice, though. Why aren't you working on the dancing? I haven't seen you with any of the choreographers yet."

Testing the edge on her blade with her thumb, Jami shrugged. "I'll get to it."

"Akira, I wouldn't be getting all friendly with her if I were you."

The only redhead in the group set her curling iron on a metal table by the lockers and smiled sweetly. "She's probably the reason you'll be heading back to Hong Kong this summer."

"My parents are from Japan." Akira ducked her head, speaking too low for anyone but Jami to catch a word. "And I was born in Calgary."

"What did you say?" Red stood and smirked at the snickering twits around her. "Speak up, girl! They need to hear you out on the ice when you're cheering the team!"

Their uniforms—black and gold mid-drift halters with the Cobra logo and black short skirts—might make them all look pretty much the same to some, but they couldn't be more different. Obvious because not one of those bitches called Red on her shit.

But I'm not one of them. Jami pressed her thumb down on the blade until it cut her thumb. The sharp bite of pain sent a cool, calming rush through her veins. She jutted her chin toward Red, then winked at Akira. "This is what happens when inbreeding becomes obvious."

Akira covered her mouth with her hands. Her porcelain features lost the little color they had.

Red's face looked like every blood vessel in her cheeks had exploded. "She said that?"

"No. I did." Jami set down her skate. "Want to make something of it?"

Please say yes.

"As if." Red snorted. "Your daddy and his fuck friend run the team. I'm not stupid."

Brow arched, Jami looked her over. "So you just wear the mask to impress people?"

Tugging at her arm, Akira muttered under her breath, "Please don't fight with her. She's the most popular girl in the group, and the judges already love her. Everyone knows why you're here, but no one can argue that you have skills. If you can dance, you're a sure bet."

"What if I can't dance?" Jami winced when she realized she'd said that out loud. Not a good thing to share with the competition. She frowned at her bloody thumb, then stuck it in her mouth. Warm copper slicked her tongue. *Yuck.* A bit too much. She looked around for somewhere to spit and nodded her thanks when Akira handed her a towel. Mouth relatively clean, pressure on her thumb, she studied Akira, trying to figure out her angle. "Why do you care if I make it or not?"

"Honestly?" Akira managed to maneuver her out of the locker room and into the hall before Red came up with a good comeback. Something about DP that was muffled by the closing door. The tiny girl released her once they were well out of hearing. "You're interesting, and so far, you're not mean. I'd rather be out there, at the end of all this, with you than her."

Fair enough. "So you don't resent me for butting in?"

"Not at all. I think you would have made it anyway." Akira's smile faded away as three huge men strode toward them. She half hid behind Jami as they paused, side by side, completely blocking the hallway.

Jami ducked her head as Dominik Mason, the Cobras big black defensemen, reached out to ruffle her hair.

"I didn't know you were back, kid. How are you?"

"Not bad. Just getting settled in." Jami couldn't tell him more. Not until she had a chance to talk to her father. He knew she was back, but that was about it. They'd argued enough about her moving into her own place—her grandmother saved her on that one by pointing out that *she'd* found the apartment and loaned Jami the money for first and last month's rent—and she really wasn't up to getting into why she was back just yet.

Dominik's lips drew into a thin line as he studied her face. "May I ask you something?"

"Sure ... ."

"Are you opposed to me telling your father we saw you here?"

Okay, that was just scary. How the hell had he figured that out? She eyed the other two players, Sloan Callahan, the freakin' team's captain, and Max Perron. These men, and several others on the team, had become like older brothers over the last five years, ever since her father had taken over as general manager. They saw her around the forum and treated her like she was still that awkward fourteen-year-old girl they'd first met. She didn't see Max telling on her. He had this sweet cowboy thing going for him, and she didn't buy that he was a "Dominant," but Dominik and Sloan . . . ?

She let out a sigh and rolled her eyes. "I'd like the chance to tell him myself."

"See that you do," Sloan said.

Max remained behind for a moment as the other men continued down the hall. He put his hand on her shoulder and squeezed lightly. "Stay out of trouble, you hear?" He grinned when she nodded and glanced over at Akira. "Don't look so scared, hon. Not one man on this team will touch you unless you want him to. Any try and you come talk to me. Understand?"

Akira must have done something besides tremble behind her, because Max inclined his head and strode off to join the others.

Jami turned around and laughed when she saw the stricken look on Akira's face. "Haven't you met any of the players before?"

Lips moving soundlessly, Akira shook her head.

"Well, as you can see, they're pretty cool—"

"They're so big." Akira hugged herself and stared down the hall. "Oh God . . . I don't know if I can do this."

At first, Jami had assumed that Akira was just overwhelmed because, like all the other girls, she idolized the players. But Max was right. She was scared.

"What is it, Akira? Is it the tryouts that scare you? Or . . ." Or what? Big hockey players? Not one girl here didn't love the game. Except Jami. But she was good at faking it. "You just said you'd rather be on the ice with me. Don't be ditching me now."

"I'm not." Akira didn't speak again until they were at the doors to the forum's workout room. Then she pressed her eyes shut and put her hand on her throat. "I just don't like men getting too close. I love watching them out there, but . . ."

Aww fuck. The poor kid. Jami gave her a one-armed hug. "You want to talk about it? We can take off for a bit, grab something to eat and chat?"

Akira shook her head. "No. I have to do this. It took forever to talk my parents into letting me try out. I'll get over it. I *told* them I was over it."

"You came all the way from Calgary by yourself?"

"Yes. But it's okay, I'm used to travelling alone." Akira wrinkled her nose. "And dealing with people like Amy Drisdain—the red-head," she added at Jami's blank look. "I've been all over for figure skating competitions, but my parents couldn't support my dream of going professional anymore and I wasn't winning any medals. Thankfully my father *loves* hockey, or he wouldn't have given me this last shot at a career on the ice. I'm hoping to use the prize money to open my own school in a few years. Help other girls succeed where I haven't. I *can't* give up now."

Jami inhaled deep. "Damn girl, you are my new idol. I wish I had half your dedication. I'm doing this because I thought it might be fun. Pretty shallow, right?"

"Is that really the only reason?"

Making a face, Jami pushed open the door to the gym and shrugged. "I've never supported my dad. Never cared about what he was doing. I figured maybe this was a good way to show I've changed."

Straightening to her full height of five foot nothing, Akira faced her. "Well, I don't think that's shallow at all."

Jami laughed and stepped into the gym, deciding that she'd made a new friend and she'd knock some teeth in if anyone else dissed her. Inside, a dozen girls stretched out on the mats, eyes fixed on the tall woman in the center of the room wearing a black leotard.

And the massive, muscular, drop-dead gorgeous stud beside her. Sebastian Ramos, the new Cobra defenseman. She might not pay much attention to hockey anymore, but she'd snatched up the magazine with him on the cover and shamelessly drooled over his photos for weeks. And he was even more mouthwatering in person. Her pulse beat double time. Her palms dampened. His black hair, done up in a low ponytail, flowed over one broad shoulder, thick and glossy as the mane of a prize stallion. His white tank top and black shorts revealed thick, tanned arms and thighs which couldn't possibly be as hard as they looked. The urge to test their solidity with her teeth made it so she couldn't even voice an apology when the dance instructor frowned and waved her and Akira into the room.

"As I was saying, please don't take it personally if you're not chosen for the pictures. The magazine has been very specific as to what they're looking for. And posing does not guarantee anyone a spot in the final round. Make sure you look your best out there and forget about the silly promo." A blush rose high on the woman's cheeks as she looked over at Sebastian. "No offense."

Silly promo? Are you kidding me? Jami took a quick look around the room at her competition. One of them would be chosen to take pictures with *him*. Unless she got herself noticed. Or . . . *Who do I have to kill to get picked?*

"No offense taken, Madame." Sebastian clasped one hand to his wrist behind his back and strolled around the room in a wide circle. Jami and Akira scrambled to the empty mats at the back of the room, barely managing to compose themselves before he reached them. His gaze didn't stay on Akira long as she cowered on her mat in a half-crouched position, but they locked on Jami as she knelt. "*Eso se ve bien, preciosa.*"

Is it horrible that I don't care what that means? As long as he kept looking at her like she was the only woman in the room. Kept talking to her in that voice that languidly melted through her like hot caramel drizzling into her core. If he did all that, he could say—*or do*—whatever he wanted to her.

The workout room had turned into a sauna. The instructor was showing the other girls a routine, but they all faded away as Sebastian moved closer to her. Her lips parted as he reached down and brushed a lightly calloused fingertip along her jaw.

"Very pretty, *mi cielo.*" The edge of his mouth tilted up as he lifted a strand of her hair. "You are different than the other girls. I will position you how I like."

The heat from his single touch spread everywhere. Her eyes widened and she barely avoided squeaking. "Position?"

His brow furrowed slightly. "I am sorry, that came out wrong. Your instructor and I have chosen you for the photo shoot. With me." He took his hand from her hair and gave Akira a tender smile. "You have been chosen as well."

Akira looked ready to pass out.

Sebastian took a knee in front of her. "Little one, take a breath for me." The alluring quality in his tone seemed to have been toned down, releasing Jami from its thrall and calming Akira. As the small girl obediently took a breath, Sebastian's smile broadened. "Very good. Now, you will not do this since it makes you uncomfortable."

"But—"

"No. We will find someone else. Stay here and dance, *pequena*." He rose to his feet and held his hand out to Jami. "You will come with me."

Her hand was almost in his before she caught herself. Her body might be willing to go wherever he took her, her brain kicked in with a great big "Slow down." She was here to prove something to her father. And herself. If she didn't learn the moves, getting bumped ahead of all the hopefuls wouldn't count for anything. It was all on her now.

Ugh. Can't you save the dedication for another time?

The naughty little voice in her head wasn't gonna win this time. Besides, she *had* changed. Last year she would have flirted shamelessly and made it clear he just had to say where and when. She'd been wild and reckless. Grandma called it stupid.

"You can have fun without getting yourself in trouble, girly," Grandma had said after Grandpa Fred found her in the old shed behind their house with the boy next door. *"Make the boys work for it; you'll both enjoy it more."*

No one would consider Sebastian a boy, but hell, if he wanted her, why make it easy for him?

She withdrew her hand slowly.

"I'm sorry, Mr. Ramos, but I haven't learned the routine yet and this is my last chance." Okay, she'd need more than one session to learn the moves and do them without coming across as a clumsy, two-left-footed monkey, but he didn't need to know that. "Can I meet up with you after you're finished with the other girls?"

His brow furrowed slightly, but he nodded. "You may. Fourth floor, office 409."

"All right."

"And, *mi cielo*?"

She shivered as that alluring timbre seeped into her skin, heating her blood enough to evaporate her token resistance. She put some pressure on her cut thumb and looked up at him. "Yes?"

"Don't make me wait too long."

* * * *

Game Misconduct

THE DARTMOUTH COBRAS #1

The game has always cast a shadow over Oriana Delgado's life. She should hate the game. But she doesn't. The passion and the energy of the sport are part of her. But so is the urge to drop the role of the Dartmouth Cobra owner's 'good daughter' and find a less . . . conventional one.

Playmaker Max Perron never expected a woman to accept him and his twisted desires. Oriana came close, but he wasn't surprised when she walked away. A girl like her needs normal. Which he can't give her. He's too much of a team player, and not just on the ice.

But then Oriana's father goes too far in trying to control her and she decides to use exposure as blackmail. Just the implication of her spending the night with the Cobras' finest should get her father to back off.

Turns out a team player is exactly what she needs.

"Ms Sommerland takes us on an extremely incredible journey as we watch Oriana's master her own sexuality. She comes to realize that there is more out there that she craves and desires, than she has ever realized." –Rhayne From Guilty Pleasures

"With a delicious storyline and kinky characters outside of the norm, Game Misconduct pushes you outside of your comfort zone and rewards your submission with phenomenally erotic sex. If you're a fan of hardcore BDSM, then this book is going to top your list of must reads!" –Silla Beaumont From Just Erotic Romance

BIANCA SOMMERLAND

Breakaway

THE DARTMOUTH COBRAS

Against some attacks, the only hope is to come out and meet the play.

Last year, Jami Richter had no plans, no goals, no future. But that's all changed. First step, make up for putting her father through hell by supporting the hockey team he manages and becoming an Ice Girl. But a photo shoot puts her right in the arms of Sebastian Ramos, a Dartmouth Cobra defenseman with a reputation for getting any woman—or, as the rumors imply, man—he desires. And the powerful dominant wants her...and Luke. Getting involved in Seb's lifestyle gives her a new understanding of the game and the bonds between players. But can she handle being caught between two men who want her, while struggling with their attraction to one another?

Luke Carter's life is about as messed up as his scarred face. His mother is sick. His girlfriend dumps him. When he goes to his favorite BDSM club to blow off some steam, his Dom status is turned upside down when a therapeutic beating puts him in a good place. He flatly denies being submissive—or, even worse, being attracted to another man. He wants Jami but can't have her without getting involved with Sebastian. Can he overcome his own prejudices long enough to admit he wants them both?

Caught between Luke and Jami, Sebastian Ramos does everything in his power to fulfill their needs. His two new submissives willingly share their bodies, but not their secrets. When his own past comes back to haunt him, the fragile foundation of their relationship is ripped apart. As he works to salvage the damage done by doubt and insecurity, he discovers that Jami is hiding something dangerous. But it may already be too late.

Ms. Sommerland has a distinctive talent in engaging her readers. She pulls you in and holds you completely captive as you live within each scene. As with all of the books in this series, the BDSM aspect is very real and very edgy. It will push your comfort level if this isn't your type of normal reading. Go into it knowing what you will get and I promise you will fall in love with this mind-blowing series. -Rhayne Riskae From Guilty Pleasures Book Reviews

About the Author

Tell you about me? Hmm, well there's not much to say. I love hockey and cars and my kids...not in that order of course! Lol! When I'm not writing—which isn't often—I'm usually watching a game or a car show while networking. Going out with my kids is my only downtime. I get to clear my head and forget everything.

As for when and why I first started writing, I guess I thought I'd get extra cookies if I was quiet for awhile—that's how young I was. I used to bring my grandmother barely legible pages filled with tales of evil unicorns. She told me then that I would be a famous author.

I hope one day to prove her right.

For more of my work, please visit: **www.ImNoAngel.com**

PRAISE FOR BIANCA SOMMERLAND'S BOOKS

"I just have to start by saying that this book is not for the faint of heart or the easily offended. Secondly, I have to say to the author, Bianca Sommerland, I give you a standing ovation. Deadly Captive was dark, sinister, erotic, intense, sexy and dangerous. Wow!"

–Karyl
Dark Diva Review of Deadly Captive

"My heart broke a little for Shawna. The entire set up made sense and from a personal note, I've been in the same situation. That's when I completely connected to the story and I was moved to tears."

–BookAddict
The Romance Reviews review of The Trip

100

JUMPERS TO FOLLOW 2006-2007

Forty-fifth year of publication
and a companion volume to
100 Winners: Horses to Follow

Edited by Ashley Rumney

The Listener (1)

Aces Tow ?

Denman 3 hch.

Kauto Star 3 ch.

Nicanor Nov ch (1)

Nickname 2-3 ch (1)

Cork All Star 2 NH (i)

Katchit 2H

Sublimity 2H (1)

Twist Magic 2 CH

~~Detroit City~~ 2H
Bu Te len 2 2 h

First published in 2006 by Raceform Ltd
Compton, Newbury, Berkshire RG20 6NL
Raceform is a wholly-owned subsidiary of Trinity Mirror plc

Copyright © Raceform Ltd 2006

A CIP catalogue record for this book is available from the British Library

ISBN 1-905153-20-1

Designed by Tracey Scarlett
Printed in Great Britain by William Clowes Ltd, Beccles, Suffolk

100 WINNERS
JUMPERS TO FOLLOW
(ages as at 2006)

ACCORDING TO JOHN (IRE) (6 years)

Having shown ability in a couple of Irish point-to-points According To John was off the mark at the first time of asking here, taking a three-mile novices' hurdle at Newcastle in December. He went on to keep his unbeaten record under Rules for new connections in three more starts, kicking off at Ayr In January and following up at Carlisle in March. On his final start at the Scottish National meeting in April he defied a mark of 123 in a novices' handicap hurdle scoring, in most decisive fashion. The Form Book commented: 'He really took the eye in the preliminaries and will be very much one to keep on the right side when sent over fences next term.'
N. G. RICHARDS

ACES FOUR (IRE) (7 years)

Off the mark on his first outing for Ferdy Murphy in a maiden hurdle at Ludlow in February, he made great strides after, following up with a wide-margin success at Ayr the following month. No match for According To John on a return trip to Ayr in April, just six days later he went to Perth for the three-mile Future Champions National Hunt Novices' Hurdle and scored easily. The Form Book reported: 'He stays well and will be interesting over fences next term.' F. MURPHY

ACES OR BETTER (IRE) (5 years)

Margaret Mullins is not the most well-known name in Irish racing, but she can certainly handle a decent horse when she gets her hands on one. Travino is an excellent example of one that has been steered in the right direction by this talented trainer, and now she has another potential top prospect on her hands. A Saddlers' Hall half-brother to Thames, a decent novice hurdler in 2004-2005, Aces or Better is described as a chaser in the making by his astute handler, but judging by the way he slammed his rivals in a bumper at Galway in early August, he can land a few prizes this term before going on to jump fences in the future. MS M. MULLINS

ALL IN THE STARS (IRE) (8 years)

Having started last season off a mark of 122, All In The Stars had improved 19lb in the eyes of the Handicapper when lining up in the Scottish National on his final start of the campaign. He ran no sort of race that day, but there was enough in his previous efforts to suggest he will be a staying chaser to follow this year. Sandwiched in between wins at Fontwell and Wincanton, he ran a fine fifth in the Hennessy and chased home Royal Auclair in a good race at Cheltenham. His connections opted to bypass the Grand National last season, but surely he will be given his chance this time and he could be worth taking a chance on ante-post. Another crack at the Hennessy and other decent handicaps will no doubt be on his agenda as well. D. P. KEANE

AMSTECOS (IRE) (6 years)

Trained in Ulster, Amstecos landed a Down Royal bumper by 15 lengths in his third and final outing of 2005, but it was his victory in a similar race at Perth in May of this year following a five-month break that brought him to prominence. Carrying a penalty for his Down Royal win, he could hardly have been more impressive in beating subsequent scorer Barton Belle by an easy 13 lengths with the rest of the 16-horse field spread out over eastern Scotland. The Presenting gelding looks a fascinating prospect for novice hurdles this season and should win his share of races on whichever side of the Irish Sea he appears. B. R. HAMILTON

ANNIE'S ANSWER (IRE) (6 years)

She may only have won a couple of summer bumpers, but Annie's Answer has created quite an impression and looks a mare to follow. Successful in a three-mile point-to-point in May 2005, she was switched to Rules racing the following month and made a pleasing introduction when fourth to three subsequent winners at Uttoxeter. She was off the track for nearly a year afterwards, but clearly benefited from her break and returned with two facile wins in bumpers, again at Uttoxeter, defying a 7lb penalty in fine style on the latter occasion. A strong, galloping type, she should have plenty of options in mares' races over hurdles this term and looks a likely type for the Mares' Final at Newbury towards the end of the season. MRS V. J. MAKIN

ARRIVE SIR CLIVE (IRE) (5 years)

An impressive winner on his debut between the flags in February 2006, this son of Un Desperado was purchased by Irish trainer Phillip Fenton for 35,000 euros, and immediately aimed at the Gigginstown House point-to-point bumper at Punchestown in April, a race famous for producing many a jumping star in the past. He duly obliged there, landing a gamble in most taking fashion, and instantly confirmed himself a very exciting prospect for the upcoming jumps season. Having handled the likes of Sher Beau and Vic Venturi last term, Fenton knows just what it takes to get the best out of this type of performer and after winning in April he stated: 'I'm not going to get carried away, but he could be a potential superstar. He's an excellent jumper and looks a real chaser in the making.' Arrive Sir Clive's versatility as regards underfoot conditions is certain to be a big advantage, as his point success came on testing ground, and it was good ground when he landed the bumper at Punchestown (indeed his dam won her bumper on a firm surface). Although his long-term future clearly lies as a chaser, it is right to expect an ambitious novice hurdling plan, which could well include Grade One events such as the Royal & SunAlliance Novice Hurdle at Cheltenham come March. P. FENTON.

ASHLEY BROOK (IRE) (8 years)

A high-class novice chaser who began last season as many people's tip for the Champion Chase, mainly due to his attacking style of racing, he only saw the track twice due to a knee injury sustained when a gallant second to Kauto Star in the Tingle Creek. However, reportedly having made a full recovery, the path is clear for him to make a return to the top level. One thing we were able to gauge from his two runs last year was that two miles is probably on the sharp side now and, having already proved himself at up to an extended two miles five furlongs, it may well be that he takes the staying route this term, with the Christmas showpiece, the King George, looking the ideal target for the eight-year-old, who is expected to begin with a spin over hurdles. K. BISHOP

AUX LE BAHNN (IRE) (5 years)

'Held up in touch, led on bit inside final furlong, not extended.' That was the close-up comment given to Aux Le Bahnn after he had hacked up in a Warwick bumper back in December 2005 on his only start under Rules to date. It was by no means a great race, but the form was given some substance with the third home winning his next two starts, and both the fourth and fifth also subsequently scoring. He was not seen out again, but is very much a staying hurdler/chaser in the making, as he showed when landing a three-mile point-to-point in Ireland before switching to his current connections. He should progress through the novice-hurdle ranks this term and, as they say, could be anything. N. T. CHANCE

BALLYTRIM (IRE) (5 years)

Ballytrim looked a serious horse in the making when winning a Thurles bumper by 25 lengths on his debut under Rules, and two subsequent defeats can be excused. His first reversal came in the Champion Bumper at Cheltenham when the mount of leading Flat jockey Johnny Murtagh, and he was basically exposed by much speedier and more nimble types. It was the same story in the big Punchestown bumper. A fine big horse, his future very much lies over obstacles and more of a trip, and he can start fulfilling his potential from this season onwards. W. P. MULLINS

BEWLEYS BERRY (IRE) (8 years)

A smart Irish pointer and a very useful novice hurdler, Bewleys Berry made no mistake on his chasing bow at Wetherby in November, jumping soundly in front and cruising home. Runner-up at Cheltenham the following month and a highly-creditable third in the Grade 1 Feltham Novices' Chase at Sandown on Boxing Day, he was clinging on to third spot when blundering two out in the Royal & SunAlliance Chase at the Cheltenham Festival, eventually passing the post sixth behind Star De Mohaison. The Form Book reckoned: 'He was staying on quite nicely in third when making the mistake and was then hampered by a casualty. But for the trouble encountered here he would surely have been third at the very worst and is a fine staying prospect.' Second-season chasers have a fine record in the big staying handicaps and he looks the ideal sort to land one this winter. J. HOWARD JOHNSON

BLACK JACK KETCHUM (IRE) (7 years)

Black Jack Ketchum was visually the most impressive winner at the 2006 Cheltenham Festival when taking the Brit Insurance Novice Hurdle by nine lengths after toying with his rivals for most of the contest. Then, a few weeks later, he repeated the trick in the Sefton Novices' Hurdle at Aintree, recording his seventh straight victory in the process. In all of those wins he has never seriously been tested and some will argue that we will not see the true level of his ability until he is forced to knuckle down and fight. It does, however, seem far more likely that he is simply an exceptional talent and it should be noted that Jonjo O'Neill rates him the best horse that he has ever trained. With that in mind, the World Hurdle, which looks like the obvious target for this season, should be his for the taking. JONJO O'NEILL

BLEAK HOUSE (IRE) (4 years)

Bleak House is a grand, big half-brother to The Duke's Speech, a bumper and novice hurdle winner for Thomas Tate, who sold this horse for 200,000gns at Doncaster Sales in May. Narrowly denied on his racecourse bow at Doncaster in December, he impressed when taking a bumper at Haydock in April in a quick time by a decisive margin. He looks a fine prospect and impresses as one bumper winner who will progress and prove himself over hurdles – plenty before him have failed and proved very expensive buys. J. HOWARD JOHNSON

BLUE SHARK (FR) (4 years)

Having got off the mark over hurdles in Listed company at Auteuil in November 2005, Blue Shark was subsequently purchased to race in the famous colours of Trevor Hemmings, and sent to trainer Nicky Henderson for a British campaign. His much-awaited debut for Henderson came in the Grade 1 Finale Juvenile Hurdle at Chepstow on Boxing Day, and he immediately went some way to repaying his purchase price by slamming a very useful benchmark in the shape of the Paul Nicholls-trained Turko by eight lengths. Quotes for the Triumph Hurdle and, more interestingly, the Royal & SunAlliance Hurdle were soon to emerge, but unfortunately Blue Shark then suffered injury and was left to sit out the rest of the season on the sidelines. There is little doubt that he rates a potentially high-class chaser for connections, trips in excess of two-and-a-half miles can be expected to suit over fences, and he clearly relishes a testing surface. The Grade 1 Feltham Novices' Chase at Kempton on Boxing Day would appeal as a likely future target. N. J. HENDERSON

CHIARO (FR) (4 years)

Chiaro already had plenty of experience in France before joining Philip Hobbs in the spring of this year, including two victories in Listed hurdles at Auteuil during 2005. He continued his decent level of form over here too, winning novice hurdles at Chepstow and Cheltenham – defeating the

Triumph Hurdle fourth Pace Shot in the second of those – and in between finishing fifth behind Natal in a Grade Two event at the Aintree Festival, when appearing to find the two and a half miles too far and the ground too quick. It is over fences that he is likely to make a name for himself this term, however, and his four-year-old allowance will be very handy in that sphere. P. J. HOBBS

CLOSED SHOP (IRE) (5 years)

Having been a comfortable winner in his point-to-point in January 2006, Closed Shop was subsequently snapped up by the powerful Philip Hobbs operation, and rewarded that faith by winning first time up in a bumper at Bangor in March. He was well backed that day, looked suited by the easy ground, and must rate an exciting prospect for novice hurdles this term. As a former point winner we can be confident that he will stay in excess of two miles, and will no doubt win his fair share, even if not able to live with the cream of this year's novices. P. J. HOBBS

CLOUDY LANE (6 years)

During the course of an eight-race campaign last season, Cloudy Lane ran three times over Haydock's "fixed brush" hurdles and won them all, culminating in the final of the Red Square Vodka Novice Hurdle series in which he defeated a talented field by upwards of six lengths. All three of those wins came over two and a half miles, but he ran well in his only try over three miles and looks very much a stayer in the making. Also, the way he took to those mini fences strongly suggests he will enjoy jumping the proper versions and he should be a real force to be reckoned with in high-class staying novice chases this term. D. McCAIN JNR

CONNA CASTLE (IRE) (7 years)

Having found only the high-class novice Straw Bear too good on his debut in graded company at Aintree last season, Conna Castle rounded off a highly-satisfactory career over hurdles with an easy victory at Killarney in May. In truth, whatever this former point-to-point winner achieved over timber should be considered a bonus, as his real future lies as a chaser and this season will see him sent over regulation fences for the first time. He is versatile as regards trip, which we know thanks to his exploits between the flags, but his trainer Jimmy Mangan has expressed that he may be leaning towards the Arkle Chase at Cheltenham in March, where the stiff two miles should prove much to his liking. One thing is for sure, Conna Castle will be some value when taking on the novices from the bigger stables this term, and he will prove a very hard nut to crack wherever he turns up. J. J. MANGAN

CROFTERS LAD (IRE) (4 years)

Venetia Williams' grey gelding made a favourable impression on his one start in 2006, a junior bumper over a mile and a half at Newbury in January. He finished a clear second to Paul Webber's Pressgang, who went on to frank the form in no uncertain terms next time out, when finishing a head behind Hairy Molly in the Champion Bumper at the Cheltenham Festival. Although the overall form of the race has not worked out that well, the fact that Crofters Lad was able to get to within five lengths of the winner, with a further 16 lengths plus back to the rest of the field, marks this performance out as one of great promise. A slight setback kept him off the track for the remainder of the season, but he is back in training again and is expected to make his comeback in the late autumn. It will be no surprise if he translates his potential to hurdles and he certainly impresses as the type to win races this season. MISS VENETIA WILLIAMS

CUAN NA GRAI (IRE) (5 years)

An easy winner of the Galway Hurdle during the summer, Cuan Na Grai has one of the most progressive profiles over hurdles on offer. Mooted as a lively Champion Hurdle outsider, he has been winning his races easily and gives the impression there is a lot more left in the locker in the way of improvement,

although all of his best form has come on a sound surface and
he has yet to prove himself as good on easy ground. The
Greatwood Hurdle at Cheltenham in November, won by his
stable companion Accordion Etoile in 2004, has been put
forward as an early-season target, after which everyone will
have a better idea of his true potential. Even if he was to fall
just short of that class, he should still be up to winning more
races before the Handicapper gets to grips with him.
P. NOLAN

DARKNESS (7 years)

Recommended by this publication two years ago, it was only
when sent chasing last season that Darkness began to fulfill his
potential, claiming the scalp of Iris's Gift and landing the
Grade One Feltham Chase at Sandown when winning four of
his first five starts over fences. The one defeat in that
sequence came to subsequent Arkle runner-up Monet's
Garden. The second half of the season did not go so well; he
only managed third having jumped poorly in the Royal &
SunAlliance Chase and had probably had enough by the time
he turned up for the Scottish National. He is obviously,
therefore, in danger of going the wrong way, so his supporters
will have to be brave this season, but it is no exaggeration to
suggest he can make a Gold Cup horse if kept sweet. He must
also be kept in mind for races like the Hennessy.
C. R. EGERTON

DENMAN (IRE) (6 years)

A high-class novice hurdler last season, Denman is expected to
perform even better over fences in 2006-2007, and this
former winning Irish pointer will take all the beating in next
year's Royal & SunAlliance Chase if the ground does not come
up too quick at the Festival. In five runs over hurdles last
season he was beaten only once, when Nicanor outbattled
him up the Cheltenham hill in the Royal & SunAlliance Hurdle.
He lost little in defeat that day as the two mile five furlong trip
was probably on the sharp side for him, while a blunder at the

third last did not help his cause. That defeat followed a run of four wins, including an impressive victory in the Grade One Challow Hurdle on New Year's Day, where he beat a quality field by 21 lengths and more. A half-brother to the useful Potter's Bay, this scopey six-year-old should take to fences like a duck to water; expect him to run up another sequence before a tilt at Cheltenham in March. P. F. NICHOLLS

DETROIT CITY (USA) (4 years)

A useful sort on the Flat for Jeremy Noseda, drew many comparisons with his owner Terry Warner's brilliant grey Rooster Booster last season, due to a striking physical resemblance, but he showed himself to be a star in his own right and never looked back following a poor debut effort at Warwick, winning impressively at Newbury and Sandown before coming clear up the Cheltenham hill to land the juvenile showpiece, the Triumph Hurdle. Considering he had a hard race at the Festival, it was quite taking the way in which he destroyed his rivals in the Grade 1 Anniversary Hurdle at Aintree three weeks later, confirming himself as the outstanding four-year-old hurdler. Whether he has the speed to develop into a Champion Hurdler this season is open to debate, and five-year-olds have a particularly poor record in the race, but as a gutsy individual with endless scope, he looks sure to give it a go, with the Fighting Fifth, Christmas, and Bula Hurdles looking likely prep races. P. J. HOBBS

DE VALIRA (IRE) (4 years)

De Valira went into many a notebook when scooting in on his debut in a Leopardstown bumper on yielding ground in March, landing strong market support in the process. Trained by the canny Michael O'Brien, it is most interesting that his dam, Valira, has already produced the high-class hurdler Valiramix (who would have most likely won the 2002 Champion Hurdle but for tragically falling) and it looks like De Valira has inherited his share of the family's ability. His hurdling debut this season, wherever it may be, will rightly be eagerly anticipated and a shot at the Supreme Novices' Hurdle at Cheltenham in March is likely to be at the back of his connections' minds. M. J. P. O'BRIEN

DOM D'ORGEVAL (FR) (6 years)

This French-bred gelding did trainer Nick Williams proud in 2005-2006. Starting off the season running off a mark of 119 after a successful novice hurdle season in modest company, he progressed so well that by the spring he was rated 156 and competing in graded races in France, including their equivalent of the Champion Hurdle, where he made the frame on each occasion and picked up over £45,000 in prizemoney. Earlier in the year he had completed a hat-trick of victories in decent handicaps at around two and a half miles before finishing third in the Coral Cup at the Cheltenham Festival. Capable of handling a sound surface but well suited by soft ground, he looks the sort who could make up into a more than useful novice chaser this season. N. WILLIAMS

DUN DOIRE (IRE) (7 years)

You would be hard pressed to name a more progressive chaser last season than this Tony Martin-trained son of Leading Counsel. His season took off in November 2005 after he gained his first win over fences at Wetherby, in seemingly workmanlike fashion from an official rating of just 79, and culminated in him recording his sixth consecutive success from a mark of 129 in the Grade 2 William Hill Trophy Handicap Chase at the Cheltenham Festival in March. He was given an incredible never-say-die ride by Ruby Walsh that day and marked himself a live candidate for this term's Grand National in the process. He finished up by coming seventh in the Irish Grand National behind Point Barrow the following month, where his come-from-behind tactics were not seen to their best effect on ground he would have found plenty fast enough. This season Dun Doire will no doubt be campaigned with a shot at Aintree in mind, and with an official rating of just 97 over hurdles, he can be expected to be campaigned

13

over the smaller obstacles, and pick up a race or two, before the weights for the world's biggest horse race are published in January. A. J. MARTIN

DZESMIN (POL) (4 years)

Richard Guest, the Grand National winning jockey, has made a colourful if not to say chequered start to his training career. He is not afraid to look far and wide in search of potential talent, as he has already enjoyed success with imports from the southern hemisphere and this one came from Poland. A multiple winner there, including their triple crown, he has shown a fair level of ability in a handful of starts on the Flat here. What he really needs is a test of stamina and some give underfoot, so it will be very disappointing if he cannot make the grade over hurdles here this winter. R. C. GUEST

EQUUS MAXIMUS (IRE) (6 years)

Sent off the 5/2 favourite for the Champion Bumper at the Cheltenham Festival, Equus Maximums could finish only 12th in the 23-strong field, but it will probably pay to forgive him that below-par effort. He has previously looked a fine prospect when bolting up on his debut at Leopardstown, and the fact he was the shortest price of Willie Mullins' four runners in the big one at Cheltenham suggests he is held in very high regard. He can show his true worth when sent over obstacles this season. W. P. MULLINS

FAR FROM TROUBLE (IRE) (7 years)

Having taken time to find his feet as a novice chaser last season, Far From Trouble lined-up for the National Hunt Challenge Chase over four miles at the Cheltenham Festival as a heavily-backed favourite. He was ultimately beaten there by a combination of an over-confident ride by his usually unflappable amateur jockey J. T. McNamara and the stiff finish over that trip proving just beyond him. His next assignment was in the Irish Grand National, where he had just started to make his move from off the pace, travelling ominously well, when falling with six left to jump. However, after a break, he finally came good and rewarded his supporters with an impressive three-length success over course specialist Ansar in the ultra-competitive Galway Plate under a strong ride from his substitute jockey Roger Loughran. There is little doubt that this Christy Roche-trained gelding has a lot more to offer as a chaser, he has improved since racing on faster ground and, with his versatility as regards distance a notable plus, strongly appeals as the type to bag another decent prize or two this term. C. ROCHE

FUNDAMENTALIST (IRE) (8 years)

It is fair to say the career of Fundamentalist has not quite gone as expected following his brilliant performance in the 2004 Royal & SunAlliance Hurdle, but rarely did he have conditions to suit last season and he is the sort who could come back with a vengeance this term. The combination of a slight drop in class and change of jockey should help him this season and he could be the sort to land a valuable handicap chase. N. TWISTON DAVIES

GLASKER MILL (IRE) (6 years)

Glasker Mill looked a progressive novice hurdler in the middle of last winter and, after winning at both Fontwell and Haydock, was asked to take on the very best staying novices around at the Cheltenham and Aintree Festivals. A decent seventh behind Nicanor in the Royal & SunAlliance in the first of those contests, he did not perform so well when stepped up to three miles behind Black Jack Ketchum at Aintree, but had probably had enough by then and was ready for a break. He looks the sort to do very well over fences this season and the way he handled the "fixed brush" hurdles when winning at Haydock was an encouraging sign for when he does eventually go over the larger obstacles. MISS H. C. KNIGHT

GOLDEN CROSS (IRE) (7 years)

In three visits to the Cheltenham Festival, Golden Cross has run exceptionally well each time without actually getting his head in front. On his first attempt in 2003, he finished third of 27

15

behind Spectroscope and Well Chief in the Triumph Hurdle, staying on strongly at the finish. A year later, he ran as well as could be expected, finishing seventh of 14 in the Champion Hurdle behind Hardy Eustace. This year, he was short-headed in the World Hurdle by My Way de Solzen in the best finish of the entire meeting. He suffered an overreach in that race which kept him off the track for the rest of the season but it was not thought to be a serious injury. Michael Halford will no doubt be looking for compensation in the same race again this term and in the build-up to Cheltenham he should be able to find a race or two for his stable star in Ireland. The Hatton's Grace Hurdle and the Boyne Hurdle would appear to be obvious targets. M. HALFORD

GOOD CITIZEN (IRE) (6 years)

Described as a promising pointer when racing between the flags, Good Citizen has run in some very decent novice hurdles under Rules, against a good calibre of rival. Not beaten far by the likes of Noland and Pirate Flagship during 2005, his season came to an abrupt end when falling at Lingfield in January of 2006. The suspicion is that he will make a much better chaser than hurdler and Tom George always seems to produce a nice novice over fences, with the likes of Lord Of Illusion and Idle Talk testament to his skills. T. R. GEORGE

HARMONY BRIG (IRE) (7 years)

A late-developing type, he was finally off the mark in a National Hunt maiden hurdle at Ayr's New Year meeting, grinding out what in the end was a decisive and overdue victory. Following up with a hard-fought win over a reliable yardstick at Newcastle in February, he completed the hat-trick on his handicap bow at Kelso the following month winning by nine lengths from a BHB mark of 122. That booked his place in the line-up for the Grade 2 Mersey Novices' Hurdle at Aintree's Grand National meeting. He found the first two much too strong but held on to a creditable third spot in this two and a half-mile event. Fences now beckon and he should prove very useful over the major obstacles for a stable very much on the up. N. G. RICHARDS

HARRINGAY (6 years)

Just two days after the tragic death of Best Mate in November 2005, the Henrietta Knight stable was back in the headlines for all the wrong reasons when Harringay was deemed a non-trier in a novice hurdle at Towcester. Stiff penalties handed out at the time to the trainer, jockey Timmy Murphy and the mare herself were rescinded later the same month and Harringay went on to show what she was truly capable of, mainly thanks to the application of a tongue tie. She landed her last three outings of the campaign, culminating in the very valuable John Smith's/E.B.F. Mares' Only Final at the Newbury March meeting. She should enjoy further success if kept over hurdles this term, but looks every inch a chaser and as mares-only novice chases are not always that competitive, she could well run up a sequence if connections decide to take that route. MISS H. C. KNIGHT

JUSTIFIED (IRE) (7 years)

One of the best novice chasers to come out of Ireland last season, Justified could take a hand in top contests at around two and a half miles in 2006-2007. He ran in seven races in his novice season, winning four times, and he improved with each outing. The only disappointing run came when he was soundly beaten by Missed That and Arteea at Punchestown in late January, but he was subsequently found to have been suffering from a viral infection. He took his revenge on his next start in the Powers Gold Cup over two and a half miles in April, where he benefited from a tremendous McCoy drive. Here he also displayed a worrying tendency to jump out to his left, which he repeated when he was narrowly beaten by Accordion Etoile over two miles on unsuitably fast ground at Punchestown later than month. His trainer is at a loss to explain the habit, but hopefully it is not a trait which will hold him back in his second season as a chaser. He is expected to

mop up races in his native Ireland before contesting one of
the major events at around two and a half miles in England,
and the Ryanair Chase at the Cheltenham Festival could be the
ideal race for him. E. SHEEHY

KARELLO BAY (5 years)

Being by the Derby-winner Kahyasi out of a full-sister to
Marello, Karello Bay is bred to be decent and she certainly did
not disappoint in three bumper outings last term. Runner-up
at Taunton on her debut, the form of which worked out well,
she went on to win her next two starts, starting with a very
easy success at Southwell and following up in the Listed
Doncaster Bloodstock Sales/E.B.F. Mares' Only Final at
Sandown. The form of that race looks strong with 14 of the
18 runners previous winners, and she scored in the style of a
stayer, very much as her pedigree would suggest. Sure to have
been well schooled, she should enjoy a profitable time of it in
mares-only novice hurdles this season. N. J. HENDERSON

KAUTO STAR (FR) (6 years)

Provided that his confidence has not been dented by a
crashing fall in the 2006 Champion Chase, Kauto Star should
continue to fulfill the promise he has shown in just five runs
over fences during this coming season. He made his
comeback last term in the Haldon Gold Cup, where he was
conceding 4lb to Monkerhostin, who just outstayed him in the
final quarter mile, but he at least demonstrated that he had
recovered from an injury sustained the previous January at the
same course. Next, he ran in the Tingle Creek at Sandown
where he beat Ashley Brook, who was better off based on the
Haldon Gold Cup form, with the minimum of fuss. As a result,
he went into the Queen Mother Champion Chase as favourite
but got no further than the third. Two falls in five starts is
obviously a worry, but otherwise Kauto Star has jumped
soundly and it would be harsh to read too much into his
errors, especially considering his inexperience. Interestingly,
connections are now planning to step him up in trip, which

means that races like the King George could be a possibility, so whether or not he will take on Well Chief or stablemate Azertyuiop over two miles at Cheltenham next spring remains to be seen. P. F. NICHOLLS

KICKS FOR FREE (IRE) (5 years)

Year upon year the Cheltenham Champion Bumper produces future stars and Kicks For Free looks to be another. Winner of two Wincanton bumpers prior to Cheltenham, he ran a blinder in the big one itself to finish two lengths third to Hairy Molly after holding every chance. He looked like gaining compensation in the Aintree champion bumper three weeks later until hanging his chance away inside the last furlong, eventually finishing third behind Pangbourne. Despite winning on soft ground on his debut, it may be that he needs a decent surface to show his best and that the ground at Aintree had gone against him. In any case, the overriding impression from his first season is that he is a very decent prospect who will make a real name for himself in novice hurdles this season and he is sure to be placed to maximum advantage by the champion trainer. P. F. NICHOLLS

KING BARRY (FR) (7 years)

This gentle giant, unbeaten in two starts in points in 2004, was back in action under Rules after injury last term. Off the mark in a maiden chase at Catterick in December, he was a bit in-and-out until finding his form in the spring. A ten-length winner of a two and a half-mile novices' handicap chase at Ayr's Scottish National meeting in April, he came good in a big way at Perth in early June, taking the three-mile Perth Gold Cup by five lengths. Trained by Pauline Robson, uncrowned queen of the northern point-to-point circuit, and her partner, former jump jockey David Parker, the seven-year-old, having proved his stamina for three miles, looks the type to get better and better with time. MISS P. ROBSON

LOCKSMITH (6 years)

A prolific novice chaser, he struggled off higher marks in
handicaps last year, but often acquitted himself with credit
and, now back down to a realistic mark of 140, he looks the
type to plunder a big handicap in David Pipe's first season.
Races such as the Paddy Power Gold Cup, Grand Annual and/or
Racing Post Plate look the likeliest races for the grey. D. E. PIPE

LORD HENRY (IRE) (7 years)

Lord Henry did not return to action last season until February,
due to numerous setbacks, but he quickly showed his quality,
running big races in hotly-contested handicap hurdles at both
the major Festivals and capitalising on the drop in grade to
score impressively at Bangor in May. A fine-looking son of Lord
America, chasing was always going to be his game, and in
what was a decent race for the course, he made his rivals look
second-rate on his chasing debut at Hereford, jumping boldly
and coasting home for a 20-length success. A horse who has a
habit of racing keenly, he has had just eight races and
possesses masses of scope, so expect him to rattle up a
sequence of wins before testing his mettle against some of
the better novices. Although a long way off, he has the look of
a Grand Annual winner and is very much one to get excited
about. P. J. HOBBS

LORD ORIEL (5 years)

This strapping son of Perugino slammed his rivals when
winning on his debut in a Fairyhouse bumper under Nina
Carberry in December 2005, and was not surprisingly
immediately promoted to near the top of the ante-post
betting for the Champion Bumper at Cheltenham. However,
connections opted to miss that event and put him away for a
novice hurdling campaign this winter. Noel Meade rarely goes
a season without handling a few high-class novice hurdlers and
surely Lord Oriel will be right at the top of the pecking order
in that division. He appreciates give underfoot and,
considering his dam was placed at up to two miles six furlongs

over timber, he can be expected to go beyond the minimum trip this term. N. MEADE

MANORSON (IRE) (7 years)

Manorson developed into a decent front-running hurdler last season, beating the useful Dom D'Orgeval in the Stan James Intermediate Hurdle at Newbury's Hennessy meeting and finishing runner-up in a handicap at the Punchestown festival in the spring in what was a light campaign. However, after that connections opted to switch him to fences but things did not go as expected. Odds-on favourite for his chasing debut at Fakenham in May, he came up against the course specialist Cool Roxy, but was travelling well enough when departing soon after halfway. Hopefully none the worse, he can soon make up for that lapse, and could pick up several races on his favoured sound surface before Christmas. O. SHERWOOD

MISSED THAT (7 years)

This Irish-trained gelding carries the Florida Pearl colours of Violet O'Leary, and has taken on the mantle of that now-retired top-class chaser in no uncertain terms. He emulated his former stable companion by winning the Cheltenham Festival bumper in 2005 and like that gelding did not race over hurdles but switched straight to fences. He took really well to chasing, winning four times including the Grade One Durkan Chase and Baileys Arkle Chase, both at Leopardstown. He was held in the Arkle at Cheltenham, but after falling at Fairyhouse over Easter, he bounced back to score at the Punchestown Festival over two miles five. He handles soft ground, but on a faster surface may need further than two miles and may even stay three miles this season. If he does he could well develop into a Gold Cup contender – both Kicking King and War Of Attrition stepped up in trip to take the chasing crown. Whatever path connections choose to take, Missed That can be expected to win more than his share of good races. W. P. MULLINS

MISTER QUASIMODO (6 years)

If ever the cliché 'Whatever he achieved over hurdles is a bonus' should be applied to a horse, then that horse is undoubtedly Mister Quasimodo. This huge son of Dubacilla was always going to make a far better staying chaser, so the fact that he was able to mix it with some of the best novice hurdlers around speaks volumes for his ability. He won twice last season, at Chepstow and Exeter, but his three second places gave even more cause for encouragement. The three horses to beat him in those races were Neptune Collonges, Noland and Senorita Rumbalita, but on all three occasions Mister Quasimodo showed plenty of raw ability before being outgunned by speedier rivals at the business end. If, as expected, he makes the grade over fences, races like the Feltham Novices' Chase will be right up his street, especially if the mud is flying on Boxing Day. C. L. TIZZARD

MODEL SON (IRE) (8 years)

Then in the charge of Heather Dalton, this big type jumped like an old hand when opening his account over fences in smooth style in a beginners' chase at Wetherby in October. Following up in effortless fashion at Carlisle two weeks later, after a change of stables he returned to finish runner-up in the three and a half-mile Grade 3 Red Square Vodka Gold Cup at Haydock in February. Sent to the Cheltenham Festival he lined up for the William Hill Trophy from a BHB mark of 133 and finished a staying-on fourth. The Form Book summed up his long-term prospects thus: 'He has time on his side and it is most unlikely that we have seen the best of him yet. It would be no surprise to see him come back for another crack at this next season and he appeals as a likely 2007 Grand National candidate.' P. C. HASLAM

MONET'S GARDEN (IRE) (8 years)

Just short of Champion Hurdle class over hurdles, this striking grey made an immediate impression on his first try over fences at Ayr in November, jumping impeccably and making

short work of Darkness. Turned out at his local track, Carlisle, in February, he cantered round in his own time scoring by a distance. With just those two public outings under his belt he was allowed to take his chance in the Arkle at the Cheltenham Festival. Never touching a twig in front, he ran out of his skin to finish runner-up, beaten a length and a quarter by Voy Por Ustedes, and five lengths ahead of Foreman in a high-class renewal. On his final start he had to work hard to take the Future Champion Novices' Chase, a Grade 2 event, at Ayr's Scottish National meeting in April. That was his first crack over two and a half miles and this time round three miles will bring out the very best in him. The plan is to go for an intermediate chase at Ayr before a crack at the King George at Kempton on Boxing Day. His front-running style is made to measure for that sharp track and in his second season over fences he looks well capable of holding his own at the highest level.
N. G. RICHARDS

MONEY TRIX (IRE) (6 years)

Narrow winner on his hurdling debut at Kelso in January, this grey son of Old Vic cruised home a wide-margin winner at Ayr the following month, and after completing the hat-trick by ten lengths at Kelso, his sights were raised considerably. Sent to Aintree for the Grade 1 Sefton Novices' Hurdle over three miles, he finished runner-up behind the brilliant and facile winner Black Jack Ketchum, beaten five lengths but ahead of some very useful prospects. The Form Book had this to say: 'Taking a big step up in class, never gave up the fight and showed much improved form to snatch second spot near the line. A grand type, he should make a fine chaser next season.'
N. G. RICHARDS

MORT DE RIRE (FR) (6 years)

Winless in 15 attempts in France, Mort De Rire quickly made a smart impression for his chase-orientated trainer, jumping his rivals into the ground to cause a surprise on his British debut at Leicester, and he followed this with a respectable effort in

defeat when third behind Halcon Genelardais in a Grade 2
event at Wetherby. Although having primarily raced in soft or
heavy ground, the Leicester win came on pretty good ground
and he could be the type to land a decent handicap this year.
He has been allotted a mark of 131 by the Handicapper, and
the Badger Ales Trophy at Wincanton looks a suitable early-
season target, before he takes his chance in races such as the
Hennessy and William Hill Handicap Chase at the Festival.
R. ALNER

MOUNTHENRY (IRE) (6 years)

Mounthenry quickly developed into a smart novice hurdler last
season, winning five races including a brace of Grade 2s,
claiming the scalp of Iktitaf on the first occasion at
Punchestown in February. Arguably his best effort of the
season though came when chasing home Royal & SunAlliance
winner Nicanor in the Grade 1 Champion Novice Hurdle at the
Punchestown Festival in April, making the Meade-trained
runner pull out all the stops. Tough and progressive, this
versatile sort with regards to ground can develop into a
leading novice chaser this season and, effective from two to
two and a half miles, he shapes as though he will get further.
C. BYRNES

MR NOSIE (IRE) (5 years)

Mr Nosie comes into this season as one of the most promising
novice chasers around. Impressive winner of his bumper in
May of last year, he quickly developed into a high-class
hurdler, scooting up at Cork before taking the Grade 2 Future
Champions Novice Hurdle at Leopardstown over Christmas.
Confirming himself a top prospect when taking the Grade 1
Deloitte Novices' Hurdle back at Leopardstown in February, he
went into the Royal & SunAlliance Hurdle as a leading
contender, but found things happening a bit too quickly at
the business end, having to settle for a keeping-on fourth
behind speedier stable companion Nicanor. Born to be a
chaser, he looks a top prospect and, although Nicanor will go

in search of the same sort of races this season, he looks to have the greater scope, especially for fences. Races such as the Grade 1 Dr P. J. Moriarty Chase at Leopardstown in February are likely to be taken in en route to a potential crack at the Royal & SunAlliance Chase. N. MEADE

MR POINTMENT (IRE) (7 years)

Darkness did the stable proud over fences last season and, although it is probably asking too much to have another high-class chaser on his hands two years in a row, Charlie Egerton definitely has a chance of doing so with Mr Pointment. Achieving a rating higher than Darkness did over hurdles, he finished his season with a career-best effort behind Nicanor in the Royal & SunAlliance Hurdle at Cheltenham in March, after an up and down season. A half-brother to the very useful chaser Ground Ball, with plenty of size and scope for improvement still, he should make his mark over fences in good company. C. R. EGERTON

MY WAY DE SOLZEN (FR) (6 years)

My Way De Solzen failed to cut it at two miles as a novice and the step up to staying distances last year could not have worked better. A real mud-lover, he showed he had improved over the summer when blitzing his rivals in the Grade 1 Long Walk Hurdle at Chepstow, and followed this with a comfy success back in trip in Fontwell's National Spirit Hurdle. Cheltenham followed and despite the ground not being ideal, he outbattled Golden Cross up the hill to claim the World Hurdle, providing his brilliant dual-purpose trainer with a deserved first success in one of the four Cheltenham majors. Below his best when second under faster conditions at Aintree, he comes into this season as a top chasing prospect and it is easy to see him racking up a string of wins, including races such as the Grade 1 Feltham Chase on Boxing Day, before going on to the Royal & SunAlliance Chase at the Festival. A. KING

NEPTUNE COLLONGES (FR) (5 years)

Already a graded winner over fences in France at the age of
four, Neptune Collonges joined Paul Nicholls last season and
made a big impression over hurdles. From seven starts for the
stable he won four races, each time on testing ground, so it
seems that plenty of cut is going to be a prerequisite when he
turns back his attention to fences this season. He lost little in
his three defeats, twice succumbing to the classy Black Jack
Ketchum and once to My Way de Solzen, who subsequently
went on to take the World Hurdle at Cheltenham. Paul
Nicholls has said that Neptune Collonges was acquired on
behalf of owner John Hales as a Gold Cup horse, and from
what we have seen so far over hurdles, there is no doubt that
he has the ability to take a very high rank over fences.
Unfortunately, he is not eligible for novice chases because of
his win in France, but connections will instead pitch him
straight into the deep end. He could run in races like the
Hennessy Gold Cup this season where he could make a big
impact, especially if the ground is soft. P. F. NICHOLLS

NEWMILL (IRE) (8 years)

Newmill has always been a useful performer, he won a
bumper on his debut and beat the top-class mare Mariah
Rollins in the Grade One Royal Bond Hurdle, one of four wins
in his novice season. He won a Grade Two over two miles five
as a novice chaser, but looked held at the highest level.
However, a spell back over hurdles in late 2005, taking on
Brave Inca no less, seemed to invigorate him, and when
returned to fences he was a revelation. He started off by
winning the two and a half-mile Kinloch Brae Chase under a
waiting ride, but then switched to front running, jumping with
panache to cause a surprise in a slightly sub-standard renewal
of the Queen Mother Champion Chase at Cheltenham. He
proved that was no fluke by taking the Kerrygold Champion
Chase at Punchestown, beating the Festival runner-up Fota
Island even further than he had at Cheltenham. Effective on
anything from good to heavy, with Moscow Flyer retired and

Azertyuiop and Well Chief due to come back from injury, he is the one they all have to beat in the two-mile division this season. J. J. MURPHY

NICANOR (FR) (5 years)

Everything about this horse shouts class but things did not go totally to plan until the latter stages of last season. He started his hurdling career with a fluent success, but failed to complete next time before returning to the track with a slightly unlucky-looking second in a Grade 1 race. Failing at odds of 1/6 in ordinary novice company on his next run, he finally announced himself as a live challenger for the staying races with an awesome display in the Golden Cygnet Hurdle at Leopardstown in January. Things had finally slotted into place, and he landed the Royal & SunAlliance Hurdle with authority on his next start before taking a Grade 1 at the Punchestown festival. A robust sort, he has the size to do well over fences, but considering he travels so well during his races, it is far from certain that he will definitely appreciate staying trips over fences, so a race such as the Dr P.J. Moriarty Chase at Leopardstown could be his best chance of Grade 1 glory. N. MEADE

NICKNAME (FR) (7 years)

Landing a huge gamble on his Irish debut after a very long break, Nickname went on to prove that success no fluke by running some really solid races in the best company in Ireland, including a Grade 2 victory on his second start. His only really disappointing effort last season was when pulled up in the Grade 1 Baileys Arkle Novice Chase, but he had a valid excuse and continued to perform with credit afterwards outside novice company. Versatile as regards to trip, his exciting style of racing makes him a horse the racing public will warm to and he looks sure to hit the target in some good races, especially if finding his much preferred easy ground. M. BRASSIL

NOBLE REQUEST (FR) (5 years)

After beginning to look exposed on a mark of 120 in the early part of last season, everything fell into place from February onwards for Noble Request, and he starts the new season on a rating of 159. His successful run included a fine second place in the County Hurdle to the progressive Desert Quest, and another solid second in the John Smith's Extra Smooth Handicap Hurdle at Aintree to stablemate Wellbeing, where he gave the winner 17lb. Finally, he recorded two victories over Faasel at Ayr and Sandown in the last week of the season, giving that rival 4lb and a length and a half beating on the second occasion. His lofty rating means that handicaps are virtually out of the question, but he is fully expected to continue climbing up the class ladder and establish himself as one of this country's leading hurdlers in 2006-2007. Presumably, his main target this season will be the Champion Hurdle and he could well emerge as the main British hope to wrest the crown away from the Irish. P. J. HOBBS

NOLAND (5 Years)

It is fair to say one could not have envisaged Festival glory for Noland when he ran a very modest race at Wincanton on his hurdling debut in October of 2005. However, given a break after that initial disappointment, he returned to the track at Cheltenham in December, thrashing some well-regarded rivals including Buena Vista and De Soto. Things progressed well from that point as he then went on to win an admittedly weak Tolworth Hurdle before landing a competitive Listed Hurdle at Exeter off a big weight. He emerged as the best of the English contingent going into the Supreme Novices' Hurdle at the Festival, and scored despite looking a less-than-likely winner rounding the home bend. Connections declared straight after the race that he would go straight over fences, and was being aimed for this coming season's Arkle Chase, with one of the owners admitting he had already backed the horse for the race. As long as his jumping holds up over the bigger obstacles, it will take a smart one to lower his colours in novice chases. P. F. NICHOLLS

OODACHEE (7 years)

A fast-ground winner on the Flat in Ireland, proved well suited by a step up in trip over hurdles in 2005-2006. Although he failed to win, he was in the frame on all five starts including two Listed races, one the Pertemps Final at the Cheltenham Festival. Switched to fences in May, he picked up two chases in five days, including a Grade Three. In the past he has wanted decent ground, although he was able to handle a yielding surface when recording the second of those two victories. He will qualify for novice chases until next spring, and having been placed on all three previous visits to Cheltenham, proving he handles the track, could be aimed at races there in the autumn and at the Festival, when ground conditions are likely to be in his favour. C. F. SWAN

OSSMOSES (IRE) (6 years)

An out-and-out stayer, this robust grey is getting better and better with age. A winner by a whisker over three miles at Kelso in December, he excelled himself in the three and a half-mile Red Square Vodka Gold Cup at Haydock in February, sprinting clear on the run-in to score by 15 lengths. Sent to Uttoxeter the following month for the highly competitive Midlands Grand National, he finished runner-up beaten four lengths conceding the Irish-trained winner 16lb, and clear of the other five who completed the extended four-mile trip in the glue-pot conditions. The apple of his six-horse Darlington permit holder's eye, he is still relatively young by staying chaser standards and stamina tests like the Eider Chase at Newcastle look perfect targets for him this time, with the Scottish National on the agenda in the spring. D. M. FORSTER

PANGBOURNE (FR) (5 years)

Pangbourne did not have the look of a high-class bumper horse when trailing in 13th of 17 on his racecourse debut at Warwick, but the application of blinkers and an eyeshield transformed the gelding, and following an improved second behind the highly-regarded Pepporoni Pete at Wincanton, he recorded back-to-back wins at Huntingdon and Folkestone, each time galloping his rivals into submission. The blinkers were replaced by a visor for the Cheltenham bumper, but he was no quite so effective and could only finish ninth. However, he showed what he is made of with the blinkers reapplied, when putting up a performance of immense toughness to win at Aintree, showing guts to get back up in a blanket finish. Staying novice hurdles are likely to be where he is seen to best effect this season, and it is not hard to see him racking up a sequence of wins before taking his chance in something like the Royal & SunAlliance Novices' Hurdle. He is most definitely one to be with in 2006-2007. A. KING

PEPPORONI PETE (IRE) (5 years)

Always held in high regard by his connections, Pepporoni Pete did not progress as one might have hoped after winning on his debut at Wincanton, finishing only third at Newbury before running down the field in the Aintree bumper, but he is surely going to come into his own when sent over hurdles, and then fences. He is likely to be kept to the smaller obstacles this term, and should take high rank amongst the novices.
P. F. NICHOLLS

PERCE ROCK (IRE) (4 years)

A mightily-impressive winner of a Leopardstown bumper on his debut and subsequently bought by J. P. McManus, Perce Rock then went on to run an excellent fourth in the Champion Bumper at the Cheltenham Festival under Tony McCoy. He would have found the ground plenty fast enough that day, and was denied a clear run at a crucial stage, so deserves extra credit. Considering he is bred for the Flat, he can be expected to be campaigned at around two miles to begin with, and his Irish trainer Tommy Stack will no doubt be hoping this four-year-old will be able to make his mark at the top level in novice hurdles this term. Soft ground would enhance his chances wherever he may turn up. T. STACK

PRESSGANG (4 years)

A half-brother to that very useful dual-purpose performer Big Moment, Pressgang never made it on to the track when owned by Khalid Abdulla and changed hands for 16,000gns before moving to Paul Webber's yard. He eventually made his debut in a 12-furlong "junior" bumper at Newbury last January and, having been well backed, he could hardly have been more impressive in gaining a five-length victory. However, he surpassed even that performance when beaten just a head by Hairy Molly in the Champion Festival Bumper at Cheltenham, a fantastic effort for a four-year-old with just one previous outing under his belt. The Cheltenham Bumper has a rich history of producing some of the best jumping performers around and there is every possibility that he will have improved again since last seen. A lucrative season in novice hurdles looks virtually assured. P. R. WEBBER

PRINCE OF SLANE (7 years)

Having had problems with his jumping when first tried over fences, it took him 16 starts to get off the mark, taking the Durham National at Sedgefield in May 2005 when officially rated just 90. Rated 102 when returning to winning ways at Catterick in January, on a return visit to that track two weeks later and 6lb higher, he excelled himself taking the three mile six furlong North Yorkshire Grand National in most decisive fashion. From a stable making great strides both on the Flat and over jumps, he looks a likely candidate to land more better-class staying chases this time round. The ground is important with him, as he does not like it on the soft side, so connections will have to pick and choose his targets.
G. A. SWINBANK

PRIZE DRAW (3 years)

Alan Swinbank knows when he has got a good horse on his hands and, although his methods may be a little unorthodox, he is a trainer to respect. He trained both subsequent Group 1 winner Collier Hill and Listed scorer Alfie Flits to win bumpers (both first-time out) before they turned their attention to the Flat, and he could have another gem in his care. 'Keep an eye on Prize Draw. He's ex-Darley and he's extra, extra special. He'll go down the bumper route,' Swinbank has been quoted as saying. G. A. SWINBANK

RASHARROW (IRE) (7 years)

A smart bumper performer, he was a 1/4 shot when easily making a winning bow over hurdles at Kelso in October. A similar performance at Ayr the following month led to him being allowed to take his chance in the Listed Agfa UK Hurdle at Sandown in February but things did not go his way that day and he managed only fifth behind much more battle-hardened and experienced horses. Run off his feet, he still managed a respectable ninth in the Supreme Novices' Hurdle at the Cheltenham Festival. Sent to Perth in April, he ended the season with a workmanlike victory in a run-of-the-mill novices' event. That will have restored his confidence and The Form Book forecast: 'he will be an interesting recruit if switching to the chasing ranks next season.' L. LUNGO

REVEILLEZ (7 years)

Having taken time to find his feet as a novice chaser last season, Reveillez belatedly came good when putting in a superb round of jumping to land the Jewson Novices' Handicap Chase at Cheltenham Festival in March for trainer James Fanshawe from an official rating of 133. He acts on a soft surface, but is probably at his best on good ground, and is fully effective at up to 2m 5f. Considering his liking for Cheltenham, he appeals as a likely sort for the Paddy Power Gold Cup at the Open meeting in November and, with time still very much on his side, should have plenty more decent prizes within his compass. He also has the option of reverting to hurdling and might even stay three miles this season.
J. R. FANSHAWE

RHACOPHORUS (5 years)

Related to the useful stayer Mountain Lodge by the St Leger winner Classic Cliché, Rhacophorus made a good start to her career in 2005-2006. She was a 100/1 chance when making her debut at Wincanton on Boxing Day, but ran on well to finish sixth of 17 behind Pepporoni Pete and the subsequent Aintree bumper winner Pangbourne. With that race under her belt she was much sharper, and took a mares-only bumper at Taunton in ready fashion from the subsequent dual winner Karello Bay. Connections gave her an 11-week break before her final outing of the season, and she returned to secure her biggest win, in the Listed mares-only bumper at Aintree's Grand National meeting. Her jumping has to be taken on trust, but she clearly possesses a good engine and looks the type to run up a sequence in novice hurdles, especially if kept to races against her own sex. C. DOWN

RING BACK (IRE) (5 years)

Ring Back raced three times in bumpers last term, showing plenty of promise on her Towcester debut before winning nicely at Warwick in her second outing, but her best performance came in her final appearance. Starting at odds of 50-1, she belied her position in the market by finishing third of 22 behind the smart pair Rhacophorus and Wyldello in the Listed mares-only bumper at the Aintree Festival. Out of a mare that won a bumper and a hurdle, she is a half-sister to that very smart chaser Feels Like Gold and it will be a surprise if she does not enjoy success in mares-only novice hurdles this season, especially when faced with a greater test of stamina. B. I. CASE

ROLL ALONG (IRE) (6 years)

This son of a half-sister to Nahthen Lad has had an abbreviated career so far, but has proved himself a gelding with plenty of ability. He made his debut in a four-horse bumper at Fontwell in October 2004 when beating the more experienced Yes Sir in clever fashion. His victim that day had previously run the unbeaten subsequent champion staying novice hurdler Black

Jack Ketchum to a neck, and has since won numerous times over hurdles and fences. Roll Along was not seen for a year following that race, but returned to take an ordinary Fakenham bumper in very easy fashion. He then stepped up in grade to take a Listed bumper at Warwick from three previous winners. Roll Along then suffered a minor setback that resulted in him missing the remainder of the season, and although the form of the Warwick contest has not worked out at all well, he still looks a horse of some potential. He can still run in bumpers in the short term, but should be switching to hurdles this season and looks an exciting prospect.

C. LLEWELLYN

ROMAN ARK (8 years)

Runner-up behind potentially smart but subsequently sidelined Villon at Uttoxeter in December on just his second start over fences, this grand type opened his account over the major obstacles in a beginners' chase at Ayr's New Year meeting. Sent to Cheltenham for the Festival, he showed his true potential staying on in determined fashion to finish fourth in the two miles five furlong Racing Post Plate. On his final start at Ayr's Scottish National meeting in April he finished runner-up in a two-mile handicap chase. An extra half-mile and some give underfoot suits him a lot better and he looks sure to add to his record in his second season over fences.

J. M. JEFFERSON

ROSS RIVER (10 years)

This talented son of Over The River was an expensive failure when brought down in the Racing Post Plate at the Cheltenham Festival in March, but he went some way to making amends when winning under a sublime ride from jockey Davy Russell on his return to hurdling at the Fairyhouse Easter meeting next time out. He was then again very well backed back over fences at Punchestown, finding only the talented Euro Leader too good on his final outing last term. They do not come any more canny than his trainer Tony

Martin, who has greatly improved this grey gelding since he was given to him by prominent Irish owner Seamus Ross, and with an official rating of 133 over fences to start his season off with, a crack at a Grand National at Aintree in April will undoubtedly be at the back of their minds. A campaign over hurdles, before the weights for the big event are announced in January, could well be on his agenda in order to preserve that mark, and he is certainly one to follow this term.
A. J. MARTIN

SCARVAGH DIAMOND (IRE) (5 years)

A springer in the market, this mare landed quite a gamble for her small Kelso-based stable on her racecourse debut in a bumper at Newcastle in January. Sent to Sandown in March for the final of a mares-only bumper series, she excelled herself despite her lack of experience, finishing a good fifth of the 18 runners, beaten only about six lengths in the end. A half-sister to the staying chaser Toulouse-Lautrec, two miles over hurdles will suit her fine and she looks sure to make her mark for her sporting syndicate. MRS R. L. ELLIOTT

SCRIBANO EILE (IRE) (5 years)

Scribano Eile only had the one run under Rules last year, but the form of his success in a Wetherby bumper worked out very well indeed. He only had half a length to spare, but the runner-up that day, Tidal Bay, went down by just a neck in the Aintree bumper on his only other start of the season, and the third home boosted the form when winning at Southwell. Previously the winner of a three-mile point-to-point in Ireland, his future very much lies over obstacles and he looks one to have on your side. N. A. TWISTON DAVIES

SKY'S THE LIMIT (FR) (5 years)

A highly-progressive hurdler last year, Sky's The Limit became the first five-year-old to land the valuable Grade 3 Coral Cup Handicap at the Cheltenham Festival for an age, when hacking up by four lengths from Strangely Brown under the burden of top weight. He was then put in his place behind the high-class mare Asian Maze on his debut in Grade 1 company in the Aintree Hurdle next time, before signing off with a well below-par effort behind that rival again at the Punchestown Festival when going over three miles for the first time. There is little doubt that trainer Edward O'Grady had him primed for Cheltenham last season and his next two efforts can simply be excused. This year Sky's The Limit is likely to be sent over fences, and can be expected to take high rank among the cream of the Irish novice chasers, with three miles expected to be more within his compass in that sphere. His versatility regarding underfoot conditions should prove a notable advantage and he really is a most exciting chase prospect for the coming season. E. J. O'GRADY

SNAKEBITE (IRE) (6 years)

Carl Llewellyn took over the reins at Weathercock House from Mark Pitman in April of this year and as a result he has inherited a number of useful prospects for the season ahead, most of which are owned by his employer, Malcolm Denmark. Among them is Snakebite, who performed well in bumpers and novice hurdles, but it is expected that he will go on to even better things over fences. Last season, the grey ran four times over hurdles, winning only once, but acquitting himself well on each occasion. His main weakness over hurdles was the lack of a finishing kick, but this will be far less significant in novice chases over extreme distances, particularly if he gets his favoured soft ground. He has reportedly strengthened up a great deal since his last run in March, and he looks an exciting prospect for novice chases. The long-term target for this season is the Royal & SunAlliance Chase at Cheltenham and hopefully he can pick up a few races along the way.
C. LLEWELLYN

STAR DE MOHAISON (FR) (5 years)

From the outset, Star De Mohaison looked a natural over fences. He was a fairly useful sort over hurdles but fences were always likely to bring the best out in him, although it is probably fair to say connections could not have envisaged such a meteoric rise to the top for their charge. He started off well, landing a fair race at Aintree in style, before a couple of slightly disappointing efforts behind The Listener in the middle of the season. He got back into the winning habit with victory in a soft race at Fontwell before going on to the Cheltenham and Aintree Festivals, winning at both tracks in the best company for novices. Things will be more difficult this year without any age allowances, but the King George in December looks absolutely tailor-made for him and would be the obvious target before the turn of the year, before Cheltenham and Aintree options are considered. P. F. NICHOLLS

STRANGELY BROWN (IRE) (5 years)

A good juvenile hurdler in 2004-2005, he rewarded connections' enterprise last summer by winning a valuable Grade One at Auteuil in June over just short of two and a half miles. He had a decent time afterwards, which is not always the case for useful juveniles in their second season, finishing second in the Coral Cup at the Cheltenham Festival before taking a similar contest at Aintree. Although another trip to France proved abortive, he looks capable of winning good staying handicaps this season, especially as he is already proven at three miles. E. McNAMARA

STRAW BEAR (USA) (5 years)

Formerly a useful handicapper on the Flat for Sir Mark Prescott, Straw Bear overcame a 16-month absence to make a very impressive winning hurdling debut from some very decent rivals at Leicester back in January. He then went on to show high-class form, including in some of the season's top novice hurdles, winning a small race at Folkestone and the Grade Two novice hurdle at the Aintree Festival in very impressive style, and losing nothing in defeat behind Noland in the Supreme Novices' at Cheltenham and Iktitaf in the Champion Novice Hurdle at Punchestown. He looks sure to prove one of the main players for the home team hoping to keep the formidable Irish challenge at bay in this season's Champion Hurdle, but whatever happens at the Festival he should at least pick up some decent prizes along the way. N. J. GIFFORD

SWEET WAKE (GER) (5 years)

Sweet Wake could manage only fifth when favourite for the Supreme Novices' Hurdle at Cheltenham, and was again below form on his final start of the season at Punchestown, but he had looked a serious horse when winning his first two starts over hurdles and should not be written off just yet. Previously a smart performer on the Flat in Germany, he looked a natural for the jumping game in his early starts and his connections will no doubt be keen to set the record straight. N. MEADE

TAMARINBLEU (FR) (6 years)

A smart hurdler on his day, Tamarinbleu looked one of last season's more interesting chasing acquisitions, and after making the highly-touted Accordion Etoile fight for his life on his chasing debut at Cheltenham's Paddy Power meeting, it was clear he had a bright future at the game. Things did not go to plan in heavy ground at Uttoxeter next time, but got back on track with an easy win at Ludlow in January and was then put away for the Arkle. However, he was unable to dominate in what was one of the best renewals in recent years and found himself outpaced from some way out. Handed a mark of 147, a step up in trip looks set to be the making of him this season and, as he is a horse who has always gone best fresh, the Paddy Power Gold Cup looks the ideal early-season target, with something like the Racing Post Plate at the Festival also likely to be on the agenda. D. E. PIPE

TARANIS (FR) (5 years)

The Nicholls stable houses any amount of chasing talent, and this incumbent could be one of the slightly darker ones, although he has proved he is very capable over fences. Some comparisons can be drawn between him and the stable's Strong Flow, who showed plenty of ability over fences at a young age. It appears as though he is being brought along very quietly, which should bring long-term benefits, and it would not be a surprise to see him make up into a genuine Hennessy Cognac Gold Cup contender by November. His official mark is high enough for that race already, so a spin over hurdles prior to the race may not be a complete surprise. Even if he does not make the big Newbury contest, there will be plenty of nice races to be won with him during the coming season. P. F. NICHOLLS

THE COOL GUY (IRE) (6 years)

A useful performer in 2004-2005, winning the Aintree champion bumper, he was immediately stepped up in trip on his switch to hurdling. Trotting up in a Uttoxeter novice hurdle on his seasonal debut, he then cruised home from the subsequent triple winner Harmony Brig at Haydock, with another five future winners well beaten. Taking his chance in the Grade One Challow Hurdle at Cheltenham's January meeting, he was taken on for the lead by the very useful Denman and his jumping suffered. He was eventually beaten a long way by the winner, but held on for second in what looked a strong contest. A subsequent setback meant he did not re-appear but, from a yard that does well with its novice chasers, the switch to fences looks the obvious route for him this season. The Royal & SunAlliance Chase is likely to be on the agenda if all goes well. N. TWISTON DAVIES

THE DUKE'S SPEECH (IRE) (5 years)

A useful bumper horse, this grand, big, chasing type steps over his hurdles rather than jumps them – he may give fences more respect. Off the mark over hurdles at the third attempt with a wide-margin success at Ayr's New Year meeting, on ground much softer than he truly cares for he made hard work of following up at Catterick in March. Sent to Aintree's Grand National meeting for the two-mile Grade 2 Top Novices'

Hurdle, he finished a respectable third behind Straw Bear
defying his 100/1 odds. Appreciating the much sounder
surface, he stayed on in dogged fashion up the home straight
to snatch third spot ahead of some very useful yardsticks. His
trainer will waste no time switching him to fences, and two
miles and decent ground should see him in the best light.
Incidentally his year-younger half-brother Bleak House, the
winner of a bumper at Haydock in April, was allowed to go for
a handy 200,000gns at Doncaster Sales in May. T. P. TATE

THE LISTENER (IRE) (7 years)
The Listener quickly developed into one of the leading staying
novice chasers around last season, hammering subsequent
Royal & SunAlliance Chase winner Star De Mohaison at Exeter
in December before winning a brace of Grade 2s at Windsor
and Cheltenham, again conquering his Exeter victim. However
his jumping, which had been simply immaculate on his first
three starts, let him down at Lingfield when taking a heavy fall
and he may still have been feeling the effects of that when
coming down two out behind Star De Mohaison at
Cheltenham. It is probably safe to forget the latter effort and
he starts the season on a mark of 150, so races such as the
Badger Ales Chase at Wincanton and the Hennessy looked
ideal early-season targets for the bold-jumping grey. R. ALNER

THE MARKET MAN (NZ) (6 years)
A winner on the Flat in his native New Zealand at the age of
three, The Market Man was bought for owner Sir Robert
Ogden as a chasing prospect in 2004, but he has had two
productive seasons over hurdles already for Nicky Henderson.
Having won twice in his novice season, he started last term on
a mark of 125 but two convincing victories in handicap
company saw him rise rapidly through the ranks. He faced his
stiffest test in the Relkeel Hurdle in December, but he
enhanced his reputation further despite narrowly losing out to
the equally progressive Mighty Man on the day. His next target
was the World Hurdle at Cheltenham, for which he was well

backed, but a bit of warmth in a tendon a few days before the race put paid to those plans. Instead, he was put away with a novice chasing campaign in mind for this season. He rates an exciting prospect in this sphere, although he must have good ground, which could restrict his options to some extent.
N. J. HENDERSON

THE PIOUS PRINCE (IRE) (5 years)

From the same family as the dual Whitbread Gold Cup winner Topsham Bay, this one made an immediate impact on his racecourse bow at Ayr in February, making light of the testing underfoot conditions and skipping home an effortless 13-length winner of a 16-runner bumper. Ridden there by Tony Dobbin, his trainer has now signed up Keith Mercer to be his stable jockey this time and together they look sure to enjoy further success. The temptation must be to keep him to bumpers until the New Year. L. LUNGO

TIDAL BAY (IRE) (5 years)

Unluckily beaten half a length on his debut in a bumper at Wetherby in March, this strong, chasing type showed his outstanding potential when failing by a neck in the champion bumper at Aintree's Grand National meeting. As on his debut he again looked a luckless loser. The Form Book commented: 'The chances are that under stronger handling he would have gone one place better, but he still ran a big race for a once-raced horse and looks a really decent prospect.' Those two runs were sufficient for him to make an incredible 300,000gns when coming under the hammer at Doncaster Sales in May. Big-spender Graham Wylie will be looking at him as a long-term chasing prospect, but in the meantime he seems sure to make a good-class hurdler. J. HOWARD JOHNSON

TIGER CRY (IRE) (8 years)

This Irish chaser had an abortive attempt at chasing in late 2004, but did much better last season after a spell back over

hurdles. He only won once, but picked up plenty of place
money, notably when runner-up in the Grand Annual at the
Cheltenham Festival, and was unlucky to come down at the
last with the race at his mercy at Punchestown in April. A
horse well suited by two miles and good ground, he will start
the new season on a mark in the high-130s, and that should
enable him to pick up a good race or two in the autumn or
spring. A. L. T. MOORE

TRABOLGAN (IRE) (8 years)

After winning the 2005 Royal & SunAlliance Chase at
Cheltenham, Trabolgan only appeared once last season, but
this one performance marked him out as one of the best
staying chasers in this country. He carried 11st 12lb in the
Hennessy Gold Cup at Newbury, conceding weight to the
three horses that he had beaten in the Royal & SunAlliance,
and he beat them all again convincingly, becoming the first
horse since 1984 to win the Hennessy off top weight. The
plan after this win was to go to the Cheltenham Gold Cup via
the King George but sadly his season was curtailed by an injury
to his near-fore tendon sustained during the Hennessy.
Connections were at pains to point out that it was not a
serious setback, and no surgery was carried out on the horse,
so it is hoped that he can return as good as ever this season.
On a line through L'Ami, who was runner-up in the Hennessy
and beaten by about ten lengths in the Gold Cup, Trabolgan
would have gone very close indeed at Cheltenham. Provided
he has not lost any of his raw ability, he should be able to play
a prominent role this season, although he is unlikely to
reappear before Christmas. N. J. HENDERSON

TRAVINO (IRE) (7 years)

There is little doubt that fences are exactly what Travino
needs. Everything he has achieved over hurdles must be
considered a massive bonus, and what a bonus it proved to
be, with the highlight a Grade 1 at Navan, beating subsequent
Royal & SunAlliance Hurdle winner Nicanor in the process,

giving him weight. He was rarely embarrassed afterwards in the face of some very stiff tasks, but his size always suggested that fences are going to see him to best advantage and, with a solid background in Irish points behind him, he should win his fair share of staying novice chases in Ireland. Soft ground is very much needed, which could limit his spring targets, but there are plenty of good prizes to be won in his homeland, where the ground is usually like a gluepot during the winter. With a slice of luck, and conditions to suit, Travino could go to the very top over fences. MS M. MULLINS

TURPIN GREEN (IRE) (6 years)

A very useful and highly-progressive hurdler, Turpin Green had to work hard to make a winning bow over fences at Carlisle in November, pushed hard all the way up the final hill by another good prospect in Rebel Rhythm. That dour struggle took a lot more out of him than thought at the time and, pulled out again less than two weeks later, he finished a jaded odds-on third at Kelso. Given two months off, he returned in the Grade 1 Scilly Isles Chase at Sandown. He was a couple of lengths up and with the race in the bag when for some reason or other he almost came to a stop at the final fence and in the end went under by a neck to Napolitain. Sent to the Cheltenham Festival for the Jewson Novices' Handicap Chase, he made too many jumping errors and weakened to finish a well-beaten fifth. However, at Aintree's Grand National meeting he showed just what he is capable of finishing runner-up behind the Royal & SunAlliance Chase winner Star De Mohaison and ahead of Copsale Lad, with the remainder well beaten off. The much flatter track at Aintree, where he won twice over hurdles, seemed to suit him a lot better than the ups and downs at Cheltenham. Second-season chasers have a fine record in the better-class handicaps and this one looks ideal material this time round for sporting owner Trevor Hemmings.
N. G. RICHARDS

TYSON (SAF) (6 years)

If David Junior was to line up for a novice hurdle, would you fancy him to win it? Well if you think that top-class horse would win over timber, how about a horse that finished only 12 lengths behind him in the 2006 Group 1 Dubai Duty Free? Not a great deal is known about Tyson in Britain, or how he might cope with some easy ground, but the bits we do know are all pretty good. He was chasing a hat-trick in Dubai in March when just coming up short in Group 2 company, but with an approximate rating of 113, he would be one of the best Flat horses to go jumping for some time. It is most interesting to note that previous trainer Mike De Kock has retained a share in the horse, and whilst it is far from certain he will take to the winter game, if he does, the sky could be the limit for him. MISS VENETIA WILLIAMS

UNGARO (FR) (7 years)

Off the mark over hurdles at the fifth attempt at Huntingdon in November, this most likeable type made steady progress after. Defying a penalty for that success in handicap company at Sedgefield a week later, he was pipped back in novice company under a double penalty at Newcastle later the same month. Back to winning ways defying a BHB mark of 128 in a two mile six furlong Grade 3 Handicap Hurdle at Sandown in February, he finished a staying-on sixth in the Coral Cup at Cheltenham. Biting off more than he could chew, he managed only a well-beaten fifth behind top-class novice Black Jack Ketchum and Money Trix in the Sefton Novices' Hurdle at Aintree. In time three miles will bring out the very best in him, but he has the speed and the ability to make his mark in novice chases this time over shorter. A tough, rugged type, he should make an even better chaser than he was a hurdler. K. G. REVELEY

VIC VENTURI (IRE) (6 years)

Vic Venturi held his form well last season and progressed into a very useful novice hurdler, winning three of his six starts and managing to make the frame on the other occasions. His last run of the year was arguably a career-best effort, when chasing home Nicanor and Mounthenry in the Champion Novice Hurdle at Punchestown. He looks capable of improving further this term, and his connections appear to have a fine chasing prospect on their hands. If he is switched to fences this season, he should develop into one of the leading novices and is likely to be contesting some decent races by the time the numerous festivals come around. P. FENTON

VOY POR USTEDES (FR) (5 years)

Every year Cheltenham's Arkle Chase seems to throw up an exciting prospect and 2006 was no exception. In what was arguably one of the best races of the whole Cheltenham Festival, Voy Por Ustedes moved with ominous ease and jumped well throughout the race before being produced to gain the upper hand just before the last. Those behind him look very decent and his ability to travel on the bridle and jump with pin-point accuracy will stand him in good stead against the best at two miles. He is almost certain to follow the usual route for two milers, so expect to see him in races such as the Haldon Gold Cup and the Tingle Creek on his way to the Queen Mother Champion Chase in March. A. KING

ZIPALONG LAD (IRE) (6 years)

There are few better trainers to follow in the jumping game than Peter Bowen, as his horses always seem trained to the minute and ready to give their running. In Zipalong Lad he appears to have a horse that epitomises what his yard is all about, and he looks one to have on your side this term. A strong, relentless galloper, he held his form well in good company last season after bolting up in a couple of minor novice hurdles and looks likely to keep progressing. It remains to be seen whether he will go chasing, or stick to the smaller obstacles, but he is likely to be well primed whatever the case and could reach a high level. P. BOWEN

INDEX TO HORSES

Published in March 2007

100 WINNERS
HORSES TO FOLLOW 2007

Companion volume to **100 Winners: Jumpers to Follow**, this book discusses the past performances and future prospects of 100 horses, selected by Raceform's expert race-readers, that are likely to perform well over the Flat in 2007.

To order post the coupon to the address below or call **01635 578080** and quote ref 100WF7. Alternatively order online at
www.racingpost.co.uk/shop

ORDER FORM

Please send me a copy of **100 WINNERS: HORSES TO FOLLOW 2007** as soon as it is published. I enclose a cheque/postal order made payable to Raceform Ltd for **£4.99** (inc. free p&p).

Name (block capitals) ....

Address ....

....

Postcode ....

SEND 100 WINNERS FLAT 2007 OFFER, RACEFORM LTD, COMPTON, NEWBURY, RG20 6NL [100WF7]